Secrets
of a
Proper
Lady

By Victoria Alexander

VICTORIA ALEXANDER

Secrets of a Proper Lady

AVON

An Imprint of HarperCollins*Publishers*

AVON BOOKS
An Imprint of HarperCollins*Publishers*
10 East 53rd Street
New York, New York 10022-5299

Copyright © 2007 by Cheryl Griffin
ISBN: 978-0-7394-8932-1

Avon Trademark Reg. U.S. Pat. Off. and in Other Countries, Marca Registrada, Hecho en U.S.A.
HarperCollins® is a registered trademark of HarperCollins Publishers.

Printed in the U.S.A.

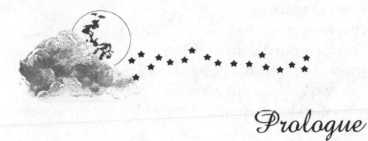

Prologue

London
June 1854

"Cursed," Daniel Sinclair said under his breath. "I have always considered myself a practical and rational sort but . . ." He shook his head. "We're cursed, it's the only explanation."

"Nonsense." Oliver Leighton, the Earl of Norcroft laughed. "We don't believe in such things."

"Still, your own Shakespeare said it." Sinclair thought for a moment. "There are more things in heaven and earth than . . . how does that go?"

"'There are more things in heaven and earth, Horatio, than are dreamt of in your philosophy,'" Oliver said with a shrug. "I thought we had agreed that this is nothing more than coincidence."

"Yes, of course." Sinclair scoffed. "It's no more than coincidence that four men, none of whom are remotely interested in marriage—"

"Actively opposed to it, I'd say," Oliver murmured.

"—form a tontine with nothing more than a handful of coins and a bottle of cognac at stake and before you know it, two of them are gone."

Oliver chuckled. "They're not dead, Sinclair. Simply married."

"Some might say it's much the same thing," Sinclair muttered darkly.

Oliver grinned at his American friend. "I had no idea your view of marriage was quite so pessimistic."

"Under other circumstances, it's not." Sinclair settled back in his chair and considered the matter. "When we first gathered here at this club of yours, there were four of us. We each contributed one shilling, a contribution more symbolic than monetary, and purchased a bottle of the club's finest cognac to be held here, in wait for the ultimate winner. You cannot tell me you didn't expect that bottle to be held for a very long time."

"I admit I didn't think our numbers would diminish so quickly."

"That was in February. It's now June and only two of us are left." Sinclair narrowed his eyes. "And frankly, I would have put their chances of winning this whole thing at better than ours."

"You do have a point."

Gideon Pearsall, Viscount Warton, was the first to go. Oliver would have bet far more than a mere shilling that Warton would have outlasted all of them, but who could have foreseen a lovely widow would have caught not merely Warton's eye but his heart? Then there was

Nigel Cavendish, now Viscount Cavendish, who married abruptly, thanks to an errant pistol shot in the night, and then proceeded to fall deeply in love with his own wife. In Oliver's opinion, given Cavendish's penchant for amorous escapades and active avoidance of responsibility of any kind, Cavendish was right on the heels of Warton as to the ultimate winner of the tontine. The last man standing as it were.

Which left only Oliver and an American entrepreneur, Daniel Sinclair, whose development of railroads in his country had a great deal of potential for profit. Oliver and the others had invested in the American's venture, and Oliver had no doubt it would ultimately be quite successful.

"I tell you, Norcroft, I feel the hot breath of matrimony on the back of my neck even as we speak."

Oliver laughed. "It might be on the back of my neck."

"But you don't seem to mind. You, among all of us, have never seemed especially adverse to marriage." Sinclair leaned toward Oliver and met his gaze firmly. "That's why you're safe and I'm doomed." He shook his head in a mournful manner. "That's how these things work."

"These things?" Oliver raised a brow. "Are you talking about curses again?"

"Curses, fate, coincidence, whatever you wish to call it. It looks around for the one least likely to appreciate whatever it has planned then singles him out for, in this case, marriage. No, I'm most certainly doomed." Sinclair tossed back the rest of his brandy then signaled a waiter for more. "I might as well walk out on the street right now and propose to the first woman who passes by."

"It's not that dire." Oliver chuckled. "Who knows what might happen. Under the proper circumstances, I could certainly marry next."

"Would you?" Sinclair accepted a fresh glass from the waiter. "I would appreciate it."

"I'm afraid not." Oliver studied the American. "It is nice to know, however, that you are preparing yourself."

"Preparing myself?"

"To lose."

Sinclair considered the other man for a long moment. "No, Norcroft, in spite of my suspicion that by forming this tontine we have shaken our fists at whatever gods rule these things and may well have brought a curse down upon our heads, I am not, by any means, surrendering." He raised his glass. "I shall fight to my last dying breath."

"Hear, hear," Oliver said and clinked his glass with Sinclair.

"But I will give you this, Norcroft, should I be lucky enough to avoid fate or coincidence or this curse, I shall be delighted to drink a toast to you at your wedding." Sinclair grinned. "With my cognac of course."

Oliver returned the grin. "I shall count on it."

Still, Sinclair had a point. It was odd that those least likely to marry were now happily wed. If they were indeed cursed, or if the American's theory as to the contrary nature of fate was accurate, then Oliver needn't concern himself with the prospect of marriage. At least not yet.

"However, if I were you." Oliver's grin widened. "I certainly wouldn't wager on it."

> *One must always be open to the possibility of adventure presented by a fork in the road.*
> An English Lady's Traveling Companion

Chapter 1

*E*ven the least astute among us, upon observing Lady Cordelia Bannister for the first, or even the second or third, time would immediately recognize that she was a young woman of sterling qualities. Properly raised, well mannered, respectful in all ways, and a credit to her parents. Even her penchant for travel, her writing about said travel, and a distinct hint of independence in her attitude would not significantly detract from that impression. Unless of course that first observation, or second or third, of the last remaining unwed daughter of the Earl of Marsham took place on a particularly overcast summer day as Cordelia stood before her father's desk in his library, her mother seated off to one side.

"No. Absolutely not. Why, the very suggestion is barbaric!" Cordelia stared at her father in stunned disbelief. "And this is why you called me here? Honestly, Father, for something of this magnitude, one should be given some sort of warning so that one might prepare oneself. I thought it was nothing more important than discussion of my latest bill at Madame Colette's."

The earl sat behind his desk, the very symbol of his authority and that of any number of earls preceding him, and closed his eyes momentarily as if to pray for strength, as he often had through the years when dealing with his daughters. "I have not yet seen that particular bill although I suspect it will not surprise me."

"It's really not that bad, dear," Mother said with an unconcerned shrug. "No worse than usual."

"That is good news," Father said sharply and directed his attention back to Cordelia. "But it's not the subject at hand."

"As for the subject at hand." Cordelia raised her chin and met her father's gaze directly. "I have absolutely no intention of doing anything of the sort and frankly, Father, I don't believe you can make me. I am of age after all." Cordelia sank down into the chair that matched her mother's. "I find the idea repugnant and offensive and really quite medieval."

"I wouldn't call it medieval," her mother murmured. "A bit out of fashion perhaps."

The earl ignored his wife and stared at his youngest daughter. "Oh, but I can make you, Cordelia. And your age is of no particular consequence as you are as firmly dependent on your family for your support and sustenance now as you were when you were a child. As your bill from your dressmaker attests."

Cordelia was hard pressed to dispute the point given that Father was right. Still, a woman approaching her twenty-sixth birthday should not be forced to take a step as drastic as marriage without her approval. "Not entirely, Father. I've managed to save quite a tidy sum from my travel articles."

His eyes narrowed. "Based on travel I paid for."

"If you wish to look at it that way . . ." She shrugged in an offhand manner even if, in truth, there was no other way to look at.

Cordelia had accompanied her parents on a tour of Europe shortly after her eighteenth birthday and had fallen passionately in love with the grand adventure of travel. Two years later she had repeated the trip with her married older sisters Amelia, Edwina, and Beatrice. Then two years ago, she had joined Aunt Lavinia on an extensive and fascinating adventure to Egypt and the Holy Lands. Indeed, Cordelia had found that area of the world to be the most amazing place and could scarcely wait to return.

While Cordelia had always kept journals and diaries about her travels, it was Lavinia who had suggested she turn them into articles for ladies' magazines. After all, Lavinia had said, if Cordelia wasn't going to listen to her advice and marry, she should do something with her life if she didn't want to end her days living with one of her sisters and caring for children that were not her own.

Cordelia had no intention of not marrying, indeed

she very much wished to marry; she simply hadn't yet found a man worth the trouble. Because, as much as Lavinia encouraged marriage, she was never reluctant to point out that men were a great deal of trouble and exceptionally difficult creatures if not managed correctly. And, as Lavinia had been married three times herself, who would know better than she?

"This tidy sum of yours," her father continued, "is it enough to support yourself? To put a roof over your head and clothes—expensive, fashionable clothes—on your back? To pay the salary of your companion? A companion, I might add, that would not be necessary if you had found yourself a husband as your sisters have done."

"Admittedly, it might not be enough for all that," Cordelia murmured.

In point of fact, the total she had accumulated from her writings was rather paltry if one looked at it as a living wage. In truth, Cordelia harbored no foolish illusions of independence. Although she was working on a compilation of her writings thus far, a travel book for the benefit of female travelers, she was realistic enough to know such an endeavor would not provide the means necessary to make her own way in the world. She'd once heard talk of a legacy from a distant aunt, but that was apparently conditional on marriage. Her only true hope for real independence lay in the possibility of a wealthy, if unknown, relative breathing his last and leaving Cordelia his entire fortune. As all relations on both sides of her family were accounted for, the possibility of that happening was extremely slim.

"I never asked for a companion, Father," Cordelia said.

"And dear, Sarah Elizabeth is as much as a member of the family as if she were one of our own daughters." Her mother pinned her father with a firm look. "And you well know it."

Father rolled his gaze toward the ceiling. "Of course, she is. I didn't mean to imply otherwise. However, I do pay her a respectable wage. And Sarah Elizabeth's position in this household is not the subject at the moment."

"You're right, Father." Cordelia crossed her arms over her chest. "The subject is your desire to arrange a marriage between me and a man I have never met."

"Arrange is such a hard word." Mother shook her head. "Encourage is a far better word."

Cordelia raised a brow. "But is it as accurate?"

"Yes," Mother said brightly.

"No." Father's voice was firm. "You need this marriage, Cordelia, as much as I do. It's not as if you have made any effort to find a husband on your own."

Cordelia sniffed. "I've made every effort. I've simply not found the right man."

"Well, I have." He leaned back in his chair and studied his daughter. "I should think you would be pleased."

Cordelia's brows pulled together. "Why on earth would I be pleased? This is a decision that affects the rest of my life and you have taken it out of my hands."

"Thus relieving you of the necessity of continuing your *efforts* in this regard. Cordelia." Her father's voice softened. "Have you or have you not had several proposals through the years?"

"I'm not sure I would use the word several," Cordelia murmured.

"Three that I am aware of." Mother glanced at her. "That would definitely be several."

Father nodded. "All of which you declined because?"

"I don't recall," Cordelia said in a lofty manner, although she did indeed recall quite clearly the reasons for rejecting each and every one.

Proposal number one came from a gentleman who was so deadly dull she envisioned a future filled with nothing more exciting than trying to keep awake as he droned on and on about topics of no consequence. Proposal number two was issued by a suitor who was quite dashing and handsome but certainly could not be trusted as, even as he'd asked for her hand, his eye was drifting elsewhere. Cordelia did not intend to be the type of wife who overlooked a husband's indiscretions. It was rather a pity really as he was quite the type of man she could easily love. Fortunately for her heart, at that particular moment, she had not. And the third came from a pleasant enough gentleman with a distinguished title and an excellent family, although, given all Cordelia had heard about his finances, she'd been certain her appeal for him lay more in her substantial dowry and family connections than in any sense of affection.

Cordelia shrugged. "Suffice it to say, Father, I simply didn't harbor any particular affection for any of them."

Her mother leaned toward her father. "She wasn't in love, dear."

"Unfortunately, the time for love has passed." Her father studied her for a long moment. "I would have thought you would understand this situation, Cordelia. Aside from your romantic notions regarding this particular subject, I have long considered you the most practical and levelheaded of all my daughters. You have a fine mind as well."

"Thank you, Father," Cordelia said in a prim manner that belied her surprise. She'd always thought Father considered her somewhat frivolous and stubborn, rather like her mother.

"You are, in truth, the most like myself of my children." He shook his head. "I too have always enjoyed the adventure of travel, the excitement of new places, the mystery of what might lie around the next corner in a foreign land. And I might add, I write a fine letter as well. In both temperament and interests I have long thought we are very much alike."

Cordelia slanted a quick glance at her mother who appeared unsurprised by this startling revelation, but as Cordelia was not one to overlook a stroke of luck, she lowered her voice in a confidential manner. "I have always thought so, Father."

"Then you will understand when I explain that a union with this man's family will be in all our best interests. Cordelia." Father paused to choose his words. "As you well know, I have any number of business interests including primary ownership of a small shipping line. It's been exceptionally profitable in the past, indeed, it has quite supported this household as well as the family estate. However, times are difficult at the moment and it's not doing especially well. My finances are currently somewhat strained."

Cordelia's eyes widened. "How strained?"

Her mother reached over and patted her hand. "We are not about to lose home and hearth. It is not as bad as all that."

"Not yet," Father said, a vaguely ominous note in his voice. "Daniel Sinclair—"

"The man you wish me to marry," Cordelia said.

Father nodded. "Is the son of American Harold Sinclair. The older Sinclair has amassed a vast fortune through various business interests around the world."

"Including shipping?" Cordelia asked. Now this was beginning to make sense.

"Shipping comprises a significant portion of his business, yes. Steamboats in particular." Father paused and tapped his fingers absently on the desk. "Mr. Sinclair and I have been corresponding for some time and I met with him a fortnight ago in Paris. He is interested in combining my company with his under the right conditions."

"The right conditions being a combining of families as well as businesses?" Cordelia said slowly.

"Aside from the financial benefits on both sides, Harold Sinclair would very much like an alliance with an old and titled family." Father said the words in a matter of fact manner, as if he were discussing nothing of importance.

"I gather Mr. Sinclair doesn't have a daughter you can foist off on Will?" Cordelia glanced at her mother. "You've long said Will needs to settle down and marry."

Mother shrugged as if her only son's marital status was of no concern at the moment.

"I have no idea if Mr. Sinclair has a daughter and it scarcely matters as Will is still in India attending to family interests there." Her father's eyes narrowed. "Doing his part to improve his family's lot."

"And it's my turn now, is it?" Cordelia struggled to keep her voice light. "To preserve the family fortune I must agree to marry a man I have never met. An American no less."

"We thought you'd like the American part of it," Mother murmured.

Her father studied his daughter silently.

"This difficulty with Father's business puts an entirely different light on it all, doesn't it?" Cordelia got to her feet, wrapped her arms around herself, and paced the room. "If I refuse, I'll be responsible for . . ." She glanced at her father.

"A detrimental reversal of family income," her father said dryly.

"And if I agree . . ." Cordelia drew a deep breath and squared her shoulders. "I can't, I just can't."

"Of course you can," Mother said.

"Mother!" Cordelia stared. "I thought you would be on my side in this."

"I am, darling, which is why I think you should look at this in a calm and rational manner." Her mother ticked the points off on her fingers. "You are twenty-five years old and while you have had every opportunity to find an appropriate match, you have yet to do so. Who knows when and if another opportunity to marry might come again. This could very well be the intervention of fate and as such should not be dismissed out of hand. You really should give this idea due consideration."

"Mother." Cordelia gasped. "This is eighteen fifty-four. This sort of thing isn't done today."

"Nonsense." Mother huffed. "It's done all the time. People simply don't talk about it the way they once did. It's really not at all uncommon and in many ways something of a family tradition." The countess leaned toward her daughter and met her gaze firmly. "You certainly don't think I wanted to marry your father, do you?"

Cordelia's eyes widened. "What?"

Her father's brow furrowed. "What?"

"Well, not at first, darling." Mother cast her husband an affectionate smile. "You and I both know our match was at the instigation of our families. It was simply blind luck that I found you wildly attractive and dashing and fell thoroughly in love with you at first sight." She paused. "Well, perhaps not at first sight but very soon and quite forever."

Father appeared somewhat mollified by her words.

"And look at how well we have turned out." She beamed at her daughter. "Cordelia dear, we're not asking you to make a decision at this very moment. You should have time to consider this. In fact, as we are leaving for Brighton within the week, I thought it would be an excellent idea if you and the younger Mr. Sinclair were to exchange notes while we are away from London. You can begin to get to know one another. One can learn a great deal about a man's nature by what he reveals on the written page."

"Why don't we just have them meet?" Father drummed his fingers on the desk. "Best to get it over and done with."

"Because, dear husband, you told me Mr. Sinclair wasn't entirely certain how his son would respond to all this. A first meeting would be exceptionally awkward at this point. Far and away too much tension with the specter of marriage hanging over their heads. He may well be no more enamored of this proposal than Cordelia is."

"He may not be? She doesn't want to?" Father's glare slid from his wife to his daughter and back. "What in the name of all that's holy has happened here? There was a time when what a man said in his own household was sacred."

Cordelia and her mother traded glances. Neither woman was about to tell the earl that his wife and daughters—especially this daughter—had always managed to wrap him around their little fingers. Still, in the past, Cordelia had always been allied with her mother. Now it appeared her parents were united.

"Very well." Father heaved a long suffering sigh. "I assume you will agree to that much?"

"Yes, of course." Cordelia nodded with relief. "I would be more than happy to write to Mr. Sinclair. Although"—she glanced at her mother—"wouldn't it be proper for him to write to me first?"

"Under other circumstances, I would agree. However as Mr. Sinclair is an American, I imagine he would appreciate a certain forthright attitude in a potential wife."

"I can certainly be forthright," Cordelia murmured.

Writing to this Daniel Sinclair would at least give her time to figure a way out of this *encouraged* match. Still, she couldn't formulate any kind of plan until she knew, well, not precisely the enemy but the opposition. Writing to him would be a step in that direction but would take entirely too long. No, she was not about to be coerced into marriage through inaction. She had to do something. She needed a brilliant plan, a smashingly good idea. Nothing came to mind at the moment but she was confident it would. After all, as her father had said, she had a fine mind. And she fully intended to put it to good use.

"Explain to me again why we are hiding in a carriage outside a park gate at what even the most stalwart of souls would consider an ungodly time of morning." Sarah stifled a yawn and glared at her friend.

"It's part of the plan," Cordelia said absently and continued to peer out the window at one of the many streets that ended, or perhaps started, depending on one's point of view and direction, at the park. "I explained the plan quite thoroughly to you last evening."

"Apparently I was not paying the proper amount of attention."

"Probably not, as you were writing yet another letter to that mysterious suitor of yours," Cordelia murmured.

"He's neither a suitor nor mysterious. Simply an old friend with whom I correspond." Sarah's tone was cool as it always was when talk turned to this particular topic. Her secrecy was most annoying as it was probably the only secret she and Cordelia did not share.

Sarah Elizabeth Palmer was a scant year older than Cordelia and the daughter of a distant cousin by marriage of Cordelia's mother. When she was left orphaned and impoverished a dozen or so years ago, Cordelia's family had taken her in. After all, her mother had said, their three oldest daughters were wed and gone and there was a certain emptiness these days in a house so well used to girls. Besides, the sister closest to Cordelia in age was still seven years older than she, and wouldn't it be lovely for Cordelia to have someone around who was closer to her own age. But when Sarah had come of age, she had stubbornly insisted on making her own way in the world as she had failed as miserably as Cordelia had to find a suitable husband. No one in the family could bear the thought of Sarah going off to work as a governess, so she had become Cordelia's paid companion. Aside from the fact that Sarah now had her own funds, her position in the family hadn't significantly changed at all.

Except that in an official sense, Cordelia was her charge. That too was most annoying.

"I tell you all my secrets," Cordelia said, still looking out the carriage window. Where was the blasted man? Cordelia could see the door of the house where her quarry lived and was confident he had not eluded her watch. Even if he had, well, there was always tomorrow.

"It's not a secret. It's simply personal and private and not the matter at hand," Sarah said firmly. "Now, explain to me again why we are lying in wait like common criminals."

"Nonsense. Common criminals would scarcely lie in wait in a carriage, especially a carriage as nice as this. No, common criminals would be skulking about behind the bushes."

"Carriage or bushes, it certainly feels as if we are skulking."

"Well, we're not. We're simply waiting." Cordelia

turned from the window, settled back in her seat, and crossed her arms over her chest. "I do so dislike a man who is not prompt."

Sarah snorted back a laugh. "I daresay, such a fault would clearly be grounds for refusal to marry. Mr. Sinclair's inability to be punctual is a serious flaw."

"Indeed it is." Cordelia huffed. "As is the inability to pay attention to the details of a plan. We are not waiting for Mr. Sinclair, we are waiting for a Mr. Lewis."

Sarah's brows drew together. "Mr. Lewis?"

"You weren't listening to me at all, were you? Very well then." Cordelia heaved a long suffering sigh. "Mr. Warren Lewis is Mr. Sinclair's secretary. Every morning without fail, Mr. Lewis takes a daily constitutional through the park. On occasion, he is accompanied by Mr. Sinclair although usually he is quite alone."

Sarah pressed her lips together. "I gather you have learned this through your usual methods?"

"You needn't look so disapproving. How else is one to learn anything in this town?" Cordelia couldn't resist a satisfied smile. "It is the simplest matter in the world to give a few shillings to the head footman who then distributes a fraction of his newfound wealth among lesser servants, who in turn make inquiries among their acquaintances, and before you know it, you have all the information you need." Cordelia's smile widened. "It was a great benefit to already know the address of the house Mr. Sinclair has leased during his stay in London, and I have my mother to thank for that."

"Did you get a description of the man as well?" Sarah asked wryly.

"Of course." Cordelia scoffed. "It would be foolish

not to. Mr. Lewis is tall, dark-haired, and an American." She shrugged. "He should be easy to spot."

"And once you have spotted him, then what?"

"Then his acquaintance needs to be made, in as natural a manner as possible, and conversation attempted in an effort to learn everything possible about Mr. Sinclair." Cordelia shook her head. "When preparing for warfare, one must know all one can about one's enemy."

"And Mr. Sinclair is the enemy?"

"I don't know. I don't know anything about him." Cordelia narrowed her eyes. "But I do intend to find out. I'll not be thrown into a marriage with a man I know nothing about."

"Isn't that why your mother suggested you and Mr. Sinclair correspond?" Sarah said slowly. "So that you may ascertain his character for yourself?"

"That's especially ridiculous and you well know it." Cordelia waved away Sarah's comment. "I can be anything I wish to be on paper. Witty, clever and altogether fascinating. As can he. Of course . . ."

"Oh, I don't like that look." Sarah shook her head. "What are you thinking?"

"If one can be far better on paper, far more than who one is in truth, one can be substantially less as well."

"Less?"

"Disagreeable, unpleasant." Cordelia widened her eyes in an innocent manner. "Not at all the type of woman a man would want to marry."

Sarah groaned. "Dear Lord, you don't intend to—"

"I don't intend to do anything until I know more about Mr. Sinclair. It was just a thought. It's entirely possible he is my one true love, the man I have always

dreamed about and fate has at last thrown us together."
Cordelia leaned forward and peered out the window.
"It is every bit as likely that he is not." A tall, dark-
haired gentleman was descending the steps in front
of the house. "There is Mr. Lewis now. We'll wait until
he passes the carriage; we don't want him to see you
getting out—"

"Me?" Sarah bolted upright. "What do you mean
me? I thought this was a *we* sort of thing."

"Don't be silly. I can't possibly be involved with
this."

"Why not?" Sarah's voice rose.

"It would be most improper. What if I were to be
found out? Father would—well, I shudder to think of
the consequences." Cordelia placed her hand on her
friend's and met her gaze. "You, however, can always
claim that you were only doing it to save me from myself, which is very nearly the truth."

Sarah stared at her.

"Come now, Sarah, please." Cordelia adopted her
most persuasive tone. "I need your assistance now
more than ever before. You are the sister I never had."

"You have three sisters!"

"Exactly, and you're the one I never had." Cordelia
glanced out the window. Mr. Lewis was passing by on
the far side of the street. "And my favorite as well."

"But I have no idea what to do or say or . . ." Sarah
sighed and reached for the door. "But I'll do it of course,
as you knew I would. On occasions such as this I rather
miss being a poor relation instead a paid companion,
responsible for keeping you out of mischief. But mind
you I don't have the least expectation of success."

"You'll be grand. I'm confident of it." Cordelia

beamed. Why some of Cordelia's best plans in the past had been refined and improved thanks to Sarah's suggestions. Cordelia's smile faltered. Still, while Sarah was clever and resourceful she did have a tendency to be reserved, even hesitant, and always tried to follow the rules of propriety. Beyond that, Sarah really didn't have the heart for deception.

What was Cordelia thinking, to send her on such a mission? It was like sending a lamb to confront a lion and the height of cowardice on Cordelia's part besides. Cordelia had never considered herself the least bit cowardly.

Sarah pushed open the door.

"Wait." Cordelia grimaced. "I have changed my mind. I can't allow you to do this. I am sorry I even asked."

"Thank goodness you've come to your senses," Sarah said with a sigh of relief. "It was an insane idea in the first place."

"Perhaps, but brilliant nonetheless. There is a fine line between brilliance and insanity and this was one of my most brilliant I think."

"Or most insane."

"We shall see." Cordelia pushed open the door and stepped out of the carriage.

Sarah's eyes widened. "What are you doing?"

"I'm doing exactly what I had planned for you to do." Cordelia caught sight of Mr. Lewis. The man certainly set a brisk pace. She'd have to hurry.

"But you said—"

"I said I couldn't allow you to do it. And I can't. I shall do this myself. However." She flashed her cousin a wicked grin. "I shall tell him I'm you."

Cordelia closed the carriage door and hurried off before Sarah could say another word. Lord knew Sarah took this whole idea of being responsible for Cordelia entirely too seriously. Regardless of Sarah's desire to provide for herself, the situation really wasn't fair to her. From the moment she had joined their family, she and Cordelia had been the closest of friends. But despite Sarah being slightly older, Cordelia had always been the one to lead and Sarah to follow.

Mr. Lewis was still ahead of her and Cordelia picked up her pace. And what would happen to Sarah once Cordelia married? Regardless of whether she wed Mr. Sinclair or someone she'd yet to meet, Cordelia was confident she would indeed marry someday. Although she would be the first to admit there might well be wagers to the contrary among more than a few gentlemen in London. Cordelia wasn't entirely sure herself why she had not yet married other than that annoying fact of not having found a man who was, well, right. A man with whom life would be more interesting than the life she now led. While Cordelia had no desire to spend the rest of her days alone, she had no doubt she could if necessary.

But Sarah needed someone to care of her. Preferably a husband. Cordelia vowed to find a suitable match for her cousin as soon as her own marital status was resolved.

Mr. Lewis had either slowed his steps or Cordelia had been walking far quicker than she had realized. Without warning she was nearly upon him. He was taller than she had anticipated, with impressively broad shoulders. Although tall and broad shouldered was precisely what she did expect in an American. No doubt he would have a somewhat rugged face as well, as befit the resident of a part of the world still relatively uncivilized and wild. It was time to find out.

She drew a deep breath. "Mr. Lewis?"

He kept walking.

She tried again. "Mr. Lewis? Mr. Warren Lewis?"

He paused and turned toward her. "I beg your pardon. Are you speaking to me?"

"Yes, well, yes, I was." She stared up at him. He had the darkest eyes she had ever seen. "You are Mr. Warren Lewis, aren't you? Secretary to Mr. Daniel Sinclair?"

He studied her for a moment. "And if I am?"

His gaze skimmed over her in an assessing and altogether impertinent manner. She ignored it. Impertinence was to be expected from an American. "Then I have a matter of great importance to discuss."

"A matter of great importance?" His brow rose and she noticed a scar directly above his eyebrow. Oddly, it wasn't the least bit disfiguring but rather gave him a rakish and even dangerous air.

"Great importance," she said firmly.

"As that is the case"—a slow, wicked grin spread across an undeniably handsome face. Good Lord, the man looked like a pirate! American or not, what kind of gentleman had a pirate in his employ?—"I am at your service."

Planning is imperative for any successful travel venture. A poorly planned trip is certain to result in unforeseen problems of a most distressing nature.

An English Lady's Traveling Companion

Chapter 2

*I*f there was one thing that Daniel Sinclair had learned in business as well as personally in his thirty-one years, it was never to ignore an unexpected opportunity. This pretty brunette with the intelligent glint in her green eyes and determined set to her shoulders was definitely an unexpected opportunity.

"I'm afraid you have me at a disadvantage. You know my name yet I am certain we have never met." His gaze swept over her. Her clothes were in the latest fashion and accentuated a nicely curved figure. An air of quality and confidence hung about her as palpable as the faint scent of roses that drifted from her on the morning breeze. "I would have remembered you."

The most becoming blush tinged her cheeks. She was obviously not accustomed to accosting strange men in the park.

She raised her chin. "That's very flattering, Mr. Lewis, but not at all necessary."

"Because you're here on a matter of great importance?"

She nodded in a firm manner. "Exactly. I should much prefer to get straight to the point."

Whatever that was. "Then, in the interest of efficiency, would you care to accompany me? I have only a limited amount of time and I hate to waste it simply standing here. I much prefer to walk."

"Yes, of course." She stepped to his side and they started off down the path.

"Now then, Miss? . . ."

"Palmer," she said quickly. "Miss Palmer."

"Very well then, Miss Palmer." He glanced at her. She was shorter than he but not at all short. Really rather a convenient height. "How may I be of assistance?"

"I need some information from you, Mr. Lewis. Confidential information." She drew a deep breath. "About your employer. Mr. Sinclair."

"Do you?" She wanted to know about him? At once the slight twinge of guilt he'd felt when he'd allowed her to believe he was Warren vanished. "Before we go any further, Miss Palmer, you should know I am intensely loyal to my employer."

"That in itself tells me a great deal," she said primly.

"A man who commands the loyalty of his employees is usually a decent sort."

"Mr. Sinclair is indeed a decent sort. In fact, I would say he was more than merely decent," Daniel said stoutly. "He is generous and kindhearted." Perhaps that was enough. He probably shouldn't overdo it. "A man of courage and intelligence and integrity." Although, why not? It wasn't every day a man had the opportunity to impress a pretty woman with his good points. "Why, those who know him consider him the salt of the earth."

"He must pay you exceptionally well," she said dryly.

"He does." Daniel shrugged. "However, my opinion as to his character has not been purchased. I have known Daniel Sinclair since we attended school together. He is not merely my employer but my friend."

"I see," she murmured.

"Well, I do not." He stopped and turned toward her. "See, that is. What is your business with Mr. Sinclair? This matter of great importance?"

"It's not really my business, it's that of my . . . my employer." Her gaze met his and again he noted that gleam of determination. "I occupy the position of companion to Lady Cordelia Bannister."

"Lady Cordelia . . ." Good Lord! That was the woman his father wanted him to marry. "That is interesting."

"I assume then that you're aware of the desire of their parents that they wed."

"Very much aware." His voice hardened. "Mr. Sinclair received a letter only yesterday informing him of his father's intentions." It was enough to infuriate even the most even tempered of men. Daniel had thought that since his father had failed in a previous attempt to marry him off to a British heiress, he would abandon the idea altogether. Apparently he had underestimated the elder Sinclair's determination.

Miss Palmer nodded. "Lady Cordelia learned of it all yesterday as well."

He narrowed his eyes. "Did she send you to quiz me about Mr. Sinclair?"

"She is, of course, curious. It's only natural that she would be. However." Miss Palmer paused. "The idea to approach you was entirely mine."

He stared down at her and smiled slowly. "How very clever of you, Miss Palmer."

"I thought so," she said under her breath.

"You seem somewhat uncertain."

"No, not at all." She shook her head. "At least not about the cleverness of the idea. I am proud to have thought of it. It's simply easier to devise a plan than to carry it through."

"Is it?"

She cast him a disapproving look. "Approaching a stranger is not an easy task."

"And yet. . ."

"One summons one's courage when necessary," she said in a staunch manner.

He resisted the urge to laugh. She was so very earnest, he suspected she would see no humor in this at all. Of course, she had no idea she was speaking to the subject of her inquiry. "Then shall we continue?"

She grimaced. "It wouldn't be at all proper to accompany you farther."

"More improper than approaching me in the first place?" He raised a brow. "Come now, Miss Palmer, I believe that ship has sailed."

"Excellent point, Mr. Lewis." She wrinkled her nose, a nice nose, just pert enough to be charming.

"I assure you, Miss Palmer, I am not the type of man to take advantage of a woman in a public park in the light of day."

She met his gaze directly. "That's very good to know, Mr. Lewis, although that was not my concern."

"If you are worried about the two of us being seen together, I have noted on my early morning strolls that only the most robust of London residents frequent the park at this time of day."

"I daresay, my acquaintances for the most part do not fall into that category."

"And if you wish to know more about Mr. Sinclair . . ."

"You are most persuasive, Mr. Lewis. Very well then." She drew a deep breath. "Why not indeed?"

They started off again and he glanced down at her. "However, I do think I should warn you that I consider turnabout to be fair play."

"What do you mean?"

"If I am to tell you Mr. Sinclair's secrets, I should expect to learn some of Lady's Cordelia's in return."

"He has secrets then?"

"We all have secrets, Miss Palmer." He bit back a smile. "I suspect even you have any number of secrets."

"Me?" Surprise sounded in her voice. "Why would you think I have secrets? There is nothing the least bit secretive about me. No, no, I have no secrets whatsoever. I am precisely as I appear. Nothing to hide, not a thing. I am very much an open book sort of person."

"For an open book sort of person, you do protest a great deal."

"Yes, well." She laughed lightly. "We open-book people are like that."

"Then tell me about yourself."

"I am not here to talk about myself. I am"—she paused to find the right words—"irrelevant in all this. Simply an observer. I am the narrator of the story as it were, nothing more than that."

"Nonsense, Miss Palmer. At the moment you are squarely at the center of the story and very much a central character."

She stopped short and frowned at him. "Well, I certainly did not intend to be."

"Nonetheless you are. Such things are inevitable when one has a clever idea and acts upon it. Especially a clever idea that requires courage." He nodded, and again started off.

It was entirely possible she wouldn't follow. She was right, of course, their walking together without any kind of chaperone probably wasn't proper. Then again, *she* was the chaperone when it came to Lady Cordelia, although she seemed both too young and too pretty for the position. Still, as much as he wasn't entirely certain as to the rules of proper behavior here in London he suspected that, as a woman who earned her own way in the world, the rules for her were less restrictive than for the virginal daughter of a noble family. He heard her hurry after him and bit back a satisfied smile. He wasn't at all sure what he thought of Lady Cordelia, but her companion was certainly intriguing. Daniel waited for her to catch up. "Now then, Miss Palmer, tell me about yourself."

"It wouldn't do any harm, I suppose. Very well." She huffed, obviously not at all pleased. "My name is Sarah Elizabeth Palmer. My mother was a very distant cousin by marriage of Lady Cordelia's mother. When I was left orphaned, Lord and Lady Marsham took me in."

Daniel's brows pulled together. "And now you are made to earn your own way?"

"I am not made to do anything," she said sharply. "My position is entirely of my own choosing. The family has always treated me as one of their own. And as for becoming Lady Cordelia's companion, that was my idea and my decision."

"Why?" He studied her out of the corner of his eye. Her chin was set in a stubborn and resolute manner.

"Because I would rather be an employee than a poor relation."

"How very independent of you."

"I am an independent sort, Mr. Lewis," she said firmly.

"Then I gather your position in the household has changed?"

"Oddly enough, it hasn't. Not really." She thought for a moment. "Lord and Lady Marsham were not in favor of my decision but Uncle Philip—Lord Marsham—did seem to understand, even though he has very definite opinions about the position of women in this world. He can be most annoying in that respect."

"Particularly to an independent sort."

"Indeed." She blew a long breath. "As much as I love

him, he can be quite stubborn. My rooms remain in the family quarters. I am still treated like a member of the family and Aunt Emma—Lady Marsham—is still as determined to see me married as she is her daughter. I was given a first season alongside Lady Cordelia and I continue to accompany her to social events as a family member."

"So, when you were unable to find a husband, you became an employee?"

"What makes you think I was unable to find a husband?" Irritation sounded in her voice.

"Well, *Miss* Palmer, companions are rarely married," he said mildly. "Therefore it's only logical to assume you were unable to find a husband."

"Nonsense. I found any number of suitable husbands."

"Then it's the word *unable* that you object to?"

"It implies a failure on my part that I am unwilling to accept. As I have yet to meet a gentleman I wished to spend the rest of my days with, I would say the failure was on their part rather than mine." Her brow furrowed. "I'm not at all sure I wish to marry if I am doing so simply to be provided for. Besides, Lady Cordelia is quite an avid traveler—"

At once the image of a sturdy woman clad in practical, sturdy clothing and equally sturdy shoes with a walking stick in one hand and a compass in the other popped into his head. God help him.

"—and has begun writing about her travels, about the adventure and excitement and history of foreign places. Articles for ladies' magazines. I do wonder if a husband, for either of us, wouldn't muck that up."

"Then Lady Cordelia does not wish to marry?"

Daniel said hopefully. It would certainly make his life less complicated.

"Oh no, she does indeed wish to marry. Very much so. But her tastes are even more discriminating than mine."

So much for hope. Daniel was not the least bit modest when it came to evaluating his own appeal as a suitable husband. He was wealthy in his own right with ambition and plans that would make his fortune grow. His mirror and the admiring glances frequently cast by the fairer sex confirmed that he was an attractive specimen. The fact that he was American as well was a strike against him in the rarified world of London society, but then since he was not actively seeking a wife, that was not a concern. Still, he had no doubt Lady Cordelia would find him more than acceptable. "Tell me about her."

Miss Palmer raised a brow. "This then is the turnabout you mentioned?"

"It does seem only fair."

She sighed. "What do you wish to know?"

"What *should* I know? Or rather," he said quickly, "what should Mr. Sinclair know?"

"Well." Her brows drew together. "I should think a man in his position would like to know about her character. She's very clever and extremely well read. Did I mention she's writing a book of her own?"

"No."

"It's a book of advice for travelers." Excitement far out of proportion to the topic at hand sounded in Miss Palmer's voice. "Specifically for lady travelers."

"How very . . . intelligent of her," he said weakly.

Spectacles appeared on the image of the sturdy woman in his head.

"Yes, it is." Miss Palmer nodded eagerly. "I suspect it will do very well too as more and more women are traveling on their own these days."

"It sounds to me as if Lady Cordelia is as independent as you are."

"Oh, she is. She quite prides herself on her independence."

The vision of lady Cordelia now grew to Amazonian proportions. "And yet she still wishes to marry?"

"Of course she wishes to marry. An independence of spirit does not negate that. Marriage is expected of her and it is as well what she expects. She has been trained from childhood for the position. I have no doubt Lady Cordelia will make an excellent mistress of a household, a perfect hostess, and an exemplary mother." She cast him a superior glance, as if he were too dim to understand the basic principles of life. "I don't know how young ladies are brought up in your country, but in England a young woman of good family understands there are responsibilities that go hand in hand with her position in life. Primary among them is the making of a good match."

"Is she confident Mr. Sinclair is a good match?" he said coolly, as if the answer were of no real importance.

"Don't be absurd." She snorted in disdain. "She is nowhere near confident of any such thing. All she really knows about Mr. Sinclair is that he has a respectable fortune, a father as interfering as her own, and that he's American."

"He is the salt of the earth," Daniel murmured.

"So you've mentioned," she said dryly. "However, as you are his friend, the veracity of your opinion is in question."

"Perhaps, Lady Cordelia should look elsewhere for her perfect match."

"It doesn't appear as if she has much choice in the matter." Miss Palmer stopped and looked at him. "Are you aware of all the details of this proposed arrangement?"

"I thought I was. I am completely in Mr. Sinclair's confidence," Daniel said slowly. Was there something else here that he should know? "But I could be mistaken."

"Then you do understand this marriage is as much a businesses arrangement as a personal match?"

"I vaguely recall something of that nature," he said under his breath. In truth, Daniel had been so annoyed by his father's actions regarding his life, he had failed to read much of the letter beyond Lady Cordelia's name and age. "Admittedly, as the details were personal I might not have given it my full attention."

"Give it your full attention now, Mr. Lewis." Miss Palmer's green eyes flashed in the morning sun. What besides annoyance might also make them flash? He pushed the thought away. Now was obviously not the time for lascivious musings about the delectable Miss Palmer.

He nodded a bow. "You have my complete and undivided attention, Miss Palmer."

"Excellent." She drew a deep breath. "Mr. Sinclair's father has extremely successful steamships. My fa— my Uncle Philip has a shipping line that is not particularly successful at the moment. But family fortunes can be salvaged if Uncle Philip's business is joined with the elder Mr. Sinclair's. The condition for such a business arrangement is the marriage of their children."

"Yes, of course, now I remember," he murmured. Damnation, how had he missed this?

She crossed her arms over her chest and studied him. "You're not very good at your job, are you?"

"I'm very good at my job." He huffed and glared at her.

"Then why didn't you know about this condition?"

"I did know. It simply slipped my mind. After all, it is a private matter of Mr. Sinclair's, the younger Mr. Sinclair that is."

She raised a skeptical brow. "I thought you were his friend as well?"

"As much as I do consider Mr. Sinclair a friend, there are boundaries I do not overstep," he said in a lofty manner. Although the real Warren certainly acknowledged no such limits when it came to Daniel's personal life.

"Why do I doubt that, Mr. Lewis?"

"I have no idea, Miss Palmer. Perhaps it's my forthright, charming manner." He flashed her a wicked grin.

"Yes, I'm certain that's it." She glanced back the way they had come. "My carriage is waiting for me, I should be off." She nodded and turned. "Good day."

"Wait, Miss Palmer." He stepped toward her. She was far too interesting to let her walk out of his life. "Do you think you've learned what you need to know about Mr. Sinclair?"

She paused.

"It seems to me, since our futures, as employees as well as friends, are tied to Mr. Sinclair and Lady Cordelia, it is in our best interest to continue this exchange of information." Or it might well be simply in his best interest. He would very much like to see her again.

She thought for a moment then nodded slowly. "I agree. There are any number of things I should still like to know about Mr. Sinclair."

"Then we should meet again."

"Yes, I suppose we should."

"Here?"

"No." She shook her head. "As much as I would not call my acquaintances robust, there is always the possibility of being seen together here. Which would be most difficult, if not impossible, to explain. I do have a reputation I should like to preserve."

"Then—"

"Do you know Murdock's? The booksellers?"

"Yes, of course." He scoffed as if it were absurd that she should ask such a question. In truth, he'd never heard of it, but Warren probably knew every bookstore in London. Of the two men, Warren had always had his nose in a book of some sort about business or law. While Daniel considered himself well-read, these days he was more inclined to devour newspapers. "I know it well."

"Good. I shall be there tomorrow, shortly after it opens I think. It's generally not busy at that time. And, if I were you, Mr. Lewis"—she leaned toward him—"I would come prepared. I would suggest compiling a list of questions about Lady Cordelia, things you think Mr. Sinclair would like to know and I shall do the same. Quite frankly, when given the opportunity to inquire about Lady Cordelia, you failed to learn anything of true significance. I daresay, Mr. Sinclair would be disappointed in you."

"You took me by surprise, that's all." He drew his brows together and glared. "I simply did not expect, well, *you*."

"One can only hope, now that the element of surprise has been eliminated, you will be somewhat more competent in your inquiry. Good day, Mr. Lewis." Miss Palmer nodded, turned, and started toward her carriage waiting outside the park gate.

"I am not incompetent," he called after her.

She didn't bother to toss back a response, but Daniel could have sworn he heard the faint sound of satisfied laughter drifting back from Miss Palmer's retreating figure.

Damnation, she was right. He hadn't learned anything important about Lady Cordelia. Why he hadn't even asked what the lady looked like, although he thought he had a pretty good idea. The Amazon in his head raised a brow in a chastising manner. It really didn't matter what she looked like, he had no intention of marrying yet another bride his father had selected for him. Still, he couldn't reject the woman out of hand. He may not be a British noble, but his family's word was just as important to him as to any titled Englishman. No, he would have to find a graceful way out. And the first step toward that was to learn as much as possible about the indomitable Lady Cordelia.

And if he forged a friendship with the lovely Miss Palmer in the process, that was certainly an unexpected benefit.

* * *

"Have you seen Mr. Lewis this morning, Gilliam?" Daniel handed his hat and gloves to the butler who, along with the rest of the staff, had come with the small town house he had leased for his stay in London.

"He is in the"—the butler's composed expression twitched as if he were trying not to grimace at the word—"*office*, sir."

Daniel bit back a smile. Gilliam was offended if not scandalized by Daniel's turning the ground floor parlor into an office, while he and Warren had suites, including their own private parlors and bedchambers, on the upper floors. But renting a house was both convenient and economical. It made no sense to Daniel to take rooms at a hotel for both him and Warren, and lease a separate office when a house served all his needs and was private as well as practical.

When Daniel had arrived in London shortly after the new year, following a brief visit to Italy, he hadn't anticipated that his stay would last any time at all and had indeed resided in a hotel. His original intention had been to stay only long enough to meet, and hopefully divest himself of, a previous fiancée his father had arranged for him, then return to America. That said fiancée was the cousin of Oliver Leighton, the Earl of Norcroft, and had already fallen in love with Jonathon Effington, Marquess of Helmsley and heir to the Duke of Roxborough, turned out to be one of those unexpected opportunities Daniel always kept his eyes open to. Helmsley and Norcroft, together with their longtime friends Viscount Cavendish and Viscount Warton, had become not only Daniel's friends but his major investors as well. The transfer of funds from one country to another, contracts, agreements, and the endless other details that accompanied arrangements and expectations between investors and enterprising businessmen had kept Daniel in London now for more than five months and had necessitated his sending for Warren to join him.

"And how is he?"

"He claims to be feeling much better, sir." Gilliam pursed his lips. "In spite of Mrs. Rumpole's protests, he insisted on leaving his bed and returning to his duties."

Daniel grinned. Mrs. Rumpole saw herself as much as a substitute mother as she did housekeeper to the two men who now resided under the roof she considered hers as well. "I would have liked to have seen that battle."

Gilliam sighed. "I daresay, it's not over, sir."

Warren claimed he was suffering from nothing more serious than a common cold, but the man had been so miserable he had finally taken to his bed yesterday and had allowed Mrs. Rumpole to minister to him with gallons of hot broth and an odd-smelling tea that she claimed would cure anything.

"Probably not." Daniel chuckled, crossed the entry hall and pushed open the doors to see his longtime friend and employee sitting at one of the two large desks that dominated the room. "Are we feeling better today?"

Warren glanced up from the notebook before him. "I no longer feel as if death would be a blessing, so, yes, I am feeling better."

Warren's eyes were red rimmed and his voice still nasal and slightly hoarse, but he wasn't nearly as pale as he had been yesterday.

"You look . . ."

Warren raised a brow.

"Better," Daniel said firmly. "Not good, mind you, but definitely better."

"Thank you. I would hate to look better than I feel." Warren managed a weak smile.

Daniel studied his friend. "Are you sure you should be out of bed?"

"If I stayed in bed another minute I would go stark, raving mad with boredom. If Mrs. Rumpole didn't drown me with soup and tea first." Warren shook his head and sighed. "Although, as much as it pains me to admit it, it is somewhat comforting when one is ill to be the object of *motherly* attention."

"And no one provides motherly attention quite the way Mrs. Rumpole does." Daniel grinned and moved to his desk.

Both men had lost their mothers at an early age and Warren's father had died shortly before he began his college studies, leaving only a small inheritance to guarantee Warren's education. Daniel, as the son of a wealthy man, had had limitless resources. That the two men met during those years was not at all odd, but both considered the fact that they had become fast friends nothing short of a miracle. Warren had studied law, Daniel commerce and finance, and now they shared a mutual ambition and a vision of a vast network of interlocking railroads that would revolutionize transportation in the United States and make them both very wealthy. While Warren was, at the moment, officially Daniel's employee with a title of secretary, it was a temporary position until their plans began bearing fruit. Then Warren would take his place as Daniel's partner. Until that time, Warren was just as stubborn as Miss Palmer when it came to earning his own way.

"Have you seen that letter from my father?" Daniel riffled through one of many untidy stacks of paper that graced both his and Warren's desks.

"The one you barely looked at yesterday before you stalked out of the room?"

"Yes, yes, I know, I know." Daniel huffed. "I should have read the entire thing and I shouldn't have lost my temper but damn it all, the man's continuing effort to control my life infuriates me. Besides, he only writes when he has something to say that is guaranteed to drive me mad."

"Then it's a good thing his travels keep him busy and your paths have not crossed in months."

"We don't seem to get on well in the same room." Where was that blasted letter anyway?

"Didn't you crumple his letter up and throw it across the room?"

"Damn." Daniel collapsed into his chair. "Mrs. Rumpole has probably—"

"I, however, being efficient even in my dying moments, rescued it before Mrs. Rumpole had the chance to tidy up." Warren glanced at the piles of papers on his desk. "It's here." His gaze shifted to Daniel's desk. "Or there. Somewhere."

"Good to know there are moments when your usual competency fails," Daniel muttered, leafing through the closest stack of documents.

"I've been ill."

"There are times when I feel quite in"—Miss Palmer's

comment as to his incompetence flashed through his mind"—intimidated by your mastery of virtually everything."

Warren scoffed. "Nothing has ever intimidated you, nor, I imagine, will anything in the future."

A vision of flashing green eyes popped into his head. "You'd be surprised," Daniel murmured. "I assume you read it?"

"Absolutely. A letter from your father in which he lays out the rest of your life for you is not to be missed." Warren chuckled in a manner that would have been described as wicked if he had sounded healthier. "And I must confess, considering all the various revelations it contained and the repercussions to come gave me a great deal of entertainment as I lay in my sickbed being force-fed soup. Why, it quite kept my mind off the ever-present possibility of Mrs. Rumpole clutching me to her bosom and rocking me to sleep."

"She wouldn't." Daniel laughed then paused. "Would she?"

"Of course she would. In spite of the fact that we are both past thirty years of age, she sees us as the sons she never had."

"At least I am spared an interfering mother. A father determined to run my life is bad enough." Daniel leaned back in his chair and mentally braced himself. "Go on then, Warren. I'm ready. What are these revelations?"

Warren chuckled. "Oh, I don't think you're at all ready."

"I'm as ready as I'll ever be. Now, tell me, was there by any chance mention of some sort of business transaction with this Lady Cordelia's father?"

"Excellent guess. I'm impressed." Warren tapped his pen on the desk. "Your father wishes to acquire half interest in Lady Cordelia's father's—I forget his name—"

"Lord Marsham," Daniel murmured.

Warren studied him. "So you did read most of it?"

"No. I'll explain in a moment. Go on."

"Very well. Lord Marsham owns a rather impressive shipping line that your father wants to merge with his steamship interests. It would give him entree into shipping in this part of the world, strengthen his position in British ports. Apparently, according to the letter, while Lord Marsham needs an influx of capital at the moment to keep from going under, the line is sound overall. So the proposition, in a business sense, is a good one."

"And how does this marriage fit in?"

"Your father thinks the joining of the son of a captain of American industry with the daughter of an old and honorable English family will benefit both sides financially and socially."

"He would think that. He's never quite gotten over the fact that he was not born with position and wealth."

"And marrying you to a titled family, aligning himself with such a family, will give him the prestige and legitimacy that he wants?"

"Exactly." Daniel shook his head. "It's times like this when I regret not having a sister he could marry off to serve his purposes."

"Don't be absurd." Warren aimed his pen at his friend. "I know you. You'd never let a beloved sister be bartered off as part of a business deal."

"I'd trade a sister's future without hesitation if doing so would save me."

Warren laughed. "Then it's fortunate you don't have a sister, although I don't believe you for a moment."

"Believe me," Daniel said firmly and ignored the thought that this was exactly what Lady Cordelia's father was doing. Poor, sturdy Lady Cordelia was in as much of a fix as he was, except that she wished to marry whereas he did not. Good God, he might well be the stout-hearted lady's only chance. Damn. Well, he certainly was not going to marry anyone out of a sense of pity. "You know," he said thoughtfully, "it strikes me that if my father's purpose is to improve his social standing, he should be the one to marry."

"You think that, do you?" Warren said slowly.

"I do indeed. It's a brilliant idea and gives everyone what he wants. I want my freedom. My father wants affiliation with a prestigious family."

"Isn't Lady Cordelia a bit young for him?"

"Not at all." Daniel waved away the objection. This really was a good idea. "She's twenty-five years old. Younger women marry older men all the time."

"That certainly does happen," Warren murmured.

"And my father has always liked younger women." Daniel thought for a moment. "She would hold more appeal for him if she were an actress or singer I suppose, but I imagine her family connections and youth would offset anything else."

"What about the lady in question? What does she get?"

"Precisely what she wants, a husband. And a wealthy one at that." Daniel snorted. "And while she is allegedly selective, I daresay one rich American will serve as well as another under these circumstances."

"And you think your father would be acceptable to a young lady?" Warren bit back a grin. "Has your father then grown taller, thinner, reacquired his hair, and adopted a charming nature since our last meeting?"

"My father has always been charming when the need arose. As for the rest of it"—Daniel waved off the comment—"appearance is not important."

Warren choked then coughed, grabbed his handkerchief and sneezed into it. "Appearance is not important? When did you come to that conclusion?"

"It's a consideration for me, not crucial but a consideration, but then I am not looking for a match to enhance my business and social positions."

"So your father should be the one to marry Lady Cordelia?"

"Why not? It was his idea, his arrangement."

"Why not indeed?" Warren paused. "However, there could be a child from such a union. Another heir to the Sinclair fortune."

"I couldn't care less and you well know it." Daniel's insistence on building his own fortune, with no help from his father, was one of many ongoing disputes between father and son. Even now, Daniel's enterprises were financed by adequate, if limited, wealth left him by his maternal grandparents. "Still, I suppose someone closer his own age might be a better idea. Which doesn't solve the question of what to do about Lady Cordelia, but would prevent any further arrangements like this in the future should I manage to extricate myself from this one. It seems to me there are any number of titled, well-connected widows in this town who would do nicely. Viscount Warton has a widowed aunt, Lady Radbury." Daniel chuckled. "Quite a spirited woman, too. She would give my father a merry chase."

Warren bit his lip. "Yes, I suppose she would."

Daniel studied his friend for a moment. He had the look of a man who knew something of great interest. Something most amusing. Daniel recognized that look. "What do you know that I don't know?"

"Any number of things, I should think." Barely suppressed amusement sparked in Warren's eyes. "You really should have read that letter."

Daniel narrowed his eyes. "Why?"

"It was filled with all sorts of interesting information."

"What?"

"I suppose I should offer my best wishes first."

"On my proposed marriage? Don't even think of it."

"I wasn't." Warren got to his feet, crossed the room, and extended his hand to Daniel. "But do let me be the first to congratulate you."

Daniel rose, grasped Warren's hand cautiously, and studied him with suspicion. "On what?"

"On marriage of course."

"I'm not—"

"Not your marriage." Warren grinned. "Your father's marriage."

"A bit premature don't you think?"

"Actually, it's overdue." Warren shook Daniel's hand. "Congratulations, old man, you have a new mother."

Daniel stared in disbelief. "A mother."

Warren nodded. "A mother."

Daniel chose his words with care. "What do you mean, a mother?"

"Stepmother is a more accurate term."

Daniel shook his head. "I don't understand."

"It's really quite simple. When a man's father remarries, the new wife becomes his stepmother."

"A know what a stepmother is, I just didn't know I had one." Daniel sank into his chair. As much as he had just proposed marriage for his father, he really hadn't given the idea serious reflection. Now or ever. He shook his head as if to clear it, then stared at his friend. "Stepmother?"

"Stepmother." Warren grinned. "You should see the look on your face."

"I didn't expect this," Daniel said under his breath. Aside from his father's occasional and unimportant involvements through the years with various women he'd seen on stage, he'd always been too busy building a financial empire to pursue any woman to the point of marriage.

"Does it upset you then?"

"No, it's just . . . Odd, the very thought of it. And shocking as well." He looked at his friend. "Did his letter say anything about her?"

"Only that she was an opera singer and you would meet her soon."

"An opera singer." Daniel groaned. "Probably younger than I am and interested in nothing more than his money."

Warren stared. "Is this concern I hear? For your father?"

"No," Daniel snapped then sighed. "Yes, of course

it is. He's my father after all. I would hate to see him taken in by a fortune hunter, there's nothing more to it than that."

"Of course not. I never thought it was anything more in spite of the bilious look on your face. You don't look at all well. I should summon Mrs. Rumpole to bring you some of her tea." Warren's brow furrowed thoughtfully. "But oddly enough, I feel better. Much better. Better than I've felt in days." He strolled back to his desk. "Imagine that."

"I'm glad my life can lift your spirits."

"You have no idea, old friend." Warren chuckled and took his seat. Although Warren had long encouraged Daniel to reconcile his differences with his father, he never failed to hide his enjoyment of the ongoing battle of wills between father and son. "No idea."

"Then perhaps this will add to your amusement."

"I would have said my cup is overflowing at the moment, but if there's more . . ." Warren grinned. "Do go on."

"In the park today, I was approached by a lovely young woman."

"And that's amusing?"

"The amusing part is," Daniel smiled slowly, "that she mistook me for you."

"That is amusing," Warren said under his breath, then looked at his friend. "How lovely?"

"Very."

"Really?" Warren's expression brightened. "And she was looking for me?"

"She was." It was Daniel's turn to feel smug. He and

Warren had competed for the same women from the first day they'd met.

Warren considered his friend for a moment. "From the expression on your face, I gather you didn't correct her mistake."

"Absolutely not." Daniel grinned. "It would have been rude of me. It might have caused her great embarrassment. Besides I was protecting you."

"Protecting me? From lovely young women?" A wry note sounded in Warren's voice. "What a good friend you are."

"You would have done the same for me."

"Saved you from a lovely young woman?" Warren nodded in an overly somber manner. "Absolutely. You may count on it. The very next time a lovely young woman approaches you, I shall throw myself between the two of you and fend her off. You have my word on it."

"She might have been a fortune hunter, you know."

"Not an especially good one." Warren laughed. "I have no fortune.

"But you will one day." Daniel shook his head. "It's never too soon to take precautions."

"Ah yes. Lord save me from lovely young women." Warren considered his friend. "Were her eyes green?"

"Yes."

"That explains a great deal. You've always had a penchant for green eyes. So what did this lovely, green-eyed young woman want with me?"

"She wanted to talk to you." Daniel paused for emphasis. "About me."

"I should have known." Warren rolled his gaze heavenward. "Well, what did she want to know about you and more to the point, why?"

"She wanted to know what kind of man I am, that sort of thing."

"Damnation. That would have been fun." Warren heaved a dramatic sigh. "One's life is filled with missed opportunities."

"As to why." Daniel crossed his arms over his chest and leaned back in his chair. "It seems the lovely young woman, a Miss Sarah Palmer, is the companion to Lady Cordelia."

Warren stared for a moment. "That is convenient."

"I'm meeting her again tomorrow," Daniel said with a note of satisfaction he made no effort to hide.

"To talk about yourself?"

"With any luck at all." Daniel grinned. "Although my ultimate goal is to learn more about Lady Cordelia."

Warren narrowed his eyes in suspicion. "Why?"

"It seems like a good idea, that's all. The more I know, the better I can decide how to escape from this proposed marriage. Besides." Daniel shrugged. "I rather enjoyed my chat with Miss Palmer. She's clever and resourceful and—"

"Pretty and green-eyed."

"That too."

Warren studied him for a long moment. "Do you know what you're doing?"

"Yes," Daniel said firmly. "I am furthering the acquaintance of an intelligent, pretty woman in hopes of saving myself from an unwanted marriage with an Amazon."

Warren stared then shrugged. "As long as you know."

"I do."

"There is, however, one more thing you should know about the letter from your father."

"Oh good, there's more. I was so afraid all the surprises were over."

"The letter was dated three days ago."

"Three days . . ." Daniel winced with realization. "Good God, that means—"

"Indeed it does." Warren chuckled. "Your father is here in London."

A thorough reading of the reports of travelers who have gone before you to any exotic land, in advance of stepping foot upon its shores, is an excellent way to avoid unpleasant surprises.
An English Lady's Traveling Companion

Chapter 3

Dear Mr. Sinclair,

Please accept my sincere apologies for the forward nature of this missive but I was assured that, as an American, you would not find it particularly offensive. As you are no doubt aware, it is the desire of our parents that we marry. This note is by way of an introduction and was suggested by my mother since it may well be several weeks before we are able to meet in person.

Each year at this time, my family takes up residence in Brighton . . .

"*I* absolutely cannot allow this." Sarah clenched her jaw. "When you told me yesterday you intended to meet this man again, I thought you would come to your senses."

"There was no need to come to my senses. My senses are just fine."

"That's open to debate. Cordelia." Sarah drew a deep breath. "This is not merely a question of propriety, but the man is a stranger. He could be dangerous."

"Don't be absurd." Cordelia sat before her dressing table, studied her reflection in the mirror, and adjusted her hat. "He's not the least bit dangerous. He's very nice although perhaps not as competent as I would have expected from someone in his position." She thought for a moment. "I probably just caught him unawares, he certainly didn't strike me as stupid."

"I don't care if he's the cleverest man in the world—"

"He's definitely handsome enough." She met Sarah's gaze in the mirror. "Did I tell you that he has the most fascinating scar above his right eyebrow?"

"You mentioned it."

"One would think a scar would detract from a man's appearance, but instead it enhances it. It makes him look quite dangerous and very much like a pirate." She grinned at Sarah. "I've always rather liked the idea of pirates."

Sarah eyes widened with dismay. "Dear Lord."

"I find them romantic and quite exciting."

Sarah groaned.

"Although I admit their appeal is strictly fictitious.

In reality, they were bloodthirsty and not at all pleasant. I doubt that I would like a real pirate if I were to meet one." Cordelia tied the ribbons of her hat and tried not to grin at Sarah's horrified expression. "I daresay, pirate is more a description of character than anything else. No, Mr. Lewis is quite like the sort of pirate one would meet in a novel. Pirate, in reference to Mr. Lewis, is an attitude. It makes him very dashing and quite intriguing."

"What about Mr. Sinclair?"

"Oh, I suspect he's probably a pirate as well."

"That's not what I meant." Sarah crossed her arms over her chest and glared. "I meant, do you find anything you've learned about Mr. Sinclair to be as intriguing as you find Mr. Lewis?"

"Not yet," Cordelia said lightly. "Which is precisely why I'm meeting Mr. Lewis again today." She swiveled to face her cousin. "I wasn't as prepared yesterday as I should have been. Indeed for a cleverly conceived plan, it was not well executed. Today, however, I am prepared."

"I'm almost afraid to ask what that means."

"I have compiled a list of specific questions I want answered about Mr. Sinclair."

"That makes sense, I suppose," Sarah said in a grudging manner. "But I don't like this at all. If your parents knew you were meeting this man, I could be let go."

"That's nonsense and you know it." Cordelia scoffed. "You're a member of the family. You only insisted on having a position in the first place because you didn't like being completely dependent."

"I should have left long ago to get a real position," Sarah muttered.

"That would be most dreadful and would make no one the least bit happy." Cordelia met the other woman's gaze firmly. "Should you ever do such a thing, Father would feel guilty. Mother would worry about you constantly. I would be quite alone and who knows what I would do. And you, dear cousin." Cordelia met her gaze firmly. "Would be nothing short of miserable."

"Yes, well, you do have a point." Sarah sighed and pulled on a short, lace-trimmed mantle that nicely matched her pale green gown. With her blond hair and brown eyes, she was most fetching even if Sarah herself did not seem to realize it. Once again, Cordelia vowed to do something about her unassuming cousin.

"What are you doing?"

Sarah stepped to one side to study her reflection. "What does it look like I'm doing?"

Cordelia widened her eyes. "Surely you do not plan on coming with me?"

Sarah snorted. "Surely you don't imagine I would let you go alone?"

"Sarah, I'm an adult. I can certainly go to a booksellers unaccompanied."

Sarah gritted her teeth. "It's my job to accompany you. Regardless of whether or not we all consider my position something of a sham, I shall do it to the best of my ability. And I do think, as I am in an official sense your companion, that you should do more with my opinion than ignore it completely."

"I can't imagine Mother or Father has ever really thought you were—"

"In charge?" Sarah said wryly, fastening the mantle. "Probably not. But I suspect they do expect me to keep you out of trouble."

"And you're doing a fine job. I am not in trouble nor do I intend to be." She cast Sarah her brightest smile. "Why, I really am doing nothing more than being a dutiful daughter."

Sarah raised a brow. "Oh?"

"I wrote Mr. Sinclair yesterday, according to my mother's suggestion, dispatched a footman to deliver my note to his residence rather than posting it, in the interest of efficiency, and all I'm doing now is trying to determine if I could indeed bow to my parents' wishes and marry the man."

Sarah stared. "You do have the remarkable ability to twist something to your benefit."

Cordelia grinned. "I shall take that as a compliment."

"It was not mean as one," Sarah snapped. She picked her hat up off the bed and jammed it on her head.

"You needn't take your frustration with me out on an innocent hat." Cordelia shook her head. "Crumpled hats are not at all in fashion these days."

"It's not crumpled," Sarah muttered, picking at a section of her hat that did appear a tiny bit crumpled. "Why don't you just meet Mr. Sinclair in person and end this farce altogether?"

"I'm not ready to meet him, that's why. A face-to-face meeting implies something on my part I am not yet ready to imply. Until I know whether or not there is the chance of, well, happiness with him, I don't intend to meet him. Besides, it will be much easier to escape this marriage if we don't meet in person."

Sarah's gaze met hers. "In spite of what you've said, is that the ultimate point of all this then? To avoid marriage to Mr. Sinclair?"

"The ultimate point, Sarah, and you should know this as well as anyone, is to find the right man. Mr. Sinclair could well be the right man. Mother suggested fate might have played a hand in all this and you must admit it is an interesting idea. When you consider that the elder Mr. Sinclair comes along just when Father's business is not doing well and each of them has a child they'd like to see suitably married, it does indeed seem as though unseen forces are at work. And, to be honest, I rather like the idea of fate presenting me with just the right man."

"Then why don't you—"

"Because fate is vague and elusive. You have no way of knowing if fate is involved or not. Fate doesn't slap you in the face and announce its presence. It's simply not practical to accept that something is fate when in truth it might be a dreadful mistake."

"But—"

"And even if you want to accept that fate brought Mr. Sinclair, the younger Mr. Sinclair that is, to me, isn't it entirely possible that fate intended for us to dispense of the notion of marriage to one another so that our true matches might appear?"

Sarah stared in obvious confusion. "What?"

"I know, I too find it confusing. Precisely why I have to take a hand in," Cordelia smiled in a satisfied manner, "determining my own fate."

"But perhaps if you were to meet him—"

"Where would be the fun in that?"

"Is that why you're continuing this masquerade of yours?" Disbelief sounded in Sarah's voice. "Because it's fun?"

"Well, it is fun." Cordelia grinned. "The most fun

I've had in a long time. I like pretending to be someone I'm not and I don't see any harm in it."

Sarah studied her cousin. "What happens when Mr. Lewis and Mr. Sinclair find out about your little charade? And they will find out eventually, you know."

"Of course they will, but only if . . ." She paused to choose just the right words. Sarah did have a tendency to be a bit skittish about things like deception. "If I decide to marry him. Then I should hope he's the kind of man who would see the humor in my actions and understand as well the practicality of knowing something about a man before promising to marry him."

"And if you decide not to marry him?" Sarah said slowly.

"We should be off." Cordelia took the other woman's elbow and steered her toward the door. "Murdock's opens in a few minutes and I told Mr. Lewis I would meet him there soon after the shop opens."

"You haven't answered my question."

"And I think it would be best if you were to stay in the carriage."

"I'm not staying in the carriage." Sarah pulled out of Cordelia's grip and stared at her. "Why on earth would I have to stay in the carriage?"

"I don't know how to explain you, who you are that is."

"Why explain me at all?"

"It simply stands to reason if I am pretending to be you, Lady Cordelia's companion that is, the woman with me would have to be Lady Cordelia."

"You want me to pretend to be you?" Sarah glared. "Absolutely not. That's taking this entirely too far."

"I thought you'd say that. Honestly, Sarah, sometimes you have no sense of adventure." Cordelia sighed. "I suppose if you were to stay on one side of the shop and pretend not to know me . . ." She nodded. "Yes, that will do."

"I do not intend to take my eyes off you." A warning sounded in Sarah's voice.

"Nor do I expect you to. It is your job after all." Cordelia cast Sarah a pleasant smile. "And I shall make your life easier by being on my best behavior."

"Beginning when?" Sarah muttered.

Cordelia hooked her arm through Sarah's and started toward the door. "Now then, let us be off."

"You still haven't answered my question. How does this deception of yours end if you decide not to marry him?"

"I'm not quite sure yet. But at that point, I suspect the easiest way to break it off with him, the best course for all concerned"—Cordelia pulled open the door—"will be to indeed have you pretend to be me."

Cordelia perused the books on the back shelves in her favorite section of Murdock's, the section devoted to foreign lands, all the while trying to keep note of where Sarah was and watching for Mr. Lewis's entrance as well. She was fairly certain he wasn't here yet unless he was hiding behind a shelf somewhere. Which was an absurd idea. What on earth did Mr. Lewis have to hide? No, he was simply late, although she probably shouldn't have expected him to be prompt. Not that it mattered. If she had to wait for anyone, this was the perfect place to do so.

Cordelia had loved Murdock's Stationers, Booksellers and Circulating Library from the moment she'd first crossed its threshold and breathed in the heady scent of old books nearly a decade ago. Certainly her family's library was extensive and sufficient for her needs in a general sense, but here were books she could purchase for her very own as well as endless volumes she could borrow for a modest annual subscription on an unimagined number of topics: foreign countries, ancient civilizations, modern inventions, and best of all, novels. Adventurous, romantic novels about star-crossed lovers or hapless governesses or, even, she grinned at the thought, pirates.

"Dare I hope that smile is for me?" A distinctly American voice sounded by her side. The oddest thrill of excitement raced up her spine. No doubt because he was standing entirely too close than was proper. Still, as he was an American, such lapses could be overlooked.

"Rather arrogant of you to think so, wouldn't you say?" she said without looking at him.

"I didn't think so." Mr. Lewis chuckled. "I merely hoped."

She stifled a smile and glanced at him. "Is Mr. Sinclair as charming as you?"

"More so. Indeed, I pale in comparison." He kept his gaze directed toward the books on the shelf in front of him but leaned slightly sideways toward her. "Tell me, Miss Palmer, are we to pretend we are searching for books and not actually speaking to one another for the length of our conversation, or are we allowed to face each other and converse like normal people?"

"I'm not sure I've decided yet, Mr. Lewis," she said

in a lofty manner. "I'm rather enjoying the clandestine nature of our conversation."

"I feel like a spy passing important military secrets to another spy."

"You look more like a pirate," Cordelia murmured.

"A pirate?" He snorted back a laugh. "I like that."

"No doubt you do." At once it struck her that she'd like nothing more than to converse and flirt with Mr. Lewis with no purpose whatsoever other than the enjoyment of matching wits with an interesting, dashing gentleman. Still, she had no business thinking of Mr. Lewis as dashing or interesting, and flirtation with this American was not her purpose here. Pity. She pushed the thought from her mind and drew a deep breath. "I think we should proceed with why we are here. I have my questions prepared."

"Do go on then."

"First of all, I think Lady Cordelia should know the extent of Mr. Sinclair's wealth."

He choked. "That's rather mercenary of her, isn't it?"

"Not at all; it's practical. She should know what lies ahead for her. Financially that is." She paused. "But do remember these are my questions, not Lady Cordelia's."

"She doesn't know about our meeting then?"

"No, of course not. Did you think she did?"

"I did wonder. There's a woman near the door who has been glaring at me since I came in and I thought—"

"I can assure you," Cordelia said with all the passion of truth, "that is not Lady Cordelia. Now then, about Mr. Sinclair's finances?"

"Ah yes, well, Lady Cordelia can rest easy on that score. Mr. Sinclair is both ambitious and intelligent. I have no doubt that he will one day be among the wealthiest men in America."

She raised a brow. "One day?"

"Fortunes are not built overnight, Miss Palmer. Mr. Sinclair inherited a tidy sum that is providing the foundation for his current venture." A smug note sounded in his voice. "It's going quite well too. He has acquired an impressive group of investors in England and we plan to return home before autumn."

"Home?" Her heart skipped a beat. "You mean America?"

He chuckled. "That is home. More specifically, Baltimore."

"He'll probably want Lady Cordelia to accompany him."

"Should they marry, I would wager on it, yes."

"I hadn't considered that," she said under her breath.

"Hadn't considered that a husband might want a wife to live in the same country, in the same house?"

"It just hadn't crossed my mind that this marriage would mean leaving England, but of course he would expect her to come with him, and she would expect to do so."

"Would Lady Cordelia be willing to leave England?" he said casually. "Possibly forever? To live the rest of her days in a foreign country?"

"The rest of her days . . ." Cordelia thought for a moment. "Yes, yes, I believe she would. She'd think it quite exciting. She loves to travel, you know."

"You've mentioned that," he murmured.

"She's never been to America and I know she's always wished to see it. And it's not like it's a true foreign country. Why, less than a century ago it was part of the empire, and Americans do speak English after all." She glanced at him. "In their fashion."

"Indeed we do." He smiled. "In our fashion."

There was something about his smile that was at once most endearing and more than a little devilish. All in all, Mr. Lewis was extremely handsome and most provocative. Not that it mattered.

"Is he handsome?" she asked without thinking.

He raised a dashing brow. "Is it important?"

"Not in the least." She shrugged. "Lady Cordelia is not so shallow as to be unduly influenced by appearance."

"Of course not."

"Still, you must admit, it's easier to spend the rest of one's life with an attractive man rather than one whose face would frighten innocent children and small animals."

"Excellent point." His brow furrowed in thought. "However, it is difficult for one man to judge whether or not another is considered handsome."

"Nonsense." She scoffed. "Women make such judgments about other women all the time."

"One of many ways in which men and women are different creatures," he said wryly.

"Simply tell me what he looks like then."

"Mr. Sinclair is about my height, with dark hair and eyes. In fact, people have said on occasion that we look as if we could be brothers." He flashed her a wicked smile. "Do you think *I'm* handsome?"

She sniffed. "I think you're entirely too arrogant

for your own good. No doubt part of that forthright, charming manner of yours."

"Probably." He laughed. "You didn't answer my question."

"Nor shall I. Besides, whether or not I find you to be attractive is of no consequence and has no place in this discussion. Our meeting is not about you and me."

"No. It's about Lady Cordelia and Mr. Sinclair." He sighed in surrender. "It's been my observation that women consider Mr. Sinclair quite handsome and charming."

"Does he like women then?"

"I would say it depends on the particular woman."

"That's not what I mean. I mean does he like the pursuit of women?"

"I think he likes the end of the pursuit better, as do we all." Amusement danced in his eyes. "Miss Palmer, you might be unaware of this but most unmarried men, and any number who are married, like the pursuit of women a great deal. Some men consider it a sport, others a fine art."

"Is Mr. Sinclair an artist then?"

Mr. Lewis choked. Again.

"Goodness, Mr. Lewis, I do hope I am not embarrassing you."

"No, not at all." His voice had an odd sort of catch in it, as if he wasn't sure if he wanted to gasp in horror or laugh in delight.

"What I mean is . . . is he the type of man who . . ." She wasn't entirely sure how to phrase this. She drew a deep breath. "Will he give up his artistic endeavors?"

He stared. "His wha—"

"Forgo the chase?"

"The ch—"

"Will he be faithful to Lady Cordelia?" she said with a huff.

"Absolutely." Indignation sounded in his voice. He looked her straight in the eye. "Mr. Sinclair is an honorable gentleman. When the day comes that he enters into marriage, it is a vow and a commitment he will not take lightly."

"I didn't mean to impugn—"

"Let me ask you." His eyes narrowed. "Will Lady Cordelia be faithful as well?"

She gasped. "How dare you suggest otherwise?"

"You suggested the same thing about Mr. Sinclair. You did far more than suggest."

"That's a different matter entirely." She waved off his comment. "Men are notorious for their faithless natures."

He snorted. "I've known any number of women who were just as faithless."

"You can rest assured, Mr. Lewis, Lady Cordelia will not be counted among them."

"Are you sure?"

"Absolutely. There isn't a doubt in my mind."

"I see." He winced. "She's not overly attractive is she?"

Cordelia widened her eyes. "Why on earth would you think that?

"Well, all that travel and her independent nature and indomitable character—"

She stared in confusion. "What are you talking about?"

"From what you've said about Lady Cordelia thus far, I have the distinct impression she has the sturdy nature and stout heart of a tweed-clad Amazon warrior." He grimaced. "And an appearance to match."

"That's what you think?"

"It does explain why she's not married," Mr. Lewis said under his breath.

"First of all, Mr. Lewis, you should know that simply because a woman is intelligent and enjoys travel and—"

"She's writing a book," he said in the same sort of hushed tone someone might use to say "she has three eyes" or "her mind is not what it should be."

"—*and* puts her observations and intelligence to use does not mean she isn't lovely as well."

"Then tell me, Miss Palmer." He crossed his arms over his chest and leaned against the bookshelves. "What does Lady Cordelia look like?"

"What does she look like?" Cordelia repeated cautiously. This was certainly awkward. But given Mr. Lewis's questions, and that her answers would ultimately be passed on to Mr. Sinclair, this was probably not the time for undue modesty. Besides, she didn't want him thinking of her as a stocky, tweed-wearing Amazon. "She's most becoming really. Indeed, while she is not a great beauty, she is pretty enough. I would say that gentlemen consider her quite lovely."

"Gentlemen blinded by her dowry and family connections."

"Wealthy gentlemen," she snapped. "Who have no need of her dowry."

"Is she as lovely as you?"

She met his gaze directly. "More so."

"I doubt that," he murmured, straightening and pulling a book from the shelf.

Heat washed up her face. "That's very flattering, Mr. Lewis, but we are here—"

"Yes, yes, to discuss Lady Cordelia and Mr. Sinclair." He flipped open the book and paged through it but directed his words to her. "How does Lady Cordelia feel about this marriage proposition?"

"She isn't yet sure how she feels about it," Cordelia said without pause. "On one hand, she realizes it's her duty to marry and ensure her family's financial stability. On the other . . ." She blew a frustrated breath. "It's difficult you know to accept a match based on practicality and responsibility rather than . . ."

"Rather than love?"

"Love is of no consequence in these circumstances, Mr. Lewis. Lady Cordelia is a dutiful daughter—"

"But surely all women wish for love?"

"Yes, but it is as elusive as the clouds in the sky. They appear solid and real and within reach but in truth they are impossible to grasp. For most of us love is very much an illusion with no substance."

He considered her thoughtfully. "Is that your opinion or Lady Cordelia's?"

She gazed into his dark eyes and, for no more than a moment, had the oddest sensation of falling. "In this, as in so many other things, we agree."

"What a shame, Miss Palmer." His gaze remained locked with hers. "For both of you."

"Perhaps," she murmured. What was this man doing to her? She shook her head and drew a deep breath. "This match is solid and practical and a matter of business."

"Initially yes, but one would hope a certain amount of affection would grow with time."

She smiled wryly. "You're something of a romantic, aren't you, Mr. Lewis?"

He chuckled. "When it comes to things like marriage and sharing the rest of one's life with someone, I suppose I am. I've never come close to marriage or love for that matter. Therefore I prefer to hang on to the illusion, as you call it. At least for now."

"Yes, well, illusion aside, one would indeed hope that affection would develop eventually between husband and wife. I understand it's not at all uncommon in arrangements of this nature." She cast him a firm glance. "However, you should be aware that, regardless of the financial benefits of this match, she won't marry him if she doesn't like him."

He laughed. "So much for being a dutiful daughter."

"Would you expect her to marry a man she found distasteful? And would you expect Mr. Sinclair to marry a woman he could not abide?" She shook her head. "Family responsibilities aside, I would wish that on no one. Nor would Lord and Lady Marsham insist on this marriage under those conditions."

"That is good to know."

She studied him curiously. "You sound relieved."

"I am relieved. I count Mr. Sinclair as one of my closest friends. I would hate for him to be trapped in a marriage with a women he could not hope to eventually care for, a woman he at the very least likes. Or a woman who doesn't like him. However." He smiled in a resigned manner. "I am confident she will like him. He's quite a likeable fellow."

"And as you've said, given her advancing years, this could well be her last chance."

"I never said that," he said staunchly. "I may have thought it but I never said it."

"She's thought it. She can't help but think it." Cordelia shrugged. "It's not a pleasant thought."

"I can imagine."

"No, Mr. Lewis, with all due respect, I don't think you can. This is another one of those instances in which men and women are different creatures." She searched for the right words. "A man can marry at very nearly any age. No one considers him past his prime until well into his elder years. It's entirely different for a woman. And for a woman with as many varied interests as Lady Cordelia—"

"Travel and writing and the like?"

She nodded. "Exactly. Her life has been eventful and adventurous and she's had a great deal of fun but the years have passed, and passed unnoticed. One day you're at your first ball and then, before you know it, you find yourself to be twenty-five years of age faced with the very real possibility that an arranged marriage may indeed be your only chance for the kind of future that deep down in your soul you've always desired."

"I see," he said slowly. "Then you're saying she will indeed marry Mr. Sinclair."

"I'm not saying that at all. Regardless of her circumstances, she hasn't decided and she doesn't want to be hurried. This is far too important a decision to make in haste." She thought for a moment. "And what of Mr. Sinclair? I haven't asked you how he feels about this proposition."

"To be perfectly honest, Miss Palmer." He paused as

if debating the wisdom of his words. "The last thing in the world Mr. Sinclair wishes is to marry."

The oddest sensation of relief washed through her. "If that is the case—"

"However, as much as he disagrees with his father on virtually every matter regarding his life or his future, he too feels a sense of responsibility as well as family honor." Mr. Lewis snapped the book in his hand closed and replaced it on the shelf. "As much as he would prefer to find a wife of his own choosing in his own time, he will not renege on a commitment made by his father. He will not withdraw from this arrangement." He paused. "If Lady Cordelia wishes to do so, however—"

"It would be a different matter entirely, wouldn't it?"

He nodded.

"That is certainly something to keep in mind," she murmured. Perhaps, if she was indeed the stouthearted Amazon Mr. Lewis had envisioned, she could reject him out of hand and not be the least bit concerned about the financial consequences of doing as she wished. As it was, her heart was rather faint at the notion of dooming her family to financial hardship. Almost as faint as it was at the idea of marrying a man not of her own choosing.

At least she had the upcoming weeks in Brighton to consider the ramifications of whatever decision she made.

"I suspect, if she finds Mr. Sinclair as charming as you claim he is, Lady Cordelia will eventually agree to marry him. I doubt that she will see any other choice." She forced a smile to her face and nodded. "Thank you for your time, Mr. Lewis. I think I have what I need."

He moved to block her way and stared down at her. "Are you sure? Perhaps we should meet again."

She shook her head. "I don't think that would be at all wise."

"I think it might be the wisest thing I have ever done." He took her hand and raised it to his lips, his gaze never leaving hers. "Meet me again, Miss Palmer."

"I . . ." She stared into his eyes. Dear Lord, there was that falling sensation again. Quickly she pulled her hand from his. "I can't, Mr. Lewis, nor do I think I should. Besides, we leave for Brighton tomorrow and we will be gone for several weeks."

"Brighton?" He nodded. "I believe Lady Cordelia mentioned that in her note to Mr. Sinclair."

"It's lovely in June. The family goes every year at this time."

"I see." He paused then cast her a noncommittal smile. "Do enjoy your holiday, Miss Palmer," he said in a formal manner. "I suspect we will meet again. Until then," he nodded a bow, "I remain your humble servant. Good day." He turned and strode toward the door.

"Good day," she murmured. Whatever had possessed Mr. Lewis? One moment he was charming and friendly and altogether too tempting in a manner she'd never experienced before and the next he was overly polite and abruptly taking his leave. Not that it wasn't an excellent idea. She found him entirely too interesting for her own good.

Mr. Lewis nodded in a pleasant manner at Sarah on his way out the door. The moment it closed behind him, Sarah caught Cordelia's gaze and raised a questioning brow. Cordelia smiled with a confidence she didn't feel and started toward her. It was past time they returned home. There was still a great deal to do today before they left for Brighton.

It would be awkward when the truth came out about her little charade. Mr. Lewis was part of Mr. Sinclair's life and no doubt always would be. Still, all in all, it was a relatively harmless deception. She'd explain to him and he would probably laugh about it. And if Daniel Sinclair wasn't the kind of man who could laugh about such things, well, that would certainly be a deciding factor in her decision.

A thought struck her and her stomach twisted. The next time she saw Mr. Lewis, she might well be on her way to the altar with his employer.

In spite of the difficulties inherent in travel to strange and exotic locales, or perhaps because of them, travel is a grand adventure. Particularly for most ladies who have little other opportunity for adventure.

An English Lady's Traveling Companion

Chapter 4

Dear Lady Cordelia,

Your apology is of course accepted but not by any means necessary. I fully understand the pressure that can be exerted by even the most well-meaning parent in a situation such as the one we find ourselves in. It would indeed be most awkward to meet face-to-face under these circumstances. Therefore allow me to tell you something of myself . . .

"Pack your bags, Warren." Daniel strode into the office and grinned at his friend. "We're leaving London."

Warren's expression brightened. "We're going home? Thank God." He got to his feet. "I can be packed within the hour. When do we leave?"

Daniel laughed. "You're obviously feeling better."

"Just the thought of Baltimore is enough to make anything that ails me vanish."

Daniel raised a brow. "I thought you were enjoying London?"

"I was, I am, but now I'm ready to return home. More than ready."

"I've never seen you quite so . . ." Daniel stared at his friend. "There's a woman, isn't there?"

"There's always a woman." Warren grinned. "Somewhere."

"There's a woman in Baltimore, isn't there? One particular woman? That's why you're so eager to go home."

"There are any number of women in Baltimore, but no, there isn't one particular one. If there is a lady I miss, it's the city herself. It will just be good to be home."

Perhaps it would have been better if Daniel had told Warren of their destination before he'd said they were leaving. He studied his friend for a moment. "Tell me, what is it that you miss most?"

"The smell of the sea," Warren said without hesitation. "I admit, it's an odd thing to miss, but there you have it."

"Well then, you're in luck." Daniel grinned. "We're going to Brighton."

"Brighton?" Warren stared in confusion. "Not Baltimore?"

"Brighton," Daniel said firmly. "You'll like it."

"Why Brighton?"

"Because," Daniel lowered his voice in a confidential manner, "I'm fairly certain it smells of the sea."

"It's not the same." Indignation sounded in Warren's voice.

"Nonsense." Daniel moved to his desk and leaned back against the edge. "Close your eyes and you'd think you were home. It will smell exactly the same, it's the very same ocean after all. Why, if you were to set out swimming from Brighton you'd eventually arrive in Baltimore."

"No you wouldn't." Warren crossed his arms over his chest. "Unless I'm thinking of the wrong town, Brighton, England, is on the Channel. You'd end up in France."

"You'd have to make a few turns."

Warren narrowed his eyes. "Why are we going to Brighton?"

"It's a famous resort and I hear it's great fun. It would be a shame not to see it before we leave this part of the world."

Warren shook his head. "I don't believe you."

"Well, it would be a shame."

"You've never been one for seeing sights." Suspicion washed across Warren's face. "Why do you want to go to Brighton?"

"I think the sea air will do you a world of good. You still aren't quite yourself, you know."

"Daniel." Warren gritted his teeth. "Why do—"

"Because." Daniel couldn't suppress a satisfied grin. "That's where Miss Palmer will be."

"Miss Palmer?" Warren raised a surprised brow. "The Miss Palmer you've been meeting to learn more about the woman you might well marry? Lady Cordelia's companion? That Miss Palmer?"

"The very one." Daniel chuckled. "She thinks I'm a pirate."

"You are a pirate," Warren snapped. "What about Lady Cordelia?"

"I doubt that she thinks I'm a pirate."

"That's not what I meant."

Daniel shrugged. "Oh, she's going to Brighton as well."

"Again, you've evaded the question." Warren studied his friend for a long moment. "Let me see if I understand this. You want to go to Brighton because Miss Palmer, the Miss Palmer who thinks you're me—"

"Who thinks I'm a pirate."

"—together with Lady Cordelia—"

"The entire family really. They go to Brighton every year."

"So Lady Cordelia's family, including Miss Palmer, will be in Brighton and the attraction of Brighton—"

"Aside from the sea air?"

Warren ignored him. "Is Miss Palmer."

"I understand there are many attractions in Brighton," Daniel said lightly.

Warren's eyes widened. "You are pursuing Miss Palmer!"

"Pursue is such a specific word." Daniel shook his head in a chastising manner. "And not entirely accurate."

"Then what is accurate?"

"I am . . . curious about the woman, that's all. I find her extremely interesting and I would like to further our acquaintance."

"To what end?"

"To what end?" Daniel drew his brows together. "I don't really know yet."

"I suggest you determine that." Warren rolled his gaze toward the ceiling. "Whether you wish to call it pursuit, and most people, myself included, would indeed consider following a woman from London to Brighton to 'further your acquaintance' pursuit, you have to decide why. This isn't just any woman, Daniel, this is Lady's Cordelia's companion as well as cousin—"

"Distant." Daniel waved off the comment. "Very distant and by marriage. There's no actual blood tie."

"Nonetheless, I would suspect they're as close as sisters. How do you think Lady Cordelia will react to discovering the man her parents wish her to marry—"

"Oh, Lady Cordelia isn't going to marry me."

"She isn't?"

"She won't marry me if she doesn't like me."

"Why wouldn't she like you?" Warren said slowly. "She's never met you."

"That's the beauty of it." Daniel slid off the desk and paced the room. "It came to me when I was on my way back from the booksellers."

Warren groaned. "I'm almost afraid to ask. What came to you?"

"How to avoid this marriage. I can't simply withdraw from an agreement made by my father, regardless of the fact that I had no say in it. It wouldn't be honorable." He paused and met Warren's gaze. "Even though a very good argument could be made that it's my father's word that's at stake rather than mine, I do have a sense of family honor. A man's word is his bond in one's personal life as much as in business. You and I count on that as do others. My own word would be worthless if I didn't uphold my father's promises."

"So how do you intend to avoid marrying Lady Cordelia?"

"It's really all in her hands. Miss Palmer has assured me she won't marry someone she doesn't like."

Warren stared in disbelief. "You plan to pursue Miss Palmer in an effort to make Lady Cordelia dislike you?"

"No, of course not," Daniel said quickly. "That would be wrong."

"You'd be lucky if Lady Cordelia, or more likely her father, doesn't shoot you."

"I said it would be wrong. Effective," Daniel added under his breath, "but definitely wrong. Besides, I have no intention of letting Miss Palmer know who I really am. She thinks I'm you."

"Excellent," Warren snapped. "Then they'll shoot me."

"No one is going to shoot anyone." Daniel scoffed. "I'm confident of that."

"Imagine my relief."

"Warren, you worry entirely too much. This is going to work extremely well." Daniel walked around his desk, sat down, and picked up Lady Cordelia's letter. He waved it at the other man. "Thanks to this."

"The letter from Lady Cordelia? Dare I hope that you read this letter thoroughly?" Warren said dryly.

"Twice." Daniel grinned. "And I've already responded, which is rather a shame really."

"You're going to use this correspondence to convince Lady Cordelia you are not the type of man she wants to marry?"

"I do intend to be subtle," Daniel said quickly.

"Of course."

"And I will avoid outright lies," Daniel added.

"As well you should." Warren nodded and considered his friend silently.

Daniel held his breath. No doubt Warren would disapprove of the idea. But damn it all, Warren wasn't about to be shepherded into a marriage with a gentlemen-find-her-lovely-tweed-wearing Amazon. "Well?"

"I have to hand it to you, Daniel." Warren smiled slowly. "It's very nearly brilliant."

"It is brilliant." Daniel leaned back in his chair and grinned. "Especially as I intend as well to convince Miss Palmer, in my guise as you, that Mr. Sinclair will not suit Lady Cordelia at all."

"I see. So it's not the actual pursuit of Miss Palmer you'll be using to deter Lady Cordelia from marriage."

"No, I said that would be wrong."

"But you do plan to persuade Miss Palmer that you are not right for Lady Cordelia. And that's why you're following her to Brighton."

"Exactly."

"It seems to me you're walking a very fine line."

"One that needs to be walked. I have no desire to marry at the moment." Determination hardened Daniel's voice. "And when I do, I much prefer to choose my own bride."

"Someone like, oh, I don't know." Warren paused. "Miss Palmer?"

"Someone exactly like Miss Palmer. She's clever and loyal. Too proud to accept charity but not too proud to earn her own living. And she's lovely as well." He drummed his fingers on top of Lady's Cordelia's letter. "All in all, she would be the perfect wife for a man in my position."

"But you're currently not interested in marriage?"

"Absolutely not."

"And you are not pursing Miss Palmer beyond furthering an acquaintance? A friendship as it were."

"Nothing more."

"How do you think Miss Palmer will react when she finds out you've been deceiving her?"

Daniel shook his head. "She's not going to find out. With any luck this matter will be resolved before I am forced to have a meeting with Lady Cordelia. And if I don't have to meet Lady Cordelia, I don't have to tell Miss Palmer."

"She'll probably hate you for deceiving her if she finds out."

"Yet another reason to make sure she doesn't."

Warren stared at him for a long moment then shrugged, returned to his desk, and took his seat.

Daniel narrowed his eyes. "What are you thinking?"

"Nothing of significance," Warren said in an off-hand way and paged through a notebook on his desk, his gaze firmly on the pages in front of him.

"What?"

"Nothing at all."

"Damn it all, Warren, tell me what has put that superior look on your face."

"Very well," Warren said mildly, his attention still on the notebook. "There's an enormous flaw in your brilliant plan."

"I don't see a flaw," Daniel said staunchly.

"No, I suspect you don't." Warren chuckled. "There's often only a matter of degree between brilliance and stupidity you know."

"What is this alleged flaw?"

"Oh no, I want nothing to do with this. This is your plan from start to finish. I will tell you one thing, though." Warren looked up and met Daniel's gaze. A wide grin stretched across his face. "I can't wait to get to Brighton."

Bracing, that's what it was. Cordelia stood on the half balcony off the small parlor she shared with Sarah in the grand house her family had leased every summer for as long as she could remember and drew in a deep breath. There was nothing like the smell of sea air and the sound of the waves. The Brighton house sat, along with other tightly packed houses, on King's Road and had an unobstructed view of the water. If, of course, one could discount the hordes of visitors sitting on benches on the beach or strolling along the promenade. Brought, for the most part, by the railway.

When Cordelia was a child, the trip to Brighton took nearly five hours by coach. Now trains had cut the travel time from London to a mere two hours, making a visit of a single day not merely possible but effortless. But even before that, Cordelia could not remember a time when Brighton had not seemed like an endless celebration, a continuous festival filled with high spirits and fun. No doubt it had much to do with the bracing aspect of the air itself.

The fact that June was not part of the official social season in Brighton made no difference to the crowds that swelled the walkways. When Cordelia's parents were first wed, the season for anyone who was anyone comprised the summer months. But that was in the day of the Prince Regent who had transformed an ordinary villa into the Royal Pavilion, modeled after fanciful Indian palaces—when grand feasts and parties hosted by the prince were the order of the day. Her mother often reminisced about those affairs; long past now that Victoria was queen and had abandoned the crowds of Brighton and the Pavilion itself for more peaceful retreats. It was the royal prerogative of course, but Cordelia never could understand why anyone wouldn't love Brighton and the Pavilion. She'd always thought the Pavilion was a magical sort of place and her mother's stories only reinforced that impression.

Even though the official social season had shifted to autumn and winter, thanks to Brighton's mild year-round climate, Mother was something of a traditionalist. Summer was when she and her family had always come to Brighton and, she had declared on any number of occasions when Cordelia's sisters had protested, always would. Although she was dismayed by the large number of common folk who now descended on Brighton, Father thought it was good for the town's merchants and good for those tourists as well to escape the confines of London for a day. Besides, he said, it made the atmosphere in the seaside resort more of an ongoing celebration, which he found most appealing. If one was going to spend a holiday anywhere, Father staunchly declared he would much rather spend it somewhere where the atmosphere was gay and light and full of fun.

It was one of the few areas in which he and Mother were not in complete agreement. Even though Mother was active in any number of charitable pursuits, Cordelia had always considered her father somewhat more egalitarian in his views regarding the social classes. When one considered it, it was extremely unusual given that Father was the product of a centuries-old British noble family and one would have thought he would have been something more of a snob than Mother whose family, while titled, was not quite as distinguished as Father's. Perhaps it was because he had always been involved in some manner in the pursuit of business that he had a more democratic view of the world around him. Perhaps as well, it was that very aspect of his nature that meant he was not averse to marrying his youngest daughter off to an American. As long as said American was acceptable in terms of both wealth and character.

Cordelia stared at the sea, her thoughts far from the sparkling blue waters. She had received her first letter from Mr. Sinclair—although she could probably think of him as Daniel now, given the circumstances—on the day they left London two days ago, and it was both informative and pleasant enough. Polite more than anything really. But then, given Mr. Lewis's assessment of his employer and friend, she had expected as much. She wasn't at all sure what she would write in her next note that would be at once personal and noncommittal. She thought perhaps she would write to him in the same style in which she wrote her articles about travel, keeping in mind she was not writing for ladies. Perhaps she'd tell him of Brighton's charms and the healthy appeal of the sea air.

"Yes, that will do," she murmured.

"Did you say something?" Sarah asked from across the room.

"Not really." She glanced over her shoulder at Sarah, who sat at the ladies' desk with pen in hand and a thoughtful expression on her face. "Are you writing to your mystery suitor again?"

"He's not . . ." Sarah cast her a pleasant smile. "Yes, I am."

"You're not going to deny it then?"

"Why? I am indeed writing a letter."

"No, I meant deny that he is your mystery suitor."

"It would do me no good. I have denied it over and over and you have completely ignored me. Therefore," Sarah's gaze returned to the letter before her, "I see no need to continue to do so."

"It would be a moot point if you simply revealed his identity to me."

"That is my business and I intend for it to remain so. Besides, it does you good not to know everything about everything. It strengthens your character."

"Most people would say my character is strong enough," Cordelia said under her breath. "Honestly, Sarah, sometimes you do take all the fun out of things."

"It's my job," Sarah said without looking up. "We have acknowledged that in most ways I am a dreadful companion but in this, at least, I do what I can."

Cordelia laughed. "Well then, be a good companion and accompany me on a walk. The sky is a brilliant blue, the air is fresh, and I hear the strains of music coming from the pier. It's far too nice a day to stay inside."

"Perhaps later," Sarah said absently.

"Couldn't you finish that later?" On any other day, regardless of how appealing the out-of-doors, Cordelia would happily occupy her time working on her book or writing her articles or planning her next trip. But today she was far too restless to sit still and too on edge to stay confined indoors. "I can't go by myself, you know."

"I do know but I'm astonished that you know it."

"I know it, I simply ignore it on occasion." In the years since Sarah had become Cordelia's official companion, there had been any number of times Cordelia had completely disregarded the requirement that properly bred young ladies be chaperoned in public at all times. Certainly when they were traveling in foreign lands, it was a question of safety never to be unaccompanied. But this was Brighton. She'd spent part of nearly every summer of her life here and knew the promenades and beaches as well as she did the streets and parks around her home in London and had always felt considerably safer in Brighton. The very atmosphere was conducive to a certain laxity of behavior. Why, even Mother was considerably more relaxed here about rules and deportment than she ever was at home.

Sarah looked at her with an overly innocent expression. "Why don't you take the boys? I'm sure they would love a walk."

"What a lovely idea," Cordelia said brightly. "Do you have a leash?"

The boys, as everyone referred to them, were the combined male offspring of Cordelia's three older sisters. Her sisters had quite efficiently provided their husbands with male heirs before they had begun producing daughters. Thus far Cordelia had six nephews, descending in age from nearly twelve to eight, and five nieces with another niece or nephew scheduled to arrive in the world any day. Mother loved having her grandchildren around her and Brighton provided the perfect opportunity to gather the entire family under one roof. Cordelia suspected it made her mother feel very much like the queen herself to be surrounded by her offspring. Cordelia's oldest sisters, Amelia and Edwina, together with their brood, as well as Beatrice's two children, had arrived this morning. Beatrice was about to give birth to her third child and had elected to remain in London this year.

Her sisters and the children were accompanied by a small army of maids, governesses, and nannies, which meant the house was now filled with the sound of children and women but lacked, for the most part, a male presence over the age of eleven. Not that anyone minded. Father was here today but he would return to London periodically. Her sisters' husbands would come for a few days now and then during their respective family's stay in Brighton, but all Cordelia's brothers-in-law pled pressing matters in London kept them from an extended stay.

It was Edwina's husband who had started begging off from the annual Brighton holiday upon noticing that Father was absent almost as often as he was in residence. Amelia's husband had next adopted the idea almost immediately—one might have thought he had simply been waiting for the opportunity—and Cordelia was fairly certain Beatrice's husband was informed by the other men of this method of avoiding too much togetherness with his new wife's family even before he had said his vows.

Would Mr. Sinclair get such instruction before they were wed?

It would be rather pleasant to have her own husband join that unique fraternity comprised only of men who had married Bannister sisters. Not that he would, of course. The oddest sense of disappointment stabbed her. If she did indeed marry Mr. Sinclair it would be rare if ever that they would join the rest of the family in Brighton. No, they would be living in America. Which would, she thought with a mental stiffening of her spine, be an adventure with grand new experiences. The very thought was exciting. Why, there were any number of sights in America she'd long wanted to see.

"I should make a list," she said under her breath.

"If you just remember kings and saints," Sarah said absently. "You should have no problem."

"Kings and . . ." Cordelia frowned in confusion then understood. "Kings and saints; yes, of course."

Amelia had named her sons after kings: Henry, Edward, and Richard. Edwina had named hers after saints, specifically apostles, and had Thomas, Matthew, and James. Thus far, Beatrice had only one son—

Philip—who could have served for king or saint but Beatrice said the boy was named for Father, which delighted him far more than it would have pleased either a king or God.

In spite of their names, the boys, particularly when they were together, had neither the dignity of kings nor the nature of saints. They were small boys and prone to do those sorts of things small boys have always done. And as such a stroll with them was tantamount to taking one's life in one's hands. Still, Cordelia had always prided herself on her courage and sense of adventure.

"Very well then." She drew a deep breath. "And Sarah."

Sarah glanced up from her letter.

"Should I never see you again." Cordelia placed the back of her hand against her forehead and adopted the overly dramatic manner of her favorite actress. "Think of me fondly in the future."

"Good Lord, you're not thinking of going without their governesses are you?" Sarah said dryly.

"Even I am not that adventurous." Cordelia grinned and left to gather the flock.

A scant half an hour later, Cordelia strolled along the promenade beside Amelia's and Edwina's governesses. Beatrice's governess had been left to care for the children, daughters really, still too young for such an outing although in truth, aunts, mothers, governesses and everyone involved had learned some time ago that it was best not to attempt even something as simple as a walk with all the children at once.

They were scarcely more than a few steps from the house when the first break with authority occurred and the governesses were forced to adopt a more than brisk pace to keep up with their scattering charges. Within moments, they were so far ahead that Cordelia found herself quite alone, if one could be considered alone on a busy walkway surrounded by countless numbers of high-spirited tourists eager to enjoy the fine summer day. If quizzed, Cordelia would have had to admit that she'd known this would happen and that perhaps she'd had this in mind. It suited her, being able to stroll along accompanied by nothing more than her own thoughts. Which inevitably turned to Mr. Sinclair—try as she might she certainly couldn't think of a man she'd never met by his given name—and oddly to Mr. Lewis as well. Warren. Rather a nice name, strong and masculine and solid. She should check on the meaning of his name. She'd always found the meaning of names, be they of people or places, to be both interesting and insightful. It was quite easy to think of Mr. Lewis by his given name.

That was no doubt due to nothing more significant than having made his acquaintance. Which probably explained as well why, when she'd read Mr. Sinclair's letter, it was Warren's voice she'd heard. Still, there was no harm to it really. It was, after all, a nice voice and went well with a gentleman who was tall and broadshouldered—with a slightly wicked look in his eye and a smile devilish but endearing. She couldn't help but smile herself at the thought.

"I know this time that smile is not for me."

She gasped and turned. "Mr. Lewis! What on earth are you doing here?"

"Well, you spoke so highly of Brighton I thought

it was a place that I definitely needed to visit." He grinned. "So I did."

She stared at him. "I don't believe I said much of anything about Brighton."

He shrugged. "It was implied."

She craned her neck to see around him, not that she knew what she looked for, although surely a handsome American would be obvious in the crowd. "Is Mr. Sinclair with you?"

"No, no." He shook his head.

"What a shame." Although it really wasn't a shame at all. The thought surprised her. But the moment she met Mr. Sinclair her charade, and any further involvement with Warren, would be at an end. And that would indeed be a shame. "Then I assume Lady Cordelia should continue to write to him in London?"

"No, my apologies. I didn't mean to imply that he wasn't here at all," Warren said quickly. "He is indeed in Brighton just not with me at the moment. He preferred to stay in his rooms. He's been . . . under the weather."

"Oh dear. I do hope it isn't serious."

"Not at all. Merely a common cold. We thought the sea air might do him a world of good." He drew an exaggerated breath. "It's so . . . so . . ."

She bit back a smile. "Bracing?"

"That's it exactly."

"It will scarcely do him any good if he doesn't leave his rooms."

"We shall leave the windows open and hope for the best. I would be happy to give you the address so that you might pass it on to Lady Cordelia." Warren's smile held the oddest touch of relief, as if he wanted to talk about anything but his employer. "Now then, as it appears you are alone . . . You are alone aren't you?"

Cordelia glanced down the promenade. Neither governesses nor boys were anywhere in sight. "I believe I am."

He offered his arm. "Then might I have the honor of accompanying you?"

It struck her that if she accepted his arm and walked with him it would put her masquerade out of the realm of an innocuous little falsehood fabricated to learn more about Mr. Sinclair and into a different category altogether. Still, she'd done nothing to encourage his appearance here. His presence was no more than mere coincidence. Wasn't it?

She studied him suspiciously. "Is this a coincidence?"

"A happy coincidence," he said firmly.

She raised a brow.

He laughed. "Other than the fact that I have been sitting on that bench over there hoping you might make an appearance, why yes, I would say it is a coincidence."

"It doesn't sound like a coincidence. How did you know where I was staying?"

"Lady Cordelia's letter to Mr. Sinclair included her address in Brighton." He grinned. "Shall we?"

She considered him for a moment. She'd never had a man lie in wait simply to walk with her before. It was most flattering and roguishly charming of him. Why shouldn't she walk with him? She was no longer a child, she'd traveled a great part of the world, she was not yet engaged, and if she wished to indulge in an innocent stroll along the promenade with an interesting man, what was wrong with that? This was Brighton after all, where rules of behavior and everything else were considerably more relaxed than London. Besides, in spite of the crowds, this wasn't the official social season and the possibility that she would be seen by anyone she knew was remote. Moreover, what might be considered improper for Lady Cordelia wasn't nearly as unseemly for Miss Palmer. And, for the moment, she was Miss Palmer.

"Very well, Mr. Lewis." She returned his grin, shifted her parasol, and took his arm. "I should like that."

He chuckled. "Not nearly as much as I will."

They started off and she realized this direction might well bring her face-to-face with the boys and their governesses. The opposite way would bring them past the house. but it was on the other side of the road and she very much doubted anyone would be out and about. Besides, spotting her in this crowd would be difficult at best. She paused and nodded back in the direction she had come. "Would you mind if we walked that way?"

"Not at all." They turned and again started off. "I am completely at your disposal."

"Are you indeed?" They walked in silence for a few minutes, although silence wasn't entirely accurate. The crash of the waves and noise of the crowd provided a constant backdrop of noise. "Why are you really in Brighton, Mr. Lewis?"

"Because you are here, Miss Palmer."

She laughed. "That's most flattering, but I'm not sure I believe you."

"Nonetheless, it's true."

"You have no other reason to be in Brighton then?"

"None whatsoever."

"And you're simply here because I am?"

"That's correct."

"Then again, I must ask why."

"Because I find you extremely interesting, Miss Palmer." He stopped and met her gaze directly. "And I should like to know you better."

"Oh." She stared into his dark eyes and for once she was at a loss for words. "I'm not sure what to say."

"I've left you speechless then?" He chuckled. "I didn't think it was possible."

"Nor did I," she murmured.

"I like that about you, that you are rarely at a loss for words, that is."

"Do you?" She studied him curiously. "I've always considered that a flaw in my character. Proper ladies should be less forthcoming than I am."

"Rubbish," he said staunchly. "You have an opinion and it's apparent you don't hesitate to share it."

"And you find that admirable?"

He nodded. "I do."

She considered him for a long moment. "It's because you're American, isn't it?"

He stared at her with surprise then laughed. "Possibly."

She nodded in a sage manner. "Americans have different attitudes about such things than the English. It's that independent nature of yours."

"Independent nature aside"—he leaned toward her, laughter twinkled in his eyes—"I suspect there are more than a few Americans who would think me completely mad and any number of English gentlemen who appreciate a forthright nature."

She scoffed. "I doubt that." They turned and resumed their walk. "I daresay, I have yet to meet one."

"Is that why you're not married?"

"I would wager it's one reason," she said wryly. "It's not at all easy to find a man who likes a woman who speaks her mind. It's not at all easy to find a man who likes a woman who has a mind of her own."

"Well, I like it." He nodded. "I like as well that when you have a good idea, you don't hesitate to act on it."

"For better or worse," she said under her breath. What was wrong with this man? He liked everything about her that everyone else had long considered a problem.

"You're hardworking, independent, and honest." He shrugged. "I find all of that appealing about you."

Honest? "Yes, well." Unease washed through her. "One is not always as one appears, you know."

"And as I have not mentioned appearance," he said lightly. "You should know, I find you lovely, Miss Palmer."

"You shall quite turn my head, Mr. Lewis."

"I very much wish to turn your head." He paused. "In my direction."

Her breath caught and her heart thudded in her chest. "What are your intentions, Mr. Lewis?"

"I have no particular intentions at the present, Miss Palmer, beyond the furtherance of an acquaintance and the pleasure of a company I find I am reluctant to abandon." His manner was firm and no nonsense, almost as if he had expected the question and had practiced his answer.

"I see." She was at once pleased and a touch disappointed although she had no idea why she should be in the least disappointed. After all, she had no particular intentions when it came to him. Indeed, she wanted no more from him than he did from her and nothing more significant than an innocent flirtation. Still . . . "I suspect you are a dangerous man."

"Dangerous?" He laughed. "I doubt it. Why, I'm as harmless as a puppy."

"An extremely flirtatious puppy."

He grinned.

"Is Mr. Sinclair as flirtatious as you?" she said, more to turn the conversation away from its current hazardous direction than to learn anything about Daniel Sinclair.

"Oh, more so. The man is incorrigible." He hesitated as if choosing his words. "I might have misled you the other day about Mr. Sinclair's pursuit of women."

"Oh?"

"He is quite active in that area. Indeed, in that regard, he's a leader among men." He leaned closer and lowered his voice. "He has something of a reputation."

"Really? I wouldn't have thought he'd been in London long enough to acquire any reputation whatsoever."

"London, Baltimore, it makes no difference." Warren shrugged in an offhand manner. "Why, not a night goes by without a different lady on his arm regardless of where he is. Actresses, widows, ladies of experience I would say. He likes them and they adore him."

She thought for a moment. "Are you now saying that you think he'll be unfaithful after he's wed?"

"I . . ." He grimaced. "I can't say that."

"Can't or won't?"

Warren shrugged.

"I see."

"I am sorry." He shook his head in a mournful manner. "I suppose Lady Cordelia won't wish to marry a man with a reputation like Mr. Sinclair's."

"Don't be absurd." She glanced at him with surprise. "I daresay, Lady Cordelia wouldn't consider him at all if he didn't. He is past thirty years of age, wealthy, and handsome. One would be somewhat suspicious of a man who didn't have a bit of a reputation."

"It's more than a bit," he warned. It was obvious that the poor man was torn between honesty and loyalty to his friend.

She shrugged. "Many women believe reformed scoundrels make the best husbands. And you did say he would be faithful."

"Yes, I did say that," he muttered. "But one never knows."

"And what of you, Mr. Lewis?" A teasing note sounded in her voice. "Do you have a bit of a reputation?"

He grinned. "Possibly."

"Are you following in Mr. Sinclair's footsteps or is he following in yours?"

"Some of both I think." He paused. "We are very similar, he and I, in many things. We both share a certain ambition and I have no doubt of our ultimate success."

"Ah yes, he will one day be one of the wealthiest men in America."

"As will I." Confidence rang in his voice.

She glanced up at him. "Are you trying to impress me, Mr. Lewis?"

"Am I?"

"Wealth does not impress me. However." She cast him a slow smile. "I do find ambition admirable. As does Lady Cordelia."

"Of course, she would," he said under his breath.

"Ambition is an interesting thing." She adjusted her parasol and considered the topic. "In this country, success has always been limited by one's original position in life. It's a rare man who can rise above the circumstances of his birth, and I admit, as a people, we tend to view such ambition and success as suspect and somewhat distasteful."

"In my country, we believe anyone can succeed with hard work and ingenuity."

"In many ways here we are mired in the past. The way things have always been done has worked well, at least for the upper classes, and no need is seen to change them." She wrinkled her nose. "It does make life awkward for a woman like Lady Cordelia whose ultimate future is out of her hands, to be determined only by what kind of match she makes."

"What does Lady Cordelia want in a husband?"

"What any woman wants I suppose." Cordelia thought for a moment. "A man who will respect her and accept her for who she is, I think, is probably to be desired above everything else. A man who will appreciate the independence of her nature. A kind and generous heart, honesty of course, those sorts of things."

He chuckled. "And so we are back to love, which you did not mention."

"There is that romantic nature of yours again." She smiled. "You forget this is not a love match."

"Still, if one finds love, it should not be ignored."

"No, but if one doesn't . . ." She shrugged.

"And what of you, Miss Palmer?" He glanced at her, his gaze meeting hers. "What are you looking for in a match?"

She laughed. "I am no different than Lady Cordelia with the exception that she has a responsibility to her family that I do not. Having no family to speak of leaves me free to marry without concern for anything save my heart. Still, I do want a man who will value my intelligence and treat me with respect and honesty. And yes, Mr. Palmer." She gazed into his dark eyes. "I would very much hope for love."

For a long moment they stared at one another, the crowds milling around them receding to nothing more than a faint hum in the background. It was an odd moment. *Intimate* was the word that came to Cordelia's mind. Personal. Private. As if they were quite alone. Her heart sped up and she wondered wildly if he would try to kiss her. It struck her that as improper and dangerous as that might be, she might well allow it. Indeed she wanted nothing more than for this virtual stranger, this pirate, to take her in his arms and kiss her quite firmly here on the promenade and damn the consequences.

"Well." He cleared his throat and abruptly the moment was lost. The noise of the crowd swelled once again. The waves crashed against the shore. The gulls cried overhead and everything was exactly as it had been.

And nothing was the same.

"Well indeed," she murmured, and ignored the fluttering of her heart. "I should—"

"We should—" he said at precisely the same time.

"Return home." Her voice had an odd, high-pitched tone and she gestured toward the direction of the house. "I've been gone entirely too long."

"Yes, of course." He nodded and they turned and headed back. "I should hate for you to be reprimanded for being gone too long."

"Oh, I daresay, I won't have any problem on that account." Indeed, even if the boys and their governesses had returned, the house was so chaotic she doubted her absence would even be noticed.

They walked for a few minutes in a companionable silence.

"You mentioned honesty a moment ago," Warren said abruptly. "Regarding what Lady Cordelia wanted in a husband.

"Yes?"

"She should understand that when it comes to business, clever and shrewd might on occasion be mistaken for dishonesty."

"And has Mr. Sinclair's cleverness been mistaken for dishonesty?"

"There is always talk," Warren said reluctantly. "Prompted more by jealousy than fact."

"I see," she murmured. How very odd for Mr. Lewis to put the idea of dishonesty in her head. Unless, of course, he didn't wish for her to marry Mr. Sinclair. Which made no sense whatsoever. Why would he care?

A moment later, Warren turned the conversation to an observation of the weather. They spoke of nothing further of importance on the way back, although they did discover a shared appreciation for Dickens and Dumas as well as the dark stories of Edgar Allan Poe. Cordelia talked about the great works of art she had seen in European museums, and he mentioned how intrigued he was by the ever-advancing science of photography and believed it might well be considered art one day. While his comments provided insight into his character, it was not as frankly personal and flirtatious as the tone of their earlier conversation. She was grateful for that. She wasn't at all sure what to say in that respect. Or what she wanted to say. Or wanted to do. It was most confusing and more than a little exciting. Still, she did feel she knew him better now and liked what she knew as well.

Within minutes they reached the point where they had first met. "I shall take my leave here, Mr. Lewis. The house is not more than a few steps away and just across the road. I shall be fine on my own from this point."

He hesitated as if he were going to argue with her, then nodded. "As you wish."

"Thank you, Mr. Lewis." She held out her hand. "I quite enjoyed our conversation. It's been—"

"Unforgettable." He raised her hand to his lips and she could have sworn heat singed her through her gloves and down to her toes. Or perhaps it was the heat of his gaze. The promise, the threat . . . the danger. "You do understand I have to see you again."

"I fear that would be a dreadful mistake." She drew a deep breath. "When?"

"Tonight? Tomorrow?" He squeezed her hand. "Soon."

"I can't tonight." A very sensible voice in the back

of her head screamed what a huge mistake this was. How very wrong it would be to meet this man again. How terribly dangerous he was to her well-being and her future and possibly her heart. She ignored it. "Every night near the Chain Pier there is music and often dancing and fireworks and great crowds. I shall make every effort to be there tomorrow night."

"And I shall make every effort to find you. And do not doubt it." His gaze caught hers. "I will find you." He released her hand and smiled. "Until then, Miss Palmer."

"Until then, Mr. Lewis." She turned and resisted the urge to run. Instead, she walked in a brisk but sedate manner that belied the frantic beat of her heart and churning of her stomach and catch in her throat. She could feel his gaze on her even as she crossed the road and approached the house.

What was she thinking? Or rather, why wasn't she thinking at all? This might well have the most disastrous consequences of anything she'd ever done in her entire life. If she realized that in a rational, practical sense, then it only made sense not to meet him tomorrow. Even as she greeted her sisters in an entirely natural manner and inquired as to whether or not the boys had returned, and climbed the stairs to her own room to discard her hat, she was trying to determine a course of action. The wisest thing to do would be to forget this nonsense, and Warren entirely.

Still, as intelligent as she considered herself, actual wisdom had never been her strong point. Surely one could argue that it would be wise to find out exactly why Warren made her feel as if something exciting and wonderful was about to happen before she married another man. Why it only made sense. And as foolish as it might be, she didn't want to stop seeing him, and Cordelia had never been very good at denying herself something she wanted.

Besides, Warren Lewis might well be something of an adventure and who knew how many of those she had left.

When deciding to embark upon serious travel one should set one's priorities and not flitter about in an untidy manner from destination to destination. A list is a handy tool for determining what one wishes to see in the span of one's lifetime.

An English Lady's Traveling Companion

Chapter 5

Dear Mr. Sinclair,

I was sorry to hear that you are unwell. I do hope the sea air in Brighton helps speed your recovery. It might interest you to know that while Brighton's origin is that of a sixth-century Saxon village, it became quite popular only a hundred years ago when it was believed bathing in the seawater could restore good health. Now,

*of course, with hundreds of tourists arriving by train
daily, it's known as London by the Sea . . .*

$\mathcal{D}$aniel sat on the sea terrace at the Albion Hotel
and stared out at the water, completely ignoring
the sunset and grateful that he was very nearly alone.
It was apparently either too early in the evening or too
late in the day or somehow unfashionable at the seaside resort to sit out of doors with a glass of whisky
in one hand and one's doubts in the other. And a fine
Scottish whisky it was too, very nearly up to the task
of dealing with his doubts. But not quite.

He sipped the liquor and gazed unseeing at the
channel. He wasn't used to having doubts of any sort
let alone doubts about whether or not he was doing the
right thing. Certainly there had been occasions when
he had been wrong and it had cost him. But those mistakes had usually involved business and had been rec-
tified quickly if not always easily. No, Daniel Sinclair
was not used to being wrong and he was certainly not
used to doubting his decisions.

He heard the door to the hotel at his back open and
footsteps approaching. Good, his glass was nearly
empty.

"You were right, Daniel." Warren pulled up a chair
and sat down. "Brighton isn't Baltimore but it's a pleasant change from London. And the air here is"—he
drew a deep breath—"not bad. Not bad at all."

"Bracing," Daniel said under his breath. "I'm glad
you like it."

"This was probably good for us, all in all." A waiter
presented Warren with a glass of whisky and he nod-

ded his thanks. "It's not a bad idea to get away from business for a few days. We have both been working entirely too hard." He lifted his glass to his friend. "I commend you for thinking of it."

"We're not staying." Daniel glanced at his friend. "I've realized the flaw."

"Have you? And so soon." Warren sipped his drink thoughtfully. "I didn't expect that."

"Regardless, I am willing to admit when I've made a mistake."

Warren raised a brow.

"I am," Daniel said staunchly.

Warren snorted.

"I know I can be stubborn on occasion." Daniel tried and failed to keep a defensive note from his voice.

"On occasion?" Warren studied the other man. "Do tell me this flaw then."

"I don't like deceiving her."

"Miss Palmer?"

Daniel shrugged. "She's very nice and strikes me as both honest and honorable. You were right. She'll hate me when she finds out."

"That didn't seem to concern you before."

"Well, it concerns me now."

"Correct me if I'm wrong, but I thought the plan was to convince Lady Cordelia, through Miss Palmer, not to marry you. And therefore you could avoid ever meeting Lady Cordelia and avoid as well Miss Palmer knowing the truth."

"It makes such sense when you say it."

"I doesn't make any sense at all." Warren scoffed. "It's the most convoluted, confusing thing you've ever come up with. Why, you can scarcely keep the players straight in this little drama of yours. It's like—I don't know—a game with no rules."

"I've always liked games," Daniel muttered.

"What you've always liked is winning. In games, in business, in everything." Warren paused. "I'm not sure winning is possible in this situation."

"Yes, well, that would be a flaw wouldn't it?" Daniel snapped.

"One of them," Warren said under his breath.

"I admit it has gotten rather tangled."

"Good word for it." Warren thought for a minute. "Maybe I can help. Wait here." Warren stood and headed back toward the door. "I saw a chess set in the lounge."

"I don't want to play chess," Daniel called after him. Warren ignored him. Daniel stared at the water and wondered how he was going to get out of this with his honor and his life intact. And without disappointing Sarah. He winced at the very thought of those green eyes flashing with disappointment. There was no question in his mind that she would indeed be disappointed in him if she learned the truth.

"Here." Warren placed a chessboard on the table, dropped a handful of chess pieces beside it, then sat down.

"I said I have no desire to play." This was absurd. Even if Warren was trying to get Daniel's mind off his problems, the last thing he wanted to do was play a silly game. Or rather, another silly game.

"We're not playing. At least we're not playing chess." Warren set the pieces upright and lined them up in a row.

"Now this"—he picked up the black king and placed him in one corner of the board—"is your father."

"It doesn't look a thing like him," Daniel muttered.

"And this"—Warren took the white king and placed him opposite the black king—"is Lord Marsham. These." He picked up a white rook and a white knight. "These are Lady Cordelia and Miss Palmer. And this"—Warren plucked a black pawn off the table and set it between the white pieces and the black king—"is you."

"I'm a pawn?"

"Somehow it seemed right," Warren murmured.

Daniel drew his brows together. "A mere pawn?"

"I thought, given the circumstances, that you probably felt like a pawn."

"Yes, I suppose I do. But I don't like it. Either feeling like it or being it." He picked up a bishop and waved it at Warren. "Couldn't I be a bishop?"

"It doesn't matter what you are, I'm just trying to illustrate your dilemma."

"Good." Daniel replaced the pawn with the bishop. "Then I'd rather be a bishop."

"Fine. So for the two kings to get what they want," Warren moved the kings together on the board. "The bishop"—he moved the bishop to stand beside the rook—"has to marry the rook."

"Only if the rook wants to marry the bishop," Daniel said quickly. "It's entirely up to the rook. The bishop is simply a—"

"A pawn?" An annoyingly innocent tone sounded in Warren's voice.

Daniel gritted his teeth. "Go on."

"However, the bishop, in his infinite wisdom, wishes to avoid marriage and so is using the knight"—he put the knight between the rook and the bishop—"as a pawn."

Daniel stared at the pieces. "Rather despicable of him isn't it?"

"I'm not sure despicable is the right word. Close but not quite right. After all, his ultimate intentions are not dishonorable."

There was something about seeing the bishop between the rook and the knight that twisted Daniel's stomach. "He's a cad. A beast."

"No, old friend, he's simply another pawn." Warren paused. "Perhaps not the cleverest pawn but a pawn nonetheless."

Daniel grimaced.

"A pawn with very few options." Warren rearranged the board, placing the bishop in a square near the center, the two kings, the rook, and the knight on each connecting diagonal square, trapping the bishop who could only move in a diagonal direction.

"Poor little fellow," Daniel murmured. "Between the devil and the deep blue sea."

"One analogy at a time, if you please."

"Still, you have to feel sorry for him."

"He's a cad, remember."

"I can scarcely forget."

"He is not, however, powerless. According to the rules of chess, the bishop is in a position to capture any of the four other pieces. By the rules of the game, both kings are now in check from at least one other piece."

Daniel studied the board. "Or they can capture the bishop." He glanced at the other man. "It all depends on whose turn it is."

"Capturing either king would end the game. If"—
Warren paused—"this was a game of chess, which it
isn't."

"Pity."

"Any move the bishop makes is bound to injure
someone."

Daniel sighed. "We're no longer speaking in terms
of chess, are we?"

"I'm afraid not. As I see it, however, the bishop—
you—does have several choices. He can hope all will
work out well and continue along the path he has already taken."

"Deceiving Sarah and avoiding Lady Cordelia?"

Warren nodded.

"It sounds so bad when put that way."

"It is bad," Warren said firmly, then continued. "Or
he can confess all to the knight, meet the rook, and
agree to the marriage arrangement."

Daniel shuddered. "Poor pawn."

"Of course, that probably means the knight will
despise him, the rook won't look upon him favorably
either and refuse the marriage, the white king will suffer great loss of fortune, and the black king will lose
financially as well. Not to mention that his word will
be suspect in the future."

"I don't think I like this game."

"You started it."

"You should have stopped me."

"Yes, I should have but," Warren shrugged, "I was
ill. Not entirely myself."

"Still—"

"I suppose there is one other choice. You can flee."
Warren flicked the bishop with his forefinger up in the

air where a sudden breeze caught it. It sailed over the balustrade of the terrace and into the sea.

"Someone is going to have to pay for that," Daniel warned.

"Someone is going to have to pay all right." Warren picked up his glass and swirled the amber liquid. "And it's up to you to decide who and how dear the price."

Daniel downed the rest of his drink and signaled a waiter for more. "Perhaps it's time for honesty. Complete, total, utter honesty."

"Honesty?" Warren paused while an efficient, silent, and no doubt curious waiter refilled their glasses. "You mean, tell your father you have no intention of honoring his word?"

Daniel nodded.

"Tell Lady Cordelia you have no desire to enter into any marriage let alone one that was arranged for you?"

"It's sounds so . . . so harsh."

"I can't imagine how to make it sound better. You could say something like 'My dear Lady Cordelia, while you are a lovely woman' "

"Amazon," Daniel muttered.

"—and I'm certain you will make some man a lovely wife—"

Daniel snorted. "Who'll run roughshod over any man no doubt."

"—I am not in the market for a wife at this time. Lovely or otherwise.' "

"Definitely otherwise," Daniel said under his breath.

"Which does sound somewhat less harsh, but I can't imagine a really good way for any man to tell a woman he doesn't want her." Warren considered his friend for a moment. "Which brings us to Miss Palmer."

Daniel sighed. "It does, doesn't it?"

"Total, complete, and utter honestly means telling Miss Palmer that you started this charade—"

"She did approach me—or rather you—first."

"And you did not correct her mistaken assumption that you were me because? . . ."

"Well, I thought, that is it seemed . . ."

Warren raised a brow.

"She was pretty. There you have it," Daniel snapped. "But she was the one who started it all."

"But if she hadn't been pretty, you would have corrected her mistake and left her to me."

"More than likely."

"Furthermore, total, complete, and utter honesty means also telling Miss Palmer you continued to deceive her because you wanted to convince Lady Cordelia not to marry you."

Daniel shook his head. "I can't tell her."

"Because? . . ."

"Because she's a nice woman and I like her." Because her eyes are green and endless. And her smile is genuine and I see it even when I close my eyes. "And she'll hate me."

"And you care about her opinion of you?"

"Lord help me, I do."

"Then you really don't have a choice do you?"

"Fleeing sounded good," Daniel muttered.

"Only in theory, not in practice." Warren shrugged. "I see no real choice other than to continue your present course."

"It does seem to be the only way to survive this mess."

"And how is it faring so far? Have you managed to convince Miss Palmer that you are not the man for Lady Cordelia?"

"Not yet. I don't seem to be doing a very good job of it. We tend to stray from the subject." Daniel hated to admit he was hard pressed to keep his ultimate object in mind when the delectable Sarah was by his side. There were always other far more interesting things to talk about. "Besides, it's damned difficult to think of reasons why a woman wouldn't want you."

"I can see where that might be a problem for you," Warren murmured.

"It wouldn't be if I was willing to let her think I was a murderer or a thief or something equally vile, but I believe fabrications—"

"Lies."

"—should at least sound legitimate."

"One should have standards," Warren said under his breath.

"I did tell Sarah—"

"Sarah?"

"I don't call her Sarah, that would be presumptuous. Even I know that. But I do think of her as Sarah. It's a lovely name don't you think? Solid and forthright and honest."

"Lovely. Go on."

"I told her I—Daniel Sinclair, that is—had an impressive reputation when it came to women."

Warren laughed. "That was a lie."

"I've scarcely been celibate."

"No, but other than the occasional frivolous encounter, you've had no time for women."

"Neither have you," Daniel said pointedly. While the

two men had always been rather competitive when it came to women, neither had had a great deal of time for the serious pursuit of the fairer sex in recent years.

"Yes, and I regret it deeply. But we're not talking about me. At least not the real me." He aimed a warning finger at his friend. "And might I request that when you are masquerading as me, you avoid any behavior that might reflect poorly on me."

"I have been, at all times, a perfect gentleman." Daniel raised his glass to his friend. "Or rather, I should say, you have."

"There wasn't a doubt in my mind." Warren touched his glass to the other man's. "So, thus far you've told her you like women."

"I also implied that I—Daniel Sinclair—might not be inclined to be faithful once married."

"Very good, Daniel. More than plausible." Warren paused. "Of course, she has no way of knowing that you find such behavior offensive."

"I have always wondered why men who consider their promises on any other subject to be sacred, don't view their marriage vows to be just as binding." Daniel shook his head. "If a man cannot be trusted to abide by his word before God and man in regards to marriage, how can his word be trusted in anything else? Which reminds me. I might have implied that there could possibly be an element of dishonesty in some of my business dealings."

Warren choked. "What?"

"In any advantageous transaction, there are always those who prefer to see dishonesty rather than brilliance on the part of one party."

"In this particular case, I don't think you need worry

about brilliance. However." Warren shook his head in a warning manner. "Given the nature of your current acquaintance, as well any future relationship you or your father might have with hers, even so much as a hint of dishonesty might be a serious mistake."

"Damn. I hadn't thought of that, but I will keep it in mind."

The two friends fell silent and gazed out at the Channel, blinding with the reflected rays of the setting sun low in the west. The quiet companionship between them was wrought from shared experience, longtime friendship, and respect. Their silence was broken only by the sound of the waves and the cry of the gulls.

Daniel would rather not be a perfect gentleman when it came to Sarah, although he didn't want to admit it aloud. He had no desire to hear what Warren would make of that admission. But Sarah was not the type of woman one dallied with unless one's intentions were honorable and, well, permanent. Still there had been that moment, that odd overwhelming moment, when he had gazed into her eyes and had felt something that went well beyond the mere furthering of her acquaintance. Something deep and intense and unsuspected. Something that carried with it a promise of excitement, a hint of forever. Something at once terrifying and damn near irresistible.

Absently, Daniel picked up the rook and the knight and rolled them in his hand. Even though he had told Warren she was exactly the type of woman who would make a perfect wife, he was not at all ready for a wife. Perfect or otherwise. And to pursue Lady Cordelia's companion with an eye toward marriage would be an even bigger muddle than the one he was currently in.

No, marriage was not for him and neither was Sarah—Miss Palmer. From now on he had to stick to his plan, no matter how flawed it might be.

"Back to the original plan then," Daniel said firmly, still staring at the water. Certainly his plan was not as brilliant as the sun upon the water, and admittedly it wasn't perfect but it would succeed if he watched his step and kept his objective in mind.

Warren chuckled. "I love moments like this when I can be justifiably superior."

"Cherish it," Daniel muttered.

He glanced at the pieces in his hand. Chess had a logic and symmetry that made it both understandable and a challenge. In spite of Warren's attempt to help clarify his situation, the game he currently played had little to do with logic. And, as he was the only one playing, it really wasn't a game unless you could count his father. Still . . .

"There might yet be an option we haven't discussed," Daniel said in a casual manner."

"Oh, I can hardly wait to hear this."

Daniel glanced at his friend. "Sarcasm does not become you."

"My apologies." Warren composed his expression but failed to hide the amusement in his eyes. "This new option?"

"It seems to me when one is involved in a game one can't possibly win . . ."

"Yes? . . ."

"The only real way to continue to play"—Daniel smiled a slow satisfied smile—"is to change the rules."

* * *

Even if, in a moral sense, one should never profit from the pain and suffering of others, it was a fortuitous accident for Cordelia. Sarah, of course, would have quite disagreed as it was her pain and suffering that had unknowingly benefited Cordelia. The poor girl had been startled by the sudden appearance of a toad, that had apparently escaped from one of the boys, and had tripped and fallen halfway down the stairs. She was currently confined to her bed with an ankle twice its normal size and a headache to match. No one knew where the toad was. The physician that Mother had insisted look at Sarah's ankle had pronounced it nothing more than a nasty sprain, had recommended Sarah stay in bed for the day and limit strenuous activity after that, but had said she would be fully recovered within the week. Which fell in nicely with Cordelia's plans.

Cordelia paced her room and considered those plans, as unformed and vague as they were at the moment. She had been racking her brains since she had left Warren yesterday afternoon, trying to determine how she could possibly escape from Sarah's watchful eyes to meet him. As lax as Sarah may be in most respects regarding her position, there was no possible way she would allow Cordelia to meet the American alone at night. Besides, Cordelia had not told Sarah that Warren and Mr. Sinclair were in Brighton nor did she intend to. Sarah wasn't the only one who could have mysterious, secret suitors.

Not that Warren was at all mysterious or her suitor for that matter. He was honest and forthright and she hadn't the faintest doubt that he was a good and honorable man. As for being her suitor, that was absurd.

They were certainly becoming friends and she did like him, and admittedly, there was some flirtation involved but there was nothing more to it than that.

She moved to the window, rested her hands on the sill, gazed out at the Channel and the fishing boats looking like giant seabirds upon the water, and heaved a heartfelt sigh. Or was there very much more to it? Even if she wished it, there could be no future for them. She was the daughter of a British earl and he was the son of . . . she had no idea who his parents were. Or where he was from. No, wait, he and Mr. Sinclair were from Baltimore in Maryland. She really should add Baltimore to her list. In truth, she knew no more about Warren than she did about Daniel Sinclair, except that the two men had a shared ambition and purpose in life. Oh, she knew Warren's shoulders were impressively broad and his eyes brown and mesmerizing, and his pirate smile altogether too wicked. And she knew as well if he had tried to kiss her yesterday she would have quite enjoyed it, and kissed him right back.

Warren Lewis was unique in her experience. She'd never had a man value her opinion or talk to her as if he were truly interested in what she had to say. And she'd never had a man look at her the way he had. It was most intoxicating.

But it was obviously time to end her charade. Past time really. It would be awkward enough when she eventually met Mr. Sinclair, and was then introduced to his employee and friend. Unfortunately, she didn't want to stop seeing Warren. He might well be the most interesting, wonderful man she'd ever met. And if she didn't watch her step, he might be the biggest mistake of her life as well. She was beginning to feel things she had no business feeling. Precisely why there really was no choice. This had to stop now. She nodded with a determination she didn't quite feel. She would meet him tonight, it would be rude not to, and then never again. Probably. Lord, this was a dangerous game.

She moved away from the window and resumed pacing. It wouldn't be at all difficult to slip out of the house, especially with Sarah already abed. Sarah had long been a favorite below stairs because of her sweet nature and the fact that she was never a bit of trouble. Thanks to the potent tea Cook had brewed that the housekeeper had plied Sarah with, she could barely keep her eyes open. She would never notice Cordelia's absence. As for the rest of the family, Cordelia would announce after dinner that she was exhausted, blame said exhaustion on the sea air, and retire for the evening. Then it would be a simple matter to slip down the back stairs and out the door. Precisely as she and Sarah had done in their youth and no doubt the very same way her older sisters had done years ago.

It was no secret among the children of the family that Amelia, Edwina, and Beatrice had all regularly stolen out of the house to join the festivities by the pier when they were younger, either as a trio or in various combinations of two. Indeed, both Will and Cordelia had earned tidy payments from their sisters simply by keeping their secrets. Cordelia would enlist her sisters' help now but, in spite of their youthful adventures, now that they were married and settled they were as well eminently proper and concerned with appearances and the possibility of scandal. Cordelia never failed to be amazed at the transformation marriage had made in her high-spirited sisters, who now confined those spirits to matters of household and entertaining, charity works and children. They certainly couldn't be trusted to keep Cordelia's secrets. And even if they could, Cordelia was confident she couldn't afford the price.

No, getting out of the house was not a problem. But Cordelia, who had once seen the full moon rise over the Pyramids in the desert night and had ridden a donkey through narrow rock-wall passages to reach the ancient city of Petra, was decidedly uncomfortable at the thought of walking the short distance to the pier at night, alone. A woman by herself might attract no end of unwanted attention. It was at moments like these that she quite appreciated the luxury of having a companion. It wasn't just a matter of propriety—the social dictum that a young unmarried woman of a certain social class should be chaperoned at all times—it was very much a matter of safety. And while Brighton wasn't Whitechapel, it would be nothing short of stupid to travel about alone at night even though the pier was a scant five-minute walk from the house.

She needed an escort. While, with the proper inducement, she could certainly convince a footman to accompany her and keep his mouth shut, one really couldn't trust anyone whose loyalty could be bought. No, one could only trust someone with a stronger bond. Someone whose best interests lay beyond mere payment. Someone who would need Cordelia's silence every bit as much as she would need his.

A flash of movement caught the corner of Cordelia's vision. She stopped in the center of the very room she had occupied on every summer to Brighton since childhood and watched a medium-sized, mottled brown toad casually emerge from beneath her bed and hop across her floor. Cordelia grabbed a straw hat, scooped up the creature, deposited toad and hat into an empty hatbox and quickly slapped the lid on the box. Unlike her older sisters, Cordelia wasn't particularly squeamish about creatures like toads and frogs, thanks to her brother, Will. They had had grand times as children, especially here in Brighton. She could remember all sorts of mischief. At once, she knew exactly who could help her. And why.

She patted the lid of the hatbox. There was a great deal to be said for family tradition.

It is imperative, gentle traveler, to be well acquainted with the various aspects of your native land so as to avoid the mortifying circumstance of being asked a question you cannot answer.
An English Lady's Traveling Companion

Chapter 6

"Well, Aunt Cordy?" Henry, her eldest sister Amelia's oldest son, eyed her in that suspicious manner of young men tottering between childhood and something as yet undefined. It had taken no time at all to find him and somewhat longer to convince him it was in his best interest to join her in her parlor. "What do you want?

"First of all, Henry, there's no need to be rude with that tone of voice. And I do hate to be called 'Cordy,' you know."

An unrepentant grin stretched across the boy's face. "I know."

"I thought you did." She studied her nephew for a moment. He was tall for his age and looked older than his eleven years. He would soon begin his studies at Eton, just as her brother, Will, had. She wasn't sure which would fare the worst in that bargain, the school or the boy. She nudged her hatbox toward him with her foot. "I believe this might be yours."

He squatted down and opened the lid. "There's nothing but a hat—" His face brightened. "You found him. You found Friday. Bloody good job, Aunt Cordy."

"Don't call me Cordy, watch your language—your mother would be appalled—and why Friday?"

"Because Friday is when we *found* him." Henry cast her a disgusted look as if the answer was obvious and she too old or too stupid or too female to understand.

"Well, put the lid back on and don't let him get away again."

Henry slipped the lid on the box and stood. "Did you tell Mother you found him?"

Cordelia shook her head.

"She and Aunt Winnie and Grandmother are angry about Sarah's taking a fall."

"As well they should be. I also know that you and the rest of the boys have professed innocence not only about where the toad—Friday—came from and whose he is, but whether he existed at all."

Henry narrowed his eyes. "Why did you think he was mine?"

"It scarcely matters who he belongs to but as you're

the ringleader of that little group of bandits you call cousins, I thought it best to speak with you."

Henry grinned. "Bandits? I quite like that."

"I thought you would."

"Are you going to tell?"

She shook her head. "Probably not."

Henry picked up the hatbox and edged toward the door. "We should be going then."

"Oh, no. Not yet." She crossed her arms over her chest. "There's a price to be paid for silence."

Henry stared at her then sighed. "What do you want?"

"I need your help."

The expression on his face battled between apprehension and curiosity. Curiosity won. "What kind of help?"

"First, I need you to agree that if I keep your secret, you will keep mine."

He hesitated. Obviously it was difficult to place one's trust in an adult and a female adult at that. He nodded slowly. "Agreed."

"Do I have your word?"

He spit on his hand and held it out to her in yet another time-honored family tradition. "You do."

She narrowed her gaze. "Did your Uncle Will teach you to do that?"

"Uncle Will says a man's word is his bond. And you need a handshake to seal that bond." Henry's voice was serious but there was a wicked challenge in his eye. Good Lord, the child was a pirate in training.

"He would." She well remembered the ritual from her childhood. She and Will had been the youngest children in the family and while he was somewhat closer in age to Beatrice than to her, the three older girls had a close-knit relationship that did not include their younger siblings.

Inevitably, Will had decided that girls, especially younger sisters, were not worth the trouble, but fortunately Sarah had come to live with them and had nicely filled the void in Cordelia's life that her brother had left. Still, she and Will had remained close. "Very well then." She spit into her palm and shook Henry's hand.

He promptly wiped his hand off on his pants and she grabbed a clean handkerchief.

"So tell me, Henry," she said in as casual a manner as she could muster while wiping off her hand. "Have you and any of the other boys ever slipped out of the house at night to go to the pier?"

He was silent for a long moment, obviously considering his answer and whether or not this was some kind of trick on his aunt's part.

"No." He drew the word out slowly.

She arched a brow.

"We've only been here for a few days," he muttered.

"Yes, of course." She waved off his comment. "And anything that might have happened last year—"

"Or the year before?"

She nodded. "Would have no bearing on this year. Why it simply wouldn't be significant."

"What's done is done?" he said hopefully.

"Absolutely," she said firmly. "Nothing need be said about past misdeeds."

"It would be unfair to do so."

"Most unfair." She heaved a dramatic sigh. "I know

I would never hold a man's past transgressions against him."

He studied her for a moment then shrugged. "We might have."

"Then if indeed you had, which neither of us is saying, but if you might have, then you might have made it there and back as well without either discovery or incident?"

"Maybe."

"Can you do it again?"

Henry snorted as if the answer was obvious.

Cordelia smiled in a manner every bit as wicked as her nephew's. "I have a proposition for you, Henry."

If she didn't get married perhaps she could have a successful career as a burglar or jewel thief. Although, Cordelia acknowledged, it was probably far easier to escape from a house than to break into one. Just as she had thought, she'd had no problem slipping out of the house. Sarah was fast asleep and neither Cordelia's mother nor her sisters had so much as looked askance at her when she'd announced she was retiring for the evening. Even if one still lived under ones parents' roof at the advanced age of twenty-five, there were certain benefits to age.

Now Cordelia waited impatiently outside the back gate for her escort. Where was Henry? If you couldn't count on a fellow conspirator to be prompt, who could you count on?

"Aunt Cordy?" Henry's voice sounded from the shadows. "Are you ready?"

"Ready and waiting," she said sharply. "Don't call me Cordy. Now then, shall we—"

"Bit of a change in plans," Henry said even as the shadows behind him stepped forward and solidified into the figures of Thomas, Edward, and Philip.

"Good Lord," she murmured.

"They caught me and I didn't have a choice but to take them along," Henry said quickly. "It's an adventure you see."

"We won't be a bit of trouble," Philip said.

Edward nodded. "It's not like we haven't—" His older brother jabbed him with his elbow. "Ouch."

"Besides," Thomas said. "Friday belongs to all of us."

"Well?" Henry asked.

Cordelia considered the rather scruffy group arrayed before her. They were dressed in clothes that had seen better days and would therefore attract no attention whatsoever. Dear Lord, the boys were probably more skilled at this sort of thing than she was. At nearly twelve, Henry was the oldest followed by Thomas, also aged eleven, Edward and Philip both ten. She wondered if her sisters, who had been so gleeful at having sons so close in age, realized what a force of nature they had created. Cordelia really had no choice. If she canceled this adventure altogether or insisted on just taking Henry, she had no doubt concerns about Friday would not be nearly enough to keep the mouths of the other boys closed. Inevitably the truth would come out, all of it. Not merely that she was sneaking out of the house but that she was meeting a gentleman, who that man was, and who she had told him she was. Add to that the charge of using her poor innocent nephews to further her own nefarious activities and . . . she had no idea what the consequences might be, but they would not be good.

"As I have little choice." She gritted her teeth. "These are the conditions under which I will allow you to accompany me. One." She met Henry's gaze. "You all stay right be my side on the way to the pier. Two." Her gaze slid to Thomas. "There will be no wandering off, no dashing about in different directions. Three." She looked firmly into Edward's eyes. "The moment I am at the pier the four of you are to return directly home. No loitering, no dallying, no distractions. And four." She stared at Philip. "When I return I shall check your room. If you are not all in your beds," she narrowed her eyes, "there will be severe consequences, the repercussions of which even I would prefer not to consider. Do not cross me, boys. Do you understand? All of you?"

The boys exchanged glances then nodded.

"And I have your word?"

Almost as one, the boys spit in their hands and held them out to her.

"No, no," she said quickly. "We shall forgo the ceremonial shaking of hands and consider it agreed nonetheless."

"She's a girl," Edward said in an aside to Philip while wiping his hand on his pants, as if no more explanation for her lack of a sense of tradition need be said.

"A cranky girl," Thomas muttered.

"And scary." Philip eyed her with obvious suspicion.

"You have no idea just how scary I can be." Cordelia nodded. "Let's go."

They started off in as sedate a manner as she could have hoped for and within minutes approached the festive crowd gathered near the pier. Lanterns were strung, laughter and music filled the air. All in all it was a fine summer night to stroll or dance or simply converse. Vendors and merchants had long ago realized there was a profit to be made by luring tourists to the Chain Pier at night by the prospect of fireworks, food, and other amusements. At the edge of the crowd she spotted Warren, who was obviously watching for her, and waved. He waved back and started toward them. She turned to the boys. "Thank you all. I do appreciate your company. Now, please return home at once."

"We didn't know you were meeting a gentleman," Thomas said.

"We think that makes this a whole different kettle of fish," Philip said with a smug smile.

"You think that, do you?" she said cautiously.

Henry grinned. "And we think it's worth more than a mere toad."

She narrowed her eyes. "I'll give you each a shilling."

"Two," Edward said.

"Four," Henry amended. "Each."

"Very well." She gritted her teeth. Once again, they had given her no choice. "I shall pay you tomorrow. And only if you abide by the rest of my conditions." She nodded toward the direction in which they'd come. "Now go."

They took off in a far more exuberant manner than that with which they'd accompanied her. She breathed a sigh of relief and turned to greet Warren.

"Miss Palmer." He took her hands and gazed into her eyes. "My apologies. I was starting toward your house to meet you, but I was very much afraid you wouldn't come."

Her breath caught at the look in his eye. "Why wouldn't I come?"

"You had said seeing me again would be a dreadful mistake." He chuckled. "I was afraid you had come to your senses."

She smiled up at him. "I'm afraid I haven't."

"Good."

It was a simple word, nothing the least bit eloquent or exceptional about it. And yet it was quite the most exciting thing she'd ever heard. "I can't stay long."

He held out his arm. "Then shall we join the crowd and listen to the music?"

"That would be delightful." She took his arm and they meandered toward the pier. "And we should probably talk about Lady Cordelia and Mr. Sinclair as well."

"No, not tonight." He put his hand over hers and looked down at her. "I'd rather talk about anything but Lady Cordelia and Mr. Sinclair."

"Very well then." She thought for a moment. Just today she was considering all the things she didn't know about Warren and yet, at this moment, it was enough merely to walk by his side, arm in arm, with his hand still improperly over hers. "Do you enjoy travel, Mr. Lewis?"

"I'm not sure I enjoy it although admittedly getting to a destination is often half the fun of it." He thought for a moment. "I can't say I've traveled extensively, most of it has been predicated on business, but I've been to Italy and I did like it a great deal. There are any number of places in the world I would like to see."

"You should make a list," she said primly.

He laughed. "Is that advice Lady Cordelia gives to travelers?"

"Indeed it is. It makes a great deal of sense." She shook her head. "But one has to act on one's list, of course. I think it would be dreadful to get to the end of one's life and still have places one wished to see but never managed to visit."

"I imagine you've traveled quite a lot with Lady Cordelia."

"I've been extremely fortunate. I've seen the Pyramids and the Coliseum and the ancient ruins of Greece."

He glanced at her. "Do you have a favorite?"

She laughed. "Not yet but there is still a considerable amount of the world I have yet to see. Although, I daresay, my days of travel and adventure are at an end."

"Why?"

"Why?" She stared at him. Blast it all, it was exceptionally difficult to pretend to be someone else and watch every word you said. "When Lady Cordelia marries, of course, my days of travel will end. As will hers, I suspect. Unless Mr. Sinclair enjoys travel as she does."

"I'm afraid he sees it as more of a necessity than an adventure," Warren said with a shake of his head. "If you did continue to travel, where would you like to go?"

"I should like to see South America. The Amazon. Fields of orchids in Columbia. I would like to see the West Indies and the jungles of Africa." She thought for a moment. "And China."

He chuckled. "You have a list then?"

"Of course."

"Is Baltimore on it?"

"No, but America is."

"You should add Baltimore," he said firmly.

"Perhaps I will," she murmured. Dear Lord, what was she doing? With every word, she was digging a deeper hole for herself. She needed to bring this particular adventure to an end, regardless of whether she wanted to or not. She drew a deep breath. "Mr. Lewis—"

"Miss Palmer—" he said at the same time, then laughed. "Do go on."

"No," she said with a distinct sense of reprieve. "I've been talking entirely too much. Please, what were you going to say?"

"Well." He paused to choose his words. "We're leaving Brighton tomorrow. We're returning to London on the morning train."

"I see." She wasn't entirely sure what to say. Putting distance between them was an excellent idea. Indeed, hadn't she just been about to tell him she couldn't see him again? Besides, she still hadn't decided what she was going to do about Mr. Sinclair. Even she could see she was using Warren as an excuse to postpone her decision. It couldn't possibly be anything more significant than that. "Well then—"

"When will you be returning to London?"

"Me?" She shook her head. "Not for a few more weeks."

"Perhaps I should come back to Brighton then."

"That would be . . . lovely," she said with a weak smile, then drew a deep breath. "There is another matter, however, that we really should talk about—"

Shouts drew his attention and he craned his neck to

see around her. "What is going on over there?"

"Where?" She turned and searched the crowd.

A large, extremely annoyed man held a struggling boy by the scruff of his neck. Several other boys were trying to free him.

"Dear God." She gasped. "That's my—er—Lady Cordelia's nephew!"

"What's he doing out at this time of night?"

"He and his cousins escorted me here, but they were supposed to go straight home." She grabbed his arm. "Warren, can—"

"Of course." Warren set his jaw and moved swiftly through the crowd. Cordelia hurried after him.

"Unhand the boy," Warren said in a commanding voice and a manner to match. He towered over the other man who nonetheless did not back down.

"I caught this little bugger trying to pick my pocket." The man lessened his hold on Philip but did not release him.

"I didn't!" Philip's frantic gaze met hers and she had no doubt as to the veracity of his statement. The child jerked his head toward a point off to one side. "I swear, it was them."

She followed his gaze to a group of laughing boys even more disreputable in appearance than her nephews. They immediately noticed the attention and melted into the crowd.

"Are you sure this was the boy?" Warren fairly growled the words. It was most impressive.

"Maybe not," the man muttered and released Philip. "But if I see the little beggars again, I shall report them to the authorities."

"See that you do." Cordelia cast a scathing glare at her nephews.

"Miss Palmer, take the boys and start back to the house. I'll handle this." Warren gave Philip an encouraging smile then steered the child toward her, and turned back to the man.

"She's not—" Edward started. Henry jabbed him again. "Ouch. Stop doing that."

"Come along," Cordelia ordered. The boys surrounded her and they started off. When they were out of range of Warren's hearing, she glared at them. "You were supposed to go home."

Edward stared at her. "He called you Miss Palmer."

"He thinks you're Sarah, doesn't he?" Henry studied her with far more perception than any child had a right to have.

"You misheard," she said quickly.

"I didn't," Thomas said. "He said it plain as day. 'Miss Palmer—'"

"That's enough," she snapped. "We're going home right this minute. And if any of you so much as stray a step out of line, I shall tell your mothers all about this little adventure of yours."

"No, you won't," Henry said confidently. "That would force us to tell your mother."

"We wouldn't want to." Philip shook his head in a regretful manner.

"But we would have no choice," Edward added.

She stopped and stared at the boys. "What do you want?"

They traded glances. Henry smirked. "A whole pound, for each of us."

"Plus, the four shillings," Philip added.

Dear Lord, they *were* pirates. "You're clever little beasts, aren't you?"

Thomas angled his head and peered around her. "He's coming. You'd better decide."

"As if I have a choice. But I shall not pay you until tomorrow." She gritted her teeth. "Now, I want you to walk ten paces in front of us and head directly home. If one of you strays from my sight for so much as a moment, the bargain is off. I shall take my chances with my mother and leave you all to your own fates with yours."

They nodded almost as one and headed off, a scant moment before Warren joined her.

"What happened?" She gazed up at him.

"I gave him a few coins and he agreed he was mistaken." Warren took her arm and they started after the boys. "That's certainly a group to be reckoned with."

"Bandits are what they are," she said through clenched teeth. "Pirates."

He laughed. "They're not that bad. Just mischievous, that's all."

"That's scarcely all," she muttered then sighed. "You were very kind to him."

Warren smiled.

"Are you always this kind to children?"

"And small dogs as well."

She laughed in spite of herself. "Mr. Lewis." She paused. "Warren."

"Yes?"

"I am most appreciative of your help. You have my undying gratitude."

"I like having you in my debt." He chuckled then sobered. "But it seems to me this was my fault entirely."

"How was it your fault? I never should have brought them with me."

In the dark, she could barely make out the boys ahead reaching the garden gate and slipping inside. Cordelia breathed a sigh of relief.

"I should have met you outside the house and escorted you myself. Or." He paused for a moment. "I should have called on you properly at the door."

"No need for that. Besides, what's done is done," she said quickly, hoping to change the subject. They reached the gate and she turned to him. "Thank you again, Mr. Lewis. I don't know what I would have—"

"Miss Palmer. Sarah." He placed his knuckle under her chin, tilted her head up toward his and leaned closer. "I have a confession to make to you."

"A confession isn't at all necessary," she said in a weak voice. Her heart pounded in her chest.

"Oh, but it is." His lips brushed against hers. "I would very much like to call on you properly."

She swallowed hard. "You would?"

"I would." His lips murmured against hers. "When I return from London—"

"We're going to London," she said without thinking and immediately wished she could take the words back.

"You are?" He straightened slightly. "I thought you said you would remain in Brighton for the month?"

"I did but I . . . I forgot." *Forgot what?* "Lady Cordelia needs to meet with a publisher who is interested in her book. Yes, that's it."

"I see." He chuckled softly and dropped his hand. "Then I shall see you in London."

"Yes, well, perhaps." Her voice had an annoying breathless quality. She turned and grabbed the gate handle.

"Miss Palmer," he said softly behind her. Her hand paused on the handle. "There is no 'perhaps' about it."

Even as she turned toward him she knew this was a dreadful mistake, but Cordelia had always had a problem when it came to resisting temptation. "Mr. Lewis."

"Miss Palmer?"

Before she could come to her senses, she slipped her arms around his neck and pulled his lips to hers. He gathered her close against him and kissed her with a pent-up passion that released a passion of her own. He deepened his kiss, his mouth opened to hers and he tasted of adventure and danger and all things exciting and forbidden. And she realized with a blinding clarity that she could stay in his arms forever regardless of the costs and consequences.

At last he pulled away and stared down at her. "I will see you in London."

"Yes, of course," she said under her breath. What else could she say? She had, in a most shameful manner, just thoroughly kissed him and had been quite thoroughly kissed in return. And no kiss had ever before made her feel as if her legs were too weak to support her body.

"Until then, Sarah." He stepped back and opened the gate for her.

"Until then." She sighed and stepped into the garden and he closed the gate behind her.

She collapsed against it and tried to catch her breath.

Dear Lord, what had she done? Why on earth had she said she too was going to London? She'd practically invited him to call on her. She had fully intended to end it with him tonight. Instead, she was in deeper than ever. She touched her fingers to her lips. She could still feel the warmth of his mouth on hers. What had the man done to her? It was nothing more than a kiss. It was certainly not the beginning of something quite remarkable. No, she couldn't allow that. But she had no idea how she would get herself out of this.

And worse, no idea why she wasn't entirely sure she wanted to.

If one has not been fortunate enough to have mastered a foreign language in one's youth, it is wise to acquire at least a smattering of the language of any country one intends to visit so as not to be thought lacking in intelligence or social graces.

An English Lady's Traveling Companion

Chapter 7

Dear Lady Cordelia,

As much as I do appreciate your discourse on the history of Brighton, I must confess I have little interest in history. What is long past and dead has always seemed to me as having little relevance to the here and now. Since arriving in England I have wondered as well if the all-encompassing presence of what has gone before

*has stifled the effort to move forward, to progress as it
were. Yours is a country wallowing in the old, mine is
a country with its vision and its people set squarely on
the future . . .*

*D*aniel really had to give Warren his due. Warren's
habit of an early morning constitutional had
seemed a waste of time when Warren had first joined
him in London and the men had begun sharing a
residence. Now, however, Daniel had found he quite
enjoyed a brisk early morning stroll with or without
Warren. It was a practice he suspected he would continue even after returning home. It was certainly invigorating in a physical sense, especially here in Brighton.
But Daniel had found it stimulated the mind as well
and promoted clear thinking. He had serious thinking
to do now, and the clearer his mind the better, as he
had obviously not been thinking at all last night.

Whatever had gotten into him? How could he have
asked to call on her? It was as if the words had come
out of his mouth without any connection to his brain
whatsoever. He couldn't recall such a thing ever happening to him before. But then he'd never encountered
anyone like Sarah Palmer before. Although, if truth
were told, he was hard pressed to explain exactly why
she was different from other women whose acquaintance he had made, other women he had kissed. She
was pretty, of course, and her green eyes were lovely,
but he had met lovely green-eyed women before. Perhaps it was her spirit that appealed to him, the independence of her nature. Or possibly it was something
he couldn't explain at all, something he couldn't name
but recognized nonetheless.

In any rational sense it was absurd to be thinking anything about Sarah at all. Why, he'd scarcely talked to her more than a handful of times. Still, the blasted woman seemed to be the only thing on his mind. It was decidedly confusing and most annoying. He would indeed call on her in London but only for the express purpose of revealing his deception to her. He certainly couldn't make any kind of commitment to one woman when he was tentatively expected to marry another. Not that he was interested in commitment of any kind to anyone.

He drew a deep breath of the fresh sea air and wondered why he didn't feel better about his newfound resolve. Instead, a heavy weight had settled in the pit of his stomach. Sarah would indeed hate him when she learned the truth and he couldn't blame her. And what if he did ultimately marry Lady Cordelia? Given Sarah's position as more a member of the family than an employee, they would certainly see one another on those occasions when he and his new wife visited England. No, it was better to end this now before someone was hurt. Before hearts were involved if they weren't already.

If one preferred solitude to crowds, this was the perfect time to stroll Brighton's promenade. The only presence besides the gulls were the fishermen setting out for the day.

"Mr. Lewis," a familiar voice called and he caught sight of Sarah approaching him at a determined pace. She wore a bright yellow gown and carried a matching parasol and looked very much the epitome of a summer day come to life. He pushed aside the fanciful thought and waited for her.

Odd that his heart could leap and sink at the same time.

He tipped his hat. "Good morning, Miss Palmer. What brings you out so early in the day?"

"You do, Mr. Lewis," she said firmly and gazed up at him. "May I join you?"

"Yes, of course." He offered her his arm and they started off. "But I must admit, Miss Palmer, you have me at a disadvantage."

"Do I?" She laughed softly. "How delightful."

"How did you know where to find me?"

"I suspected a man who takes a constitutional every morning would not be able to resist doing so in Brighton as well." She gazed at the boats putting out to sea. "It's a thoroughly marvelous time of day here, quiet and peaceful and yet filled with light and promise. Even the cries of the gulls seem less intrusive. Don't you think?"

"I do indeed, but how did you know about my morning walk?"

She hesitated then shrugged. "You must have mentioned it in passing."

"Yes, of course." Although he doubted it since he had only recently adopted the habit. Still, it was of no consequence. "Which explains my presence but not yours."

"I wished to thank you again for last night. I had a lovely time."

"As did I, although it was entirely too brief."

"And I wished to talk to you as well." She paused. "About your request to call on me."

"Yes?"

"I fear, Mr. Lewis, that might not be wise."

"Oh?" Not that he hadn't already realized the same thing, although his reasons were likely decidedly different than hers.

"I think it would be most awkward for you to call on me in any sort of formal manner."

"Why?" he said before he could stop himself. If he was half as intelligent as he thought he was, he would keep his mouth shut.

She chose her words carefully. "My position in the household is unique and this, our . . . our friendship, simply complicates everything. Until Lady Cordelia's future is resolved, I think it would be best if you and I were to refrain from seeing one another."

"I don't understand."

"I didn't expect you to." She glanced up at him. "What I do hope, however, is that you will honor my wishes without question."

"That's not entirely fair, Miss Palmer."

"No, Mr. Lewis." She heaved a heartfelt sigh. "It's not fair. It's not fair at all, but then little in life is."

"What if I would prefer not to honor your wishes without question? What if I prefer to ignore your wishes altogether?" he said without thinking. What was he saying? She was giving him exactly what he had decided was necessary. And yet, it wasn't what he wanted and he couldn't seem to accept it.

"Then you are not nearly as honorable a man as I had thought."

"You don't know me very well. I might be the most dishonorable man you've ever met."

"I doubt that. I have seen you rescue small children." She shook her head. "This is complicated, Mr. Lewis."

"Warren." He squeezed her hand. "I thought we were becoming friends?"

"We were. We are. It's just . . ." She paused. "As I said it's complicated. And every minute I'm with you it just becomes more complicated."

Little did she know just how complicated it all really was. Still, she was right. "You should know, Sarah, I do not kiss every lovely young woman who crosses my path."

"That is good to know." She smiled. "And you should know as well, that I do not make it a habit of kissing every handsome pirate who comes my way."

He laughed. "It seems to me we have a great deal in common then."

"No, Warren. Mr. Lewis." She stopped, stepped back and met his gaze directly. "We have nothing in common except a . . an attraction that I cannot account for."

He raised a brow. "And do you need to account for it?"

"Yes, I do." She shifted her parasol and gazed out at the water. "You must understand I have obligations to . . . to Lady Cordelia and her family that do not allow for anything of this nature. At least not at the present time." She glanced at him. "I have disregarded them up until now, but I can do so no longer."

"I see."

"Do you?"

"Not really." He chuckled wryly.

"Nothing can come of whatever this is between us." Regret shone in her eyes and he realized she was as reluctant to stop seeing him as he was to stop seeing her. She was right, nothing could come of it.

Still . . . "Perhaps, if we change the rules."

"What?" Her brow furrowed with confusion.

"Something that recently occurred to me. It's of no consequence at the moment I suppose." He paused. "So then is this goodbye?"

"I'm afraid it must be."

Abruptly it struck him that regardless of the fact that agreeing not to see her was absolutely the right thing to do, he didn't want to give her up. At least not yet. "You asked me to honor your wishes, will you do the same for me?"

She shook her head slowly. "I don't think that would be wise."

"I think the time for wisdom is past."

"Even so—"

"Didn't you say last night that I had your undying gratitude?"

"Yes?" Caution sounded in her voice.

"I will agree not to call on you formally or pursue you with any intent beyond friendship, but grant my wish and allow me to see you again as nothing more than a friend."

"A friend?"

"You did say we had become friends. Didn't you mean it?"

"Certainly, I meant it but—"

"Surely there's no harm in continuing an innocent friendship?"

She stared at him. "Is this an innocent friendship then?"

"Yes," he said staunchly. "Or it can be."

"I'm not sure I believe you nor am I sure you believe that either. This is a dangerous idea, Mr. Lewis. It can lead to nothing of any good whatsoever. Still, I suppose if the idea of friendship is kept firmly in mind . . ." She studied him for a moment then blew a resigned breath. "I have always been fond of the Egyptian gallery at the British Museum. Indeed, I go there regularly and fully intend to do so this coming Thursday.

"Three days from now?"

"That would be Thursday, yes. I am usually there early to avoid crowds."

"Avoiding crowds seems like a good idea."

"And if I should happen to cross paths with a friend . . ." She shrugged. "Well, that sort of thing can't be helped."

"No, not at all."

"However," her tone was firm, "I would expect a friend to behave in a respectable manner."

"Absolutely." He nodded.

"I would anticipate that there would be no repeat of anything at all improper."

"No pulling you into his arms behind the giant sculpture of an Egyptian god, you mean?"

"Yes, that's exactly what I mean."

"No pressing his lips to yours until your breath mingles with his in a manner exciting and intimate?"

She stared up at him. "Certainly not."

"No kissing you until you melt against him and you wonder if you can ever stand unaided again?" He gazed into her green eyes. "And he wonders the same?"

"No." She swallowed hard. "None of that."

"Very well." He grinned down at her. "Should I happen to be in the vicinity of the British Museum on this coming Wednesday—"

"Thursday."

"Yes, of course, and should I happen to wander into the Egyptian gallery on Thursday, and if I then crossed paths with a friend, I will resist all impulses toward anything beyond intellectual discussion of a civilization long dead."

"I doubt that," she said under her breath. Her brows drew together and she glared up at him. "You might well be the most annoying man I have ever met."

"And the most determined."

"Which in and of itself is annoying," she said sharply. "As well as confusing." She sighed. "Good day, Mr. Lewis." With that she turned and started off.

Daniel chuckled. "Good day, Miss Palmer."

He watched her walk off, watched until in the distance she crossed the road and entered her house. His smile faded. What was the matter with him? When had he become such an idiot? She had given him the perfect opportunity to gracefully stop seeing her without having to tell her the truth. And he had ignored it. Tossed it aside without so such as a moment of consideration.

She'd bewitched him, that's what she'd done. Miss Sarah Palmer with the magic green eyes had put him under some sort of spell. He'd told Norcroft he thought that blasted tontine was cursed and here was the proof. From the very beginning, Daniel had thought he'd be the last man standing. There hadn't been a doubt in his mind. And yet here he was—damn near engaged to one woman with another making him think thoughts dangerously close to things like permanence and forever. Because a woman like Sarah Palmer wasn't the type one dallied with, she was the type one married.

Whether one wanted to marry or not.

* * *

"I'm returning to London today," Cordelia announced in a casual manner and glanced around the breakfast table for the inevitable reaction. "There is a publisher interested in my book and I should like to meet with him. Sarah will accompany me, of course."

Sarah glanced at Cordelia and smiled but otherwise held her tongue. After all, this was not her battle.

"Oh, I don't think so dear," her mother said with a pleasant smile and passed the rack of toast to Amelia.

Cordelia had expected as much and had her argument already prepared. First, she was twenty-five years of age, scarcely a child, and regardless of her position as the youngest in the family, should certainly be treated as an adult. Indeed, this was a conversation long overdue. And, as an adult, if she wished to return to London, there was no reason why she shouldn't. Secondly, she had traveled extensively with Aunt Lavinia and Sarah. And on those travels, she'd been very much a person of independence and confidence. A two-hour train ride to London was scarcely significant. Third, well, Cordelia wasn't sure what the third reason was but she was certain it would come to mind when needed. "Why—"

"Why ever not, Mother?" Amelia said casually. "She's no longer a child. She's twenty-five."

"And I would think, if she wishes to return to London, she should be allowed to do so," Edwina added. "It's not as if she'll be alone. Sarah will be with her and there's an entire house full of servants in London."

Her mother, Cordelia, and Sarah stared at the other women. Cordelia couldn't remember any of her sisters ever taking her side in anything. Even more surprising, they'd just presented reasons number one and three—even if number three hadn't yet occurred to Cordelia—which was remarkably significant given Cordelia never imagined they understood anything about her at all.

Father was reading his paper and apparently ignoring the conversation entirely as was his custom regarding discussions among the female members of his family.

"Nonetheless, I think it's entirely improper for a young, unmarried woman to reside in London without her family," Mother said firmly. "What will people think?"

"I daresay, no one will think anything worse than they already do," Edwina said. "Cordelia has always trod her own path. All that travel and writing, she's long been far more independent than anyone else in the family."

"And look where it's led her." Mother sniffed. "She should be married by now with children of her own."

"And yet she seems quite content with her life." Amelia looked at her youngest sister. "Are you content?"

"I haven't really considered the question of contentment." Cordelia thought for a moment. "I suppose I am content with my life thus far. Certainly, I would like to marry, but I would like to continue my travels as well. I'm not sure both marriage and travel are possible."

"Sacrifices, Cordelia. It's not easy but one must make certain sacrifices." Mother's tone was prim. "One cannot have everything one wants in this life."

"Why not?" Amelia asked.

"It doesn't seem at all fair," Edwina added.

Mother sputtered. "Fair?"

Amelia nodded. "Fair."

"Nothing in life is especially fair. *Fair* is a lovely word but has very little to do with the realities of life." Mother rose to her feet in a manner the queen herself might well have envied and glared at her daughters. "Cordelia will not return to London. She will marry Mr. Sinclair. And until such time comes as she is no longer under her father's roof, she shall do precisely as she is told." Mother nodded regally and resumed her seat.

"It seems to me that particular ship has long since sailed," Edwina said under her breath.

"What?" Mother snapped.

"Mother," Amelia said in a mollifying tone. "Cordelia has always done precisely as she's pleased."

Cordelia drew her brows together. "No, I haven't."

Amelia cast her a tolerant smile. "My dear, we've watched you do exactly that through the years. Oh, you've never been openly rebellious, but all in all you've done just as you've wished."

"We think you're extremely spoiled." Edwina's smile tempered her words. "On occasion we've been quite jealous."

"Jealous." Cordelia stared. "Of me?"

"Of course," Amelia said. "You've traveled to fascinating parts of the world we'll probably never see. One can scarcely pick up a ladies' magazine these days without seeing one of your pieces. Your life is very much an adventure while ours are, well, not. As much as we love our husbands and our children, it has long seemed to us that you have followed your, I don't know, desires I suppose, heart if you will, more so than anyone else we know."

"I would have liked to have studied art in Paris," Edwina said in an aside to Cordelia.

"Bea has mentioned on more than one occasion how much she would have liked to have dug for ancient artifacts in Greece. And I," Amelia drew a deep breath. "I should have quite liked to have learned how to operate a camera and take photographs."

Mother's eyes widened with horror.

Sarah tried and failed to hide a smile.

"I never imagined," Cordelia murmured.

"No, of course not." Amelia reached her hand across the table and patted Cordelia's hand. "My dear little sister, a full eleven years separates my age from yours. Winnie, Bea, and I are very close in age and therefore we have been very close as sisters. I regret that we have never included you in that particular bond but it doesn't mean we don't care for you, and aren't proud of you as well. And then you have had Sarah who has hopefully made up for our failures in that respect."

"However, it's past time to do something to show you how we feel." Edwina met her mother's gaze directly. "We've discussed this with Beatrice and the three of us agree that Cordelia should not be forced to marry Mr. Sinclair. It is her life after all."

"What?" Mother's forehead furrowed.

Father's paper rustled.

"We don't think it's right." Amelia drew a deep breath. "You're bartering her off as if she were so much excess farm stock."

Sarah choked.

"That's a lovely vision," Cordelia said under her breath.

"And to an American, Mother. *An American.*" Amelia

shook her head as if the word *American* was inter-changeable with *savage* or *cannibal* or *heathen*. "How could you?"

"Quite easily," Mother said sharply. "The girl needs to marry and this is her opportunity. You've said it yourself, she's done exactly as she's wished up to now. It's past time she live up to her familial responsibilities. Besides, right here at this very table not five minutes ago she admitted she does indeed wish to marry."

"No doubt to a man of her own choosing," Edwina scoffed. "Precisely as we did."

"But she hasn't as of yet, has she? Chosen a man, that is. Cordelia has failed to find a husband on her own and she's fast approaching an age where her chances of ever doing so diminish dramatically." Mother shook her head in a warning manner. "Men might well over-look a woman's obvious intelligence if she is pretty enough and Cordelia is, at the moment. But she is get-ting older and old and smart is not an attractive com-bination."

"But an American, Mother." Amelia glared.

"A *wealthy* American. Do keep that in mind." Mother huffed. "Marriage to your sister will not be an inex-pensive proposition. Regardless of nationality, she cer-tainly couldn't marry a poor man."

A vision of Warren flashed through Cordelia's mind. He wasn't poor—although Mother would no doubt think him so—and he did have excellent prospects. It was one thing to marry a wealthy American and quite another to marry an American who had to work for his living. Still, Warren had no business being in her head at all and she reluctantly banished him.

"No, poor wouldn't suit her," Edwina murmured.

"Nor would it suit any of us." She glanced at her older sister and nodded.

"Mother." Amelia chose her words with care. "We, Winnie and Bea and I, are quite well off in a financial sense—"

"You married wisely," Mother said pointedly.

"We've all three spoken to our husbands and we are in agreement." Amelia squared her shoulders and met her mother's gaze directly. "We shall provide whatever funding is necessary to save Father's business and eliminate the need for Cordelia to marry the American."

For a moment no one said anything. Mother looked stunned, Sarah only mildly surprised, and Cordelia was shocked. Not so much by the generosity of the offer but by the fact that her sisters had made it to save her. She hadn't even thought her sisters particularly liked her.

"That's very generous of you, dear." Father lowered his paper. "Please express my appreciation to your husbands." He folded his paper in a thoughtful manner. "Certainly, an influx of cash would be helpful at the moment but it does not solve all my problems. The best hope for that is this arrangement with the elder Mr. Sinclair." His gaze skimmed the circle of women. "You should all realize as well that, regardless of the consequences, Cordelia is not being forced to marry. For good or ill." His gaze met his youngest daughter's. "We have left the ultimate decision in her hands as it is, as you have all pointed out, her life. We believe she will reach the decision best for her future and the futures of all concerned."

Cordelia smiled weakly. What real choice did she have? She had begun to believe she could avoid this marriage but perhaps that was nothing more than wishful thinking on her part helped along by the memory of the dark eyes of a pirate.

"I had already planned on taking the train to London myself tomorrow to attend to business," Father continued. "If Cordelia can wait until tomorrow, I should be happy to accompany her and Sarah. I shall return to Brighton the following day."

Mother gasped. "You'll leave them home alone? What will," she narrowed her eyes, "what will Mr. Sinclair think?"

"I doubt Mr. Sinclair will think anything of it one way or the other," Father said firmly.

"He's an American after all," Amelia said under her breath.

"Besides, they'll scarcely be alone in a house full of servants." Father heaved a resigned sigh. "My sister is in residence in London at the moment and if you wish, I shall call on Lavinia and ask her to stay at the house."

Mother pressed her lips together but held her tongue, although Cordelia expected she'd have words with Father later.

The rest of the meal was finished in silence. Cordelia suspected everyone else at the table had as much to reflect upon as she did. Obviously she would have to tell Warren the truth and tell him as well whatever was growing between them was at an end. The oddest pain stabbed her heart at the thought. Nonsense, they'd shared little more than a few conversations and one mere kiss. Although mere was not entirely accurate. Heat pooled in her stomach at the very thought of his lips on hers. Well, whether she wished it to be or not, that particular adventure was at an end. She should never have begun it in the first place. She'd known from the start it was a silly escapade that would end badly. It was frivolous and irresponsible and far more exciting than it should have been.

Besides, she wanted her parents to treat her as an adult although even she could see her behavior wasn't always up to adult standards. Her sisters were right. She was indeed spoiled and had always managed to get whatever she'd wanted without ever having to truly stand up for herself. Today her sisters had done that for her.

It was past time Cordelia Victoria Williams Bannister became an adult. Past time she realized that adulthood brought with it certain responsibilities. Past time she accepted them.

And probably past time as well to at last meet Mr. Daniel Sinclair.

There remain today places in the world where natives live exactly as they did eons ago. A clever traveler will not look askance at such ways of life but rather appreciate them as expressions of a foreign heritage that, while different from our own, are no less worthy.

An English Lady's Traveling Companion

Chapter 8

Mr. Sinclair,

I was sorry to read what little value you place on history. Understandable, perhaps, as your country has so little history of its own. I should think it must be rather sad not to have the richness of heritage we so cherish in my country. As to any stifling of progress, as you so eloquently phrased it, perhaps, in your country, you

*did not hear of the Great Exposition? Or perhaps you
are unaware as to the current breadth of the British
Empire . . .*

*T*he day after his return to London, Daniel stood
before the door of a suite at Claridge's Hotel and
tried to summon up his courage to knock. Not that
he needed courage, of course, but a certain strength
of character was required. He hadn't seen his father
for months, not since they'd met in Italy and the elder
Sinclair had informed him he'd arranged for Daniel to
marry the daughter of a deceased British gentleman.
That Daniel had escaped that arrangement could be
attributed to little more than good timing and sheer
luck.

"Change the rules," Daniel said under his breath.

It wasn't that Daniel didn't love his father, they simply disagreed about virtually everything. Nowhere
was that conflict more intense than when it came to
Daniel's life. He and his father had been engaged in a
war of sorts nearly from the time he had been as young
as those mischievous nephews of Lady Cordelia's.
Which did not make it easy to ask for his help now.

Daniel drew a deep breath and knocked on the door.
He was about to knock again when it jerked open.

"Yes?" A tall woman stood in the doorway and
stared at him in a haughty manner. Her eyes were
piercing, her hair was a red color Daniel would not
have thought could be produced by nature, and her
complexion flawless. She couldn't have been more
than perhaps ten years older than he. Good God, he
groaned to himself, this must be his new mother. "Did
you want something?"

He cleared his throat. "I was told these are Mr. Sinclair's rooms?"

"Indeed, they are." Her gaze slid over him in an assessing and distinctly personal manner. He resisted the odd urge to shift from foot to foot. "And you are?"

"Daniel Sinclair."

She arched a perfectly formed brow. "You're the son? You don't look at all like your father, fortunately. Do come in."

He stepped into a large, well-appointed sitting room. She closed the door behind him and took his hat from his hand. "Sit down, Mr. Sinclair." She seated herself on a chair and gestured at a nearby sofa. "Or may I call you Daniel? Now that we're family."

"Of course . . ." And what was he supposed to call her? Surely she didn't expect him to call her *Mother*? "Er, Mrs. Sinclair."

"Mrs. Sinclair?" She laughed. "I daresay, I never thought I'd hear anyone call me Mrs. Sinclair."

"I wasn't sure what to call you," he said under his breath.

"You may call her Countess Paretti." A female voice sounded from the open door to his right. "Or Ursula."

Ursula leaned toward him and lowered her voice in a decidedly seductive manner. "Auntie Ursula."

He jumped to his feet and turned toward the door. A short, plump, mature woman with dark red hair and a friendly smile sailed toward him. "But her sister calls her 'most annoying.' I am Felice Di Mecurio Sinclair."

He stared and realized he must look like something of an idiot.

She took his hands in hers. Her eyes were a lovely clear shade of blue and abruptly Daniel realized, while not as striking as the other woman, she was beautiful nonetheless. "Your father's wife and your . . ." She laughed. "Well, I'm not entirely sure. Stepmother I suppose, although you're obviously past the age of needing a stepmother. You may call me Felice if you like, but my friends have always called me Daisy."

"I should be honored," he murmured.

"I'm not what you expected, am I?" Amusement danced in her blue eyes.

"I thought you were an opera singer," he blurted.

"I am. Or rather I was."

"There's a vast difference between an operatic soprano and a tart in the chorus, although most men don't seem to realize it," Ursula said dryly.

Daisy leaned toward him in a confidential manner. "Would you like to see me break a glass with a single note?"

Ursula groaned. "Do say no. It makes a nasty mess." She paused. "Good trick, though."

He chuckled in spite of himself. "Although I would like to see that, I'll forgo the pleasure today."

"Another time then. Now." Daisy settled in the chair opposite her sister's and gestured for him to retake his seat. "I expect your father to return at any minute. Until then, we can get to know one another."

He sat down, still trying to reconcile his preconceived notions of the type of woman his father would marry with this delightful and charming lady.

"I suspect you have any number of questions for me. I imagine you're quite curious." She studied him with a sympathetic eye. "It must be awkward to find oneself with a new mother at your age."

"Oh, it's certainly awkward," he said under his breath. Still, his gaze slipped to Ursula, it could have been much worse. "I barely remember my own mother. I must confess I never expected my father to marry again."

"I never expected to marry again either," Daisy said with a shrug. "I married when I was very young to a brilliant maestro who died tragically—"

"Run through with a sword by a jealous husband," Ursula said in a conversational manner, as if she were relating nothing of particular significance. "And well deserved I might add."

Daisy cast her sister a quelling glance. "We'd been married less than two years—"

Ursula huffed. "I said it was well deserved."

"From then on I concentrated on my work."

"Are you very famous?" Daniel said without thinking. "My apologies if you are. I have to admit I am not well versed in opera."

"Indeed she is," Ursula said staunchly.

"Nonsense, Ursula, I wouldn't say that at all, but I do appreciate the sentiment." She smiled at her sister and Daniel realized no matter how at odds the two women appeared, they were really very close. "In terms of fame, I would say I am well known in operatic circles, particularly in Europe. Critics have always liked me as have directors, and, of course, audiences. I have a modicum of fame, perhaps. But of course, that's at an end now."

"Pity," Ursula muttered.

Daniel drew his brows together. "Why is it at an end?"

Surprise crossed Daisy's face. "Because I've married your father. I'm very much looking forward to being a wife and managing a household. I never have, you know. In the future, I will confine my singing to charitable endeavors. I'm quite eager to return to America to live."

"We were born in Philadelphia," Ursula added. "Although we have spent most of our lives in Italy."

"And I am looking forward as well to being as much of a mother as you wish. And perhaps someday a grandmother." She smiled. "I have always wanted to be a mother and I'm delighted, even at this late juncture, to finally have the opportunity."

"Auntie Ursula would be happy to bounce you on her knee," Ursula said with a wicked light in her eye that was more than a little frightening.

"Stop it, Ursula," Daisy said firmly. "You'll give Daniel the wrong idea entirely. He doesn't know that you're teasing."

"Teasing?" Her sister raised a brow. "Yes, of course. That's exactly what I was doing." Ursula leaned forward and put her hand on his knee. "I can be quite a tease."

"I should warn you, Ursula has always been partial to handsome young men for amusement." Daisy pinned her sister with a hard look. "But she does understand nephews are prohibited."

"Yes, of course." His new aunt removed her hand and said under her breath, "but I don't see why."

"Because it's improper, impolite, and any flirtation would put the poor boy in an extremely awkward position. He's a relative now and one should try not to seduce one's relations, and because," Daisy's voice hardened, "I said so."

"Oh, well then . . ." Ursula rolled her gaze toward the ceiling.

"You must forgive my sister, she has no sense of . . . well, she has no sense."

"But she has a great deal of fun." Ursula flashed her sister an unrepentant smile. "Between husbands, that is."

"Regardless of Ursula's definition of fun, she has a distinct mercenary streak when it comes to marriage. She has always married for money and position, and always men considerably older. Three times now, dear?"

"Yes, but I quite liked the last one," Ursula sighed. "Count Paretti was a charming man. Pity, he had to pass on so soon."

"Men of advanced age tend to do that," Daisy said wryly.

"Might I ask, and I mean no offense by the question." Daniel looked at Daisy and chose his words carefully. "Why did you marry my father?"

"I don't mind the question at all." Daisy smiled. "The usual reasons, I think."

"He has a great deal of money," Ursula said in an offhand manner.

"Yes, but I have a great deal of money as well, which negates that. Although I wouldn't have wed anyone who was not wealthy in his own right." Daisy shook her head slowly. "When one is financially well off, one is always aware that potential suitors may be more interested in one's fortune than one's character. Money was not a serious consideration."

She thought for a moment. "Your father and I are not so far apart in age that we do not share a mutual history of the world, as it were. Indeed, in terms of our likes and dislikes, we have a great deal in common. Beyond that, he has a kind heart and a generous nature. He's tolerant and intelligent and amusing." She met Daniel's gaze directly. "He makes me laugh and makes me feel as if I were a girl again. I quite fell in love with him, and I have every intention of making him happy for the rest of our days."

Daniel said the first thing that came to mind. "This is Harold Sinclair you're speaking of?"

"Indeed it is." Daisy laughed. "I don't expect that you would see him the way I do. I know the two of you have not been especially close in recent years."

Daniel snorted. "Not especially, no."

"Which is why I'm somewhat surprised to see you here," Daisy said slowly. "Pleased but surprised."

"As am I," Daniel murmured. Still, facing his father might not be as much of an ordeal as he had anticipated. His stepmother had certainly come as an unexpected, and most welcome, surprise. "He might not feel the same."

"Nonsense." Daisy beamed at him. "He'll be delighted. He's quite proud of you, you know."

"He is?" Here was yet another surprise.

"Of course he is." Daisy's eyes widened. "I can't believe you didn't know that."

"I wasn't aware—"

"Well, you should be." Indignation rang in Daisy's voice. "He's told me all about you. How you've refused his help, financially and in every other way ever since you finished your studies. How you've used a small inheritance from your mother's family to fund your ventures. How you have gone off on your own to build your own fortune, find your own success, rather than wait to inherit his. He's said more than once how your ambition reminds him of his own at your age and he feels you come by it naturally. Indeed, he thinks you're exactly like he was."

"Am I?" Daniel said weakly. He'd never for so much as a moment considered he might be the least bit like his father.

She nodded. "He thinks your scheme of purchasing small railroads with an eye toward consolidation is nothing short of brilliant. In fact, I have heard him compare you to Vanderbilt."

"Really? How . . . unexpected." Not merely his father's pride but the extent of his knowledge about Daniel's business pursuits. "How does he know all this?"

"Goodness, Daniel. Your father is a captain of industry. He makes it his business to know such things. And, I daresay, when it comes to the world of business, especially anything having to do with the transport of goods or people, he probably knows everything worth knowing." Daisy leaned toward him and rested her hand on his. "My dear boy, you needn't be concerned as to what your father has told me about your business. While I have no idea whether or not your activities require secrecy, I can assure you your father would not say anything to anyone that might compromise your success."

He stared. "I didn't think—"

"No, you certainly did not." She removed her hand

and straightened in her chair. "I know full well your father can be extremely stubborn and he rarely, if ever, admits when he is wrong. I have no doubt you take after him in that respect."

Ursula choked back a laugh. Her sister glared at her. Ursula coughed, then tried and failed to look entirely innocent of anything beyond a tickle in the throat.

"There have been any number of occasions when I have admitted that I might have been wrong." Daniel couldn't quite hide the defensive note in his voice although he had nothing to be defensive about.

"You must understand something about me, Daniel. When I said I have always wanted to be a mother that was entirely accurate but only as far as it went. Ursula and I have been quite alone in the world, aside from whatever husband she happened to have at the moment, for a very long time. I have wanted to be part of a family again for as long as I can remember. Your father is now my family, as are you." She narrowed her eyes. "And I will not permit dissension in my family."

"You won't?" he said cautiously. He really had no idea what else to say. "You do understand that I am an adult. I am not a child."

"Then stop behaving like one," Daisy said sharply. "You and your father both. Daniel." Her tone softened and she met his gaze. "You're over thirty, your father is past fifty. There will come a time when he will no longer be here. You—both of you—have the opportunity now to make peace with one another. Before it's too late."

The truth of her comment struck him with an unexpected clarity. Hadn't he just seen exactly what she was talking about? Nigel Cavendish had lost his father barely more than a month ago. Cavendish had long thought his father saw him as something of a disappointment. It was only recently that he had learned otherwise. But he and his father had had the opportunity to grow close in the final months before the older man's death. Cavendish had mentioned on more than one occasion how grateful he was for that.

Daniel had never before considered that the time he and his father had was finite. Certainly he was well aware of the inevitability of death, but he had never thought about it in terms of his relationship with his father. If truth were told he'd been far too busy resenting his father's interference for far too long to consider the consequences of that resentment.

"Daniel," her voice was soft but intense. "You might not be given another chance. If you miss this opportunity, mark my words, one day you will regret it."

Hadn't Cavendish said much the same thing? That if he had not reconciled his differences with his father, he would have regretted it for the rest of his life?

Were Harold Sinclair's crimes against his son so heinous they could not be forgiven? Of course not. The worst was the elder Sinclair's determination to see Daniel in an advantageous marriage. Still, if Daniel looked at his father's actions with a rational eye, with the eye of an adult, he might well see that the older man had always simply wanted what was best for his son. That he thought he knew what that was could be forgiven. Wouldn't Daniel some day want only the best for his own son? And wouldn't he think he knew better than his son what that was?

Was that the real problem between them then? That as much as Daniel was a grown man, he had never quite stopped seeing his father from the point of view of a rebellious youth? Had never stopped responding to him the same way he had as a child? That it took an observer who recognized the value of family, the value of what the Sinclairs might have, and more, what they might lose, to make him realize it was past time to reconcile their differences would have been somewhat discomforting had it not been for the nature of the observer herself. Daisy might well be the smartest move his father had ever made. For himself and for his son.

"You're right." Daniel blew a long breath.

Daisy favored him with a brilliant smile. "I know."

"You're very lucky to have her," Ursula murmured.

Daniel grinned. "I'm convinced of it." He paused. "You do realize, this might not be easy."

Daisy waved off his comment. "Undoubtedly. But your father and I have discussed it, and he has promised to make an effort."

"Then I can do no less. Still—"

A key sounded in the lock and Daniel got to his feet. A strange mix of apprehension and anticipation gripped him. He had no idea what to expect. He glanced at Daisy and she smiled in an encouraging manner.

The door opened and Harold Sinclair strode into the room.

"Daniel!" A wide grin broke over his father's face. He started toward his son then hesitated.

"Father." Daniel stepped toward him. "It's . . . it's

good to see you." Even as he said the words he knew they were true.

His father's grin widened if possible. He moved to his son and took one of Daniel's hands in both of his. "It's good to see you too, son."

The oddest sense of relief and well-being swept through Daniel as he gazed down at his father. As if he was once again a small boy looking at the one man in the whole world he could trust to be there for him always. Of course, in those days his father wasn't the portly, balding gentlemen nearly half a foot shorter than Daniel that stood before him now.

Daniel smiled a genuine smile. "You look ten years younger, Father."

His father chuckled. "That's what the love of a good woman will do for you, son. It won't restore your hair but other than that . . ." He leaned toward his son and lowered his voice. "She makes me feel young. Wish I'd met her years ago."

"She is a prize."

"Indeed she is." The elder Sinclair straightened and studied his son. "You, however, look ten years older. I suspect you've been working entirely too hard."

"I feel ten years older," Daniel said wryly. "You're right, I have been working hard."

"If you want my advice—"

"Harold." A warning note sounded in Daisy's voice.

"My apologies, my dear." He squared his shoulders and looked up at his son. "Daniel, we need to talk. If that's amenable to you?"

"I would like that," Daniel said firmly.

Daisy rose to her feet. "I believe Ursula and I have some errands—"

"Oh no, this is your doing, Daisy, and I will not permit you to avoid the end result of it now. Besides," Harold cast a private sort of smile at his wife and Daniel realized this was very much a love match. Ironic, as the older man had never given love any consideration when trying to marry off Daniel. Perhaps it wasn't as much ironic as it was fitting. "This is not merely between father and son, it's a family matter and you are a part of this family."

"Yes of course. Still, it does seem rather personal and perhaps Ursula . . ." She glanced pointedly at her sister. "If you don't leave now, Ursula, you shall miss your appointment."

"Canceled," Ursula said with a ring in her voice and a blithe wave of her hand.

Daisy narrowed her eyes. "Surely you do have somewhere you have to be?"

"No, no, not at all." Ursula cast them a brilliant smile. "Nowhere to go, nothing to do. Not a thing."

"Even so, I'm certain—"

"If your new husband, an arrogant beast of a father, is about to reconcile with your new son, his ungrateful, if handsome, offspring, I can't think of anywhere else I should rather be. Unless"—Ursula's eyes widened in disbelief—"I am not considered part of your newfound family? Your own sister? If you are tossing me aside like so much discarded rubbish—"

"For goodness sakes, Ursula, you needn't be so dramatic." Daisy sighed and glanced at her husband.

"She can stay," Father said and added in a low tone. "Part and parcel of for-better-or-worse, I suppose."

Daniel bit back a grin.

Ursula beamed. "I shall just sit over here in the corner quiet as a little mouse. Why, you won't even know I'm here."

"Impossible," the elder Sinclair said under his breath. He settled on the sofa and gestured for Daniel to join him. Daisy retook her seat. "You should know, Daniel, that Daisy and I have had several conversations on this subject. She has some very definite opinions about family."

"So I've heard." Daniel smiled at his stepmother.

"She is aware this rift between us has weighed heavily on my mind—"

"On your heart," Daisy corrected.

"On my heart." Father sighed. "Furthermore she thinks it is, for the most part, entirely my fault."

Daniel's eyes widened in surprise. "She does?"

"Indeed she does." Father nodded. "So I have a proposition of sorts for you. I have promised Daisy, and I will now promise you, that I will no longer offer unsolicited advice. I will refrain as well from expressing my belief that my opinions are more valid than yours. And I will resist the urge, should the opportunity ever again present itself, to arrange a marriage for you."

Daniel stared. "You will?"

His father hesitated, glanced at Daisy, then smiled weakly. "I will. You should know that it will take a great deal of effort on my part, but I will. My intent has always been to make your life easier and better. To help you avoid the mistakes I have made. Daisy has helped me to see that I may never have accepted that you are now an intelligent adult and more than capable of handling your own affairs. But I have always viewed my actions as being those of a concerned, loving parent."

Daisy cleared her throat.

"Although I have come to realize that perhaps they might have been construed as . . ." He rolled his gaze toward the ceiling. "As somewhat overbearing and heavy-handed and domineering."

"You have?" Daniel said slowly. He wasn't sure what he had expected but this admission certainly wasn't it.

"So my proposition is that I will endeavor to change." He winced. "I *will* change."

Daniel stared.

"I wish to be part of your life and to accomplish that I need to resist my more annoying tendencies. Oh, I will always be available should you need advice or funding or merely to talk. Or anything else, but it will be entirely up to you."

"I see." Daniel drew a deep breath. "What I'd like is a favor."

"A favor?" His father considered him for a moment. Daniel had never asked him for anything, let alone a favor. "Name it."

"I need you to get me out of this marriage."

"This marriage?" His father's forehead furrowed in confusion, then his expression cleared. "Oh, you're talking about the arrangement with Lord Marsham?"

Daniel drew his brows together. "Is there another arrangement?"

"Absolutely not," his father said staunchly. "Just this one."

"Then do something about this one."

"Daniel, I would if I could but . . ."

"But?" Daniel's voice rose.

"But, I gave my word." He shook his head in a regretful manner. "I can't renege on it now."

"I'm not asking you to. I'm simply asking you to change the rules."

"Change the rules," his father said cautiously. "I don't understand."

"How good is this deal with Lord Marsham?"

"Very good. If he wasn't in a bit of a financial bind at the moment, he'd never consider it. His company is otherwise sound."

"Then if he didn't have a marriageable daughter, you'd still be interested?"

"Yes." Father drew the word out slowly.

"Lord Marsham will not force his daughter to marry me if she doesn't wish to."

"And?"

"She feels compelled to marry me to save her family's fortune."

"Go on."

"If you withdraw that stipulation to the deal, it will alleviate any pressure she may feel to agree to a marriage."

His father considered the idea for a moment. "I suspect you've given this a great deal of thought. Precisely how do you propose I do that?"

"You simply tell Lord Marsham, while you still think an alliance with his family is an excellent idea, you have realized that business matters should not be contingent on personal issues." Daniel grinned in triumph. "Therefore, while you are still eager to merge his interests with yours, a marriage between your children is no longer a condition of the deal."

His father narrowed his eyes. "And I have come to that realization because? . . ."

"Because . . ." Daniel searched for an answer.

"Because," Ursula leaned forward eagerly, "you have recently found happiness in a marriage with a wife of your own choosing therefore you have realized you cannot deny your son the same opportunity."

Three pairs of eyes stared at Ursula in surprise.

"Brava, Ursula," Daisy murmured. "Well said."

Ursula shrugged and settled back in her chair. "I thought it was obvious."

"Obvious perhaps, but it might not be as easy as that," his father said. "The suggestion as to a match between you and Lady—what was her name?"

"Cordelia," Daniel said.

"That's it. Lady Cordelia. The proposal was Lord Marsham's, not mine." Reluctance sounded in his father's voice. "Although I did think it was a splendid idea."

"Because he had not yet come to his senses," Daisy said firmly. "Indeed, it was when I learned of this arrangement that he and I had our most serious talk about you and he."

"That's something at any rate." Daniel got to his feet and paced the room. "But it still doesn't get me out of this."

Daisy wrinkled her nose. "It sounds to me as if the man is eager to get the girl off his hands."

"Of course he is." Daniel huffed. "The woman is twenty-five, a stout and sturdy sort of . . . Amazon if you will, and she's writing a book."

"We would hate to have a woman of undue intelligence in the family," Ursula said under her breath.

Daniel glared at his new aunt. "I have no difficulties with her intelligence. Indeed, my intentions have always been to marry a woman with a good mind. I just want to find her on my own rather than having her thrust upon me."

"That's completely understandable, Daniel," Daisy said in a soothing manner. "So you've met Lady Cordelia then?"

"Not exactly," Daniel muttered.

His father frowned. "How do you not exactly meet someone?"

Daniel shrugged. "We've been corresponding. But I have met her companion, a distant cousin by marriage. Miss Palmer. Sarah Palmer. She's a lovely woman." He pinned Ursula with a firm look. "With an exceptionally fine mind."

His father and stepmother traded glances. Daisy chose her words with care. "I gather you like this Miss Palmer?"

"Indeed I do. I like her a great deal. In fact . . ."

In fact what? He had impulsively told Sarah he would like to call on her and when he'd said it, he'd meant it. At that moment, he'd paid no heed at all to the consequences of such an act. And then she had kissed him and he'd been able to think of very little else since then, but the feel of her lips beneath his and her supple body pressed against his and the growing conviction that, regardless of his wish to avoid marriage, this might well be the one woman in the world for him. Even her request the morning that he left Brighton that he not call on her did little to dampen his growing feelings. In truth, he simply thought her all the more honorable for choosing her responsibilities to Lady Cordelia and her family over her own desires.

But he could do nothing about Sarah, indeed, he couldn't even reveal his true identity to her, until he resolved the matter of Lady Cordelia. Sarah's employer, cousin, and dear friend.

"This is so delicious," Ursula murmured.

"Did you say something?" Daisy aimed a sharp look at her sister.

"No, no, not me." Ursula smiled innocently. "Not a word. Nothing at all."

"In fact what, Daniel?" his father asked.

"In fact." Daniel chose his words carefully. "Right now, I'm not entirely certain how I feel about Sarah—Miss Palmer. But I would like the opportunity to find out."

"And you can't until the question of Lady Cordelia is laid to rest. I see. It's my fault you're in the position you're in and I wish . . ." He shrugged in a helpless manner. "To be perfectly honest, Daniel, I need this transaction almost as much as Marsham does." He paused for a long moment. "As do you."

"What I need is the freedom to choose my own wife when and if I wish for a wife and not to be shackled to a female as part of a business deal."

"It does sound bad when you put it that way," Ursula murmured.

"You may need that shackling," Father said under his breath, then met Daniel's gaze. "I was glad to see you here today, son, for more than the obvious reasons. I was going to send you a note requesting a meeting."

Daniel narrowed his eyes. "Why?"

His father studied him carefully. "I received a letter

this morning from a business associate in New York. He had some disturbing information concerning your plans."

"My plans?" a finger of unease teased Daniel's stomach. "What do you mean my plans?"

"Your railroads." His father leaned toward him and lowered his voice in a confidential manner. "I know that in additions to the railroads you own outright or have controlling interest in, you currently have tentative agreements to purchase three more. There may be a challenge in the wind to those transactions."

"What?" Daniel shook his head. "That's impossible. Those agreements are ironclad."

"No agreement is ironclad when enough money is on the table."

The full impact of what the older man said hit him with a physical force, and he stared at his father. The railroads in question had been chosen after long study and consideration of specific factors including location and potential. Each fit into his and Warren's overall design with the precision of a puzzle. When they had begun, adjustments could be made but now the loss of even one, let alone three, would spell disaster.

"Without those railroads"—Daniel chose his words with care—"it all falls apart. Warren and I will lose everything, our futures as well as my money and the money of friends who have put their faith in me."

"You need a great deal of money and you need it quickly, at least within the next few months." A grim note sounded in his father's voice. "You should plan on returning home as well. Within the month I would say."

"Father." Daniel met his father's gaze. Damnation this was hard. "I believe I need another favor."

His father shook his head. "I wish I could assist you but most of my uncommitted funding is tied up in this deal with Lord Marsham. Once that is finalized, I will have the money available and be more than willing to help. But that will take as long as half a year."

"Unfortunately, that does not solve my current problem." His father hadn't mentioned specific figures but Daniel had a good idea of how much he would need.

"In spite of her father's financial problems, Lady Cordelia has a substantial dowry set aside and the man she marries receives a significant inheritance immediately upon her marriage as well," the elder Sinclair said in an offhand manner.

Daisy gasped. "Harold."

Daniel braced himself. "How significant?"

"Extremely, according to her father. It can be signed over to you, the moment the vows are said."

"Harold." Daisy glared at her husband. "I can't believe you're encouraging the boy to marry this woman for her money."

"There are worse reasons," Ursula said mildly.

"I'm encouraging the boy to do what he needs to do," Father said firmly. "And it was the lady's father who offered this bit of incentive in the first place. A carrot as it were. It comes from a great aunt, I believe. I'm not sure even the lady herself is aware of it." He then turned to Daniel. "But didn't you say Lord Marsham will leave the decision as to whether or not she'll marry you up to her?"

"I did and I've been trying to convince her, through Miss Palmer, that I am not the man for her."

Daisy's eyes widened. "Daniel!"

"How charmingly devious of you," Ursula murmured.

"I tell you what I can do, Daniel. If Lady Cordelia refuses to marry you, I'll do everything I can to make certain this deal goes through, but without the marriage I'm not sure that's possible. Lord Marsham wants his daughter married and you're apparently the best that's come along."

"Lucky me," Daniel said under his breath.

"Although, by that time my assistance might be too late. Your most expedient move—"

"Would be to marry Lady Cordelia." An awful sense of inevitability settled in the pit of Daniel's stomach and with it, regret and an acute feeling of loss.

"What about Miss Palmer?" Daisy asked. "Surely she'll be upset when she realizes you've been using her to manipulate Lady Cordelia?"

"I doubt that will be at the top of the list of things she'll be angry about," Daniel muttered.

Daisy studied her stepson. "Is there another problem then?"

"You could call it a problem." Daniel ran his hand through his hair. "Miss Palmer thinks I'm somebody else."

Ursula choked back a laugh. "This just gets better and better."

His father stared at him. "Who does she think you are?"

Daniel grimaced. "Warren."

"You mentioned him before. Who is Warren?" Daisy asked her husband.

"Warren Lewis. Daniel's right-hand man. Brilliant

young man. I would give a great deal to have him working for me." He looked at his son. "Why does Miss Palmer think you're Warren?"

"It's a long story," Daniel warned.

"We have time," Ursula said brightly.

Her sister narrowed her eyes. "You promised to be quiet."

"I know but I can't seem to help myself." Ursula raised a shoulder in a casual shrug. Laughter sparkled in her eyes. "This is so much better than opera."

A journal is an excellent accompaniment for any traveler to record one's thoughts and impressions as they occur. It is a pity to attempt to recall those memories upon returning home only to find they have faded.

An English Lady's Traveling Companion

Chapter 9

A few hours after her return home, Cordelia paced the hall outside the library door. It had taken her this long to marshal her courage.

The train ride to London had been uneventful if overly hot. Father had occupied his time with a newspaper, Sarah had read her favorite poetry, a book she never traveled without, and Cordelia had worked on a recollection of the bazaars of Cairo. Although her mind had been anywhere but on merchants sitting cross-legged surrounded by their goods, or water carriers bearing freshly filled goatskins.

She had to speak to her father before she confessed to Warren or at last met Daniel Sinclair. Father had been altogether too vague about the repercussions of her decision as to whether or not she would marry Mr. Sinclair. She wanted—no, needed—to know in no uncertain terms exactly how important this business proposal was to her family. And exactly how dire the consequences would be if she did not agree to the marriage. Regardless of Father's assertion that the decision was up to her, her choice was entirely dependent on his answer.

Not that she had a choice. She'd never doubted her father's love and the very fact that he'd put her in this position in the first place indicated the serious nature of the situation. Indeed, hadn't she just been delaying the inevitable? If her family's future depended on this marriage, she would face her fate—if not willingly then at least with a certain amount of courage. And she would put any thought of dark-eyed pirates out of her head.

She squared her shoulders, rapped sharply on the door, waited for her father's response, then entered the library.

"Good evening, Father. Might I have a word with you?"

Father looked up from the papers before him on his desk. "Of course."

Cordelia crossed the room to take her usual seat in the chair positioned in front of her father's desk.

He waved for her to sit down. "I was wondering when you'd ask."

"You were?" she said cautiously and settled herself in the chair.

"You're here to discuss this arrangement of marriage, aren't you?"

"Well, yes, I am. How did you know?"

"I've been expecting it. Indeed, I'm surprised it has not come before now. You've been remarkably quiet on the subject since our first discussion." He studied his daughter for a long moment. "I must admit I have wondered why although I did consider the possibility you were planning some form of escape."

She widened her eyes in an innocent manner. "Me?"

"You," he said firmly. "Why haven't you hounded me on this subject?"

"Why?"

He nodded. "Why."

"I'm not sure it would have done me any good. It seemed wiser to bide my time. However, I have been giving it a great deal of thought." She drew a deep breath. "Father, I am not a child."

"Yes, I think mention of that was made yesterday."

"Before I make any decision I need to understand the true importance of this business arrangement." She met her father's gaze directly. "If it does not take place, what are the consequences?"

"I thought I made that clear."

"Not entirely. I recall you saying something about a detrimental reversal of family income, which, quite frankly, Father, could mean anything from having to forgo new ball gowns to having to sell Marsham Hall."

"Do you know anything about business?"

"No." She paused. "But I am not stupid."

Father smiled. "No, you're not. Very well then. Allow me to start from the beginning." He folded his hands on top of his desk and paused to pull his thoughts together. "The title of Earl of Marsham goes back nearly two centuries. When I was a young man I realized the way the aristocracy in this country had prospered for generations was coming to an end. Times were changing and we had to change with them if we were to survive. My father disagreed, of course, but then he was firmly mired in the past. He couldn't imagine his world not remaining as it had always been.

"At any rate, I began investing in various enterprises. Some quite successful, others not as much. Eventually, I focused my efforts and funding on shipping, and it has proven profitable up to now. But once again, times are changing. Most of my fleet is wind driven, and while I think there will always be a place for sailing ships, I believe the future is in steam . . ."

For the next half an hour or so, Father discussed the intricacies and assorted aspects of wind versus steam: the need to carry fuel in the form of coal, the dependability of scheduling, the development of screw propellers to replace paddle wheels, the sheer weight of steam engines and the accompanying stress on wooden ships, and any number of other concerns. The issues Father detailed were complicated but understandable. By the time he had finished Cordelia had an acceptable grasp of the problems he faced and why merging his interests with the elder Mr. Sinclair was not merely an excellent idea but, in many ways, a salvation.

"Even the offers made by your sisters, and most appreciated I might add—"

"By both of us," Cordelia murmured.

"Would provide, at best, a temporary solution. However, Mr. Sinclair has the vast resources to provide for modernization I do not."

"I see," Cordelia said slowly. "So if this transaction is contingent upon this marriage, there really is no choice."

"I would not take that choice away from you, Cordelia. It is, as it must be, ultimately your decision."

"Still . . ."

"Do understand, my dear girl, this is not easy for me either, which is precisely why I waited so long to tell you of this arrangement." His tone was serious but a smile twinkled in his eye. "It's difficult to barter off one's favorite daughter like excess farm stock."

She raised a delighted brow. "Am I your favorite?"

Father chuckled. "You always have been. I would ask, however, that you not let your sisters know." He paused. "Beyond the benefits of a good marriage for you, Mr. Sinclair or any man would be lucky to have you. I consider you one of my greatest achievements."

She wrinkled her nose. "Mother doesn't. She doesn't see anything but my failure to wed."

"Your mother sees things from only a narrow, feminine point of view and in many ways, she's living in the past. She measures a woman's accomplishments by the prestige of her marriage."

"And you?"

"I like the woman you've become. I quite enjoy reading your accounts of camel rides in the desert or balloon flights over Paris. I am extremely proud that you are my daughter. Unfortunately, however, the world is what it is and the opportunities for an unmarried woman in this day and age are limited."

She sighed. "It's not the least bit fair."

"No, of course it isn't, which doesn't change a thing." He chose his words with care. "Have you considered the effect of this marriage on your future?"

She grimaced. "I've thought of little else."

"I fully understand the desire of a young woman to marry for affection, yet love has not come your way." He considered her carefully. "Unless I'm mistaken?"

"No." Warren's devilish smile flashed through her mind. Not that she was in love with him. No, love would be sweet and serene and completely without doubt. Whenever she so much as thought of Warren her feelings were tumultuous and uncertain and not at all what love would surely be like. Worse, everything with Warren was predicated on a lie. No, what, if anything, they shared was certainly not love. She pushed him out of her thoughts, ignored the odd ache accompanying it, and smiled reluctantly. "You're not mistaken."

"Then let us be practical. You've said you do indeed wish to marry."

She nodded.

"Therefore, in a practical sense, you need to marry well. You need a man who can, to be blunt, afford you. Daniel Sinclair is that man. He has the resources to pay for the travel you so dearly love. To pay as well for a good home and servants and fine clothes."

"I do so love hats," she said under her breath.

"And hats are surprisingly expensive." He studied

his daughter. "What would you do with your life if you don't marry, Cordelia?"

"Ever, you mean?"

He nodded.

"I don't know." She thought for a moment. "I would continue my travels—"

"Which, even if we were to give up all hope of marriage and use the funds of your dowry, is still an expense I will not be able to afford indefinitely."

"I would continue my writing—"

"Which might, one day, allow you to eek out a meager living. Writers do not make a great deal of money, my dear."

"Pity." She shook her head. "I suppose I could become a governess—"

Father bit back a grin. "Yes, I've seen how well you get along with your sister's children."

"There must be something wrong with me, Father." Cordelia pulled her brows together. "While I do want children of my own, I don't seem to like theirs all that much."

He laughed. "I suspect you will like yours when the time comes."

"So I would not suit as a governess." She thought for a moment. "I could become a companion like Sarah."

"Not like Sarah," Father said firmly. "Let us be honest, Cordelia. Sarah has the position of companion only to salvage her own pride. I admire the girl for not wanting to be fully dependent on us and I admit it is cheaper to pay her a salary than it is to underwrite her expenses as I do yours, but as companions go, I do not think she is as effective as someone you did not have entirely under your thumb."

Heat washed up Cordelia's face. "Father!"

He narrowed his eyes. "You disagree."

She huffed. "Not entirely. It just sounds so calculating."

"We wouldn't want that." He chuckled. "I daresay Sarah won't be your companion for much longer at any rate."

Cordelia stared. "What do you mean?"

"Nothing of significance." Father waved off her comment. "Just an odd thought really. How goes your correspondence with Mr. Sinclair? Have you come to know him at all?"

Only that he is most annoying. Cordelia shrugged. "One can be so many things on paper, Father. I fear it's not at all fair to judge him by his letters." She drew a deep breath. "It's probably time I met him in person."

"Excellent." Surprise sounded in Father's voice. "When the rest of the family returns from Brighton, we shall have . . ." His brow furrowed, "A dinner perhaps. With his family and ours. Yes, your mother will like that. I suspect it would be better for you and Mr. Sinclair to meet in an atmosphere of cordiality rather than something more serious."

She forced a smile. "That sounds lovely, Father."

His gaze searched hers. "I am sorry that it has come to this, Cordelia. But I believe it's the best course for all concerned."

She picked absently at the arm of the chair. "Yes, well, I suppose that's part and parcel of being an adult, isn't it?"

"What?"

"Why, doing what's best." She met her Father's gaze and raised her chin. "Whether one wants to or not."

* * *

"I don't know what to do, Warren." Daniel paced the width of the office.

"That's not exactly accurate," Warren said mildly.

Daniel stopped and stared at his friend. "What do you mean?"

"What I mean is that you know exactly what to do, what you have to do." Warren shrugged. "You just don't want to do it."

"Of course I don't want to do it." Daniel resumed pacing. He had always thought better on his feet and he had some serious thinking to do now. "I have no desire to marry at all, let alone to a woman not of my choosing, to facilitate a business deal for my father, to assure financing—"

"To save our respective futures, our reputations as well as all of your money and the money of our investors, which includes a fair number of men you call 'friend'."

Daniel ran his hand through his hair. "I don't seem to have a choice do I?"

"You have any number of choices, Daniel, you always have. One, you can continue to try to convince Lady Cordelia she doesn't want to marry you and hope her father will nonetheless go through with his merger with your father, thus freeing up your father's funds to help us, although by then it will be too late and we'll be ruined, impoverished." Warren's brow furrowed. "No, I'll be the only one impoverished. You'll still be the son of a wealthy man although you will be an abject failure and have to turn to your father for support." Warren shuddered. "There's a nasty prospect for your pride."

"You won't be impoverished," Daniel said with an

absent wave of his hand. "My father will jump at the chance to hire you. He thinks very highly of you. Nor will he think of either of us as failures."

Warren raised a brow. "I would say that he's changed but I suspect the change has been in you."

"In both of us, I think." Daniel sighed and dropped into the nearest chair. "He has seen the error of his ways regarding his interference in my life, thanks to Daisy. And I now understand his intentions were well meant. I also see that our similarities are greater than our differences and that we are lucky to have one another."

Warren stared. "Apparently your meeting this morning produced far greater results than you've mentioned thus far."

"It's hard to admit, even to an old friend, that you've behaved badly in regards to a parent."

"Especially as this particular old friend already knew and has not hesitated to—"

"Yes, yes, and admittedly I should have listened."

"To my advice about your father and so many other words of wisdom. Although I have to admit, you're right about one thing." Warren grimaced. "You don't really have a choice other than to marry Lady Cordelia. Well." Warren shrugged. "It can't be helped I suppose."

"I'm glad you're taking this so well."

"I'm not taking it at all well. I feel dreadful about it, and yet I am willing to set aside my personal feelings and bravely sacrifice you on the altar of holy matrimony."

"How selfless of you."

"I think so." Warren studied his friend for a moment. "It could be worse you know."

"Worse than marrying a woman I've never met to satisfy a promise I didn't make and acquire money I haven't earned?" Daniel snorted. "How?"

"You could be in love." Warren paused. "With Miss Palmer that is."

Daniel started to deny it, then shrugged as if Warren's charge was of no consequence.

Warren opened his bottom desk drawer, drew out a bottle and two glasses, filled them and got to his feet, crossed the room, and handed one to Daniel.

Daniel glanced skeptically from the glass in his hand to the other man. "When did you begin keeping whisky in your desk?"

"Shortly after you left to meet your father this morning. It seemed like a good idea."

"It's an excellent idea."

Warren pulled up a chair, sat down, and considered his friend. "You didn't answer my question."

"You didn't ask a question."

"Then I'll ask one now." He met Daniel's gaze. "Are you in love with Miss Palmer?"

"No, of course not." Daniel tossed back the contents of the glass, scarcely noting the burn of the liquor in his throat. "That would be the height of stupidity."

"And your actions of late have been the epitome of intelligence?"

"Apparently not. I admit that I like her. I like her a lot." Now that he'd said it aloud, Daniel was shocked to realize just how much he did like her and liked as well the pleasure of her company. Walking with her, talking to her—he wasn't entirely sure he'd ever really talked to a woman before in anything but the depth required of casual conversation at a party or in passing. And when he'd kissed her . . . It was entirely possible he more than merely liked her. "The more I'm with her, the more I like her."

"And therein lies the biggest flaw," Warren said softly and refilled Daniel's glass.

"The flaw?" Daniel stared at the other man and abruptly saw exactly what Warren had warned him of all along. "That I would come to care for her?"

Warren nodded. "And worse."

"That she would come to care for me," Daniel said slowly. Good God, what had he done?

"Do you think she does?"

"No, no, of course not," Daniel said quickly. "She's far too sensible for that. Certainly she kissed me—"

"You kissed her?"

"No, she kissed me, although I admit I kissed her back."

Warren's eyes widened in disbelief. "And you don't think that's an indication of her feelings? Sensible young women don't kiss gentlemen they don't have some feeling for."

"But she refused to let me call on her," Daniel added quickly.

"You asked to call on her?"

"A momentary lapse in judgment."

Warren scoffed. "Scarcely momentary."

"Yes, yes, well I've made a mess of all this, haven't I?" Daniel stood and resumed pacing, glass in hand. "Sarah's going to despise me and I can't say that I blame her. As for Lady Cordelia—"

"If Miss Palmer tells Lady Cordelia that you kissed her—"

"She kissed me," Daniel said firmly, "and with a great deal of enthusiasm I might add."

"Regardless of who kissed whom and the degree of enthusiasm involved, I can't imagine Lady Cordelia would take it at all well." Warren raised his glass pointedly. "She might even see it as a reason to reject your suit altogether."

"Wouldn't that be ironic?" Daniel swirled the liquor in his glass. "Just when I realize I have to marry her, I've come up with the perfect way to avoid it." He downed his whisky, moved to Warren's desk, and sloshed more liquor into his glass. "Not that my plan wasn't proceeding nicely. Based on our correspondence, I think Lady Cordelia would have soon decided she wants nothing whatsoever to do with me. I found her Achilles heel and she now considers me pompous, arrogant, narrow-minded and, no doubt, irritating as well."

"A match made in heaven."

"Or somewhere considerably lower." Daniel sank back into his chair.

"And what do you think of her?"

At once Daniel's original impression of a sturdy Amazonian traveler complete with walking stick, compass, and chastising expression popped back into his head. "She writes a fine letter."

Warren laughed. "She writes more than that." He got up, stepped to his desk, picked up a pile of bound papers, and dropped them on Daniel's desk in front of him. "You should read these."

Daniel eyed the stack. "What are they?"

"Ladies' magazines." Warren retook his seat and refilled his glass.

Daniel glanced at the top copy of *Cadwallender's Monthly Lady's Cabinet.* "As much as I appreciate the gesture, I'm not overly interested in the latest style of frocks."

"The magazines have articles written by your," Warren cleared his throat, "fiancée."

Daniel flipped open the cover. "Why do you have these?"

"I thought they would come in handy." Warren paused. "I've read them."

Daniel cast his gaze over Warren. "And yet you are as unfashionable as ever."

"I beg to differ, however that is beside the point. I didn't read everything." He rolled his gaze toward the ceiling. "Just those articles written by Lady Cordelia. While they're obviously directed toward a female readership, her observances and descriptions are quite acute. I have to admit, I found her writing most amusing." Warren chuckled. "She has a dry wit and a lively style. Indeed, her account of an Italian countess' first ride on a camel made me laugh aloud."

"Wonderful," Daniel muttered. The Amazon in his head smiled smugly.

"Although I have never known a writer, I would imagine you could learn a great deal about a person from their work." Warren sipped his whisky. "From what I've read, I like her."

"Excellent. Then you can marry her." Daniel aimed his glass at his friend. "As I've been pretending to be you, you can be me."

"For the rest of my life?" Warren shook his head. "Thank you, but no. I have plans for the rest of my life, especially when it comes to whom I might or might not marry at some time in the far distant future. And I should point out that when that time comes, I would much prefer to call her Mrs. Lewis rather than Mrs. Sinclair, although again, I do appreciate the offer."

Daniel shrugged. "It seemed like a good idea to me."

"I can see where it would," Warren said under his breath.

For a long moment neither man said a word. Daniel stared into his glass as if the solutions to all his problems could be found there. Although past experience had taught him there was a price to be paid for the respite from his troubles to be found in the bottom of a glass. Still, at the moment drowning his sorrows seemed like an excellent idea. He emptied the rest of his glass and held it out for Warren to refill.

How could he have been so stupid? No matter how much he denied it to Warren, he had feelings for Sarah he had no business feeling. Unintentional of course, but there it was.

Shouldn't he have expected something like this? Wasn't this just one of those things life liked to throw at you unawares? Why was it that at the very moment you thought everything was going along quite nicely in your life, all of your business matters were in order, you were inches away from escaping marriage to an Amazon, and a lovely green-eyed girl looked at you with a look that seemed quite remarkable, something had to happen to muck it up. Certainly in this case an argument could be made that that particular *something* was him. Even so, he didn't deserve this. Still, there were Eastern religions that believed in reincarnation of the soul and that the circumstances of your new life were the result of the sins of the past. "I must have done something very, very bad in a previous life."

Warren snorted. "I'm not sure it's fair to blame a previous life."

"Probably not." Daniel heaved a resigned sigh and for the first time seriously considered the prospect of marriage to a stout-hearted Amazon. While the vision in his head wasn't at all the type of woman he thought he'd marry, she probably wasn't nearly as bad as the female his imagination had produced. A female who relished travel and its accompanying discomforts with the enthusiasm Lady Cordelia apparently did was probably a decent enough sort. Still, did she have flashing green eyes and a smile that warmed even the coldest hearts?

"You have to tell her the truth now, you know," Warren said casually. "Miss Palmer that is. You can no longer avoid it."

"No, I suppose not."

"You wouldn't want her to come face–to-face with Lady Cordelia's new fiancé—"

"No, no, of course not." Just the thought of the look of disbelief and betrayal and hurt in Sarah's green eyes stabbed his heart. And there was no doubt in his mind she would indeed feel betrayed and hurt. Wouldn't he if the situation were reversed?

"When?"

"As soon as the bottle is empty," Daniel muttered. It was going to take a fair amount of courage to face Sarah. He wasn't even ready to think about his inevitable first meeting with Lady Cordelia. He drew a deep breath and grabbed the bottle. "Tomorrow. I'll talk to Sarah tomorrow."

"You certainly won't be in any condition to speak with her tonight," Warren said wryly.

"Or think about her." Daniel peered at the other man. "And that, Warren, old friend, is precisely the idea."

Travel is fraught with surprise and revelation. Much of it quite wonderful although on occasion it can be somewhat bothersome and even unpleasant.

An English Lady's Traveling Companion

Chapter 10

Dear Lady Cordelia,

Upon further reflection, I fear my previous missive might have seemed somewhat pompous, even arrogant. I assure you that was not my intent. However, I am extremely proud of my country and its people. It was a mere seventy-three years ago that we threw off the bonds of tyranny imposed upon us by a government that had grown unresponsive and intolerable. And

*in this century, we were again forced to protect our
people and our homes against the excesses of that same
foreign power. Not once but twice we have faced what
you describe one of the greatest countries on earth and
have emerged strong and victorious. Perhaps my view
is not arrogant as much as realistic . . .*

*D*aniel stood in the foyer of Lord Marsham's grand
London house and resisted the urge to pace impatiently. Still, every moment he was kept waiting was
another moment put toward trying to find the right
words. The butler who had commanded him to wait
while Sarah was fetched now eyed him with obvious
suspicion. It was apparent that the servant saw himself as guardian of the household and its occupants,
the unflappable, undefeatable protector of his charges.
The man probably had a bias against Americans as
well or perhaps he just didn't like Daniel. Given the
ache in his head and the strange, heavy weight in the
vicinity of his heart, Daniel wasn't especially fond of
himself at the moment.

Without warning the front door flew open and a tall,
fair-haired man strode into the house.

"My lord." The butler gasped. "We were not expecting you. We had no idea. We—"

The man laughed. "I do so enjoy it when I can surprise you, Hodges."

"You always have, my lord." The butler—Hodges—
stared for another moment, then regained his composure. "The family is in Brighton, sir."

"As is to be expected at this time of year." The man
chuckled. "I thought I would stop at the house first
then proceed on to Brighton."

"Lord Marsham was here yesterday. He returned to Brighton this morning, but Lady Cordelia and Miss Palmer are still in residence. Your aunt is expected to join them today. Lady Cordelia is at her dressmaker's and is not expected back for several hours." Hodges paused in a significant manner. "However, *Miss Palmer* is here."

"A stroke of luck then." The man grinned. "Send for Miss Palmer if you would, Hodges."

Send for Miss Palmer?

"I already have, sir." Hodges slanted a pointed look at Daniel and the newcomer noticed him for the first time.

"Good day." Daniel stepped forward.

"Good day," the man said in a pleasant if cool manner. "Forgive me for being abrupt but have we met?"

"I doubt it." He extended his hand. "Daniel Sinclair."

"Viscount Creswell." The viscount shook Daniel's hand. "Daniel Sinclair did you say?"

Daniel nodded.

Creswell's brow furrowed, then his expression cleared. "The American?"

"I am *an* American," Daniel said slowly.

"I have heard of you."

Daniel's brows drew together. "You have?"

"Indeed I have. Lord Norcroft is an old friend of mine and we correspond regularly. I've been out of the country for more than a year." His lordship chuckled. "Damn interesting wager you and Norcroft and the others have."

"The tontine?" Daniel smiled reluctantly. "I think the thing is cursed. Only Norcroft and I are left."

"I knew about Warton but Cavendish comes as something of a shock." Creswell shook his head. "I would have placed my money on him." He studied Daniel with an admiring eye. "I understand Norcroft and the others have invested in a venture of yours involving railroads in America. He seems to think it will be quite profitable."

"It will." Daniel raised a brow. "Are you interested?"

"I would be, but my personal funds are limited and the family coffers are a bit strained at the moment." Creswell blew a long breath. "It's a bloody shame really. I would like nothing better than to—"

"Will?" A shocked female voice sounded from the stairway.

Both men looked up. A vaguely familiar blond woman hobbled down the stairs.

"Sarah!"

Sarah?

The newcomer stepped forward eagerly and the woman stumbled into his arms. Hodges discretely averted his eyes, but there was a definite hint of a smile on his lips. Daniel and a footman stared openly.

At last Daniel cleared his throat and the couple reluctantly broke apart.

"Dear Lord." This Miss Palmer stared at him, her eyes wide with surprise. "What are *you* doing here?"

"I'm here to call on Miss Palmer," Daniel said slowly. "Miss Sarah Palmer."

"This is Miss Sarah Palmer," Creswell said. "Sarah, do you know this man?"

"No," Daniel said quickly.

"Not exactly," this Miss Palmer said far more slowly.

Creswell stared at the woman. "What do you mean not exactly?"

She shrugged in a helpless manner. "It's hard to explain."

"You were the woman at the booksellers," Daniel said.

They ignored him.

Disbelief shadowed his lordship's face. "Sarah, I know I've been gone for a long time, but I thought we had a certain understanding . . ."

She stared at him. "Are you jealous?"

"Yes, I suppose I am." The viscount huffed.

Daniel leaned toward Creswell and lowered his voice confidentially. "I really don't know her."

Again he was ignored.

Miss Palmer's eyes narrowed. "Don't you trust me?"

"Yes, of course I trust you. This is just very confusing." Creswell paused. "But it doesn't matter. Whatever this man may mean to you—"

"Nothing," Daniel said vehemently. "I mean nothing to her. Not a thing. We've never even met." It was as if he was talking to himself.

"—I don't care. I love you, Sarah. I want to marry you as soon as it can be arranged and I don't care about this man or any other."

"Any other?" Miss Palmer raised a brow. "You forgive me then? For this man and any others?"

"Careful, Creswell," Daniel said under his breath. At last the viscount seemed to notice him. "You can't win with this question."

Creswell was silent for a moment then drew a deep breath. "I don't see anything to forgive you for. There is some confusion here, but I am as confident of your affection for me as I am of mine for you. Therefore I am confident as well that there is a rational explanation. You, Sarah, are the love of my life. I have long trusted you with my heart and nothing will ever change that."

"Excellent answer," Daniel murmured.

Miss Palmer studied Creswell then smiled. "A very good answer indeed." She sighed. "I admit this might be somewhat confusing."

"Somewhat?" Daniel scoffed. "Tell me, is there another Miss Sarah Palmer?"

"Not at the moment," she said slowly.

"Of course there isn't another Miss Sarah Palmer," Creswell said firmly. "This is *the* only Miss Sarah Palmer."

She winced. "Not exactly." She drew a deep breath. "It's rather complicated. Will, this is Mr. Lewis."

Creswell drew his brows together. "No, it isn't."

"Not exactly," Daniel said under his breath.

Creswell's confused gaze shifted between Daniel and Sarah. "What in the name of all that's holy is going on here? *Exactly?*"

"Quite honestly, I'm as confused as you are." Daniel shook his head.

Creswell's gaze narrowed. "Let us start from the beginning then. I know who I am. I am Viscount Creswell and this is my family's home. I know who this is. This is Miss Sarah Palmer. The only Sarah Palmer I know of. And you say you are Daniel Sinclair."

"No, he isn't," Miss Palmer said firmly. "He's Mr. Lewis, Mr. Sinclair's secretary."

"No, I'm not," Daniel said reluctantly. "I am Daniel Sinclair."

Sarah stared. "You're not."

"I'm afraid I am."

Sarah's face paled. "Good Lord."

"And I'm here to see Miss Palmer. Not this Miss Palmer," Daniel added quickly. "The other Miss Palmer."

"There is no other Miss Palmer!" Exasperation rang in Creswell's voice.

"That's not entirely true," the new Miss Palmer said. She looked at the viscount. "I don't think you're going to like this, but I doubt you'll be overly surprised." She cast Daniel a disgusted look. "I daresay, you won't like it either but I suspect you deserve it."

"Out with it, Sarah," Creswell said.

"It all has to do with Cordelia," Miss Palmer began.

Creswell snorted. "Who else?"

"The Amazon," Daniel said in an aside to Creswell.

"The what?" Creswell stared.

"Amazon. Sturdy, stout-hearted, carries a walking stick." Daniel nodded. "That sort of thing."

Creswell's eyes narrowed. "I'll have you know that Amazon is my sister."

"Sorry," Daniel muttered.

"Because you called her an Amazon or because she's my sister? Although." Creswell turned a suspicious gaze on Miss Palmer. "In a moment, I daresay, I will agree with you on the latter. Sarah?"

"It's a long story," she murmured and threw Daniel a pointed glance, "and apparently more complicated than I thought."

Creswell crossed his arms over his chest. "I have time."

Daniel mirrored Creswell's actions. "I'm not going anywhere."

"Very well then." Miss Palmer thought for a moment. "It began when your father and his father came to a business agreement that included the marriage of their children."

Creswell stared. "Me?"

"No, not you." Miss Palmer rolled her gaze toward the ceiling.

"Thank God," Daniel murmured.

"Cordelia, of course. However, while your father was strongly encouraging the match, he said the fate of the family fortune depended on the success of this business transaction, he left the ultimate decision up to her. She decided she needed to know more about Daniel Sinclair before she could decide anything and thought the best way to do that was to speak to someone in his employ. So she approached him—" Miss Palmer gestured in Daniel's direction—"thinking he was Mr. Lewis—"

Creswell held up a hand. "And Mr. Lewis is your secretary?"

Daniel nodded. "Secretary, attorney, longtime friend, one day to be my partner."

"An impression, I might add," Miss Palmer glared at Daniel, "that you did nothing to correct."

"Don't blame this on me. Who initiated all of this? Who approached whom? Who—"

"Why didn't you inform her of her mistake right away?" Creswell asked.

Daniel stared at the viscount. "If a very pretty, determined, green-eyed woman came up to you in the park and thought you were someone else, what would you do?"

"I can see your dilemma," Creswell murmured, then

slanted a quick glance at Miss Palmer. His shoulders squared. "Although I certainly would have told her of her mistake at once."

"No doubt," Daniel muttered, although he would have wagered a great deal of money as to whether or not that would have been the case. At once the import of Miss Palmer's words—apparently the real Miss Palmer— struck him and he stared. "You mean the woman I've been seeing this entire time is really Lady Cordelia?"

"You mean the woman you've been seeing who thinks you're Mr. Lewis?" Miss Palmer's voice was deceptively pleasant. "That would be Lady Cordelia, yes."

"What do you mean, *seeing*?" Creswell frowned.

"Only twice," Miss Palmer said quickly. "Nothing especially improper. In the park and at the booksellers.

"And in Brighton," Daniel said under his breath.

Miss Palmer stared in surprise. "You were in Brighton?"

"For the sea air." Daniel glanced at Creswell. "It's quite bracing you know."

"Always has been." The viscount studied him. "You followed my sister to Brighton?"

"Absolutely not." Indignation sounded in Daniel's voice. "I followed *Miss Palmer* to Brighton. That she turned out to be your sister has nothing to do with me." He looked at Miss Palmer. "Are you sure about all this?"

"That I am the only Miss Palmer?" she said sharply. "Reasonably sure, yes."

"And the woman I've been seeing—"

"I still want to know what you mean by seeing," Creswell muttered.

"The charming, witty, *honest* woman—"

"I wouldn't bring up *honesty* if I were you, Mr. Sinclair," Miss Palmer said pointedly.

"Perhaps not." It was entirely possible his faculties were still muddled from last night's liquor. He couldn't seem to quite grasp what this Miss Palmer was saying. "So you're telling me that my Miss Palmer is then actually Lady Cordelia?"

"You're not very quick are you?" Miss Palmer snapped.

Daniel clenched his jaw. "I'm very quick in a rational, logical world where people are who they're supposed to be. Where lovely, honest women don't abruptly became traveling Amazons."

Creswell frowned. "Why do you keep calling her that?"

"It's really not important now, I suppose." Daniel waved off the question with an impatient gesture. "Something she said in the way she spoke about Lady Cordelia, or rather herself, brought the idea of a sturdy, stout-hearted Amazonian traveler to mind. It's an image that's now stuck in my head."

A snort sounded off to one side. Daniel glanced at Hodges whose expression remained impassive, but a definite twinkle of amusement shone in his eye.

"Are your intentions honorable?" Creswell asked in a deceptively cool manner.

"Of course my intentions are honorable," Daniel said without thinking. "I'm here, aren't I?"

"Why *are* you here?" Miss Palmer frowned.

"Why?" Daniel stared. "Complete, total, and utter honesty, that's why. I thought it was time."

Miss Palmer huffed. "Rather too late for that I would think."

"Not at all," Daniel said staunchly. "I came today to confess everything. To tell her who I really am and ask her to forgive me for deceiving her. And now that I learn that she has been deceiving me as well . . ." There was far more to Miss Palmer—or rather Lady Cordelia—than he had suspected. That she had the nerve or courage or daring to carry on the same kind of charade he had was far more intriguing than he had imagined. He rather liked her obvious spirit of adventure. This was a woman who would be a challenge to a man. Not easy but always exciting. "I should be indignant, even outraged, furious perhaps." He grinned in spite of himself. "I might well be mad but this strikes me as being, well, funny."

"It does have all the elements of a French farce." Creswell chuckled.

"It's not the least bit amusing." Miss Palmer glared. "She hates him!"

"Oh, I don't think she hates me."

"Not you as Mr. Lewis but you as Daniel Sinclair." She shook her head. "Cordelia has found your letters most annoying."

Daniel winced. "That was the original plan."

"What plan?" Creswell said.

"If you know about the tontine, then no doubt you've surmised that I've not been especially interested in marriage. Especially a marriage I had no say in. I couldn't just tell your sister I didn't want to marry her."

Miss Palmer scoffed. "Oh no, honesty would be rude."

"It would certainly be rude," Daniel said in a lofty manner.

"Rude would be an improvement. She thinks you're an arrogant, pompous ass." She cast an apologetic glance at the viscount. "Her words. I can't imagine what she'll think when she finds out you've been lying to her."

"As she's been lying to me."

"Then you're remarkably well suited to one another, aren't you?" Miss Palmer glared. "An arrogant, pompous ass and a—"

"Stout-hearted Amazon?" Creswell suggested in an innocent manner.

An odd choking sound came from Hodges.

"I thought if she didn't like me, she would decline this marriage." He met Miss Palmer's accusing gaze. "It seemed kinder, to allow her to refuse me rather than me refuse her."

"Hah." Miss Palmer snorted.

"I see," the viscount said thoughtfully. "This is something of a mess, isn't it? Mr. Sinclair, if we are to continue this conversation with any hope of resolving this quagmire, liquid refreshment is obviously in order. Will you join me?"

"If liquid refreshment means what I think it does, I should be delighted."

"Hodges." Miss Palmer turned toward the butler. "Would you have tea served? In the parlor, I think."

"In the library, Hodges, and just tea for one." Creswell smiled at Miss Palmer. "This discussion calls for the library, my dear, as well as something significantly stronger than tea."

"Yes, of course," Miss Palmer said in a pleasant manner, but Daniel suspected she wasn't especially pleased. She led the two men into the library.

Creswell chuckled and said under his breath to Daniel, "She's going to make an excellent countess."

"It's a little frightening," Daniel murmured.

"My mother has trained her well."

They took their seats near the fireplace at one end of the library. It was an impressive room, large and book lined with a desk and chairs in front of floor-to-ceiling windows, as well as a sofa and chairs before a fireplace and a long library table at the other end of the room. Daniel could almost see Sarah—or rather—Cordelia sitting at the table and writing her travel book. A maid brought tea for Miss Palmer and Hodges poured glasses of whisky for the men, leaving the decanter on the table at his lordship's request. Creswell waited until the butler had quietly, if reluctantly, left the room.

Creswell studied Daniel. "So, what is your plan now?"

"I have no plan." Daniel thought for a moment. "I came with the intention of telling her the truth—"

"Still an excellent idea," Miss Palmer murmured.

"Now, however . . ." Daniel shook his head.

Creswell sipped his drink thoughtfully. "I'm not sure honesty is the best course at this point."

Miss Palmer gasped. "William! Honesty is always—"

"Not always, my dear, as Mr. Sinclair has already pointed out. If he had been honest initially, and had told Cordelia he had no desire to marry her, she would have been dreadfully hurt." He met Daniel's gaze. "How do you feel about my sister?"

"As honesty does seem to be called for at this particular moment, I have to admit I don't know." Daniel thought for a moment. "I liked the woman I was getting to know. Enough to want to make a clean breast of it." He shrugged. "Enough to ask to call on her."

"She didn't tell me that either. I didn't know about Brighton, I don't know about this." Miss Palmer huffed. "She used to tell me everything. She's getting even with me, you know. Just because I wouldn't tell her I was writing to you. She thinks I have a secret suitor."

"You do have a secret suitor." Creswell cast her a private sort of smile. "Although Father knows about our feelings and I would wager Mother suspects." He sipped his whisky and studied Daniel. "You need a plan, Sinclair."

"I've had several," Daniel said wryly.

"A *good* plan."

"Yes, well, that's where I've apparently fallen short. I am open to any suggestions. You should know, I have realized that I have no choice but to go through with this marriage to your sister. Now, however." Sarah, *his* *Sarah*, was the Amazon. It was still hard to believe. Daniel chuckled. "It is not quite the sacrifice it once was."

"Cordelia needs to be taught a lesson," the viscount said firmly.

Daniel shrugged. "I wasn't entirely honest myself."

"You were turned by a pretty face. That's understandable."

"You are a man after all," Miss Palmer said under her breath.

"Until a few minutes ago," Daniel chose his words carefully. "My intentions, aside from telling her—as

Miss Palmer, that is—everything, were to introduce myself to Lady Cordelia as soon as possible."

"And what are your intentions now?" Creswell said slowly.

"Now?" Daniel shook his head. "I'm not sure what to do now."

"You said you liked her," Creswell said.

"I did, or rather I do." Daniel paused. "Quite a lot actually."

"And your feelings are not unchanged by learning of her deception?"

"I suppose they should be, shouldn't they?" Daniel thought for a moment. The fact that the woman he had finally realized he cared for, the woman he wanted, was the very woman he needed to marry was an unquestioned relief. And he couldn't help but see the humor in it all. "It seems I find it just makes her more . . . interesting."

"You are mad," Miss Palmer said sharply and sipped her tea. "The two of you probably deserve one another."

"Let me tell you a few things about my sister," Creswell began. "She's the youngest of five children. We have three older sisters, all of which were so much older than Cordelia that her only real companion when she was a child was me. Until Sarah came to live with us, of course. She's therefore somewhat spoiled."

"Somewhat," Miss Palmer muttered.

"Although, she's never been prone to tantrums. That's not what I mean by spoiled. But she has always managed to get her own way, especially with Father. She's quite subtle and more than a little devious and before you know it, she's off riding camels in the desert with his permission. And taking Sarah with her."

"I rather liked Egypt," Sarah said under her breath. "Although I could do without camels."

"Cordelia is far too independent for a female as well. In spirit as well as behavior. It would be admirable if she were a man." Creswell shrugged. "When she discovered traveling, it was as if she'd found her calling in life. That too fostered the independence of her nature."

Miss Palmer leaned toward Daniel. "There's a certain freedom inherent in traveling, Mr. Sinclair. Especially for a woman. Even I have felt the invigorating effects of independence and self-reliance when we've been navigating ancient Greek ruins that I have never known on the streets of London. It's quite intoxicating."

"But you have never been especially intoxicated by it." Creswell met the lady's gaze, a slight anxious note in his voice. The viscount probably had no desire to have the woman he planned to marry follow in his sister's footsteps.

"No, Will," Miss Palmer said smoothly. "I am intoxicated only by you."

"Good answer," Daniel said under his breath.

Miss Palmer cast him a smug smile.

Creswell grinned then turned his attention back to Daniel. "While Cordelia has never behaved in a seriously improper manner—" He glanced at Miss Palmer for confirmation and she nodded. "Indeed aside from the articles she writes or that book of hers, her behavior has never been cause for scandal."

"Although it's only a matter of time," Miss Palmer murmured.

"She's never, to my knowledge, been involved in a situation where the repercussions could indeed be scandalous. Probably because her various escapades have never involved questionable behavior with men." The viscount's gaze met Daniel's. "Until now."

Daniel ignored the charge and sipped his whisky. "And the lesson you propose we teach her?"

"I propose." Creswell grinned. "That we do nothing at all."

Miss Palmer started. "We can't do nothing. Cordelia needs to know the truth. And she needs to be," she searched for the right word, "chastised for her behavior."

"No she doesn't, at least not yet." The viscount shook his head. "I suggest we allow her to carry on her charade."

"And I should continue to see her as I have?" Daniel said slowly.

"Absolutely. At some point she has to accept the consequences of her actions. As you've said, she started this whole thing. It should be up to her to finish it. She should be the one to tell you the truth." Creswell chuckled. "It will be difficult for her and will serve her right."

"Oh that's good, Creswell. That's very good." Daniel raised his glass to the other man. "I should have thought of it myself."

Miss Palmer's eyes widened. "I can't believe you are trusting this man, possibly with your sister's heart."

"I have always been an excellent judge of character, my dear, and I suspect her heart is in capable hands. One way or another, he's probably going to be my brother-in-law and I should welcome him with a certain amount of trust." Creswell cast him a confident smile. "Besides, Norcroft speaks highly of him and I value his opinion. Sinclair strikes me as an honorable man—"

"He's been lying to her!"

"*She's* been lying to *him*. Cordelia is nearly twenty-six years of age and is responsible for her own actions or should be anyway."

"What about his actions?"

"He came here today to confess all. He's taken the first step toward honesty. To my way of thinking that act alone absolves him." Creswell turned to Daniel. "I would suggest, if you are amenable, that you pursue her with eagerness and enthusiasm. As Miss Palmer that is. Allow her to think this man she's deceived has serious intentions about her."

"I did ask to call on her," Daniel murmured.

Miss Palmer huffed.

The viscount pinned her with a firm glance. "This will require a certain amount of secrecy on your part as well."

"Now you want *me* to lie?" Miss Palmer crossed her arms over her chest. "I don't think so."

"Only by omission," Creswell said quickly. "I'm not asking you to do anything overt at all. Simply keep what you know to yourself."

Miss Palmer's brow furrowed. "Even so . . ."

"It's not as if she has taken you into her confidence," Creswell said pointedly.

Miss Palmer sighed. "No, I suppose she hasn't."

"So you'll do it?"

"I'll agree not to do anything up to a point." Miss Palmer snatched his lordship's glass, downed his whisky, smacked the glass back down on the table and glared at the viscount. "But if she asks me a direct question, I will not lie to her."

Creswell stared and Daniel suspected the man was now wondering just how much of an influence his independent, spoiled sister had been on the love of his life. "Fair enough."

"I am not as convinced of the cleverness of this plan as the two of you are." She met Daniel's gaze firmly. "I suggest you give this further consideration before you agree."

"I—"

"Come now, Sinclair, what other choice do you have?" The viscount refilled his glass. "If you tell her the truth now, she'll despise you for lying to her regardless of her own actions. If you somehow maneuver her into a confession of her own and then tell her the truth, she'll detest you for making her feel like a fool. Any move you make spells your doom."

Daniel raised a brow. "And not doing anything is a good idea?"

"It might not be good but it's definitely better." The viscount met Daniel's gaze firmly. "Think of this as a game."

"Of chess perhaps?" Daniel said wryly.

"Yes, that will do." The viscount chuckled. "She doesn't know it yet, but she's in check with very few salvaging moves. And make no mistake, Sinclair, it is her move."

"Yes, I suppose it is." While initially, Daniel had liked the proposal, now he wasn't at all sure what he thought of the viscount's plan to allow his sister to find her way out of this hole she had dug herself into. It was most annoying as he was never this indecisive. But then he'd never been in a situation even remotely like this before and the stakes had never been greater. He certainly didn't have a better idea at the moment. And Creswell was right. Anything Daniel did now would surely destroy any chance of a future with her.

"Well?" Creswell said.

"It does seem to me, if indeed I were to confess all to her now, it would give her the upper hand." Daniel chose his words with care. "I'm not sure that's a good way to start a future together."

Daniel wasn't entirely sure when he had decided he wanted a future with her if he had decided at all. Perhaps the mere act of asking to call on Sarah—Cordelia—was significant even if he hadn't realized it at the time. Or possibly, the decision had been made before that when Daniel had followed her to Brighton. Or maybe even when he had met her in the bookstore. More likely his fate had been sealed the very first time he'd gazed into her green eyes and had seen, but not recognized, his future. Every single action he'd taken since the moment he'd met her had been a mistake if his intention was to indeed avoid marriage to Sarah or Cordelia or anyone else. A more romantic man might have said his heart was leading his head all along and his head was just too stupid to realize it.

The ultimate question to be answered now was what he wanted. Not what he had to do out of necessity but what he truly wanted. It was something of a shock to realize what he wanted was this woman, whether he called her Sarah or Cordelia, in his life forever. And forever meant only one thing. Still, the game had become far more complicated than he had expected. And the outcome was not the least bit assured.

There was a certain irony to the fact that the woman he had actively avoided was the same one he had actively pursued. Warren would say it was no more than Daniel deserved, once he stopped laughing of course. Now Daniel needed to win the heart of that same woman because like it or not, she had already won his.

"It seems to me it's not enough simply to continue the deception. Somehow, I need to engage her affections as well." Daniel drew a deep breath. "Miss Palmer, perhaps you could give me a bit of advice."

"Advice?" She studied him for a long moment then heaved a reluctant sigh. "What do you want to know?"

"I suspect you know Lady Cordelia better than anyone." Daniel leaned toward her and met her gaze directly. "How would you suggest an arrogant, pompous ass go about the task of winning the affections of a stout-hearted Amazon?"

When visiting a land whose ruins or monuments of antiquity are as great an attraction to visitors as anything of a more modern nature, it is beneficial to know as much about a country's history as possible.

An English Lady's Traveling Companion

Chapter 11

Mr. Sinclair,

Under other circumstances, I might consider opinions such as yours to be the expression of an ill-mannered, uncivilized twit, but I can well understand how a man of your limited historical perspective might confuse arrogance with accuracy. As for pride, Mr. Sinclair, it should not be misplaced. Certainly a handful of victo-

*ries when one has so little to choose from might instill
pride. However, when one has centuries of successes
to avail oneself of, it would be most immodest to single
out more than a few. Does one point to the Battle of
Poitiers in 1356? Or the defeat of the Spanish Armada
in 1588? Or perhaps, in more recent memory, the
trouncing of Napoleon at Waterloo?*

*I would think that rebellion, insolence and a com-
plete lack of gratitude as well as respect would provoke
feelings of embarrassment rather than pride . . .*

"*I* can't believe I didn't know about this. It was
right under my nose the entire time and I never
so much as suspected." Cordelia paced the width of the
parlor. "Did everyone know about this except me?"

Aunt Lavinia sat on the sofa sipping a cup of tea lib-
erally laced with brandy. "Not everyone, dear."

"Did Father know?"

"Yes, of course, and he quite approves."

"What about Mother?"

"She had her suspicions," Lavinia said thoughtfully.
"She wasn't certain but she was optimistic."

Cordelia crossed her arms over her chest and glared
at her aunt. "Did you know?"

"One only had to look at Sarah and Will to know. Or,
at least, to suspect."

"I didn't." Indeed it came as something of a shock
when Cordelia returned home from the dressmaker's
today to discover that not only had Will returned from
India but he and Sarah were planning to marry. Will
was Sarah's mysterious suitor. They had apparently
had some feelings for each other long before he left

England, but a year of correspondence solidified those emotions into love. "Why didn't I see it?"

"One doesn't always see what one doesn't expect to see." Aunt Lavinia sipped her tea. "It's what magicians depend on, you know."

"But she is my dearest friend." Cordelia sank down on the sofa beside her aunt. "I should have noticed something."

"Well," Aunt Lavinia said casually, "it didn't really have anything to do with you, now did it?"

Cordelia frowned. "What do you mean?"

"Cordelia, you're an exceptional young woman. Talented and intelligent and pretty as well. However, how to put this delicately." Lavinia chose her words with care. "While I have never known you to be deliberately unkind, you do have a tendency to be unaware of anyone's circumstances save your own."

Shock coursed through Cordelia. "Are you saying I'm selfish?"

"No darling. You've always been quite generous and you have a kind heart. You're just very . . ." Aunt Lavinia winced. "Self . . . centered. Yes, that's it. You've always trod your own path, Cordelia, and I don't believe you've ever considered that others might not wish to tread it as well."

"I had no idea," Cordelia said under her breath and considered her aunt's comment. Rather a difficult thing to accept about oneself, but Aunt Lavinia was right. While Cordelia cared deeply for Sarah she certainly had never put Sarah's interests above her own. Even now, while she should be happy for her friend and her brother, and indeed she was, she was upset that Sarah hadn't confided in her. "I shall try to do better in the future." She met her aunt's gaze. "But at the moment, while I realize it is," she grimaced, *"self-centered* of me, I can't help but be hurt that Sarah did not tell me her secret."

"My dear, all of us have secrets of some sort or other." Aunt Lavinia patted her hand. "Why, even the most proper of ladies have secrets. I daresay, I can't name a single lady who doesn't. Indeed, I suspect some of those secrets are such that the ladies in question would no longer be considered at all proper if they were known."

"Who?"

Aunt Lavinia laughed. "I would never tell you someone else's secrets, my dear. They're not meant to be told. That's why they call them secrets. Besides, I do love a good secret and if I were to reveal any of the secrets I'm privy to, even to you, no one would ever tell me a secret again."

"Of course not," Cordelia murmured. "Do you have secrets?"

"Oh my, yes. I have any number of secrets. Some of them insignificant, of no real consequence whatsoever, some more than a little embarrassing and a fair number," she smiled in a serene manner, "rather naughty."

Cordelia's eyes widened although she wasn't really surprised.

"I suspect even you have secrets."

"No, no, I have no secrets," Cordelia said quickly. She grabbed the brandy decanter and poured a healthy dollop into her own cup of tea. "None at all. Not a one. Nothing. No secrets."

"Really?" Aunt Lavinia's gaze slipped to Cordelia

teacup. "I'm very trustworthy when it comes to keeping secrets."

"I shall keep that in mind should I ever have secrets that need keeping," Cordelia said brightly and sipped her tea.

Oh, certainly there was that somewhat massive secret about Warren. Why, at this very moment, he was no doubt receiving her note reminding him she would be at the British Museum tomorrow morning if he cared to join her. It was terribly forward of her but she didn't want to run the risk of him showing up at the house to call on her. Especially now that she knew she had no choice but to marry his employer. Even though he had agreed not to call on her, there was a look in the man's eye that fairly screamed he might well do exactly as he wanted. He was a pirate after all.

"What is on your mind then?"

Now was perhaps not the best time for Cordelia to bring up her own problems. "Nothing of significance."

"Really? I would think a young woman being encouraged to marry a wealthy American, the son of an even wealthier American as I understand it, would have any number of questions and concerns on her mind."

"You know about that then?"

Aunt Lavinia raised a brow. "It's not a secret is it?"

"Not within the family, although I would prefer the rest of the world not know about it." Cordelia wrinkled her nose. "It's rather embarrassing."

"Why would it be embarrassing?"

"To have one's father select one's husband . . ." Cordelia shuddered.

"My dear Cordelia, any number of us have had no choice in the selection of our first husbands. Why, there was a day when it was unheard of to choose your own husband. Marriages were for political or financial alliances. Parents arranged those sorts of things and the parties involved had nothing to say about it."

"Thank goodness, times have changed," Cordelia murmured.

"The majority of those marriages turned out quite well." Aunt Lavinia paused. "You're probably unaware of this, it was long before you were born, but my first marriage was more or less arranged."

"Oh?"

"My family and his family had long planned for us to marry even though we had no idea of their intentions until after my first season. As I rather liked Charles from the moment I met him, it was not an objectionable arrangement." She smiled at the memory. "I think we could have happily spent the rest of our lives together. Unfortunately while Charles was quite handsome and most amusing, he was not as intelligent as he appeared. He died in an accident that was no less tragic for the stupidity of it."

Cordelia widened her eyes. "How?"

"Oh, I never discuss it." Aunt Lavinia waved off the question. "Even after all these years, I still find it most annoying. If the man were alive I'd probably have to kill him for being such an idiot."

"I see," Cordelia murmured and wondered if her mother would tell her how Uncle Charles died.

"Although his death did leave me free to pursue my own interests. My second husband, again before you were born, was Italian and quite the most romantic man I had ever met. Understand, I was younger than you are now when I married for the second time. Marcello was tall and dashing and had the darkest eyes I had ever seen. Can you imagine eyes so dark you thought you could drown in them?"

Immediately Warren's dark eyes came to mind and Cordelia nodded.

"I daresay, the man would never have remained faithful had the marriage lasted any length of time at all. But a scant year and a half after we wed, we were caught in a sudden rainstorm during a tryst in the garden of his villa on the outskirts of Rome. He fell ill and died after that." Aunt Lavinia sighed, whether with regret for his loss or at the memory of that tryst, Cordelia wasn't sure.

"And then I married Walter who was a very nice man, an excellent companion, great fun and loved me more than I deserved."

"I remember Uncle Walter."

"We were married for nearly twenty years and I miss him more than any of the others. But I don't regret any of my marriages or any of my husbands." Aunt Lavinia patted her hand. "Especially not Charles, even if that was a marriage I had very little say in."

"Yes, but you said yourself that you liked him."

"From what your father had said I was under the impression you had not met this Daniel Sinclair. How do you know you don't like him?"

"I haven't met him in person but we've been corresponding." Cordelia narrowed her eyes. "Thus far he has not endeared himself to me. In fact, I find him arrogant and annoying."

"Excellent. He sounds like an Englishman." Aunt

Lavinia freshened her cup with tea from the pot. "I was afraid you objected to the fact that he was American."

"Oh no. I very much like Americans." There was an odd wistful note in Cordelia's voice. One American in particular, but unfortunately not the right American. She cleared her throat.

"I see." Aunt Lavinia added brandy to her cup. "Are you certain there isn't anything else you wish to talk about?"

"No." Cordelia paused. "Yes, actually." Regardless of her aunt's avowed ability to keep secrets, Cordelia preferred not to reveal hers. Besides, confiding in Aunt Lavinia would put her aunt in an awkward position. Self-centered indeed. Still, advice would be most welcome. "I'm considering . . . writing a story." Yes that was good. "Nothing to do with travel, a fictional story."

"Like Mr. Dickens?"

"Exactly. It's about a . . . a . . . a princess who meets a knight and for various reasons allows him to think she's someone she's not. Her lady in waiting, I think. It's all quite innocent in the beginning," Cordelia added quickly. "Not much more than a lark.

Aunt Lavinia nodded. "As such things often are."

"But as time goes on and she continues to meet with him, she discovers he's a very nice knight. Honest and kind. So while she knows she should tell him the truth, she can't seem to be able to do so."

"I can see where that would be difficult," Aunt Lavinia murmured.

"There's something of a complication."

"I like stories with complications."

"She's more or less expected to marry . . . the duke. A rather unpleasant fellow. The knight is in his service."

"That is a complication."

"Worse yet, if she doesn't marry the duke, her fam— her country will be ruined. Financially that is. She's an orphan princess, she doesn't have any family." Good Lord, was this making any sense whatsoever? "It all has to do with exchange rates and national indebtedness and that sort of thing. The consequences for her country could be quite dire."

"As well they should be." Aunt Lavinia nodded thoughtfully. "For a good story that is."

"There's more."

"Oh, good, another twist."

"Even if the financial difficulties magically disappear." Cordelia thought for a moment. "The discovery of a long-lost treasure or something of that sort. Yes, I like that. But even then, the knight is not the kind of man she's expected to marry."

"Why ever not? Is he a villain?"

"No, no." Cordelia shook her head. "I'm fairly sure he's the hero of the piece."

"That's right, you did say he was very nice and honest. Handsome too, I would imagine."

"Quite."

"What would be the point of a hero who wasn't kind, honorable, and handsome?" Aunt Lavinia scoffed. "Go on."

"Even disregarding the duke, she's expected to marry a prince. The knight is really only a commoner."

"That is a problem." Aunt Lavinia's brow furrowed. "Does she love him?"

"She doesn't know. She's never been in love."

"Well, you have to decide that of course." Aunt Lavinia paused. "For the story."

"Yes, I suppose I do."

"Then what happens? How does it end?"

Cordelia sighed. "I don't know. I haven't written it yet. But I'm afraid the princess has no real choice." She glanced at her aunt. "I thought perhaps you might have some ideas."

"Well, she can sacrifice her happiness for the well-being of her country. Even a princess can't have everything she wants."

"Princesses do have great responsibilities," Cordelia murmured, a heavy weight lodging in the pit of her stomach. "And my princess is very aware of her duty to her country."

"Still, while noble, it's not a very happy ending, for the princess that is. Perhaps she could find the lost treasure?"

"I'm afraid my princess is not that clever."

"That is a problem." Aunt Lavinia thought for a moment. "What happens when the knight finds out she's not a lady in waiting?"

"I daresay, he won't like it, he's very loyal to the duke. Besides, he won't be pleased to discover she's deceived him."

"One way or the other, he will find out. They always find out." Aunt Lavinia paused. "Perhaps it's wise for the princess to tell him herself."

"Wise, yes, but the princess is afraid of what might happen if she tells him." Cordelia sighed. "She has only begun to realize she might indeed have feelings for him she did not expect. She would hate to lose him, even if she realizes he can never truly be hers."

"Why don't you have him find the treasure and have him discover as well that he's a long-lost prince?" Aunt Lavinia smiled triumphantly. "He would forgive the princess for her deceit because he is the hero after all and heroes are prone to forgiveness. Besides, she only continued her deception because she cared for him. And they would live the rest of their days happily ruling her country."

"Yes, that would do." Cordelia smiled weakly.

"Or, perhaps your princess could discover the duke is not such a bad sort after all."

"I doubt that."

"Well, if as you say, the princess has no choice, she must make the best of it then."

"Yes." Cordelia raised her chin a notch. "I suppose she must."

"It's only a story, my dear. You can do almost anything you want in a story."

"Yes, of course."

"Cordelia." Her aunt studied her for a long moment. "You don't have to marry this Mr. Sinclair. Your father has faced financial difficulties before and with or without this business arrangement will no doubt face them again. You've not asked for my advice, but if you don't think you can be reasonably happy in this marriage, I would advise that you tell your father."

"No, Aunt Lavinia, I've spoken to Father. He needs this marriage and he feels I need it as well. He's probably right, I do want to marry and this might well be my last chance for an acceptable match." Cordelia adopted her brightest smile. "I have until the family returns from Brighton the week after next to make my decision. Who knows what might happen between now and then."

Her aunt smiled wryly. "A long-lost treasure could be found."

And a commoner could become a prince. Cordelia shook her head. "We can certainly hope."

Aunt Lavinia laid her hand over Cordelia's. "It's not easy being a princess, is it my dear?"

Cordelia forced a laugh. "As you said, it's just a story, Aunt Lavinia."

"I never thought otherwise." Aunt Lavinia removed her hand and picked up her cup. "Although it does seem to me, if the princess is going to do what she has to do and sacrifice her own happiness for the good of her country, perhaps she should follow her heart for as long as possible and enjoy the company of the knight." Aunt Lavinia's gaze met Cordelia's. "As long as that did not involve anything of an improper or scandalous or untoward nature. Meetings in the royal park, at coronation balls or other public places, that sort of thing. Even a princess needs a bit of freedom as well as fond memories. But we wouldn't want our princess's reputation to be ruined."

Cordelia nodded slowly. "Of course not."

"Now then, let's talk about your book, shall we? Your father told me a publisher has expressed interest. How is it progressing? And Cordelia, do drink your tea." Aunt Lavinia cast her a pleasant smile. "It will do you a world of good."

"Does it make you feel as if you're back in Egypt?" Warren's voice sounded behind her. But even before he'd said a word, she'd somehow known he was there.

Odd how in the British Museum's huge Egyptian gallery, filled with colossal sculptures and fragments of statuary as well as the vague presence of the kings and priests depicted here in cold granite, she'd sensed his very real presence before he had said a word. What had the man done to her?

"No, I'm afraid not. Although I wish it did." Cordelia heaved a resigned sigh. "I loved Egypt. More so perhaps than anywhere else I've visited. Although," she glanced over her shoulder at Warren. He smiled down at her with his dark eyes and her heart skipped a beat. "Have you ever heard of Petra?"

"I don't think so."

"It's in Arabia and is quite the most amazing place I've ever seen. The city is all tombs and palaces hewn from rose-colored rock walls. It fairly glows at certain times of the day, depending on where the sun is. It's exceptionally difficult to get to but well worth it. One can't help but believe in magic in a place like that."

"Do you believe in magic, Sarah?"

Good Lord, he was calling her Sarah now in a most casual and personal manner. As if it were the most natural thing in the world. And why not? He had kissed her and asked to call on her. She certainly thought of him as Warren. And she did think of him, a great deal.

"Magic, Warren, is nothing more than seeing only what one expects to see or not seeing what one doesn't expect to see. Misdirection as it were." Even as she said the words she wanted to take them back. She sounded so prim and more like a governess than anything else. "Still, there are places in the world where magic does indeed seem not only possible but inevitable."

"I like that." He laughed. "Inevitable magic." He paused. "And what about magic between people?"

"Between people?" She forced a lighthearted note to her voice. "Are you speaking of love?"

"I'm not entirely sure," he said under his breath. He stared at her and she realized he was as unsure about whatever was happening between them as she was.

"Do you like history, Warren?" she said abruptly, breaking the tension that now hung in the air.

"Do I like the study of names of those who are long dead and dates of battles long past? Not especially. I've always found it quite dull. But this," he waved at the Egyptian kings and queens surrounding them. "This is different. This is, I don't know, alive if you will."

"I think that's why I like to travel. In many parts of the world, life is as it has been for centuries. It is as though one is walking through history."

"You like history then?"

"I do. Even before I had so much as stepped a foot out of England, I've always been fascinated by the past." She glanced at him. "We have a rather impressive history in this country you know."

"I am well aware of that." He chuckled. "It's almost impossible not to be. London is an ancient city and in spite of the modern bustle of its streets today, one still has the sense of being surrounded by history. One can't help but appreciate it."

"It's a pity Mr. Sinclair doesn't feel the same," she said dryly. "His letters to Lady Cordelia indicate he has no appreciation whatsoever for history or heritage. And no particular respect for hers."

Warren paused for a long moment. "It's a sham, you know."

Cordelia scoffed. "I doubt that."

"You should understand, about Mr. Sinclair, that he is, well, scared I think."

"Scared? Of what? Surely not of Lady Cordelia?"

"Of the situation." Warren shook his head. "Believe it or not, this is as awkward for him as it is for her."

"She's the one with the most to lose. She's faced with marriage to a man she doesn't know as well as the prospect of leaving the land of her birth for life in a country she's never seen."

"His position is no less difficult. Aside from everything else, he is in this spot not out of his choice but because his father has given his word. Regardless of his own feelings, he would not renege on his father's promise." Warren shrugged. "Beyond that, he feels much the same way she does. Apprehensive, to say the least, about marriage to a woman he doesn't know. About taking her to a country that's remarkably different from her own. And wondering if he can make her happy."

"Does he care about her happiness?"

"Very much so," Warren said staunchly. "He wonders as well if eventually affection might grow between them or if they will spend the rest of their lives resenting one another. It's not a pleasant prospect and it is a cause for concern. He has no desire to be unhappy for the rest of his days or see her unhappy. However, as he is an honorable man, there's nothing he can do about it, the marriage that is." He paused. "The decision is in Lady Cordelia's hands. She does have a choice."

"Even princesses can't have everything they want," she said under her breath.

"I'm sorry. Did you say something?"

"No." She drew a deep breath. "She has no choice, Warren. The terms of the business agreement between her father and the elder Mr. Sinclair added to the fact that her family's finances are at stake means she can't refuse this marriage. How could she? It would be terribly," she wrinkled her nose, "self-centered of her to think only of her own desires."

"What are her desires?"

"She wants what any woman wants. She wishes to marry for love."

"Does she? I thought you told me love was of no consequence in this situation?"

"It's not, but as the inevitable meeting between the two of them grows closer, I believe she is beginning to realize love is of great importance after all."

He paused for a long moment. "If the stipulation for marriage was removed from their father's arrangement—"

"She would dance in the streets with sheer joy and utter relief," Cordelia said without thinking. "Wouldn't Mr. Sinclair be relieved as well?"

"I don't know," he said slowly. "I think he's starting to, well, admire her."

"Admire her?" She raised a brow. "She gets no sense of admiration from his letters."

"Sometimes, he's not as smart as he should be."

"Only sometimes?"

"He's been known to get into difficult situations that he is then hard-pressed to extricate himself from."

"Then they may well suit one another after all," Cordelia muttered.

"And what of you and I?" His gaze meshed with hers, his eyes intense and endless and once again she felt as if she were falling. And, as much as she knew it was foolish, this time she had no desire to save herself. "Do we suit one another?"

"I really haven't given it any thought," she lied.

"It seems to me we have a great deal in common."

"Do we?"

He leaned closer, his voice was low. "I think I'm falling in love with you."

Her breath caught.

"And what's more, I think you're falling in love with me as well."

"I think that assumption is rather . . . arrogant of you, Mr. Lewis."

He grinned. "Or accurate."

"And what if I am?" She raised her chin.

"We should talk about it, don't you think?"

"There's nothing to talk about."

"Although I don't hear you deny it."

She should deny it but somehow the words wouldn't come. "We really don't know anything about each other."

"We know enough," he said in the manner of a man who had already made up his mind.

She ignored him. "I have no idea of your likes or your dislikes or anything of that sort."

"Very well." He thought for a moment. "I like sweets, the occasional good cigar, a fine bottle of cognac. I like history when it surrounds me but not as much when I simply read about it."

She smiled. "I did know that."

"I like to travel but I'm ready to return home. I was born in a small town called St. Dennis and my family home is still there, I now reside in Baltimore and have for many years. I find I miss it. I like the theater and I'm particularly fond of Shakespeare. I can be prevailed upon to go to the opera but I'm unenthusiastic about it, although I might have to reconsider that. I like large families, mine is very small, and large dogs. I think small dogs are a waste of time."

She laughed.

"I like the direction of my life. I like my vision of the future. I like the idea of trains, my trains, linked together to get people and goods quickly and efficiently and easily from one point to another. Even you must agree one of the more unpleasant aspects of visiting new places is the difficulty of travel."

"Yes, although that can be quite adventurous."

"If one is traveling for pleasure. But if one if traveling for purpose, it should be less of an adventure and more of a convenience, don't you think?"

She considered the comment then nodded. "I will concede your point."

"I like . . ." He gazed off into the far end of the gallery and his brow furrowed thoughtfully. "I like the smell of the air right before snow, so crisp and clean you can almost taste it. And storms over the ocean, like the angry hand of God. I like . . ." His gaze met hers. "Green eyes the color of the sea just before that storm." His gaze slid to her mouth. "Lips that look as if they aren't sure whether to pout or invite."

She resisted the urge to bite her lips.

"I like how the absurd hats that would look silly on anyone else don't look the least bit silly on you. I like the way your hair." He reached forward and tucked an errant strand of hair behind her ear. "Seems determined to escape those hats. He chuckled. "One can scarcely blame them."

"It's the latest fashion," she murmured.

"I like the way determination squares your shoulders and resolve lifts your chin and you get this stubborn look in your eye." He leaned closer and lowered his voice. "And I very much like the way you felt in my arms when I kissed you, as if you were meant to be there."

She stared in stunned silence.

He straightened and grinned. "And what do you like, Miss Palmer?"

"I like . . . I like . . ." She swallowed hard. This was absurd. It didn't matter what she did or didn't like. "Travel, of course. And history and, um . . . hats." Dear Lord she could scarcely think straight. All she wanted was to throw herself into his arms this very minute right in front of the handful of tourists in the gallery and Osiris and Horus and whatever other Egyptian gods might be watching. But regardless of what she wanted, what she should do is leave. Turn right now and flee through the hallowed halls of the museum and all the glories of ancient Egypt itself, and not stop running until she was far, far away from the dark eyes of a pirate and the promises they held.

Still, even a princess needed memories.

"I like autumn and champagne and chocolates. I like . . ." She thought for a moment. "Not knowing what's around the next corner in a city I've never been to before or around the next bend in a country I've never before visited. I like waking up in a new place and for just a fraction of a moment not being entirely sure where I am. Then realizing I'm in Athens or Rome or Vienna and it's just the start of a glorious new day of adventure. I like having seen the sun rise over the sea and I like having seen the sun set over the sea.

"I like being in places like this and understanding that I am insignificant in respect to those who came before me, and I like standing at the edge of an endless desert and realizing that I am insignificant in respect to the vastness of God's creations." She smiled slowly. "And I like storms over the ocean."

"And?" he said in a low tone rich with meaning.

"And," she drew a deep breath and disregarded any thought of caution. "And I like the way you look at me as if you had a hunger only I could satisfy. I like the dark richness of your eyes and I like that I have to look up to gaze into them, and when I do I feel as if something inside me is melting. I like the sound of your laugh and how I know you're near even when I've yet to see you.

"And I liked how when you kissed me, the rest of the world vanished." She met his gaze firmly and steeled herself against the effect of the dark heat of his eyes. "And how in your arms I felt as if I were exactly where I was supposed to be."

He smiled slowly. "I would say we know a lot about each other, Miss Palmer."

"Perhaps we do, Mr. Lewis."

"Although there is always more to learn."

"Indeed."

"It might take a great deal of time." He paused. "Years perhaps."

"That is a great deal of time." If he was about to say what she thought he might be about to say, time had run out. She drew a deep breath. "Mr. Lewis."

"Miss Palmer," he said at the same time, then nodded. "I've come to a decision—"

"I really should tell you—"

"I think it's only right—"

"Before we go any further—" She stopped. "If we're both going to talk at the same time we shall never get anything resolved."

"And there is much to be resolved," he murmured. "But perhaps this is not the place or the time."

She glanced around at the stone figures still keeping their secrets after thousands of years of silence. "Perhaps not."

"I know you're reluctant to allow me to call on you. I assume that's because of your position in the household."

"Yes, well, my position does make things a bit awkward," she said under her breath.

"Nonetheless, I will call on you tomorrow." His decided gaze met hers. "Frankly, I'm tired of whatever game we've been playing."

"Really?" She forced a weak smile. "I've thought it was something of an adventure. I'd hate to see it end."

"Yes, I suppose it has been and I too hate to see it end. However, it strikes me that the very best of adventures are often just the beginning." He smiled and offered her his arm. "But enough talk of the present. I suspect you know a great deal more about all of this than I."

Her eyes widened. "All of what?"

"The statues, the sculptures, the remnants of ancient Egypt." He studied her curiously. "What did you think I meant?"

"I thought you meant all of this as it pertains to . . . to the nature of adventure, in which case perhaps I do." She groaned to herself. How could an intelligent woman sound like such an idiot? "Not to ancient Egypt although I probably do know a great deal about it." She paused. "And to modern Egypt itself of course."

"Then, Miss Palmer," he paused in a solemn manner, "would you do me the very great honor of becoming"— she stared up at him, he grinned down at her—"my tour guide?"

For the longest moment their gazes locked, then she smiled slowly. "I should be delighted, Mr. Lewis." She took his arm and indicated the closest sculpture. "Let us then begin here. This colossal head was found in Karnak and is believed to be that of Thothmes the third . . ."

For the next few hours, Cordelia led him through the galleries devoted to Egyptian deities and royalty. They passed sphinxes with human heads or heads of hawks or lions. They wandered through the room devoted to Lycia and saw the Xanthian marbles. They debated the differences between Egyptian sculpture and the more refined style of the Greeks. All in all, Cordelia couldn't remember the last time she'd had such an enjoyable morning. Warren's questions were intelligent, his observations astute, and his sense of the absurd most amusing. It struck her that they were indeed well suited for one another. Not that it mattered.

Today she and Warren had wandered through the

past. Tomorrow she was certain he wanted to talk about the future. Which left only tonight for her to straighten out this mess, to confess all, to tell him there was no future. And someone was going to be hurt. Her heart twisted at the fear that she might possibly break his heart.

And twisted as well at knowing that his heart would not break alone.

When, on occasion, one finds native customs to be distasteful to English sensibilities, remember, gentle traveler, that you are a guest in a foreign land and keep your opinions on such matters to yourself.

An English Lady's Traveling Companion

Chapter 12

My Dear Lady Cordelia,

I have obviously offended you and for that you have my apologies. Indeed, your point is well taken and while I cannot wholeheartedly agree with you, I do accept that your perspective and mine are shaped by our respective histories and surroundings. Out of a misplaced sense of loyalty, I chose to emphasize the clashes between our countries rather than the ties that bind us together. For that I must ask your forgiveness.

Our similarities are far more significant than our differences. Indeed, we have a great deal in common . . .

$\mathcal{C}$ordelia sat in her carriage a few doors down from the house Warren resided in with Mr. Sinclair and gathered her courage. She absolutely could not allow him to call on her. Between Hodges, Aunt Lavinia, Sarah, and now Will, someone would surely tell him the truth before Cordelia had the opportunity. And as bad as this was, that would make it all much worse. No, Cordelia had to tell him and she had to tell him now. It could be put off no longer.

A tall, dark-haired man left the house and she realized this must be Mr. Sinclair. He was indeed handsome enough, she reluctantly admitted to herself. Well, if she had to marry a pompous, arrogant ass, he might as well be attractive. Still, his last letter had been surprisingly conciliatory in tone. She supposed it was possible that Warren was right. The man might well be as apprehensive about this marriage as she was. It would be two weeks until her family returned from Brighton and she had to meet him in person. Hopefully, by then she would be able to accept her inevitable fate.

Tonight she had to do what she'd already waited far too long to do. She had to face as well the fact that she was in love with Warren Lewis. Madly, passionately, and irrevocably in love. And now, she had to say goodbye.

She could indeed reject marriage to Mr. Sinclair and her family's fortune would be damaged but probably not ruined. But her family—her father—had given her everything she had ever wanted. Her father had made it possible for her to travel. In many ways he had given her the world. The least she could do in return was ease the lines of worry from his face, the resignation in his eyes. Such were the obligations of a daughter or an adult or a princess.

Now, she had to tell Warren the truth before he found out from someone else.

Her driver assisted her out of the carriage. She stepped up to the front door and knocked. It was entirely improper to arrive sans chaperone, but what difference did it make now? Propriety was the least of her concerns. She was about to tell the man she loved she wasn't who he thought she was and she was going to marry someone else to boot. His employer as well as his friend. In a few minutes, he would no doubt detest her, her heart would break and it was entirely her own doing.

A butler opened the door and she forced a pleasant smile. "I should like to see Mr. Lewis if you please."

The butler cast an appraising glance over her, obviously judged her to be of quality, and ushered her into the foyer. "I am sorry, Miss. Mr. Lewis is not here."

She frowned. "Are you certain?"

"Quite certain. He left through this very door not more than two minutes ago."

"Two minutes ago, you say?" She stared at the butler. "The gentleman who left was Mr. Lewis? Mr. Warren Lewis?"

"The only Mr. Lewis in residence here."

"You're certain it wasn't Mr. Sinclair? Could you possibly be confused?"

The butler sniffed. "I am never confused, Miss."

"And no one else has left? In the last few minutes, that is?"

"No one has come or gone, Miss."

A horrendous thought occurred to her. Surely she was mistaken. "Is Mr. . . . . Sinclair here?

"Yes, Miss, he's in the office."

"Tell me." She lowered her voice in a confidential manner. "Does he resemble Mr. Lewis?"

"They share a similarity of height and build and coloring. They could indeed be brothers, Miss, yes." He inclined his head toward her and matched his tone to hers. "Although I have it on very good authority that not all Americans look alike."

"That is good to know." She thought for a moment. Surely, this wasn't possible. "But does Mr. Sinclair look like a pirate?"

The butler's brow arched. "A pirate, Miss?"

"Does he have a scar." She touched her forehead above her right eyebrow. "Here?"

"Yes, Miss, he does."

"I see." Shock stole her breath. *The man she knew as Warren Lewis was actually Daniel Sinclair? Daniel Sinclair? The man she was supposed to marry?*

"Miss?"

Her pirate was the pompous, arrogant ass? He'd been deceiving her all this time? Lying to her? He was indeed an ass as well as a pirate.

"Are you ill, Miss?" Cautious concern sounded in the butler's voice. "You look rather pale."

"Do I?" she murmured absently, barely noting his words.

Warren or Daniel or whoever he was had kissed her!

The nerve of the man! He'd kissed her, and worse, she'd kissed him never knowing she was kissing Daniel Sinclair. She'd thought she was kissing Warren Lewis. Nice, honorable, *honest* Warren Lewis.

And who had Daniel Sinclair been kissing? Not the woman he was expected to marry. Oh no, he'd been kissing another woman entirely. He'd been kissing Sarah Palmer. The cad! The beast! Why, Cordelia's indiscretion in kissing a man other than the one she was supposed to marry wasn't nearly as significant in comparison. The fact that she'd been just as deceitful as he was scarcely worth mentioning. She was furious. Incensed. Outraged.

"Are you feeling better now, Miss?"

"What?"

"The color has returned to your face." The butler frowned. "But perhaps you would like to sit down?"

"Thank you, but no, I'm fine," she said firmly and realized it was true. Apparently, anger of this magnitude brought with it an amazing sense of calm. All the better to absorb her discovery and consider the repercussions.

Good God, she'd fallen in love with the right American after all! What a shame that now she'd have to strangle him with her bare hands.

She drew a steadying breath and cast the butler her most pleasant smile. The very one she used on porters and doormen and hotel managers that never failed to provoke excellent service. "And you are?"

"Gilliam, Miss."

"Well, Gilliam, would you be so good as to inform Mr. Sinclair that Miss Palmer is here to see Mr. Lewis."

"Of course, Miss, but Mr. Lewis isn't here."

"I know that and you know that and Mr. Sinclair probably knows it as well, but what he doesn't know is that I know. And I think the fact that I do know should remain our secret."

He stared for a moment. "As you wish, Miss."

"And do try not to look surprised by anything you may hear.

"My dear young woman, even in a household of Americans." Gilliam sniffed. "I never look surprised. If you will excuse me." With that, he crossed the foyer to a closed door, knocked and let himself into the room.

Cordelia wished she could have just a fraction of his composure. She would need it. The implications of all of this were still hard to grasp.

Not only *could* the princess have everything she wanted, the princess *would* have everything she wanted. The commoner had turned out to be a prince after all. But there was a price to be paid for said transformation. She wasn't entirely sure what it was yet but like so many of her smashing ideas in the past, she was confident inspiration would strike just when she needed it most.

Gilliam returned to the foyer. "Might I take your hat and wrap, Miss?"

"Yes, thank you." She untied the ribbons of her hat, handed it to the butler, slipped off the short mantle, hesitated, then removed her gloves.

Gilliam nodded and passed everything to a footman. "One moment, please, Miss." He returned to the door that obviously led into the office, failing to close it completely behind him. She stepped closer.

"Brown, sir," Gilliam said on the other side of the

door apparently in response to a question. "I can certainly tell blond from brown and Miss Palmer's hair is definitely a dark brown."

Warren—or rather Daniel—asked a question Cordelia couldn't quite make out.

"Green, sir," Gilliam added. "Definitely green. Quite unique, sir." He paused. "I'm not sure I've seen the ocean before a storm, sir."

Cordelia moved away from the door. Warren— Daniel—was obviously asking about the hair and eye color of the woman asking for Mr. Lewis. *Why on earth—*

At once the answer struck her. The real Sarah's hair was blond and her eyes were brown. But Warren— Daniel—would have no way of knowing that unless . . .

Unless he'd met the real Sarah Palmer. Which meant he knew who Cordelia really was!

Angry indignation swept through her. This was worse than she'd thought. The question now was how long had he known? And what was she going to do about it?

Gilliam returned to the foyer, ushered her into the office, then closed the door behind her.

Warren—Daniel, she had to start thinking of him as Daniel—started toward her from behind a desk across the room. He had discarded his coat, his shirt was open at the neck, and he looked both relaxed and delicious. Except for the surprised and vaguely apprehensive smile on his face. "Sarah, what an unexpected pleasure."

At once she realized what she had to do. What she wanted to do. And what would serve him right.

"Warren!" She flew across the room and into his arms.

"Sarah," Daniel murmured, just as her lips met his. Surprise turned to pleasure and desire. Immediate and intense and damn near irresistible. Her lips were warm and full, her kiss most enthusiastic. He gathered her closer and for a moment lost himself in the absolute delight of having her in his arms. The heat of her body against his, her lips pressed eagerly to his own. He'd wanted her from very nearly the first moment they'd met. Now—

Now, this was a huge mistake. What was he doing? What was he thinking? No, he wasn't thinking at all, which always got him in trouble. He gently untangled her arms from around his neck and stepped back, catching her hands in his.

"Co—Sarah," he said firmly and reminded himself to call her Sarah even though he'd started thinking of her as Cordelia. He'd had a devil of a time this morning keeping her names straight. "This isn't really proper behavior, is it? Aside from the fact that you shouldn't be here. Alone."

"Oh, Warren, Warren, Warren." She sighed deeply and fluttered her lashes at him. "I think we're far past concerns of propriety, don't you?"

"I don't see why," he said cautiously.

"Goodness, Warren, nearly every time we have met it has been in secret." She did have a point.

"Even so, it has always been in a public place. One could argue that there wasn't anything the least bit improper with our . . . encounters." God, he sounded stuffy. Obviously he'd been in England far too long.

She leaned toward him. "Rather a shame, don't you think. Warren?"

"What do you mean, a shame?"

"Oh, I think you know what I mean, Warren."

He stared down at her. "Why do you keep saying my name like that?"

"I like saying your name. I like the way it rolls off the tongue. Warrrr." She drew a deep breath after the first syllable and exhaled slowly with the second. "Rennn."

He swallowed hard. He'd never imagined a simple name could sound so provocative.

"Indeed, I like your name. No, I adore your name. Warren." She fairly sighed the word. "It's a wonderful name. Strong and masculine and honest. Did you know it means loyal in German? Exactly like the man himself."

"It's just a name like any other name. Like . . . like Daniel. Daniel is a nice name. And Daniel means . . ." He had no idea.

"It means God is my judge. In Hebrew." She smiled in an innocent manner. Too innocent. It was more than a little frightening.

"I would think that ultimately God is everyone's judge," he said slowly.

"Then we should probably all be called Daniel." She cast him a brilliant smile. "Although, I daresay, it might be rather confusing. Daniel Sinclair, Daniel Lewis, Daniel Palmer, Daniel here, Daniel there, Daniel everywhere you look. Why, one could call out Daniel in a crowd and everyone would answer."

He smiled in spite of himself. "That's ridiculous."

"But amusing." She pulled her hands from his, rested them on his chest, and sighed up at him. "Still, I do like loyal so much more than wrath of God."

He frowned. "You said it meant God is my judge."

"And once he's judged no doubt there will be hell to pay." She patted his chest for emphasis then turned away. "Although I suppose one name is just as good as another."

"Shakespeare thought so." When in doubt, fall back on the tried and true. No one was more tried and true than Shakespeare and at the moment, no one more in doubt than Daniel himself. No matter what she called him. "'What's in a name? That which we call a rose by any other name would smell as sweet.'"

"You're resorting to Shakespeare? My goodness, my unexpected appearance must have you more ill at ease than I thought." She grinned. "I find it charming of you. But if you wish to invoke Shakespeare . . ." She shrugged. "He said any number of things usually appropriate to the occasion, whatever that occasion may be. Let me think." She paused and tapped her forefinger against her chin. " 'Love all, trust a few. Do wrong to none.' From *All's Well That Ends Well.* Or 'No legacy is so rich as honesty.' Again from *All's Well that Ends Well.*" She raised a brow. "Well?"

"Well what?"

"Well, it's your turn, for a quote. Don't you have one?"

"Nothing comes to mind," Daniel muttered.

"I thought you liked Shakespeare?" She wandered around the room idly glancing at the framed engravings on the wall. "And you did start this."

"I do like Shakespeare and I didn't realize I was starting something." A defensive note sounded in his voice. "I just can't think of anything appropriately Shakespearean at the moment." How could she possibly expect him to think about Shakespeare when all he could think about was why she was here. What she wanted. How to get rid of her. And what would surely happen if he didn't. He furrowed his brow and tried to think of something intelligent to say. "I have it. 'Alas, poor Yorick, I knew him well.' "

"Not that well, Yorick," she murmured absently, her gaze drifting over Warren's desk. "The quote is actually 'Alas, poor Yorick! I knew him, Horatio.' "

"I knew that." He scoffed. "It just slipped my mind for a minute. It's from *Hamlet*."

"Very good, Warren, indeed it is. As is 'Something is rotten in the state of Denmark.' " She glanced at him and smiled. "How very lucky we are then not to be in Denmark."

"Yes, I suppose."

"Although I do like Denmark. I've only been there once and I didn't think there was anything rotten at all."

"I've never—"

"Is this your desk?" She waved at Warren's desk.

"Yes." He nodded. "Yes, it is."

"Weren't you at the other desk when I came in? Isn't that desk Mr. Sinclair's?"

"I use both desks," he said quickly. "I move from desk to desk depending on what needs to be accomplished."

"I know nothing about business of course, but that doesn't sound very efficient to me." She continued her casual meander around the room.

"Oh, it's extremely efficient. It cuts down on the

loss of important documents because they stay in one place." He nodded firmly and felt every bit as idiotic as he sounded.

"Who ever would have imagined."

"Sarah." He drew a steadying breath. "Why are you here?"

"Why?" She trailed her fingers along the edge of his desk.

"Why?"

"I missed you, Warren."

"We were together only this morning.

She tilted her head and glanced at him from beneath lowered lashes. "And yet, it seems a lifetime ago."

"And yet, it was only this morning," he said, his voice sharper than he had intended.

She shrugged off his comment. "It wasn't enough. It simply," she paused, "whet my appetite."

"It did what?"

"For goodness sakes, you needn't look so shocked." She smiled in a pleasant manner as if she were discussing something far less . . . well, far less. "One would think you've never had a woman tell you she's missed you before."

"It isn't the missing that concerns me. It's the appetite."

"And isn't that interesting?" She shook her head as if she couldn't quite believe it herself. "I never dreamed I'd have an appetite for whatever it is I have an appetite for." She met his gaze. "I'm actually quite pleased about it."

His brows drew together and he stared. "What?"

"Your face will freeze that way, Warren, if you're not careful."

"What exactly do you mean?"

"I mean it's not an attractive look and it would be quite a shame if your very handsome face were to stay—"

"That's not what I meant and you know it."

"For someone who is so astute when it comes to business, you do appear to have a difficult time understanding something really quite simple. It must be the element of surprise. You did not expect me and I've taken you unawares." Her brows drew together thoughtfully. "We shall have to proceed at a slower pace then."

"Proceed to what?"

She ignored him. "But first, I find I am rather parched."

He nodded. "I'll ring for tea."

"Honestly, Warren, tea is not appropriate for an evening like this. I should think brandy would be much better." She glanced around the room. "Nor is an office. Surely you don't spend all your time in here. You must have a parlor? Someplace less of business and more of . . . relaxation. Pleasure if you will. We would be much more comfortable in a parlor, I think."

"I have a suite of rooms on the next floor," he said without thinking.

The woman didn't hesitate for so much as a second. "Excellent. We have a great deal to discuss, and as it is not of a business nature, I would much prefer not to be surrounded by business. Do you mind?"

"I suppose not." Although he probably should mind. He should mind very much. But he wanted to know what she was up to. While he was intrigued and cautious, he wasn't especially worried at the moment. After all, she was a properly bred young lady from a respectable family.

She started toward the door then glanced back at him over her shoulder, her voice lowered in a most seductive manner. "Shall we then?"

"Probably not," he muttered and trailed after her.

A properly bred young lady with an independent streak and a history of getting what she wanted. What she wanted now was the question. He could end this by confronting her with the truth about her deception and his but that might well lead to disaster. He had very nearly confessed all at the museum. But he had agreed with her brother's proposal to leave what happened next up to her. He had agreed as well with the argument that as she had begun their charade, it should be up to her to end it. That it would teach her a well-deserved lesson. Even so, Daniel was fairly confident her brother had not anticipated this. Still, the argument for not telling her the truth was as valid now as it was when he and Creswell and the real Miss Palmer had discussed it yesterday. Daniel really had no choice at the moment but to wait and see what Cordelia was up to.

He instructed Gilliam to bring up a decanter of brandy then escorted Cordelia up the stairs, to what the English called the first floor, and into his parlor. It was large and well furnished with sofa, chairs, and a small desk. It struck him, not for the first time, how very impersonal the room was. There was nothing of himself here. Usually he was too busy to pay attention to such things, but on those few occasions he had noticed, it had reminded him that Warren wasn't the only one who missed home. Still, at the moment, he was grateful for the lack of personal effects.

Cordelia glanced around the room. "Are Mr. Sinclair's rooms on this floor?"

"No, they're upstairs."

"Really? How unique. Usually the rooms of the head of the house are on the lower floors. Servants or employees are higher up in the house."

"Mr. Sinclair likes the view from the upper floors," Daniel said quickly. "As an American in a foreign city, a good view is preferable to acquiescing to the restrictions of social class, although I should point out Daniel Sinclair considers me very much his equal in all things with the possible exception of net wealth."

"How very democratic of him." She smiled.

Gilliam entered the parlor, deposited a tray with decanter and glasses on the desk, then took his leave, pointedly leaving the door open behind him. Daniel made a mental note to give the butler a bonus for that.

"However." Daniel stepped to the desk and filled the glasses. "I should add, the disparity in the sizes of our relative fortunes will narrow in the coming years with the success of our railroads."

"Your relative fortunes?" Cordelia moved to him and accepted a glass. "I thought you had no fortune, Warren." She took a sip and gazed at him over the rim of her glass. "Only prospects."

"Excellent prospects," he said firmly.

"Of course," she murmured. "And what of your future, Warren, aside from your prospects that is."

"My future," he said slowly. "One cannot foretell the future.

"But surely you have expectations?" She wandered away from him in an aimless manner. "In addition to prospects."

"Expectations?"

"Yes, expectations. What do you hope to get out of your life beyond being a railroad king?" She reached the door and nudged it closed with her foot.

"What are you doing?"

"Nothing." She leaned back against the door and sipped her brandy. "Not a thing."

"If you're not concerned about your reputation—"

"I'm not." She smiled slowly. "Are you?"

"Yes, of course. There could be talk."

"About Mr. Sinclair's secretary and Lady Cordelia's companion?" She shrugged. "I daresay, such talk would be of no particular concern to anyone."

"Nonetheless, I think—"

"You're just trying to change the subject." She aimed her glass at him. "It won't work." There was a gleam in her eye he couldn't quite recognize. Of determination perhaps. Or resolve. Or desire. His stomach tightened and he downed his brandy.

She sauntered toward him. "What do you want, Warren? What are your hopes, your wishes?"

I wish for you to stop calling me Warren! He refilled his glass.

"Your dreams?" She stopped in front of him. Her voice was low and sultry. "Your desires?"

"My desires?" His voice cracked with the word.

She reached around him and set her glass on the desk. "What do you want, Warren?"

"You asked that once."

"It bears repeating." She plucked his glass from

his hand, took a sip and then brushed her lips over his. The fire of the liquor and the heat of the woman meshed and melded and swept through him.

He braced his hands against the desk behind him, as much to support himself as to keep from reaching for her. In a moment, it would be quite apparent even to the inexperienced Lady Cordelia exactly what he wanted. "Are you trying to seduce me, Miss Palmer?"

"That wasn't my original plan." Surprise shaded her green eyes as if she hadn't been planning seduction at all. Nonetheless, seduction hovered in the room. "Although, perhaps it was, in the back of my head." She stared at him for a long moment then smiled wickedly. "I think it's a smashingly good idea."

He pulled a deep, shuddering breath. "You haven't thought this through."

"Frankly, Warren, all I ever do is think and I'm quite tired of it. I think about where I'm traveling next. I write—I *assist* Lady Cordelia in thinking about where we've been. Do you want to know what I'm thinking now?"

He stared down at her. "I'm not sure."

"I'm thinking that for the first time in my nearly twenty-six years I am alone in a room with a gentlemen I am not related to." She took a long sip of his brandy. "With his glass of quite tasty and probably highly potent brandy in my hand and little possibility of interruption."

"We should probably do something about that." What he should do was open the door. Or send her on her way. At the very least, he should put more than a few inches between them. But Cordelia's green eyes held a promise he didn't think he could resist and, with every passing moment, didn't want to. He reclaimed his glass, tossed back the rest of the drink, then set the empty glass on the desk behind him.

Regardless of what she had planned, seduction was definitely in the air. So thick he could almost touch it, taste it, feel it.

She slid her arms around his neck and again brushed her lips across his. "What should we do about that?"

"We should open the door. We should take you home." His arms wrapped around her. "We should come to our senses."

"Why?" Her lips sighed against his.

"Why indeed?" he murmured and pressed his lips harder to hers. For a long moment he savored the feel of her mouth against his. The heavy taste of brandy, the faint scent of roses. For a moment it was enough just to take pleasure in taste and scent and feel. Her mouth opened to his and his tongue met hers and sensation coursed through him. His body tightened with desire.

He pulled his lips from hers and trailed kisses along the line of her jaw and nibbled lightly at the lobe of her ear. She gasped and her head fell back and he kissed her neck and her throat. Her hands clutched at his shoulders and he knew she shared the desire that gripped him. He pulled her tighter against him and his mouth again claimed hers. Harder now, insistent and demanding. Her fingers twined through the hair at the nape of his neck and she met his demands with her own.

She pulled her mouth from his and murmured along

his cheek. "I have no intention of opening the door."

Daniel hesitated but a man could only fight for so long. "Nor should you."

Besides, he had every intention of marrying her. Did it matter if their first time together was tonight or tomorrow or next month? He tasted the curve between neck and shoulder and felt her shudder beneath him.

"Nor do I plan on returning home at the moment."

"Entirely your decision," he said, his voice as breathless as hers. Indeed, he'd marry her tomorrow if she'd have him. At once he realized that regardless of what happened when she discovered the truth, she would have to marry him now. Why, she'd be ruined and ruined by him. Ruined by a pirate. He certainly felt like a pirate at the moment. His hands roamed over her back.

"And I have no desire to come to my senses," she murmured.

"I couldn't if I wanted to." In some part of his mind not completely obscured by passion and need and desire a small voice noted she might not be thrilled at having no choice about marrying him. Still, she had no real choice at the moment anyway. Her responsibility to her family dictated a marriage to him. That insistent voice added that she thought the man whose bed she was obviously about to share was someone else. He ignored it.

His mouth returned to hers, to plunder and claim and it was not nearly enough. A frantic edge tinged her response as if her passion finally unleashed could not now be controlled.

At last she pulled her lips away from his and gasped.

"I have entirely too many clothes on, you know. You shall have to help me with these."

"It will be my pleasure." He quickly spun her around and swiftly unhooked the fastenings at the back of her bodice. "I should protest." Usually he was all thumbs at this. "Defend my honor, that sort of thing." But tonight, his fingers were deft and sure and quick. "Resist your seduction of me."

"*My* seduction of *you*?" She laughed, a low, breathless, erotic kind of laugh.

"Absolutely." Her dress opened and he pushed it over her shoulders and slid it down past her hips to pool at her feet. "Do you think you should reconsider this?" He untied her petticoats, unbuttoned her drawers and let them fall to join her dress.

"Seducing you?" she scoffed. "Absolutely not." She fumbled at the hooks on the front of her corset. "Although it does seem as though you are doing more of the seducing than I. You should know I have no experience at seducing."

"You're doing a fine job." He tugged his shirt over his head and tossed it aside.

"No, I'm not." Frustration rang in her voice. "I take a blasted corset on and off every day of my life and now I can't seem to get the nasty thing undone!"

"Allow me." He knelt before her and finished unfastening the remaining hooks until the corset was fully opened and slid to the floor.

Her chemise was of a material so fine he could see the dark circles of her nipples and the shadow between her thighs. He slipped his hands around her waist and pulled her closer, then leaned forward and pressed a kiss in the valley between her breasts. His hands skimmed slowly over her bottom to the back of her thighs and down her legs until he reached the hem of her chemise and her naked flesh. She gasped at his touch.

"You're very good at this. You must have a great deal of experience."

Daniel was smart enough to know there was no good way to answer that particular question at this particular moment so he ignored it and slid his hands upward over her thighs to her nicely rounded bottom. He marveled at the silken softness of her skin, the creamy smoothness of her flesh beneath his fingers. He ran his hands higher up her body, along her sides until his thumbs lightly touched the undersides of her breasts.

Her breath came in little gasps but she held herself still, waiting, expectant. He cupped her breasts under her chemise, reveling in the full, ripe weight of them in his hands. There was something intensely exciting about the sight of his hands cupping her breasts beneath the delicate fabric of her undergarment. He circled her nipples with his thumbs and felt them harden with his touch. He slipped one hand to the small of her back then leaned forward and claimed a nipple with his mouth, fabric and all, and sucked in a slow, deliberate manner until she moaned with pleasure and her fingers on his shoulders dug into his flesh. He shifted his attention to the other breast and teased and toyed until it seemed she might collapse against him.

He straightened and stared down at her. "Have you given any thought to marriage?"

Her eyes were glazed with passion and she reached

out to trail her fingers across his naked chest. "Not in the last few minutes."

He unbuttoned his trousers and slipped them off. "Perhaps you—"

"No. All I've done recently is think about marriage. Tonight, I don't want to think about anything but you and me." Her hand trailed down his abdomen to his stomach and she studied him in a frankly appraising manner. He resisted the urge to cover himself with his hands. "You're naked, you know."

He braced himself against the feel of her touch on his skin. "I did notice that, yes."

With one finger she traced teasing lines and circles and God knew what else on his stomach, just inches above his erection and he resisted the urge to grab her hand. For a woman who had no idea what she was doing, she certainly had a natural talent for it.

"Did you know there are many places in the world where the natives wear very little clothing whatsoever?" Her voice was absent, her touch light, curious and unrelenting.

He gritted his teeth. "I suspect their winters are milder than ours."

Her gaze drifted to his erection. "I suppose that's the reason, yes. Did I mention that you are naked?"

"Yes." The word was a slow hiss.

"It doesn't seem quite fair does it?" Her gaze slid up to his and she smiled a slow, wicked smile. She pulled her chemise off over her head and discarded it. "Is this better?"

"Better?" Better than what? Paradise? She was curved and lush in precisely the areas where he preferred curved and lush. Her ivory skin was shadowed

with peach and he wanted nothing more than to . . .
No, he wanted much, much more.

"Now that I'm naked as well?"

"You still have your stockings on." He scooped her
into his arms and started toward the bedroom. "This
will only complicate things you know."

"Then I shall be happy to take my stockings off."

He shoved the door of his bedroom open with his
foot. "That's not what I meant and you know it."

"Perhaps. Nonetheless, I suspect." She nibbled lightly
on the lobe of his ear and desire shivered through him.
"It will be a glorious complication."

The greatest adventure of travel lies in the discovery of the unexpected and the anticipation of what might be around the next corner.

An English Lady's Traveling Companion

Chapter 13

My Dear Mr. Sinclair,

Your apology is accepted and no more need be said on the subject. Although I do feel it necessary to offer an apology of my own. Not for my opinions but for my intolerance of yours. You take pride in your country's accomplishments, as well you should, and you express your pride with great passion.

There is much to be admired about passion . . .

*T*hey tumbled onto the bed in a tangled mass of limbs and heated desire. Cordelia had never been this close to a man before and certainly never without clothes. It was at once odd and liberating. She'd been kissed by a man before, any number of times. But a man had never kissed her where Daniel had already kissed her and where she suspected he might still kiss her.

Right now, his mouth was trailing kisses over her neck and throat. His hand was lightly caressing her breasts in far too teasing a manner but most delightful nonetheless. Oh, he was very good at this. She really hadn't intended seduction when she'd thrown herself into his arms. She really hadn't intended much of anything beyond making him think how fond she had become of Warren in a probably misguided attempt to teach him a lesson.

He moved to take a nipple in his mouth and his hand trailed over her stomach. She caught her breath. Of course, if she'd had any idea seduction would feel quite this remarkable perhaps she would have intended it from the beginning. She still wasn't sure at what moment flirtation had turned to something far more serious. At which second some wanton, never before suspected aspect of her nature had swept away all sense of reason. Perhaps the turning point was the very instant he had asked if she were trying to seduce him. Or when the most intense sense of desire had swept through her and heat had pooled low in her body.

His hand drifted lower and she wanted . . . everything. She might well be inexperienced but she was well aware of what everything entailed. And while she might once have thought it all sounded rather nasty, she could certainly see the appeal of it now. She wasn't used to being wanton although—his hand slipped between her legs and she gasped—there certainly was a great deal to say for it, and had no idea how to proceed. Still, given she was lying on his bed naked and he was lying beside her, equally naked, with a rather impressive appendage aimed—and truly there was no other word for it but *aimed*—directly at her, with his tongue caressing her breast and his hand between her legs, she was probably proceeding just fine. She did plan to marry him after all and even though, in a strictly moral sense, she well knew this was wrong, it seemed to her that it scarcely made any difference whether he took her innocence tonight or later. Although, one could argue he was not so much taking as accepting.

His fingers found that point of sheer sensitivity between her legs that she had long been aware of and her body jerked. Her hand clutched at his but she did not push it away. Perhaps she had always been somewhat wanton after all. Her legs fell open and he caressed her slowly in a manner obviously designed to torture. She gasped for breath and arched upward and pressed his hand harder against her. His fingers were slick and slid over her in an increasing rhythm. The most exquisite sensations coursed through her and she could think of nothing save that spiraling tension within her and the source of pleasure between her legs. Her breath came in short choppy huffs and she ceased to exist outside the touch of his hand and the need gripping her.

Without warning he stopped, shifted to kneel between her legs and before she could protest the absence of his hand, guided his erection slowly into her. While she was tight around him, he slid into her with an ease she attributed to years of riding horses and camels and donkeys and noted how amazing the information one accumulated through travel was. Indeed, while there was a touch of discomfort, and the sensation of fullness was odd, it was not unpleasant. And when he was fully sheathed in her she thought this wasn't anywhere near as painful as she'd been warned. Indeed, it really wasn't painful at all, rather unique and not unpleasant. He withdrew slowly then slid back into her. No, definitely not unpleasant. He repeated the action. Not unpleasant at all, really rather nice.

The rhythm of his movements increased. Rather nice indeed and growing nicer with each passing moment. She arched her hips upwards to meet his and urge him on. They moved together in tandem, in ever increasing measure like a primitive dance, as old as time as natural as the stars. Her body throbbed with pleasure and an ever mounting need for something just out of reach. For something unknown, something unimagined, something magnificent. She lost herself in the feel of his body hot against hers, the surge of the blood in her veins, the intensity of the desire growing ever stronger within her. She existed only in sensation, remarkable and intoxicating. She struggled for breath and yearned for release and strained for more. She had never imagined, never dreamed, never suspected. He thrust harder and her body jerked upward of its own accord. Abruptly pure delight shattered within her and wave after wave of ecstasy washed through her. Dimly, through the roar of blood in her ears, she heard him gasp and felt him shudder against her. A moment later he stilled, his breathing labored, his heart thudding against her own and she reveled in his heat, of being surrounded and filled by him. Of being one with him. And the loveliest sense of contentment claimed her.

He pulled out of her, shifted to one side but continued to hold her close. When her breathing had at last returned to normal she considered the situation. What was she going to do now?

Certainly she could tell him the truth but then he already knew the truth. And while she hadn't intended seduction she had intended a lesson of some sort. This was not exactly a lesson although she had certainly learned quite a bit. Even now, flushed in the warm aftermath of their lovemaking it did seem some sort of retribution was in order. Unfortunately at the moment she didn't feel like doing much of anything beyond staying right where she was, curled up in his arms.

"We have a great deal to talk about," he said softly

"Do we?" Her head rested on his chest and she could hear the beat of his heart in harmony with her own.

"Yes, I think we do. What do you want to talk about?"

"Oh, I don't know. This seems like the perfect time to discuss Egyptian funeral practices or Lycian sculpture."

She laughed. "I believe we've done that."

"Then we might wish to discuss the future rather than the past although it's often difficult to move forward until what's gone before has been resolved." He paused. "This might be the right time for secrets, revelations, confessions that sort of thing."

"Confessions?" She pulled away from him, rolled

on her side, and propped her head in her hand. "You mean of our sins?"

"Of our sins and . . . other things." he said slowly.

"We already know our sins. Quite well I would say. Enjoyable sins at that." She cast him a wicked grin. "I would imagine God already knows our sins as well so we needn't confess to him. As for the rest of the world, I would just as soon keep our sins to ourselves, if you don't mind."

"I didn't mean confess to the world. I just meant confess to each other. If there was anything one felt compelled to confess."

"Do you feel the need for confession then? The baring of your soul. The revelation of all your secrets?" She studied him carefully.

She'd been deceiving him as to who she really was but then he'd been deceiving her as well. Worse, he knew of her deception and might well have known all along. For some reason that, more than anything else, was the most upsetting part of all this. She felt like a fool. No, he still needed to be taught some sort of lesson. She fully intended to spend the rest of her life with him, but giving him the upper hand from the start of their lives together did not seem like a wise idea.

Of course, if he were to confess all right now, she'd be more than willing to confess as well. And apologize. Admittedly, she did owe him that.

"Go on then," she said brightly. "Confess."

He paused for a moment. "I suppose I don't really have anything to confess."

She stared at him. "Nothing at all?"

He shook his head slowly. "No."

"How disappointing," she said lightly, although she was indeed disappointed. She hadn't realized it, but she wouldn't mind ending this entire charade right now. Tell the man she loved that she did indeed love him. That she did as well wish to marry him and make her father and everyone else, including herself, happy. "I do love hearing other people's secrets."

"Do you have any secrets? Anything you'd like to confess?" he asked casually.

"I have any number of secrets and probably all sorts of things I should confess." She cast him a brilliant smile. If he was going to continue to play this game, so would she. And she'd play it better. She had the advantage now. She sat up and scooted to the edge of the bed. "The first thing I should confess is that it's getting late and I should be going before my absence is noted." She scanned the floor, looking for her undergarments and realized her clothes were all in the parlor.

Well, this was awkward. She didn't want to leap out of bed stark naked. Odd, when one considered that Daniel had certainly seen her naked, as well as touched very nearly every naked part of her.

He scoffed. "That's not much of a confession."

"Well then, here's another. I confess that I'm somewhat, well, embarrassed at the thought of you watching me wander around without clothes trying to find my clothes."

He laughed, threw the covers back, and got out of bed. Daniel strode across the room without so much as a moment of hesitation. He certainly didn't suffer embarrassment of any sort. Probably an American attitude. He was rather magnificent and was obviously well aware of it. Who was he really? Was he the kind, funny, clever man she'd grown to know? To love? Or was he the arrogant beast of his letters?

Good God—what had she done?

Her stomach twisted. She'd never been swept away by passion before. Indeed, she'd never so much as tasted passion before. Perhaps she'd allowed herself to give in to desire because she knew he was the man she would ultimately marry. Still, that was no excuse. She should have kept her head. Or her heart. Or both. Now she was ruined and he, whomever he really was, had ruined her. Worse, she'd been a willing, eager participant.

Daniel returned with her clothes in his arms and dumped them on the bed. He had taken the time to put his own clothes back on. He nodded toward the parlor. "Would you prefer that I wait—"

"Yes, please," she said gratefully. "Although I might need your help."

"Always at your service." He grinned and took his leave.

She quickly scrambled into her undergarments, fastened her corset, and slipped into her dress. Then she stepped into the other room. "Would you be so kind as to do what you undid?"

"I'd be honored." He moved behind her and began to fasten her bodice.

How very odd that after all they had shared, his assistance now struck her as more intimate than anything else. More personal somehow, more . . . binding. Maybe a bit of confession really was good for the soul. Her soul would certainly feel better if everything were out in the open. If one looked at the situation objectively, one might say that, as she had started their masquerade, she should be the one to end it. It wouldn't be easy but what in life worth doing was? Still, before tonight she'd been worried that revealing the truth would hurt him. Now that she knew of his deception and knew that he had known of hers, that was no longer a concern. Why, they might even laugh about it someday.

She drew a deep breath. "I do have a confession of sorts."

"Do you?"

"I have not been completely honest with you."

"You haven't?"

"I'm not who you think I am."

"Oh?" He kissed the back of her neck. "Finished."

This was more difficult than she'd expected. She summoned her resolve and turned to face him. "I'm not Sarah Palmer." She lifted her chin and met his gaze directly. "I'm Lady Cordelia Bannister."

"You are?" He gasped, feigned shock on his face. "That *is* a confession."

"And?" she prompted.

"And I'm shocked, stunned." He drew his brows together in apparent dismay. The man was an awful actor. How had he managed to keep up the pretense of being someone else for so long? "I certainly did not expect that."

She stared at him for a long moment. She had confessed, why hadn't he? What was he up to now? "Don't you have anything to say?"

"Absolutely." He nodded firmly. "Why were you pretending to be Miss Palmer?"

"It was an error in judgment. A mistake on my part." *And apparently not my only mistake.*

"Well, this does make things awkward doesn't it?" He shook his head in a chastising manner. *He* was chastising *her*?

"Awkward?" Her voice rose. "Yes, I would say it does indeed make things awkward. As does the fact that I've fallen in love with you." At once it struck her exactly what kind of lesson he should be taught. "I love you . . . *Warren.*"

The look of shock on his face was most gratifying. "Do you?"

"Without question. I've never felt like this before. And you said it yourself, only this morning. You said you thought I was falling in love with you. And you further said." She leaned close and brushed her lips across his. "That you were falling in love with me."

"I might have said something like that," he murmured.

She widened her eyes. "Didn't you mean it?"

"Yes, yes, I meant it."

"Good." She forced her brightest smile. "Then everything will be quite wonderful. I love you, you love me. And after all this," she gestured at the bed. "I assume when you suggest we talk about the future you're talking about marriage."

"Absolutely," he said staunchly. "I would never have"—he gestured at the bed—"with you had my intentions not been strictly honorable."

She raised a brow.

"Relatively honorable," he said under his breath

"I knew you were an honorable, honest man, Warren." She straightened the neck of his shirt. "And that's what I shall tell my family as well."

"What?" Something very much like horror shone in his eyes.

"I will have to tell them. Sooner rather than later I expect." She brushed invisible lint off his shoulders. "After all, there could be additional consequences from tonight."

"Beyond marriage?"

She cast him a tolerant smile.

"Children, of course," he muttered.

"We shall have to keep our fingers crossed on that score. I would prefer not to have children until we are safely wed. I would hate to have gossips adding up the months on their fingers." She shrugged. "This will be enough of a shock for my family as it is. Although that's to be expected."

"What's to be expected?"

"Have you forgotten? I am supposed to marry Mr. Sinclair. To save my father's business and all that." She heaved an exaggerated sigh. "It can't be helped, I suppose. Certainly my mother had always hoped I would marry well, a titled gentleman or at least great wealth. But you do have excellent prospects. They will come to accept you in time. And even then it scarcely matters as we will be living in America." She gasped. "You will still have your position, won't you? Mr. Sinclair won't discharge you, will he? He's not that vindictive, is he? After all, he might consider that you have stolen his bride." She grimaced. "Not that I really would have married the arrogant beast. I have come to detest him."

"No, my position is safe." Daniel smiled weakly.

"Now, Warren, if you would be so good as to escort

me out. I have a carriage waiting." She gave his shirt a final smoothing pat and resisted the urge to crack her hand across his face. "Although I did take a bit longer than I had expected. Still." She gazed at him in an adoring manner. "It was a remarkable evening."

"Remarkable," he echoed.

Poor man, he looked as if he had just eaten something quite nasty that disagreed with him. Good. Indigestion was the very least he deserved.

The moment she was safely in her carriage and on her way home, Cordelia allowed the smile she'd kept firmly plastered on her face to fade. Why was Daniel continuing this charade? Why hadn't he told her the truth? She had taken the first difficult step and confessed to him. At this very moment they could be planning the rest of their lives together. Instead, she was miserable and, with any luck at all, he was miserable as well.

Well, let the wretched man think she had fallen in love with the man he was pretending to be. Let him stew in those juices for a while. And let him think as well that she hated the man he really was.

In both cases at the moment, it was no more than the truth.

"There, now you know everything. I need advice or maybe just a fresh perspective." Daniel paced to and fro in Norcroft's library. "I can't talk to Warren, he's predicted disaster from the beginning, flaws in my plan that I didn't see."

"I'd say there are any number of flaws." Norcroft handed Daniel a glass of whisky as he passed by.

"Besides, I think Warren would be hard pressed to say anything through his laughter."

"I'm having a difficult time myself," Norcroft murmured. "You certainly can't discuss this with her brother."

Daniel grimaced. "That does seem like a bad idea."

Norcroft propped his hip on a long library table and bit back a smile. "One of many I would say."

Daniel glanced at him. "You're the only one I can talk to about this."

"What luck for me." Norcroft sipped his whisky. "You've told me everything except why you didn't tell her the truth last night when you had the chance."

"I don't know." Daniel still couldn't believe it himself. "I started to tell her at the museum but that didn't seem quite right. And last night, after she confessed to me, it was the perfect opportunity but I . . . I froze. I knew I should tell her but I couldn't seem to get the words out. In that moment I realized what a true cad she'd think I was—"

"To have seduced her as another man?"

"Well, yes." Daniel paused. "Although one could argue she seduced me."

"Virgins rarely do the seducing."

"This one did." Indeed, Cordelia had been quite insistent, shockingly seductive, and absolutely irresistible. Certainly he could have resisted, he should have resisted, but damn it all, he wanted her. Had wanted her since the beginning even if he hadn't realized it until recently. And his intentions were honorable. Ultimately.

"And even worse." Norcroft raised his glass to Daniel. "You didn't seduce Lady Cordelia. You seduced Miss Palmer."

"But I knew who she was," Daniel said quickly.

"But she didn't know that. As far as she knew, you didn't know who she really was until afterward."

"Good God, I hadn't thought of that."

"It's something to consider."

"The only way out of this is to admit I knew who she was." He shook his head. "And that seems even worse."

"I can see your dilemma."

"Then she told me she loved me."

"Which you?"

"Warren. She's willing to give up everything for him. For me." Daniel took a sip of his whisky. "She doesn't even like me. Daniel Sinclair that is."

"I daresay, she'll like you even less when she learns the truth." Norcroft shook his head. "And she will learn the truth. This mess will come to a head soon enough."

"Unless I pretend to be Warren Lewis for the rest of my life," Daniel muttered.

"Oh, that's another good idea if rather impractical." Norcroft thought for a moment. "It seems to me your biggest problem at the moment isn't so much your deception—"

Daniel raised a brow.

"Although that is significant. But a bigger problem is the fact that she's fallen in love with the wrong man."

"What if . . ." The vague beginning of an idea glimmered in the back of Daniel's mind. "What if she fell out of love with the wrong man and in love with the right man?"

"The right man and the wrong man being the same man?"

"I didn't say it would be easy," Daniel muttered.

"No, you passed easy long ago."

"What if she were to find out something dreadful about Warren? Something so awful she would never want to marry him?"

"What? That he's married with a dozen children?" Daniel stared. "That's very good."

Norcroft snorted. "No it's not."

"She wouldn't want to have anything more to do with me, with him, which would leave the way clear for me, as me."

"Don't forget at some point she has to meet you in person. I suspect she'll realize everything when that happens."

"Yes, but by then she'll have rejected Warren and be in love with me. And we can laugh about this whole thing."

Norcroft stared. "You're deranged, aren't you?"

"Probably." Daniel thought for a moment. "We've been corresponding. I can do much of this through letters, although I am running out of time."

"Let me repeat, and it bears repeating, there will come a day when you have to meet her in person. As you."

"I realize that," Daniel snapped. "There's got to be a way . . ." The answer hit him. "What if she doesn't know it's me?"

Norcroft stared. "Who are you going to pretend to be now?"

"I won't pretend to be anyone, I just won't let her see my face."

"How will you manage that? Hide behind a potted palm?"

"That would be silly." Daniel scoffed. "Besides, it probably wouldn't work." He considered the problem. "You remember the masquerade we attended in May?"

"Yes?" Caution sounded in Norcroft's voice.

"That's what I need," Daniel said slowly. "Another masquerade."

"With costumes?"

"We needn't go that far." This wasn't half bad. "Just masks would do."

"Then you need a masked ball."

"Exactly." Daniel grinned in triumph. "It's perfect."

"Pity, there's never a masked ball around when you need one," Norcroft said wryly.

Daniel pinned his friend with a firm look. "That's where you come in."

"Me? I thought my only role was to lend a sympathetic ear. Perhaps offer some sage advice. The benefit of my wisdom. That sort of thing."

"This is better."

Norcroft's eyes narrowed. "Define better."

"Norcroft, I need you to give a masked ball."

"Oh no." Norcroft shook his head. "I don't know the first thing about throwing a masked ball. Or any ball for that matter."

Daniel forced an offended note to his voice. "I thought we had become friends."

"We have." Indignation furrowed Norcroft's forehead. "We drink together, we play cards together, we make stupid wagers together, and we make sure each of us makes it to our respective homes alive at the end of an evening. I don't know what happens in America, but in this country, that's what friends—male friends—do. We do not throw masked balls for one another."

"Even in an emergency? To resolve a crisis?"

"No." Norcroft glared. "Besides, even if I were inclined to do such a thing, I haven't the vaguest idea how to go about—"

"No, but your mother does."

"Yes and she quite enjoys it, but even I know something of this nature takes a great deal of planning. Months and months. And I assume you want this ball as soon as possible."

"The longer this deception goes on the worse it will be." Daniel met the other man's gaze. "Keep in mind, aside from the fact that I've apparently fallen in love with the woman, I need her inheritance to salvage my plans as well as your investment."

Norcroft grimaced. "Your best point so far."

"Tomorrow would be good, for the ball that is, but next week will do."

"It can't be done." Norcroft paused. "And even if it could, how do you propose I talk my mother into doing such a thing?"

Daniel bit back a triumphant grin. "I don't know. I've never had to manipulate a mother. I would think you'd be experienced at this. I only have a new stepmother that I've just met although she is a very motherly sort of person." Daniel paced the width of the library and back. Daisy could probably be talked into something of this nature if Daniel simply told her why he needed it. Norcroft's mother was a different matter entirely. Abruptly Daniel stopped and stared at the other man. "I think the key word here is emergency."

"What?"

"Are there any charities that your mother is especially fond of?"

"Dozens."

"Any that are in dire need of money at the moment?"

"They're always in dire need of money."

"Then your mother can host a masked ball to raise emergency funds for her favorite charity." Daniel strode to the window and gestured toward Norcroft's gardens. "It can be held out of doors, with lanterns and that sort of thing. I would think there isn't as much preparation involved for an outside event."

"Probably." Norcroft sipped his whisky thoughtfully. "That's not a bad idea."

"Thank you," Daniel said in a modest manner. "I do think well under pressure."

"Thank God," Norcroft murmured. "It might well work. Mother always has loved a social challenge. Remember how quickly she pulled together my cousin's wedding."

"This can be hosted by your mother for the benefit of whatever charity she wants. And sponsored by," Daniel paused for effect, "Mr. Henry Sinclair with a special appearance by a famous operatic soprano."

Norcroft stared. "Your father will sponsor this?"

"He'll pay for everything and make a sizable donation as well."

"I thought you and your father didn't get along?"

Daniel shrugged. "We've reconciled our differences."

"And he'll do this?"

"He'll jump at the chance to help me. Just my asking will probably make him happy." Daniel grinned. "Besides, your mother is a countess and, even with little notice, I would bet her guest list will be full of lords and ladies and whatnot. My father will love that."

"I suppose he will." Norcroft studied him. "But I thought you said he was short on funds?"

"He can't provide me with what I need, but this is a pittance in comparison."

"And I suppose you have an operatic soprano in mind as well?"

Daniel grinned. "Felice Di Mecurio is my new step-mother. I met her the other day."

Norcroft stared. "You have been busy haven't you?"

Daniel chuckled. "Surprisingly so."

"I should speak to my mother. If we are to pull this off, invitations should be sent out no later than tomorrow. Unfortunately, a lot of those in my mother's circle of friends are in the country at this time of year, but on the other hand, there are not a lot of social events in London for those who remain in the city. We should be able to manage a nice-sized crowd."

"It is for charity after all." Daniel nodded and downed his drink. "And I should be off. I have to inform my father he's sponsoring a charity ball and ask my new mother if she would be so kind as to perform."

"Before we are too far along with this, let me ask you something else."

"Anything."

"You failed to tell Lady Cordelia the truth yesterday and I do understand why. But why don't you tell her the truth today? Confess everything to her. Won't continued deception just make matters worse?"

"Maybe. Frankly Norcroft." Daniel met his friend's

gaze. "I'm afraid to tell her the truth now. I'm afraid of losing her. She thinks she's in love with Warren Lewis but she's really in love with me. I may have lied to her about my name but I never pretended to be someone I wasn't."

"That's a very fine line."

"I know." Daniel struggled to find the right words. "I was always myself with her even while pretending to be someone else. That's who she fell in love with. I need her to realize, regardless of what she calls me, I'm the man she loves. I need to win her heart as Daniel Sinclair. And I can't do that unless I can be with her as me. And the only way I can think of to do that is behind a mask." He grimaced. "Another mask."

"You do plan to marry her, I presume?"

"As soon as she'll have me."

"And not merely for the money?"

"As much as I need her money . . ." Daniel shrugged. "I wish we could leave money out of this altogether."

"You did say you loved her although it was obvious." Norcroft chuckled. "Only a man in love would be quite this stupid."

Daniel grinned. "Thank you."

"You realize this means I'll be drinking the cognac alone?"

"Sorry about that, old man, but it seems to me when one finds the one right woman in the world for him, he would be an idiot to let her slip away."

"And you wouldn't want to be an idiot."

"Not merely an idiot." Daniel shook his head. "More of an idiot, Norcroft, more of an idiot."

A prepared traveler should be armed with knowledge as well as the necessities of life.
An English Lady's Traveling Companion

Chapter 14

The nice thing about a masked ball was that one could be very nearly whomever one wanted behind a mask. Cordelia considered the three gowns laid out on her bed and which would be the best for tonight's charity ball. Immediately, she eliminated the pink satin on the right. This was a dress one would choose to please one's father. It was entirely too sweet, innocent, *virginal*. She knew precisely who she wanted to be tonight and it had nothing to do with sweet.

Who Daniel intended to be was another question entirely.

Her heart sped up at the mere thought of him. It wasn't that she hadn't wanted to see him in the two weeks since the night she had discovered the truth. On more than one occasion she had stopped herself from directing her carriage toward his house. It had taken every bit of willpower she'd possessed to stay away from him. Dear Lord, what had he done to her? She wanted him. Wanted to be in his arms, in his bed. Wanted to smack him hard for lying to her. Wanted to forgive him. There wasn't a moment that passed when he wasn't in her thoughts and sleep brought only dreams of him, thanks in part to the letters that arrived nearly every day. Amusing and interesting and more than a little romantic. Even though she did think the next step was up to him, two weeks was a horribly long time to wait for that step. *Blasted pirate.*

The yellow moiré in the middle was a shade too bright and entirely too lighthearted. This was a dress one would choose to please one's mother but not at all the look Cordelia intended for this evening. And neither her mother nor her father would be present. She certainly didn't want to appear too serious, but lighthearted was not what she wanted.

Still, these last two weeks had not been wasted. Cordelia had made it her mission to learn everything there was to learn about Mr. Daniel Sinclair. She went about studying him just as she did any new country she intended to visit or, in this case, to take up residence in. It had been remarkably easy to acquire information as virtually everyone assumed it was only natural for Cordelia to be curious about the man she would more than likely marry. Father had been back and forth between London and Brighton three times since escorting Cordelia home and he'd been more than willing to tell her everything he knew about both the elder and younger Sinclairs. She was pleased to learn Daniel had not exaggerated either his plans or the potential for success. That much at least was true. Even her father was impressed with him and pleased as well that his youngest daughter had apparently accepted her responsibilities and with such determination too. He was especially relieved since Mother had already planned an informal dinner party for her family and Daniel's, for the day after the family returned to London.

Servants were, as always, excellent sources and Cordelia discovered, in contrast to Daniel's assertions about his pursuit of women, he and Mr. Lewis in truth lived a fairly quiet life with work filling most of their hours. That too was good to know.

Her brother had provided the most interesting bits of information. After the invitation had come to a charity ball to be hosted by Lady Norcroft, that no one had so much as heard a whisper about before the arrival of the invitation itself, Will had said Lady Norcroft's son, the Earl of Norcroft, had not only invested in Daniel's railroads but considered the American a friend. Will had also let slip mention of a wager between Norcroft and Daniel regarding which of them would be the last to wed and had chuckled over Norcroft being the ultimate winner. Whoever would have thought Norcroft, who had always seemed inclined toward marriage, would be the last man left standing?

But it was Aunt Lavinia who had discovered the most enlightening details. No sooner had the invitation been delivered than Aunt Lavinia had paid a call on her old friend Lady Norcroft. An unexpected ball, even to raise funds for a charity in dire need, triggered Aunt Lavinia's instinct for gossip. She knew at once there was a story behind it all and she was right. Apparently this sudden fete to raise money for wayward girls or homeless orphans or wayward homeless girl orphans was prompted by Lord Norcroft and was being sponsored, if quietly, by the elder Mr. Sinclair. In addition, the ball was to be masked at his lordship's urging. And, Aunt Lavinia delivered this final bon mot with a gleam in her eye, in addition to his father, Mr. Daniel Sinclair was expected to attend. And wasn't that interesting?

Indeed it was.

The green silk from Paris was the obvious choice. Cordelia wasn't sure why she had hesitated. Even though it had arrived months ago she'd never actually worn it in public. It was a touch more risqué than she had expected. Not that she didn't like it, she had simply planned to save it for the appropriate occasion. A masked ball at which she was certain to meet the man she was expected to marry, the man she already loved, the man who had lied to her, seemed to fit the category of appropriate. Would he tell her the truth tonight? Take off his mask and confess all? Or would he pretend they had never met? Continue his charade? One could do almost anything with one's true face concealed.

When she had first heard about the party she had agreed with Aunt Lavinia that it was unusual for Lady Norcroft to host something of this nature without months of preparation, but then had dismissed it from her thoughts. The invitation had come a mere two days after she had shared Daniel's bed and Cordelia had had any number of other concerns pressing on her mind. But when she'd learned of his father's involvement, Daniel's friendship with Norcroft, and the earl's insistence on a masked event it was as if the pieces of a puzzle suddenly fell into place.

Cordelia was convinced Daniel was behind it all. Obviously the man wanted to hide behind a mask for their first real meeting. Probably because he believed she had fallen in love with Warren. Or rather, with him masquerading as Warren, but he didn't know that she knew that. It made perfect sense. Well, not perfect sense but what about the two of them thus far had?

Oh, this was going to be fun.

She did wish she had someone to talk to about it all, though. As free spirited as Aunt Lavinia was, and as much as she claimed to be excellent at keeping secrets, there was only so much Cordelia was willing to confide in the older woman and a great deal she was certain her aunt might not understand.

As for Sarah, while she'd always been Cordelia's confidant, the two hadn't said anything of note to one another since Will's return home. Sarah was spending every free minute with him, which was to be expected of course. Beyond that, she seemed vaguely uncomfortable around Cordelia, as if she were keeping something from her. And indeed she was. The front hall footman had confided in the cook's assistant who told Cordelia's maid who couldn't wait to tell Cordelia that on the very day Will had arrived home, there was a gentleman, an American, asking for Sarah. The footman had said there had been some confusion over the real identity of both Sarah and the American and that they and Will had retired to the library for a significant amount of time. Sarah hadn't said a word to Cordelia. Obviously, her loyalty now was to the man she loved rather than to his sister and that was as it should be. Sarah was her dearest friend and Cordelia was happy that she and Will had found each other, even if Cordelia couldn't help but regret the loss of the closeness that had been part of their lives nearly forever. It left Cordelia without anyone to share her secrets with, no one to give her advice that she probably wouldn't listen to anyway, and surprisingly lonely as well. Still, Sarah was obviously blissful and if this was the price Cordelia had to pay for her cousin's happiness, so be it.

She ran her fingertips lightly over the green silk. When she had realized Daniel had already known the truth when they'd met at the museum, she had been furious. Everything he'd said to her then had seemed a lie. But every passing day, every new piece of information brought further reflection. The man had lied about his name, but she wasn't at all sure he'd lied about himself. He might not quite be the salt of the earth, but she hadn't learned anything that indicated he wasn't a decent sort. Exactly as she'd thought he was when she'd thought he was Warren. The kind of man one could depend on for the rest of one's life.

A knock sounded at her door.

Still, one did have to wonder what he had planned for tonight and why he didn't simply confess all and be done with it.

"Cordelia?" The door opened slightly and Amelia popped her head in. "Are you in here?"

"Yes?" Cordelia stared. The last person she expected to see today was her oldest sister. Amelia pushed the door wider and stepped into the room, Edwina right on her heels. "What are you doing here? I thought the family wasn't coming back to London for another few days. How did you get here? Is Mother with you?"

Amelia carefully pulled off her hat. "The rest of the family isn't coming home until tomorrow. We arrived on this morning's train. Mother is still in Brighton, and a good day to you too."

"We've been invited to a charity ball." Edwina peeled off her gloves. "We would hate to miss a charitable event."

"We are most charitable you know." Amelia smiled pleasantly. "Besides, Bea is certain she's going to give birth any day now and she wrote practically begging us to come back to London."

Edwina snorted. "She's the size of a small cottage but, I daresay, nothing will happen for a good month. I wasn't silly enough to tell her that to her face, though. She'd quite bite my head off." Edwina grimaced and took off her hat. "We stopped to see her before we came here. She's rather cranky these days."

"Yes, I visited with her the other day," Cordelia murmured.

"However, it gave us the perfect excuse to return home," Amelia said, placed her hat and gloves on top of a chest of drawers and casually meandered around the room. "I daresay this room hasn't changed a bit since it was mine."

Cordelia ignored her. "I thought you came home because you were going to a charity ball?"

Edwina smiled brightly. "And wasn't that an excellent reason."

Cordelia studied her sisters. Admittedly, she didn't

know them well, but their behavior was definitely odd. "What are you up to?"

"She's a suspicious sort, isn't she?" Amelia said to Edwina. "I had no idea she was so suspicious."

Edwina shook her head. "It does prove the point, though, doesn't it?"

Cordelia narrowed her eyes. "What point?"

Amelia's gaze slid around the room. "Although the room used to be yellow, didn't it?"

Edwina looked around. "I think so, but I do like this peachy color."

"What point?" Cordelia said again.

"Simply that you are as intelligent and perceptive as we suspected." Amelia glanced out the window. "Ever since you left Brighton, we've been thinking."

"And talking," Edwina added.

"About you," Amelia said lightly.

"What about me?" Cordelia said slowly

Amelia heaved a heartfelt sigh. "We regret that we haven't been closer. That we've, well—"

"Ignored you all these years." Edwina settled herself on the fainting couch. "Treated you as something of an afterthought."

"I never felt like an afterthought," Cordelia muttered. "Although now that you've brought it up . . ."

"We've discussed this with Bea and she agrees." Edwina shrugged. "In a cranky sort of way of course."

"We'd like to make it up to you," Amelia said firmly. "Now that you are about to be married, we'll have all sorts of things in common."

"We can be quite helpful, you know." Edwina smiled in an encouraging manner. "About setting up a household and managing servants and any number of other things."

Amelia caught Cordelia's gaze. "And managing husbands."

"You'd be surprised just how much managing a husband needs." Edwina sighed. "But, between the three of us, we have a great deal of experience in such matters."

"And even though you'll be in America," Amelia added, "we intend to write."

"Every day." Edwina paused. "Or maybe every week."

"We can be the sisters we've never been," Amelia declared.

Edwina nodded. "Unburden ourselves to one another."

"Share our lives. Our thoughts," Amelia said. "Our troubles. Our secrets . . ."

"Oh, yes, that's good." Edwina patted the seat beside her. "Do sit down, Cordelia, and we can begin sharing right this very moment."

Cordelia sat cautiously. "Sharing what?"

"Our secrets of course."

"I don't have any secrets." Cordelia shook her head. "No, no, no secrets. Not even one. I wish I did. I should think it would be quite fun to have secrets but, as much of a shame as it is, I don't have any." She forced a pleasant smile.

Edwina and Amelia traded glances. Amelia sighed and produced a small pouch from somewhere in the folds of her wide skirts. She moved to the dressing table, opened the pouch, and tipped it over. A handful of coins clinked onto the table.

Cordelia frowned. "What's that?"

"That is what's left of four pounds, sixteen shillings."

"Four pounds, sixteen . . ." At once Cordelia realized the significance of the amount. "Oh dear."

"Blood money," Edwina said in an ominous voice.

"Don't be absurd. It was a simple bribe." Amelia rolled her gaze toward the ceiling. "In many ways I'm embarrassed that our sons did not live up to their agreement."

"Perhaps if you had paid them as much as we used to pay you and Will . . ." Edwina said under her breath.

"Nonetheless." Amelia sank into a nearby chair. "The boys said they escorted you to meet a man."

"Did they?" Cordelia said weakly.

Amelia studied Cordelia carefully. "And that man called you Miss Palmer."

"It was dark," Cordelia murmured.

"And." Edwina paused dramatically. "He kissed you."

"They were spying on me? Those wicked beasts!" Indignation swept through Cordelia. "They were supposed to go directly into the house. I trusted them. They gave me their word. And they certainly took my money under false pretenses, the little bandits."

"They're children, Cordelia, and worse, male children. A certain amount of deception is to be expected." Amelia shrugged. "One day they'll be men."

"And then there will be hell to pay," Edwina muttered.

"Regardless of how we found out, we did find out." Amelia leaned toward the younger woman. "Now we want to know if you're in some sort of trouble. Involved in something of a scandalous nature."

"Or if you're having a grand time." Edwina glanced at her older sister and winced. "Which, of course, would be wrong."

"We're not here to judge, we just want to help." Amelia leaned toward Cordelia and met her gaze firmly. "We meant everything we said in Brighton. We do feel you're old enough to make your own decisions. And we'll stand by you, no matter what."

"Besides, we're much better at keeping secrets than our sons are." Edwina grinned. "And you won't have to pay us even a penny."

Amelia nodded. "Which means our rates are extremely reasonable. Only a certain amount of sisterly trust is required." Amelia paused. "We haven't earned it up to now, but we do intend to make up for that from this point on. Well?"

"Well?" Edwina added.

"Well . . ." Cordelia's gaze slipped from one sister to the next. She had absolutely no reason to trust them, but then she had no reason not to trust them either. It would be nice to have someone to talk to about Daniel. And even if they proved to be no better at keeping secrets than their sons, it would scarcely matter soon at any rate. If her sisters were willing to make this sort of gesture, Cordelia should be willing to accept it. "It's a long story and somewhat complicated."

Amelia patted her younger sister's hand. "We thought it might be."

"And not entirely proper," Cordelia added.

"Oh good." Edwina smiled in a wicked manner. "Do go on then."

Cordelia drew a deep breath. "It all started when Father told me he wished me to marry . . ."

Within minutes, Cordelia had explained everything from the moment she mistook Daniel for Warren in the park to her discovery of his true identity to her belief that tonight's ball was his doing. She skirted around the part about sharing his bed. That was a secret even the most trustworthy of sisters should not have to keep. "And that brings us to tonight."

"I agree with you," Amelia said slowly. "Mr. Sinclair has definitely had a hand in tonight's event. And I think you're right. The next step should be his."

"Still." Edwina gaze met Cordelia's. "You should probably have some sort of plan."

"I do, more or less." Cordelia slanted a quick glance at the green silk. "I am perfectly willing to confess to him, even to apologize but—"

"But only after he does." Amelia's voice was firm. "It won't do at all for you to do it first. It sets a bad precedent for a marriage. It would give him the upper hand and once that happens, you will have a devil of a time getting it back."

"Nor should you ever, ever admit you're wrong," Edwina said. "About anything."

"But what if I am?"

"Whether you are or not is beside the point. Regardless, it's entirely possible to apologize for a transgression without actually admitting you were wrong." Edwina nodded. "It's one of the first things a clever woman learns about managing a man in marriage."

"The trick, however, Cordelia dear," Amelia said, "is to let him think he does indeed have the upper hand. To allow him to believe he is the captain of his ship, so to speak, the master of his household and all that."

"It sounds rather manipulative," Cordelia murmured.

"Do keep in mind, this world of ours belongs to men. You should know that better than anyone. If you were a man, you could earn your own way and spend the rest of your life pursuing travel or whatever else you wished. However we, as women, are not helpless. But we do need to use every weapon at our disposal to ensure our place in the world." Amelia raised a brow. "And I can't imagine manipulation would bother you of all people."

"In truth, Amelia." Cordelia smiled slowly. "It doesn't."

"Good." Amelia beamed. "Now about tonight—"

"But we haven't asked her the most important question of all." Edwina frowned. "She's going to marry this American but does she want to? Does she love him?"

Amelia's eyes widened with surprise. "I thought that was obvious. One doesn't go through this kind of effort for a man one doesn't love." Amelia met Cordelia's gaze directly. "And a man doesn't go through this kind of trouble for a woman he doesn't love."

"Do you really think so?"

Amelia nodded. "I'm confident of it."

"I fell in love with him when I thought he was someone he wasn't," Cordelia said slowly. "And now that I know who he really is . . ." Cordelia wrinkled her nose. "Nothing has changed except for his name. I don't believe I can live without him nor do I wish to."

"Excellent." Edwina nodded with satisfaction and got to her feet, Amelia and Cordelia following suit. "That's that then."

"As for tonight"—Amelia collected her hat and gloves and started for the door—"I would suggest you don't do anything beyond acting as if nothing has changed from the last time you saw him. Pretend you don't know who he really is. It shouldn't be at all difficult given he'll be wearing a mask." She gave her youngest sister a quick hug. "And do remember, Cordelia, in this game you and Mr. Sinclair are playing, it is definitely his move."

"We must be off." Edwina too embraced Cordelia. "Neither of us has the vaguest idea what we're going to wear tonight." Edwina gathered her things and turned to leave.

Amelia opened the door and cast her little sister an affectionate smile. The oddest lump formed in Cordelia's throat. For the first time, possibly in her entire life, she felt like she did indeed have sisters who cared about her and liked her and didn't consider her an afterthought. For the first time she truly felt like one of the Bannister sisters. It was a pity it had taken this long, but then given the differences in their ages perhaps it was unavoidable. Still, it had happened now and Cordelia was both grateful and more than a little touched.

"One more thing, little sister." Amelia nodded toward the bed. "Wear the green silk. It's an excellent weapon."

Lady Norcroft had produced nothing short of a miracle.

Daniel gazed over the Norcroft terrace and beyond to the gardens with as much pride as if he had had a hand in this himself. He hadn't of course. Still, it was perfect.

The doors between ballroom and terrace had been

thrown open and the inside of the house melted seamlessly into the out of doors. Refreshments and tables were positioned at one end of the ballroom, chairs were arranged in rows at the other in preparation for Daisy's performance. Outside, music from barely glimpsed musicians floated down from a balcony above the terrace, as if from on high. Lanterns were strung from the terrace well out into the gardens.

The crowd was no less impressive than the setting. Norcroft's mother had worried that a ball at this time of year, when nearly everyone who was anyone was in residence at their country homes rather than in London, would attract enough guests to make it worthwhile. But apparently there was something to be said for throwing a party out of season.

Daniel had spotted Cordelia almost immediately upon her arrival a quarter of an hour or so ago and now surreptitiously watched her stroll around the perimeter of the terrace, greeting acquaintances. Creswell had sent word as to the color of her gown and mask, as well as what Miss Palmer would be wearing should Daniel be inclined to confuse the two of them again. Daniel liked Creswell, which, since they would soon be related, seemed a good omen.

Still, Creswell might not have the good sense Daniel had credited him with. What was he thinking to allow his sister, *his youngest sister*, to appear in public in such a dress? He didn't care if it was the latest fashion, her shoulders were bare and her bodice was definitely too low, revealing entirely too much, well, too much Cordelia. It didn't matter that very nearly every other woman present had exposed shoulders and bosoms that looked as if they might spring free of their garments at any minute. This was Cordelia. His Cordelia! And the color. Good God. Daniel had never thought of a color as being particularly scandalous, but the rich sea green silk was downright decadent. The shade made Cordelia's dark hair look richer and her peach tinged skin seem creamier. What kind of dress did things like that? How could a responsible brother allow it? And why wasn't every man in the place besieging her at this very moment? Daniel shook his head in disgust. As much as there were several Englishmen he now considered friends, he certainly didn't understand them. How could an entire country of intelligent men have allowed Cordelia to get to the advanced age of twenty-five without being snapped up? Still, it was fortunate for him that her fellow countrymen had failed to recognize a jewel in their midst.

He watched her pause to exchange words with a small group of guests. Norcroft and Creswell had both said he needed a plan. Pity he didn't have one beyond Creswell's suggestion to continue his deception and his own questionable idea of making her turn away from him as Warren and toward him as . . . *him*. Unfortunately, he still hadn't the vaguest idea how he was going to accomplish that. He had to be his most charming of course, sweep her off her feet if possible. If he could just get her to like him a little, then when he confessed all maybe she wouldn't completely detest him. Hopefully she'd find it in her heart to forgive him sooner rather than later. With luck she'd even find it amusing. After all, he had.

Of course, he wasn't the one who had given his virginity and his heart to someone who'd been lying to him.

Daniel summoned his courage and started to make his way in her direction. He'd never considered himself the least bit cowardly but telling Cordelia the truth terrified him. He could very well lose her and now that he'd at last realized how much she meant to him, he didn't think he could bear that. And then there was the question of the inheritance she was apparently unaware of. As much as he needed it, he'd sacrifice it in a heartbeat to avoid losing her. Still, with luck, she wouldn't know anything about it until they were wed and on their way back to Baltimore. Warren was already making arrangements for them to sail within the week. Daniel brushed aside the thought that keeping silent might be the tiniest bit deceitful. But hopefully, by the time she learned of her inheritance, she would have transferred her affection from Warren to him. She was in love with him after all and the only thing that had changed was his name and his position in life. Besides, when all was considered rationally, he was a much better catch than Warren. Surely, she'd see that eventually.

Or she'd strangle him with her bare hands.

He stepped up behind her and resisted the impulse to lean forward and kiss the back of her neck. Daniel adopted his most charming smile. "Might I be so bold as to ask for this dance?" He braced himself. "Lady Cordelia."

She turned toward him. "Apparently, my mask has not provided an adequate disguise." Cordelia gazed up at him and he thought his heart would stop. "Mr. Sinclair."

He chuckled with as much relief as amusement. Perhaps this wouldn't be as bad as he'd thought. "How did you know?"

"I might ask you the same."

I would know you with my eyes closed. From across a room or a city or a sea. "I made it my business to know."

She smiled politely. "How very efficient of you."

"I can be most efficient." *I can be most efficient?* He cringed to himself. No, no, he needed to be charming not efficient. "But I see your glass is empty." He signaled a passing waiter, exchanged her empty glass for a filled one, and took one for himself.

"That was efficient," she murmured.

"And thoughtful," he said without thinking.

"Yes, of course. Most thoughtful." She laughed, and why wouldn't she? He was a bumbling idiot.

Charming, he needed to be charming. He raised a glass to her. "I find there's nothing more refreshing on a warm summer evening than champagne."

"Or any evening." She touched her glass to his and took a sip.

"You haven't answered my question," he said and immediately regretted it. There was nothing charming about being overeager.

"Which question was that, Mr. Sinclair?"

"How did you know who I was?" He tried and failed to hide the note of hope in his voice. Was it even remotely possible that she already knew everything? It would certainly make his life less difficult.

"Your accent, Mr. Sinclair," she said coolly and his spirits sank. "Your mask merely covers your eyes, not your mouth, and an American accent is quite distinct.

Besides, I suspect, aside from your father, there are no other Americans present."

He smiled weakly. "I've been told we all sound alike."

"Now that you mention it, I believe you do. How very remarkable."

Damnation. Of course Americans would sound alike if the only ones she knew were the same man. He really had to be more careful with his words. "I've been looking forward to meeting you."

"Come now, Mr. Sinclair, falsehoods, even pleasant ones, are not the way to begin our acquaintance."

"I *have* been looking forward to meeting you," he said staunchly.

"And yet you've made no effort to do so. You haven't called on me here in London, nor did you appear at my door in Brighton."

"I was . . ." He coughed. "Not well in Brighton."

"And how is your health now?"

"Excellent." He nodded. "I've never felt better."

"It's probably the sea air in Brighton. It's so—"

"Bracing?"

She nodded. "That's exactly the word I was going to use."

This was going well. His tension eased and he leaned toward her in a confidential manner. "I suspect we have a great deal in common."

"Besides word usage and finding the air in Brighton to be bracing? I daresay, I haven't noticed any similarities between us thus far."

"You haven't had the opportunity."

"We've been writing to one another for weeks now."

Yet another ill-fated plan. He chose his words carefully. "Admittedly, in the beginning, my letters might have been somewhat—"

"Annoying? Irritating? Infuriating?"

"They could have been so much worse," he said under his breath.

"I don't see how."

Perhaps it was best to drop this particular subject. "May I ask you something, Lady Cordelia?"

"Of course, Mr. Sinclair."

He studied her for a moment. "When you first learned of this arrangement of marriage between us, how did you feel about it?"

"Shall I respond in the polite, flirtatious manner of party banter, Mr. Sinclair, or do you want the truth?"

He chuckled. "I'd prefer polite, flirtatious banter but I think, at this point, honesty between us might be best."

"I quite agree, Mr. Sinclair." She stared at him in a direct manner. "And I should say, in the interest of honesty, I was not at all pleased that my father had seen fit to take my life in his hands and arrange a marriage for me."

"And now?"

"Now, I find it no less annoying even given its inevitability."

"It's inevitability," he said slowly. "Dare I take that to mean that you do indeed intend to marry me?"

"How businesslike of you, Mr. Sinclair, and very American I would think, to be so direct and efficient. To dispense with silliness like romance or flirtation. To make no effort whatsoever to be charming."

He drew his brows together. "Wasn't I being charming?"

"I'm afraid not."

"I can be very charming." An indignant note sounded in his voice.

"Can you?"

"Indeed, I have never had a woman complain about my lack of charm before."

She laid a hand on his arm, sympathy sounded in her voice. "Perhaps the tension inherent in our first meeting has taken a toll on your charm."

"I wasn't aware of any tension," he said with a huff.

"Might I suggest, Mr. Sinclair, it might be best if you were to be yourself and didn't try quite so hard to be someone you are not. Charming, as it were."

She was right. He was trying entirely too hard. Still, he was charming. Naturally charming. He sipped his champagne and studied her. "You should know, under other circumstances, I am considered to have a forth-right, charming manner."

"I have no doubt of it and I am most relieved. All women want a man who can be charming. I am no exception."

"And do you want romance as well?"

"Well, it seems to me if we are to spend the rest of our lives together, a certain element of romance would be nice."

"I see." He paused to choose his words. "Are we to spend the rest of our lives together then?"

She laughed. "You are persistent, aren't you?"

"When there is something I want, yes."

"Something you want? If you're speaking of me, I'm flattered. Possibly even charmed." She considered him for a moment. "You want to know right this very minute?"

"That would be nice."

"You are an impatient man, Mr. Sinclair."

"Not at all. I consider myself extremely patient under most circumstances. These however are not most circumstances. You can scarcely blame me for being eager to know my fate."

"Your fate?" She sipped her wine. "It sounds so dire."

He chuckled. "I suppose it does."

"Is it? Dire that is? Marrying someone you scarcely know for reasons you had no say in." She sighed. "Yes, I suppose it is."

"It was in the beginning," he said quickly. "But now." He took her hand and raised it to his lips. "Now I can see that things work out remarkably well just when one least expects them to."

"My, my, Mr. Sinclair, that was charming and most romantic."

"I told you," he said with a smug smile. He lowered her hand but continued to hold it. It was most improper but she didn't object. That was a good sign. "Now, then, Lady Cordelia, are you going to marry me?"

"So much for charming and romantic." She pulled her hand from his. "I'm afraid, Mr. Sinclair, that it simply isn't done this way. One doesn't announce a decision of this magnitude at the beginning of a party."

"One doesn't?"

"Of course not. It would be like knowing the end of a play shortly after the curtain rises on the first act. Or reading the end of a book before one is finished with the first chapter. Regardless of the circumstances, you and I have really just met. Why, whatever decision I might have made prior to meeting you face-to-face—"

"Or mask to mask."

"—might not be at all what I want to do once I have shared an evening with you. Besides, it would take all the excitement out of the night, the anticipation as it were, the uncertainty."

He smiled in a wry manner. "I've never been fond of uncertainty."

"Then this will be good for your character." She nodded firmly and sipped her champagne.

"But you will tell me tonight?"

"You assume I've already made my decision, but perhaps I haven't. It might well be contingent on what happens tonight. One never knows how one might feel after an intriguing evening of flirtation and conversation that sounds most proper on the surface but is actually fraught with all sorts of innuendo and promises."

"And charm and romance?"

"Most certainly." She smiled. "Preferably under the stars—"

He glanced up. "We are under the stars."

"With music playing somewhere off in the distance."

He nodded in the direction of the balcony. "There is music."

"And dancing." She shook her head. "I could never agree to marry a man I haven't danced with."

"Then we shall have to remedy that." He drained his glass, plucked hers from her hand, set both glasses on the balustrade, and offered his arm. "They are playing a Viennese waltz, Lady Cordelia, and I confess the waltz is my favorite dance."

"There now, you were right. That is something else we have in common." She took his arm. "Do you know the waltz was once considered quite scandalous?"

They took their position on the floor. "I can certainly see why."

"Can you?" She placed her right hand on his shoulder and his muscles tensed with the memory of her fingers on his bare flesh.

"I can indeed." He took her left hand in his right, his left hand rested lightly on the small of her back.

"It doesn't seem at all scandalous to me."

"Doesn't it, Lady Cordelia?" Was there anything more scandalous than the desire that had swept through him the moment he had taken her in his arms? "Holding a lovely woman in your arms, in what amounts to public with the implied consent of said public." He pulled her closer and stared down at her. "It's quite intoxicating."

Cordelia's tone was cool. "You're holding me entirely tighter than is proper, Mr. Sinclair."

He leaned close to her ear. "I am well aware of that, Lady Cordelia."

"You should really loosen your grip, Mr. Sinclair."

"Yes, I suppose I should, Lady Cordelia." He grinned a slow wicked grin. "But I have no intention of doing so." Not now, not ever.

With that he swept her into the dance. The music swelled around them and without warning the perfection of the moment struck him. The three-quarter time of the music, the swirl of the dance, the night sky, and the woman in his arms. The woman he loved who loved him back, even if she didn't yet realize he was the one she loved.

She would. He was confident of that. He hadn't been confident of much of anything since he had learned of his pressing need for funds coupled with the revelation of Cordelia's identity. Cordelia laughed, whether with the exhilaration of the dance or some secret thought of her own, he didn't know and didn't care. But he laughed with her. Yes, at this moment there wasn't a doubt in his mind that everything between them would ultimately be . . . perfect.

The dance drew to a close and he held her a moment longer than was proper. And she didn't pull away.

Maybe he would even tell her the truth tonight. He hadn't intended to, but then his intentions were rather vague and ill formed. Still, the sooner they put all this behind them, the sooner they could get on with their lives. The sooner she would be permanently in his arms, in his bed, in his life.

At last he reluctantly released her and stared down at her. "That was delightful, Lady Cordelia."

"I must agree, Mr. Sinclair."

"I will remember our first dance together always. Under the stars. On a warm summer night."

For a moment, she stared at him. "Congratulations, Mr. Sinclair, that was most charming."

He raised his brow under his mask. "And romantic?"

"Definitely romantic," she said in a satisfyingly breathless way. This was going better than he had hoped.

He drew a deep breath. "We have a great deal to talk about, you and I."

"I suspect we do." Her gaze strayed to a point behind him. "However, I believe guests are being ushered toward the ballroom. It appears the entertainment is about to begin. We should join—"

"No," he said quickly, grabbed her hand, and led her down the terrace steps toward the gardens.

"But I understand the lady who is to sing is quite wonderful and—"

"And I will arrange for you to hear her at another time," he said over his shoulder.

They passed any number of people heading for the ballroom who might have looked at them with curiosity as to why they were headed in the opposite direction and just what the tall, dark-haired man pulling the lady in the fashionable, but scandalous, green gown had on his mind. He might not have had a lot of good ideas when it came to what to do about Cordelia, but wearing masks tonight was definitely brilliant.

"Where are we going?"

"We need to speak privately."

"I thought we were speaking privately."

"Not privately enough," he muttered. "We have a matter of great importance to discuss."

In spite of his lack of a definitive plan, Daniel had taken the opportunity before her arrival to explore the various garden paths and knew this one, although lit as they all were with lanterns, ended in a secluded spot complete with bench and appropriately romantic garden statue of a scantily clad Greek couple entwined in each other's arm. "This will do."

"This will do for what?" She yanked her hand from his. "You should know I do not appreciate being hauled through a garden like a child. And furthermore, Mr. Sinclair—"

"Daniel."

"What?"

"You should call me Daniel. Given the circumstances, you and I should call one another by our given names. From this moment on, I want you to call me Daniel and I fully intend to call you Cordelia."

She crossed her arms over her chest. "I have not given you permission to call me Cordelia."

"And yet, I will call you Cordelia," he snapped, trying and failing to keep his mind on the matter at hand. It was remarkably difficult to think about anything other than what her crossed arms were doing to her bosom in that dress. "And you will call me Daniel."

"Very well then." She fairly spit the word. "Daniel."

"I like the way you say it, the way it rolls lightly off your tongue," he said sharply. "Perhaps you could say it again?"

She stared at him for a moment and he wasn't sure but he thought the corners of her lips might have tipped upward just a bit. "Daniel." She unfolded her arms—thank God—and flicked open the fan that dangled from a loop at her wrist. "Did you know your name means wrath of God in Hebrew."

"It means God is my judge."

"Are you sure?"

"Yes," he said firmly.

She snorted in disdain. "And not your only judge."

"What do you mean?"

"I mean there are probably many people passing judgment on your behavior. Your father perhaps, your investors, me—"

"You?"

"Your letters." She pointed the fan at him.

"Yes, of course, you're right. I do owe you an apology, Cordelia. Initially, it seemed to me we would both be better served if you didn't like me and therefore rejected this marriage."

"I see." She thought for a long moment. "That was really rather clever of you. I have to admit, the same idea occurred to me in the beginning although I did not actively carry it out."

"You called me an ill-mannered, uncivilized twit." He snorted. "That sounds remarkably active to me."

"That was only on paper, Daniel," she said in a lofty manner. "When talking about you in person I preferred the phrase *arrogant, pompous ass.*"

He chuckled. "Obviously, I was doing a better job than I'd thought."

"Indeed, I didn't like you at all and I certainly had no desire to marry you. But you're right, as annoying as your letters were they could have been much worse."

"Regardless, you have my apologies."

"However, your most recent notes . . ." She smiled a reluctant smile. "One might even call them charming."

"And romantic?" He flashed her a grin.

She laughed. "There might have been a suggestion of romance, yes."

"I shall endeavor to do better in the future."

She fanned her face thoughtfully. "So you did wish to avoid this marriage in the beginning?"

In this, at least, he could be completely honest. "Yes, Cordelia, I did."

"I would assume, given what you've said and your efforts at charm thus far this evening, not to mention your last letters, that you have changed your mind."

"You've changed it, Cordelia." He moved to her and took her free hand.

"As we've never met, how could I have changed your mind?" she said cautiously.

"I've read your work."

"You've what?"

"I've read your articles on travel. I had to wade through a fair number of ladies'magazines in order to do so."

"And?"

"And I liked them. I liked your witty style of writing and the cleverness of your observations. I think your writing is wonderful. I have always thought you can tell a great deal about a person from the way they write, my own letters to you notwithstanding, and I like the person who wrote those articles. Very much so. I think that person and I would suit as if we were made one for the other. Furthermore, I am confident I can spend the rest of my life with the author of those articles and not regret it for so much as a single second."

"Oh my," she murmured. "I didn't expect this."

"It was romantic wasn't it?" He grinned.

"Surprisingly so," she said under her breath.

"I might point out as well, those magazines are showing fashions that are not quite as," he cleared his throat, "revealing as the gown you're wearing tonight. In the future it might be best if you forgo this particular dress."

She stared at him. "Are you telling me what I can or cannot wear?"

"I'm just suggesting that this particular gown might be too . . . too provocative."

"Daniel." She drew a deep breath, obviously fighting the urge to smack him with her fan, and stepped back. "*If* we marry, I should be most willing to listen to your opinions and suggestions, even seek your guidance on occasion. But until you become as well versed on fashion as you are on railroads, you will have no say in what I choose to wear. This gown is French, terribly expensive, the latest fashion and looks quite well on me. Why on earth would I agree to not wear it again?"

"Because it encourages every man in the room to wonder exactly what perfection is beneath it." He stepped closer. "And every man in the room to want that perfection."

"And isn't that precisely why—"

"Cordelia, I've never considered myself a jealous man, but I must be honest. I find myself experiencing what can only be jealousy when it comes to you." The moment the words were out of his mouth he realized they were true, even if the man he was most jealous of was himself. "I know it sounds odd, since we've only really met tonight, but I do feel I know you very well."

"Because of my writing," she said slowly.

"Yes, of course." *And hours walking the corridors of a museum and walks on the beach and an ill-fated night on a pier.*

"And you're telling me all this in the interest of honesty?"

"Absolutely." Certainly, it wasn't everything he could say but it was a start. And it was true as far as it went. "Do you think you could care for me, Cordelia? Someday?"

"Someday? I'm not at all—"

"Are your affections engaged then? Elsewhere that is."

"Does it matter? Our match is the result of business. Affection has nothing to do with it."

"Still, it is preferable to like the person you marry."

"Preferable but not necessary."

"I very much want you to like me, Cordelia."

"Why wouldn't I like you, Daniel?" She cast him a brilliant smile. "You have a forthright, charming manner."

He drew a deep breath. "I have something to tell you."

"Go on."

"It's a bit awkward." What if she couldn't forgive him?

"Then say it, Daniel, just say it."

"And unpleasant." What if the love she felt for Warren had nothing to do with Daniel?

"Then it's best to get it over with."

Say it, Daniel say it. "It's about Warren." What if the truth destroyed any chance of a future?

"Yes?" She leaned toward him.

"Warren is . . ."

"Yes, yes." She rested her fan on his chest and gazed up at him.

"Warren is," he repeated and stared down at her. And he realized he was not as brave as he'd always thought he was. Fear twisted his stomach. Still, the words that leapt from his mouth as if of their own accord surprised even him. "Warren Lewis is married."

When invited to partake of native customs or celebrations one should do so with enthusiasm and an openness of spirit.

An English Lady's Traveling Companion

Chapter 15

"What?"

Cordelia stared at Daniel in utter disbelief. This was his matter of great importance? This, in the interest of honesty, was all he had to say? She would have laughed if it hadn't been so annoying.

"Warren Lewis is married," Daniel muttered in the manner of a man who had said something he shouldn't have and was now stuck with it.

She chose her words with care. "Why are you telling me this?"

He shrugged. "I thought you should know."

She narrowed her eyes behind her mask. "Why?"

"Because you—your companion, Miss Palmer that is." He straightened his shoulders. "I think she's been seeing him."

"Seeing him?" Cordelia gasped with feigned surprise. "What do you mean by seeing him?"

"Meeting with him. Privately. That sort of thing."

"In a romantic sense?"

"That's it exactly." Daniel nodded. "And most improper too, I would think."

"And he's married." Contrived shock rang in her voice and she sank down on a nearby bench. This made no sense at all. Why on earth would Daniel want her to think poorly of "Warren" rather than simply tell her the truth about his deception? It was certainly possible he was as apprehensive about confessing to her as she was about confessing to him. Still, this nonsense about "Warren" was absurd. One would think . . . At once the answer occurred to her. The dear man was indeed jealous—of himself! After all, she had told "Warren" she loved him. Clearly Daniel thought if he tempered her affection for him as Warren she'd be inclined to turn said affection toward him as Daniel. It was exactly the sort of idea she might have had. At once smashingly brilliant and completely stupid. "Oh dear."

"He's a cad, Cordelia, and you—your Miss Palmer should have nothing more to do with him. Furthermore, if she has developed any feelings for him—"

"Feelings?"

"Affection, love if you will," he said firmly. "It is misplaced."

She sighed. "Because he's married."

"With children," Daniel added in an ominous manner.

"Dear Lord." She paused to compose her features. Now Warren had children? Just how far would Daniel take this? "How many children?"

"Quite a few. So many I forget the actual number." He shook his head in a mournful manner. "Mrs. Lewis is always having another child."

"What's her name?"

"Who?

"Mrs. Lewis." Cordelia did wish she could see Daniel's entire face. Still, the blasted masks were appreciated at the moment. She couldn't see what she suspected was probably desperation on his face, but then he couldn't see how amusing she was finding this either.

"Her name," he said uneasily.

"I was under the impression you and Mr. Lewis were great friends."

"How did you know that?" Suspicion sounded in his voice.

"You must have mentioned it in your letters." She shrugged. "Surely you know Mrs. Lewis's given name?"

"Of course I do. It just escapes me at the moment. I have been ill," he said in a haughty manner.

"Ah yes. Lingering effects of the . . . cold was it?"

"Yes." He coughed in a completely unrealistic way. "The fever, you know. It must have affected my mind."

"Poor man," she murmured and bit her lip to keep from laughing aloud. "You probably can't remember the names of any of the children then."

"No, no. Except for the one who is named after me," he added quickly. "But other than little Daniel—"

She choked back a laugh.

"—I'm afraid I can't."

"Well . . ." She sighed, shook her head, and was silent for a long moment. Let him think she was considering this revelation of his. "Well . . ."

"Well?" he said hopefully.

"That's that then." She cast him her brightest smile and rose to her feet. "We should get back to the ballroom."

"That's that?" Disbelief rang in his voice. "That's all you're going to say?"

She adopted an innocent tone. "What else should I say?"

"Something other than that's that. This man may well have broken the heart of the woman who is your companion, your cousin, and your dear friend. Surely that calls for some justifiable indignation on your part."

"One would think so." She thought for a moment. "But I don't seem to have any indignation, justifiable or otherwise, within me. No." She nodded. "In fact, it seems to me it's all worked out for the best."

"The best?" His voice rose.

"Yes, of course."

"But, but—"

"Besides, I doubt that Sarah's heart is so much as cracked. Indeed, I've never seen her happier." She leaned toward Daniel in a confidential manner. "It hasn't been announced yet but she is going to marry my brother."

"What about you?"

"What about me?"

"Aren't you upset?"

"Not at all. I've never had any desire to marry my brother. That would be illegal and immoral and most disturbing. Ancient Egyptian kings and queens, however, often married siblings."

"I don't care about ancient Egyptians. I care about you!"

"How very sweet of you, Daniel. And charming. And romantic." She tapped the lapel of his coat with her fan. "I'm really quite impressed with how charming you can be."

His jaw clenched. "Then you don't care that Warren Lewis is married?"

She raised a shoulder in a casual shrug. "Not particularly."

"And you don't think you should?" he said slowly. "All things considered?"

"Not really. All things considered." She paused. "What's done is done and it's best to move on. Sarah certainly has." She studied him curiously. "Can you give me one good reason why I should care about Mr. Lewis's marital state?" *Now, Daniel, this is the perfect opportunity to confess all.*

He was silent for a long moment then finally sighed. "No, I suppose not."

Cordelia ignored an immediate stab of disappointment. It would have been quite nice if he had confessed. She would have promptly done the same then this game of theirs would be at an end. Still, she could certainly understand his reluctance and apprehension.

She would feel precisely the same if she didn't already know that he knew of her deception.

"Then we should return to the others. It wouldn't do for anyone to notice our absence. Gossip you know." She smiled pleasantly and turned toward the house.

"Cordelia." He caught her arm.

She turned back to him. "Yes."

He stared at her. "Are you going to tell me tonight?"

"Tell you what?"

"Whether you intend to marry me?"

"I don't know." She moved closer to him, so close he could easily kiss her if he wished. "Do you intend to take off your mask tonight? Reveal all as it were? In what amounts to a very public setting?"

He shook his head. "I'm not sure that would be wise."

Or she could kiss him. "Very well. You keep your secrets and I shall keep mine. At least for the moment."

"For the moment."

She'd rather like to kiss him. She knew she'd enjoy it and it certainly couldn't make the situation any worse. He probably already thought she was the worst sort of tart and completely lacking in morals for having shared "Warren's" bed and not being especially bothered by his marital status. She wasn't completely lacking in morals, she did have some standards. After all, the bed she had shared was that of her soon-to-be husband. He just didn't know it yet. Or rather he didn't know she knew. Blast it all, this was getting most confusing. Still, if he hadn't started with all that 'Warren is married' nonsense and had just come out and finally confessed. Or if he had just taken his mask off.

"Daniel Sinclair." She sighed. "You are a stubborn, stubborn man." She slipped her arm around his neck and pressed her lips to his in a kiss just long enough for desire to flutter in her stomach. Dear Lord, no matter what name he used, the man was irresistable. She released him and stepped back.

"My mother returns home tomorrow, Daniel, and I understand you and your family are joining us for dinner the next day. It was supposed to be for the purpose of introducing us, formally that is." She thought for a moment. "I think it might be best if we both pretend that it is."

"Pretend we didn't meet tonight you mean?"

She laughed. "Exactly. When we meet for the first time at dinner we can act as if it is indeed for the first time."

He nodded slowly.

"Now, I for one would like to return to the festivities and enjoy the rest of the evening." She smiled, turned, and started back the way they had come. The moment she returned home, she intended to have a long talk with Sarah. It was past time she knew exactly what Daniel knew and when he had known it. "And I shall quite look forward to hearing all your secrets."

"I wouldn't wager on that," he said under his breath and trailed after her.

She laughed.

"And I'm not stubborn," he muttered behind her.

"Oh, but you are, Daniel." She grinned. "I find it adds to your charm."

Warren lit the lamp on his desk in the office, settled into his chair and paged through the nearest ledger.

"You do know what they say about men who drink alone in the dark, don't you?"

"Not specifically but I can imagine." Daniel sat in the shadows at the far end of the room, his feet propped on his desk, a whisky in his hand. "I suspect it's true. And probably similar to what they say about men who work at their desks in the dead of night."

"I couldn't sleep." Warren turned a page, his tone was mild. "I gather the ball did not go well."

"Actually, Warren, it went surprisingly well. You should have changed your mind and come. Cordelia and I had a lovely evening."

"And what did she say when you told her—"

"I didn't." Daniel swirled the whisky in his glass. There was something to be said for good whisky after a night of dancing and deception and fear.

Warren looked up. "You didn't take off your mask?"

"I couldn't." Daniel took a long swallow of his drink. "I didn't have the courage. I came very close to telling her but I couldn't get the right words out. I ended up saying something remarkably stupid."

"Again."

"Yes, again." Daniel blew a long breath. "I don't recall my being this stupid with women before, do you? Unless excess alcohol has at last dimmed my memory, it seems to me I was always rather successful with women, wasn't I? Clever and charming and amusing, without any particular effort mind you. And great fun to be with. I'd say women always liked me, wouldn't you? Now I've become . . ."

"A befuddled, confused, pathetic shell of a man?" Warren suggested in an overly pleasant manner.

Daniel slumped farther down in his chair. "She's

done this to me. Even when I thought she was Sarah Palmer, I wondered if she had bewitched me. Now I know. She's turned me into a babbling idiot."

"You didn't have far to go," Warren said under his breath.

"I heard that and I did have far to go. I was competent and confident when it came to the fairer sex." A mournful note sounded in his voice. "But you're right, she's turned me into a pathetic shell of a man."

Warren laughed.

"It's not funny."

"It's very funny and I'd bet that someday you'll laugh about it."

Daniel snorted.

"And in answer to your questions, no, you've never been this stupid with women. Yes, you were most successful with women. And indeed women have always liked you."

"That's what I thought." Indignation sounded in his voice. "It's Cordelia, she's the problem. She's not a normal woman, Warren."

Warren choked back a laugh.

"First, she managed to engage my heart, which was never intended to be engaged. And then she sucked the confidence right out of me."

"Thus leaving in her wake the man we see today."

"Bewitched." Daniel shook his head in disgust. "Cursed."

"Still, all is not lost." Warren adopted a serious note Daniel didn't believe for a moment. His old friend was enjoying this entirely too much. "Now tell me what happened. I thought the whole purpose of this evening was to tell her the truth."

"No, the purpose of the evening was to try to engage her affections."

"I see." Warren paused. "And did you?"

"I think so, to a certain extent. She did seem to like me, as me. But . . ."

"But?"

"But." Daniel shook his head. "She didn't react at all as I thought she would when I told her you—me—Warren that is, was married."

"You told her what?" Warren bolted upright in his chair. "You told her I was married?"

"Not you, *me* pretending to be you. It's an entirely different thing." Daniel huffed. "I told her *Warren* was married—"

"I am Warren!"

"You know what I mean. She thinks I'm you so she now thinks I'm the one who is married." Daniel paused. "With children."

"Good God." Warren groaned. "How many children?"

"Too many to count."

Warren stared. "You just keep digging this hole deeper, don't you?"

"Apparently." Daniel shook his head. "I thought she'd hate him or at the very least be upset when I told her that her *lover*—"

"Her what?" Shock sounded in Warren's voice. "By lover do you mean what I think you mean?"

Daniel grimaced. "Perhaps I haven't mentioned that part of all this."

"It's a rather significant part," Warren snapped. "You seduced her?"

"I most certainly did not," Daniel said in an indignant manner. "One could accurately say that she seduced me. She was most . . . *seductive*. And persistent. The woman would not take no for answer."

Warren raised a skeptical brow.

"Admittedly I never actually said no."

"And that didn't strike you as unusual?"

"Not at all. I would never say no in a situation like—"

"Not you. Her. Her seductive, persistent manner that is." Warren stared in disbelief. "A well-bred young woman, from all accounts, a virtuous young woman, being most seductive and persistent? That didn't seem odd?"

"She was very good at it. Besides, she was swept away by passion. I know I was," Daniel added under his breath.

Warren heaved a long suffering sigh. "Go on."

"I thought telling her Warren was married would diminish her feelings for him—"

"For you."

"As you, so it scarcely counts." Daniel waved his glass at the other man. "After all, she'd declared her love for him—for me—and she was willing to give up everything for him—for me." He sighed. "But she didn't seem at all bothered by his marital state."

"Really," Warren said thoughtfully. "That is odd. One would think a woman in her circumstances would be devastated to learn the man she loved had betrayed her in such a way."

"One would think," Daniel muttered.

"Unless of course . . ."

Daniel glanced up. "What?"

"No." Warren's brow furrowed. "It couldn't possibly . . ."

"What couldn't possibly?"

"Although she is certainly clever enough," Warren said more to himself than to Daniel.

"Clever enough for what?" Daniel glared

Warren chuckled. "That would be too, too amusing."

"What would be amusing?"

"But perfect, absolutely perfect."

"What?" Daniel glared.

"When one thinks about it—"

"Thinks about what?"

"Consider it, Daniel. Why wouldn't the knowledge that her lover is married upset her?"

"I don't know." Daniel ran his hand through his hair. "Because she has questionable morals?"

"Given the time you've spent with her, regardless of the names used, do you believe that?"

Daniel thought for a moment. "She is somewhat spoiled. But no." In spite of one rather remarkable night. "No, I don't think she's the least bit immoral. She shared the bed of the man she loved, I can't fault her for that."

"Nor should you, considering you are that man. Still, one would expect a revelation of this nature to have a certain effect." Warren studied his friend thoughtfully. "Unless, of course she already knew the man she loved wasn't married at all and has known since before sharing his bed."

"And how would she know that?" Daniel scoffed. "I've become very good at playing you, you know."

"I've no doubt of it," Warren said wryly. "Even so, you stumbled onto the truth, are you sure she didn't as well?"

"Of course, I'm sure. She couldn't possibly have known that night. Why, she went on and on about how much she liked the name Warren as opposed to Daniel. Warren, Warren, Warren." Daniel shook his head in disgust.

"As if she were, I don't know, trying to make a point?"

"Exactly. I can tell you, she was quite obnoxious about it. Did you know the name Warren means loyalty—"

"Appropriately enough." Warren grinned.

"And Daniel means . . ."

"And once he's judged no doubt there will be hell to pay."

"Wrath of God," Daniel said under his breath. Surely she couldn't have known the truth?

"What?"

"Daniel means God is my judge," Daniel said slowly. Of course, he had known everything. Wasn't it possible she had known as well? "But she kept saying wrath of God."

"Or wrath of Cordelia?"

Daniel stared. "And she quoted Shakespeare!"

"The nerve of the woman."

"You don't understand. Every quote had to do with honesty or deception." Daniel narrowed his eyes. "She knew then, didn't she?"

"It would appear so."

"It explains so much," Daniel muttered. Indeed, it explained everything. Her behavior the night they were together, her reactions tonight.

Good God! He slid his feet off the desk and sat upright. How could he have been so blind? Now that he thought about, it made perfect sense. His spirits rose. There was no need to worry if she already knew the truth. No need to fear telling her what she already knew. The very fact she hadn't confronted him with it thus far was a sure sign she wasn't at all upset about his deception. And why should she be? Hadn't she been doing exactly the same thing?

Of course, until this minute, it appeared she had been doing it better.

Daniel smiled slowly. "She's very good, isn't she?"

Warren chuckled.

"One has to appreciate a woman like that.

"I would say you are well suited to one another."

"I shall have to remember to thank my father."

"As well you should."

"My family is expected to join her family for dinner the day after—or rather—tomorrow now. Cordelia suggested, since that was to be our official introduction, that we act as if we haven't met before."

"So the masquerade is to continue?"

"Not a masquerade. At this point, I'd say it was more of a performance."

"All the world's a stage, and all the men and women merely players." Warren grinned. "Shakespeare."

"And always appropriate." Daniel returned his grin. "I find it rather remarkable how one significant piece of information changes everything."

"Not everything." Warren drummed his fingers on his desk. "Don't forget we're supposed to sail home in five days. You need to be married by then and in possession of her inheritance if we aren't going to lose everything."

"I love her and I'm confident she loves me. She'll think it's quite romantic of me to want to marry immediately."

"And what will she think when she finds out about the inheritance?

"I hadn't planned on telling her until we were married." Daniel grimaced. "I can see now that might be a mistake."

"You can see that can you?" Warren said mildly.

"It's time we were honest with one another." Daniel drew a deep breath. "She should know about this before we marry."

"What if she then decides against marrying you?"

"She won't," Daniel said firmly.

Warren raised a brow. "You're certain?"

"Absolutely," Daniel lied. He already knew better than to be absolutely certain about anything when it came to Cordelia. Still, he knew he loved her and he didn't have a doubt that she loved him. "Why is it, Warren, that from the beginning you've seen all of this so clearly whereas I haven't seen it at all?"

"Daniel, my good friend, any number of reasons. Most importantly, you fell in love with the girl."

"The flaw in the plan," Daniel said with a wry chuckle.

Warren grinned. "Always."

When on occasion one encounters difficulties in
arriving at one's destination in a timely manner,
one should always keep one's wits about her.
There is nothing more distressing than the sight
of a properly bred Englishwoman in a public
display of outrage. No matter how justified.

An English Lady's Traveling Companion

Chapter 16

Dear Cordelia,

*I can't tell you how much I am looking forward to to-
morrow evening and meeting you again for the first
time. Without masks between us. Or secrets . . .*

My dear Daniel,

Even though it's a scant few hours until we meet one another again for the first time, I did feel it necessary to share one thought with you about your previous missive. I found it utterly charming and quite, quite romantic. Until tonight I remain,

Yours,
Cordelia

*C*ordelia clasped her hands together and tried to maintain a semblance of calm. Amelia and Edwina stood a half step behind her, one on each side as if to give her their silent support.

She and Daniel had agreed to greet one another as if this was their first meeting, which had seemed a good idea when she'd proposed it. It would eliminate any unpleasant accusations on either side in front of their families. Not that he had anything to accuse her of, although admittedly she had known who he was when she'd told "Warren" she'd loved him.

She heard her father greet Daniel and his family in the front entry. She shouldn't be the least bit nervous. After all, she was the one who had the upper hand. She knew more than Daniel did and knowledge was a most powerful asset. Still, she wasn't entirely sure what would happen tonight. Daniel could have confessed everything the night they'd been together. Indeed, he'd had every opportunity then as well as at the ball to tell her. While she was quite looking forward to the look on his face when he realized she wasn't the least bit shocked by the revelation of his identity, at the moment, she couldn't help but be a tiny bit apprehensive.

From across the room, Sarah, standing next to Will, offered Cordelia an encouraging smile. She and Sarah had had a long talk in which Sarah had told her everything that had transpired on the day Daniel had come to call on her and had offered a tearful apology for not telling her sooner. And now they were friends again.

Her father accompanied Daniel's father, his stepmother, and another woman into the parlor. Daniel followed a step behind.

"My goodness," Amelia said quietly to her youngest sister. "I wouldn't think marrying him would be much of a sacrifice."

"He looks absolutely delicious," Edwina murmured on Cordelia's other side. "And just a little wicked."

"It's the scar," Cordelia said under her breath.

Amelia snorted. "No it's not."

It was lovely to have sisters.

From across the room Cordelia's gaze met his and her heart leapt. She moved toward him.

"Cordelia," her father said. "This is Mr. Daniel Sinclair. Mr. Sinclair, may I at last introduce my daughter, Cordelia."

"How nice to finally meet you in person, Mr. Sinclair." Cordelia held her hand out to Daniel and tried to keep her smile from being entirely too satisfied.

"The pleasure is all mine, Lady Cordelia." Daniel took her hand and raised it to his lips, his gaze never leaving hers. There wasn't so much as a flicker of surprise in his dark eyes. Not even the tiniest spark of revelation. "I can't tell you how eagerly I've waited for this moment."

Cordelia stared at him. Gone was the endearingly uncertain man of the other night. Here was her pirate. Strong, self-assured, and nicely wicked. A man in control of his world. A man who obviously knew now what he hadn't known before. A delightful sense of anticipation shivered through her. She wondered how quickly her mother would swoon if Cordelia threw herself into his arms.

Cordelia smiled slowly. "Might I ask how you acquired that scar, Mr. Sinclair?"

He lowered his voice and leaned toward her. "Pirating, Lady Cordelia."

She leaned toward him. "I assumed as much, Mr. Sinclair. Or do you prefer Warren?"

He chuckled. "It's been an interesting game, Cordelia."

"Indeed it has, Daniel." She grinned. "You do realize everyone is watching us."

"I do indeed."

"They're wondering what we're saying to one another that no one else can hear."

"And why I haven't let go of your hand?"

"And why I haven't pulled my hand away." She started to do just that, but he held it tight.

"Will you marry me, Cordelia?"

"That's it?" She shook her head in a chiding manner. "So much potential for romance and that's all you can say?"

"I thought the time for games was over."

"My dear, Daniel, I suspect we will always have time for games."

Someone cleared his throat and Cordelia straightened, pulled her hand from Daniel's, and stepped back.

Father's gaze slid from Cordelia to Daniel and back. "Dare I hope this means your correspondence has been successful?"

Daniel grinned. "I do feel I have come to know Lady Cordelia quite well."

"Excellent." Mother beamed as if somehow this was all her doing and turned toward the elder Mr. Sinclair and his wife. "And you must be Mr. Harold Sinclair."

"As much as I would prefer with every passing year to deny it." Mr. Sinclair chuckled. "Indeed I am. May I present my wife, Mrs. Sinclair—"

"The soprano," Amelia murmured from somewhere behind Cordelia. "Felice Di Mecurio. From the ball."

"But you must call me Daisy." Daisy turned to Cordelia and took her hand. "I'm delighted to meet you, my dear, although I must admit you are not entirely what I expected."

"Not quite as stout and sturdy as you have been led to believe perhaps?" Cordelia said mildly.

Daisy stared then laughed. "No, but as clever as I expected." She leaned close to Cordelia. "I have read your articles and I find them fascinating and most amusing. Perhaps later we can have a long talk about some of the places we have both visited and where we would still like to go."

"I'd enjoy that," Cordelia said with a smile.

Daisy turned to the striking, red-haired woman at her side. "May I present my sister . . ."

The next few minutes were filled with a flurry of introductions. The presence of the Countess Paretti delighted Cordelia's mother, as having an Italian countess in the family apparently took the sting out of her youngest daughter's necessary marriage to a common American. Wealthy but nonetheless common.

Daniel and Will greeted one another and acted as if they too had just met. Sarah caught Cordelia's gaze and she raised a knowing brow. Cordelia bit back a laugh. Amelia and Edwina, their respective husbands, and Aunt Lavinia were introduced. Explanations were made as to Beatrice's absence. Aunt Lavinia and Countess Paretti soon discovered they had a great deal in common and knew any number of the same people. The only odd moment occurred when the Sinclairs met Sarah. Daisy slanted Daniel a questioning look. He grinned and whispered something to her. All in all it was a most affable gathering.

Pity it was entirely too small. There was no opportunity to spend any time alone with Daniel therefore no opportunity to discuss anything of a personal nature. Still, they would have time for that. The rest of their lives.

Dinner was announced and the gathering filed into the dining room in an informal manner, which under other circumstances would have brought a rather pinched look to Mother's face. But she had earlier said that a certain amount of informality was unavoidable tonight as their guests were American and couldn't be expected to completely conform to English rules regarding such things. Besides, they were all soon to be family so they should become acquainted with one another.

Daniel offered his arm to Cordelia to escort her to the table.

"Of course I will," she said under her breath to him.

"Will . . ." He stared down at her then grinned.

"Did you have any doubt?"

"I am fraught with doubt, Cordelia." He chuckled. But only when it comes to you." He sobered. "However, there is something I should tell you."

"No doubt there are any number of things you still need to tell me." She squeezed his arm. "We have time, Daniel."

"Not as much as you think," he muttered.

Cordelia took her seat directly across the table from Daniel, between the countess and Will, her sisters on either side of Daniel. Both sets of parents were seated toward the head of the table. Her mother had arranged the seating with an eye toward conversational groups instead of position, which again went against her innate sense of propriety. Still, from the look on her face, she was pleased by the buzz of congenial, lighthearted discussion that filled the room.

"Tell me, Mr. Sinclair," Amelia said the moment the first course had been served. "Do you like children? Boys in particular?"

"Boys?" Daniel cast a quick glance at Cordelia, who smiled in an innocent manner. "I must confess I have not had a great deal of experience with children, boys or girls, although I was once a boy myself."

"No doubt you were quite a scamp as a boy," Edwina murmured.

"If I recall correctly." Daniel grinned. "I might have been."

"There are a great number of children in this family, Mr. Sinclair. When we are all together we are quite overrun with them, most of them boys." Amelia met

Daniel's gaze firmly. "On occasion they have been known to pursue adventures that might get them in a great deal of trouble."

"And on those occasions," Edwina cut in, "they may well need rescue by an adult."

A choking noise sounded from one of the husbands.

"You should know, regardless of the circumstances leading to such adventures, the poor decisions made by whomever." Amelia cast Daniel a knowing smile. "Rescue is always greatly appreciated."

Daniel nodded, obviously trying to hide a grin. "That's very good to know."

"And do you like to travel, Mr. Sinclair?" Amelia said abruptly and idly stirred her soup. "Cordelia is quite passionate about travel."

"I know." Daniel's gaze met Cordelia's. "I've read her articles."

"Have you?" Edwina studied him. "How very clever of you."

Amelia smiled in a cool manner. "And what did you think?"

"I thought they were exceptional," Daniel said firmly. "Well written, amusing, and most enjoyable."

"Did you know she's writing a book about travel?" Edwina shook her head. "It would be a pity if it were never finished."

"A great pity," Amelia said firmly. "But you haven't answered my question, Mr. Sinclair. Do you like travel?"

"Cordelia loves travel," Edwina added as if it could not be said enough.

At once Cordelia realized this was not merely polite

conversation on the part of her sisters. This was something of an interrogation and, as such, quite touching.

"I must confess I have not traveled as extensively as
your sister has. Not for pleasure that is," Daniel said
smoothly. "Right now, the demands of business leave
me little time for pleasurable travel. However, I expect
that will change in the future."

Cordelia tried not to smile.

"You're from Baltimore, is it?" Edwina asked. "In
America?"

Daniel nodded.

"And do you plan to reside there?" Amelia paused.
"Permanently?"

"I do indeed," Daniel said firmly. "Frankly, I have
never considered living anywhere else, permanently
that is. However, I have pressing business concerns
here in London that mean we shall probably have to
return periodically. Perhaps as often as once a year."

We. He said *we.* Was there ever a more delightful
word?

Amelia and Edwina traded glances. Amelia nodded.
"You should plan on joining us one summer in Brighton."

Amelia's husband cleared his throat, no doubt planning on advising Daniel as to the best way to avoid
that family gathering.

Edwina smiled. "And how long have you been in
London?"

"It's been." He thought for a moment. "Seven months
now. Since the beginning of the year."

"Are you planning to return home soon?" Amelia
said lightly.

Daniel's gaze met Cordelia's and he winced. He rose

to his feet, all conversation stopped. "Cordelia, might I speak to you privately for a moment?"

Cordelia stared up at him. "What is it?"

"If we could step into the parlor." He nodded toward the door.

"Nonsense," the countess said. "We'll all soon be family. Surely you can say whatever it is in front of us."

"Unless it's something quite personal, and dreadful and devastating," Aunt Lavinia said. "In which case, privacy is an excellent idea."

Daniel looked distinctly uneasy. Cordelia's breath caught. "Is it dreadful?"

"No, no of course not. Awkward but not dreadful. Business, something of a crisis really, demands that I return home. I have already put it off too long." His gaze met hers. "I am set to sail at the end of the week. Cordelia, do you think . . . is it possible . . . would you consider . . ." He drew a deep breath. "Will you marry me as soon as possible and accompany me as my wife?"

"Oh no, that's entirely too soon," Mother said. "Why, there are arrangements to be made and—"

"Daniel." Cordelia rose to her feet and wondered that they were still planted firmly on the ground. In spite of the fact that he already had his answer, that it was inevitable and necessary for all involved, she couldn't recall ever having been happier than she was at this very moment. "I should like nothing better."

Daniel stared at her, a slow grin spreading across his face. He'd been confident of her answer, indeed she'd already said it. But it was now official, in front of her family and his. And she would marry him at once.

Still, until she knew everything. He straightened his shoulders. "Cordelia—"

"Excellent." At the end of the table, Father stood and raised a glass. "Congratulations and best wishes to you both."

Mr. Sinclair got to his feet and did the same. "To all of us."

"Cordelia," Daniel started. "I really must speak to you—"

"I shall arrange for the funds to be transferred immediately upon the marriage," Father said to Mr. Sinclair.

"Cordelia." He had to tell her before—

"What funds?" Cordelia looked at her father. "Are you speaking of my dowry?"

"That and the inheritance," Lady Marsham said in an offhand manner.

"Cordelia," Daniel tried again. "We need to—"

"What inheritance?" Cordelia said slowly.

"You know, darling," Lady Marsham said, "the inheritance from your great-aunt Cordelia."

Cordelia shook her head. "I'm not aware of any inheritance."

Lady Marsham's brow furrowed. "I'm certain you were told of it although it really wasn't significant until now."

"Refresh my memory, if you please." A sharp note sounded in Cordelia's voice.

"In spite of the fact that she never married, so I have always wondered how she came by it, when your great-aunt Cordelia died she left behind a significant fortune," Lord Marsham began. "She was quite pleased that we had named you after her."

Cordelia's eyes widened. "And she left me her money?"

"Not directly." Lord Marsham paused to choose his words. "She stipulated that her fortune would go to the man you married."

"The man I married," Cordelia repeated, shock evident in her voice. "Not me but the man I married?"

"I believe she regretted not marrying and thought it was in your best interest to . . ." Lord Marsham grimaced.

"To make marrying me more palatable?" Cordelia glared at her father. "It wasn't enough simply to trade me off as part of a business arrangement? You had to offer a . . . a *bonus* as well?" Her gaze shot to Daniel. "Did you know about this?"

"I—"

"I knew," his father said quickly. "Your father told me when we first agreed to arrange a marriage between the two of you. Daniel didn't know anything about it." The elder Sinclair winced. "In the beginning."

"In the beginning!" Cordelia stared at Daniel with disbelief. "In the beginning when you were doing everything you could to avoid marrying me?"

"That would be the beginning, yes, but—"

"Did you know in Brighton?"

"Brighton?" Lady Marsham said. "What does Brighton have to do with anything?"

"No." Daniel shook his head firmly. "I didn't know in Brighton."

"You don't need to know about Brighton, Mother," Amelia said firmly.

"No, of course you didn't know then. In Brighton

you were still . . ." Cordelia's eyes narrowed. "Trying to seduce Sarah Palmer!"

"Not this Sarah Palmer," Miss Palmer said quickly.

"The other Sarah Palmer," Will added. "Cordelia that is."

"The princess," Aunt Lavinia murmured.

"Is there another Sarah Palmer?" Ursula asked. "How delightfully twisted."

"Quiet, Ursula," Daisy snapped.

"I was not trying to seduce Sarah Palmer," Daniel said indignantly."

"Oh?" Cordelia glared at him. "What do you call 'I would like to call on you properly, Miss Palmer?' 'I shall see you in London, Miss Palmer?' 'I promise to refrain from pulling you into my arms behind Egyptian statues!' "

"Well, he did promise," Ursula said under her breath.

"My intentions were honorable." He thought for a moment. "Entirely honorable."

"Hah!" Cordelia huffed. "You kissed me!"

"I would say you kissed me."

"He kissed her?" Aunt Lavinia raised a brow. "Where?"

"Directly on the lips." Edwina smirked. "According to witnesses."

Amelia rolled her eyes toward the ceiling. "In Brighton."

"Cordelia, I didn't know about the money until the day before I went to call on Miss Palmer, or rather you. That's when I found out I needed money, a great deal of money, in order to salvage everything I had worked for. And I realized I had no choice other than to marry Lady Cordelia. Which, as it turns out, was you."

"But I still had to agree to marry you!" Cordelia shook her head. "You knew at the museum and at the ball—"

"I don't know anything about a museum," Lady Marsham muttered.

Daisy patted her hand. "I daresay, there's quite a lot we don't know."

Cordelia gasped. "And the night I came to see you! You knew then!"

Abruptly, Daniel had had quite enough. This was not entirely his doing. "About that night, Cordelia, did *you* know the truth then? Who I really was? Before we—"

Lady Marsham groaned. "Dear Lord, I knew it was only a matter of time."

"Before you what?" Ursula asked innocently.

"I knew exactly who you were." Anger flashed in Cordelia's green eyes.

"You let me think you were in love with Warren! You did it deliberately because you knew it would drive me mad."

"Warren?" Lady Marsham said weakly.

"And you didn't correct me, did you? Even though you had every opportunity to do so. You deserved to be driven mad." Realization flashed in Cordelia's eyes. "And your letters! There was a distinct change of attitude in those letters that can be dated directly to when you found out about the money. They became . . ." She practically spit the word. "Pleasant, even engaging."

"Forgive me for trying to make amends!"

"Amends?" She snorted in disdain.

Daniel clenched his jaw. "You're missing the most important point, Cordelia."

"Oh?" Her brow rose. "And what would that be?"

"The point is I found out about the inheritance the day before I found out that the woman I had fallen in love with was actually the woman I was expected to marry!"

"And that makes this all," Cordelia gestured angrily, "acceptable?"

"No, what makes it acceptable, what makes it damn near perfect is that, in spite of our fathers, in spite of the games we've played with one another, we've fallen in love with each other!" Daniel braced his hands on the table and leaned toward her. "I love you and you love me and the money has nothing to do with that."

"Well then." She mimicked his actions and leaned over the table toward him. "Give it up."

He glared at her. "Give what up?"

"The inheritance!" Her eyes narrowed. "If you do indeed want to marry me for reasons that have nothing to do with money, then give it up."

"Very well," he snapped. "If it will prove—"

"You can't. He can't." His father shook his head. "I realize this is all most distressing to the course of true love and all that, but I'm sorry, Lady Cordelia, he can't give it up. Without your money everything he has worked for will collapse and people who have trusted him will lose a great deal. Perhaps if time wasn't a factor he could be noble and do what you ask, but at the moment he has no choice."

Cordelia stared at his father. "He'd be ruined?"

"I'm afraid so."

"Good." Cordelia straightened and drew a deep breath. At once she seemed remarkably calm. Fear twisted his stomach. "Mr. Sinclair, will you go through with this business arrangement with my father if I don't marry your son?"

His father's gaze slid from Cordelia to Daniel and back and he nodded. "Yes, Lady Cordelia, I will."

"I, however, will not," the Earl of Marsham said in a hard voice. "The marriage was my stipulation not Mr. Sinclair's. My dear daughter, you are brilliant and independent and I cherish everything about you. But with every passing year you are headed down a path that will lead you to the same fate as my aunt. She died bitter and alone. I will not see you spend your life without someone to share it with."

"What if I refuse?"

"If you refuse, I will not do business with Mr. Sinclair. Eventually, my enterprises will fail. There will be no extra money for travel or anything else." Lord Marsham's gaze bored into his daughter. "I need you to save this family, but more, I need you to save yourself." His voice softened. "I'm not sure how it happened, it's all most confusing—"

Ursula snorted.

"—but this man has apparently fallen in love with you and it's clear to all of us here that you care for him as well. I think he's a fine young man and regardless of what has occurred between you, I don't want to see him ruined. And I don't want to see you let pride destroy what you've always said you wanted and did not expect to find."

"So then I really have no choice," Cordelia said coolly.

"Cordelia," Daniel started. "Please listen—"

She held out a hand to stop him. "I will marry you as soon as it can be arranged. I'm certain there are ways to expedite these things." She glanced at her father. He nodded. Her gaze turned back to Daniel's. "However, I will not accompany you to America and aside from the necessity of a ceremony, I intend never to see you again." Her polite smile belied the unshed tears in her eyes and Daniel thought his heart would break. "Good evening." She nodded curtly and headed out of the room.

"Cordelia." He started after her. Amelia grabbed his arm.

"I think it might be best if we spoke with her." Amelia nodded to Edwina and they hurried after their sister.

Daniel stared after them. What had he done? If he hadn't been so stupid he would have ended the charade between them as soon as he'd found out about it and told her about the inheritance as well. If he hadn't let it go on, she would be in his arms right now. And now he had no time left to make it right.

"Well," Ursula said brightly. "It seems we have a wedding to plan.

It was really rather startling how quickly something like a wedding could be arranged if women like her mother and Aunt Lavinia set their minds to it. And if there was a great deal of money at stake.

Three days after the ill-fated dinner that had already taken its place in the annals of legendary family gatherings, Cordelia found herself about to wed a man who would sail out of her life by sunset. The same family members who had witnessed their betrothal, for want of a better word, now waited uneasily in the parlor ready to witness their marriage.

"There, that will do, I suppose." Amelia studied her sister. "Although I do think you should have worn something more festive."

"And yet, I don't feel the least bit festive," Cordelia muttered, although she wasn't entirely sure how she did feel. It was as if she'd been living in something of a fog since the night of the dinner.

"It's a nice enough dress, if a bit ordinary," Edwina said with a helpful smile. "But you do look lovely."

Her family had tried to help. Amelia and Edwina had both agreed that Daniel did seem a good sort all in all. And he was certainly dashing enough with a wonderfully wicked smile. Aunt Lavinia had pointed out money was not a bad reason to marry one's first husband. Will had said much of this disaster could be laid directly at her feet. Cordelia had not taken that well. Mother had continued to murmur that at least Cordelia would be married, regardless of the circumstances of the marriage. Sarah had simply offered her shoulder to cry on. And Father had wisely refrained from saying anything at all. She still couldn't quite get over the fact that this arrangement was her father's doing. With the best of intentions, admittedly, but it was still her life.

As for Daniel, she squared her shoulders. She would marry him, of course, she had no choice. But too many conflicting emotions warred within her to make any decisions beyond that. Cordelia couldn't recall ever having been the least bit indecisive. But now the only thing she knew for certain was that she was still angry with him. He should have told her everything when he had the chance. In spite of his declaration of love, she wasn't at all sure his love didn't go hand in hand with his need for the inheritance. It was most confusing and upsetting. She needed time to clear her mind, to sort through her thoughts and emotions in a rational manner. Time to get over the pain that had lingered in her heart since she'd found out his desire for her might not have anything to do with love. To consider whether or not she wanted to spend the rest of her life with him or without him. Pity, there was no time.

Amelia held out her hand. "Are you ready?"

"No." Cordelia uttered a weak laugh and took her older sister's hand. "But the papers have all been signed so it's best to get on with it."

Her sisters accompanied her from the library into the parlor. Daniel stood near the vicar, the real Warren Lewis by his side.

Cordelia avoided Daniel's gaze, took her place beside him, and the vicar began the ceremony.

Daniel leaned toward her and murmured into her ear. "You haven't answered my letter."

"I didn't read your letter," she said under her breath.

"I don't want things to end this way."

"You should have thought of that."

The vicar cleared his throat. "Lady Cordelia?"

"Yes, yes," she said sharply. "I will, I do. Go on."

The vicar raised a brow but continued.

"You're not going to give me any opportunity to make this right are you?" Daniel's voice was low and tinged with anger. He certainly had no right to be angry.

"Not today."

"Mr. Sinclair?" the vicar said. "It's your turn."

"I do too," Daniel snapped.

"I never doubted otherwise," the vicar murmured and continued.

"You wanted to ruin me," Daniel said in a low voice for her alone.

"Why not?" She clenched her jaw. "You ruined me."

"One might say you ruined yourself."

"With your help!"

"Ring!" The vicar's voice rose. "I assume there's a ring."

"I have it." Daniel grabbed her hand and shoved an emerald encrusted band on her finger. It was perfect, exactly what she would have wanted, or would have under other circumstances.

She stared at it. "Where did you get this?"

"It was my mother's."

Her gaze snapped to his. "Do you carry it around with you in the off chance you find an heiress to marry?"

A groan sounded from the gathering behind them.

"No." He gritted his teeth. "My father had it."

"How very convenient!"

His eyes narrowed. "Not really."

"You are now man and wife!" The vicar glared at them. "Although it is not required, often at this point a kiss is exchanged. I assume you'll forgo that."

"Absolutely," Daniel said.

"I'd rather die," Cordelia said at the same time.

"Very well then." The vicar snapped his prayer book closed. "And may God have mercy on you both. You're going to need it." With that he stalked from the room.

"And a grand time was had by all," the countess murmured.

Cordelia turned toward her father. "It that it then? Is everything signed and in order?"

Father nodded.

"There is a lovely breakfast prepared in the dining room," Mother said brightly.

"You do realize I'm leaving today," Daniel said quietly. "I don't know when I'll be back."

She met his gaze firmly. "I'm certain I'll be able to bravely carry on."

His jaw tightened. "I have arranged for a solicitor here to take care of anything you might need."

"How very thoughtful of you."

He stared at her for a long moment and she saw genuine regret in his dark eyes and something that might have been sorrow. And for an instant she wanted nothing more than to throw herself into his arms and wasn't sure why she didn't. He nodded in a curt manner. "Good day then, Cordelia."

"Good day." There was an awful ache at the back of her throat and she knew if she remained here one second longer her resolve would shatter. She nodded, turned, and swept from the room.

"Breakfast," her mother's hopeful voice called after her.

Cordelia didn't so much as pause until she had reached her room and shut the door behind her. The enormity of what she had done washed through her. She had just married the man she loved and she was about to let him sail out of her life.

Why? Because she was angry? Because she was hurt? Because he had wounded her pride? She sniffed back tears. For a woman everyone considered intelligent, she apparently wasn't the least bit clever when it came to matters of the heart. All she really knew was that her heart had broken.

She crossed to the window and gazed out. Below her on the street, Daniel and Mr. Lewis entered a carriage. She recalled the look in his eyes. Had his heart broken as well?

She watched his carriage drive off and her breath caught. She might just have made the biggest mistake of her life.

Did it truly matter what he'd done or why? Or what she'd done? Neither of them were blameless. Perhaps the only thing that mattered was that in spite of fathers and deception and heretofore unknown inheritances, they had found one another.

She stepped to her dressing table and picked up the letter that had lain there since yesterday. Cordelia drew a deep breath, unfolded it and began to read.

Chapter 17

My dearest Cordelia,

I may have forfeited the right to call you my dearest and yet I refuse to forfeit hope as well. I understand your anger. The revelation of your inheritance coupled with my need for funds is more than enough to condemn even the most innocent of men. And I am certainly not among them.

But know this, Cordelia, I loved you when I knew you as Sarah, when I thought you were penniless. The worst moment of my life was when I realized my financial circumstances meant I could not be with the woman who had stolen my heart. The very best moment was discovering the woman I had to marry and the woman I wanted to marry were one and the same.

I should have told you everything at once but the longer I allowed things to continue, the more I feared *my mistakes in judgment would cost me what I wanted most. You, by my side, as my wife for the rest of my days. I hope someday you will forgive me.*

You told me you loved me when I was using another man's name and I know now that was said to teach me a lesson. It's one I have learned, dear Cordelia. But, regardless of the circumstances, I believe that you did mean those words. Because I cannot believe that what my heart feels is not shared. The enormity of it is not enough for one person. Surely my heart is not alone?

Tomorrow we will become man and wife and of necessity I must return home. I regret that I have no choice. It is my fervent prayer that you will choose to accompany me. If not, however, you must know without question or doubt, I will return.

Regardless of whether we are separated by an ocean or our own foolish mistakes I will forever remain,

Yours,
Daniel

"*I*t was a lovely ceremony," Warren said in an idle manner, his gaze fixed on the ship they were about to board. It was the first time either man had mentioned the wedding since they had left Cordelia's house this morning.

"There was nothing lovely about it." Daniel shrugged. "With the possible exception of the bride. Her eyes flash when she's angry."

"They must have been flashing a great deal."

"She has a temper, you know."

"She hides it well," Warren murmured.

"And she's quite stubborn."

"I never would have suspected."

Daniel slanted a glance at his friend. "I can be rather stubborn on occasion."

Warren gasped in mock surprise. "Surely not."

"And my temper might, on occasion, be somewhat quick."

"Yours?" Warren scoffed. "Hard to believe."

Daniel blew a long breath. "I love her, Warren."

"And therein lies the problem and not the only one." Warren paused. "Might I ask why we've been standing here staring at this ship for a good quarter of an hour. It appears sound and seaworthy. Is there some reason why we haven't boarded her?"

"Hope," Daniel said simply.

"I see," Warren murmured.

"It's futile, I know, but there you have it." Daniel glanced at his friend. "The moment I set foot on that ship, my fate is sealed."

"Are you giving up?"

"Of course not. I am . . . retreating, as it were, temporarily. I fully intend to return as soon as I can but . . ." Daniel shook his head. "The more time we spend apart, the more time she has to realize she can easily live her life without me."

"Or, what's more likely, is that she'll see she can't live without you at all. Absence making the heart grow fonder and all that."

"How can I go? How could she let me go?"

"You have no choice and she's obviously mad," Warren said with a somber shake of his head. "Mad as a hatter."

Daniel laughed in spite of himself. "I suspect we both are."

"I was going to say you are well suited."

"If I didn't have to leave . . ." Then what? It scarcely mattered, he did have to leave. They should have returned home weeks ago, although it would have been pointless. He didn't have the funds he needed weeks ago.

"There's another ship tomorrow, you know," Warren said casually. "It advertises to make the voyage in a shorter time than this one. It would give you another day here."

"A day is scarcely enough . . ."

A day is scarcely enough? What was he thinking? He'd managed to accomplish quite impressive achievements in the span of a single day. Why, he was poised at the threshold of becoming one of the most successful entrepreneurs of the century. A day, why he could do damn near anything in a day. Including win the heart of the woman he loved. And a day was certainly better than no time at all.

He stared at the other man. "Damnation, Warren, I should have thought of this myself."

"You can't expect to be your usual self. After all you are now a pathetic shell of a man."

"No, a minute ago I was a pathetic shell of a man. Now I am a man of resolve and determination who clearly sees what must be done."

"A man of vision?"

"Absolutely." Daniel thought for a moment. "This is not a good way to start a marriage. She should know that."

"Indeed she should."

"She should understand as well that a wife should be by her husband's side."

"What's the point of having a wife otherwise?"

Daniel nodded. "A husband needs to be with his wife to protect her and guide her and advise her."

Warren winced. "I'm not sure that's your best argument." His gazed slipped past Daniel then back. The corners of his lips quirked upward with amusement. "You should work on that."

"Probably." Daniel drew his brows together. "It seems to me the best point, the one thing she can't really debate, is the simple fact that I love her and I don't want to be without her. Not for a minute, not for a day."

"She should know that as well."

"Indeed she should!"

"You should tell her."

"Indeed I shall." Determination swept through him. He would return to her house and make her listen to him. And this time, he absolutely would not allow her to ignore him or leave the room in a huff. No, if he had to, he'd tie her up and throw her on the ship. Two weeks at sea would make her listen to reason. To him.

"Now would be a good time."

"Hah," Daniel scoffed. "I'd say it's past time for me to have a serious talk with my wife. And when you arrange passage on that other ship, arrange it for three." Daniel turned on his heel, took a step, and pulled up short.

"I see I haven't missed the ship." Cordelia walked toward him in a leisurely manner, as if she were strolling along the promenade at Brighton. "It took a surprisingly long time to pack."

A grin sounded in Warren's voice behind Daniel. "I'll go see to . . . the luggage or something."

Daniel's heart thudded in his chest but he forced a casual note to his voice. "What are you doing here?"

"I considered the situation, in a calm and rational manner, taking into account all the facts on both sides of the conflict as it were, and I decided it would be silly of me to pass up the opportunity to travel to America." She shrugged. "I've never been there and it is on my list."

"It's a nice place to visit," he said cautiously. Behind her, porters were unloading what appeared to be an endless stream of trunks and bags. "You have a great deal of luggage."

"I anticipate being gone a long time. Permanently, in fact."

"Do you?" The desire to grin in a most insane manner washed through him and he ignored it.

"Indeed I do." She took a deep breath. "Your letters have improved a great deal since the first one."

"Oh?"

"This last one was most . . ." She swallowed hard. "Romantic."

"That was not my intent."

"What was your intent?"

He studied her for a moment. "Honesty."

"I see." She paused to choose her words. "In the interest of honesty then, there may have been some misstatements on my part, lies if you will, and I believe I may owe you an apology."

"For masquerading as someone else?"

"Of course not." She sniffed. "That deception on my part was offset by yours."

He raised a brow. "Therefore no apology is necessary?"

"I don't think so."

She was really quite remarkable. "Then you wish to apologize for making me believe you loved Warren?"

"Not at all," she said in a lofty manner. "You deserved that, as I had given you every opportunity to confess. Besides, the only part of that evening that was a lie were the names used—as I do, well, love you."

"I see." And remarkably stubborn as well. "Then what precisely do you wish to apologize for?"

"When I said I never wanted to see you again, that was a lie and I do apologize for that."

"Apology accepted." He stifled a grin.

"When I said I could carry on without you." She squared her shoulders and met his gaze firmly. "That was a lie as well. I'm fairly certain I can't live so much as another day of my life without you."

"Then you're apologizing for that too?"

She nodded. "Yes."

"Is there anything else?"

"A few minor things." She stepped closer. "I didn't really want you to be ruined. That was simply one of those things one says without thinking. I know how passionate you are about your railroads and while my comment might have been justifiable at that moment, it was very nearly unforgivable."

"And yet." He bit back a smile. "I will forgive it."

She considered him carefully. "And obviously I lied when I said I wouldn't accompany you to America."

"I have never been more delighted to discover something I feared was true was a lie."

The slightest hint of a smile curved the corners of her lips. "When I called you an ill-mannered, uncivilized twit—"

"Or an arrogant, pompous ass?"

"Yes, although they weren't actually lies because I did mean them at the time and they did seem accurate, again at the time, however I admit I may have been wrong. So I do apologize for that too."

"Is that it?"

"No, there's one more thing." She lifted her chin and gazed into his eyes. "When I said I would rather die than kiss you, that was definitely a lie. I would rather kiss you than do anything else in the world. Now, and for the rest of my life."

"I see," he murmured.

"Well?" Her green eyes flashed, this time with apprehension and . . . hope.

He smiled slowly and pulled her into his arms. "I have a great deal to apologize for as well."

"Yes, you do." The prim note in her voice belied the way she wrapped her arms around his neck. "And your letter was an excellent beginning. Furthermore, I intend to allow you to apologize every day from this day until the day you breathe your last."

"Agreed." He grinned.

"I think we should also agree as well that there will be no more secrets between us."

"No secrets," he murmured and bent his lips to hers.

She drew her head back and stared into his eyes. "Do not think of this as any sort of victory, Daniel."

"But it is a victory, my dear, darling Cordelia." His grin widened. "My victory." His lips met hers. "And yours."

And finally, gentle traveler, never forget that the destination of any journey is very nearly always worth the effort undertaken to get there.

An English Lady's Traveling Companion

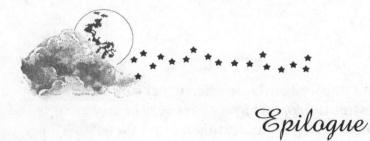

Epilogue

Three weeks later

Oliver sat in his usual chair at his usual table in the club he and his friends had long declared their favorite and considered that he was quite alone. Oh, certainly, he had other friends but he'd shared a bond with the three who had filled the now-empty chairs at his table that he suspected would not come again. Even so, he chuckled to himself, it wasn't as if they were dead, and he shouldn't behave as if they were. They were simply married.

He toyed with the four coins that lay on the table. The club had held the shillings as well as the bottle of cognac for the winner of the tontine and today Oliver had claimed his prize. Still, a fine bottle like this was meant to be shared, not drunk alone by a man feeling a bit more melancholy than was warranted. Oliver signaled a waiter for another brandy. The cognac could wait.

There was no need to feel anything but pleased for his friends. After all, each had found a joy they had not expected and indeed Oliver was happy for them even if he realized he was more than a little envious at what they had found that he had not.

Regardless of the fact that he was now alone, there was a tradition to be maintained. Oliver rose to his feet, stepped up on the table, and wished he had had considerably more to drink than he'd had thus far this afternoon. He drew a deep breath and addressed the other club members.

"Gentlemen, I should like to propose a toast. To your feet, if you please."

A low grumble passed through the sparse crowd but those present stood. The tontine had not been a secret.

"To Viscount Warton." Oliver held up his glass. "Who found what he didn't believe existed."

"Hear, hear," someone called.

"To Viscount Cavendish." Oliver chuckled. "Who discovered the prize is sometimes worth the sacrifice."

"To Cavendish," the crowd echoed.

"And to Mr. Daniel Sinclair," Oliver said with a grin. "Who learned if you're very lucky, what you want will turn out to be exactly what you need."

"And what of you, Norcroft?" a gentleman from a far table called.

"Me?" He stared at the other man. Well, why not? "You're right, as the winner I deserve acknowledgment." He raised his glass higher. "To the winner then, of a handful of coins and a fine bottle of cognac. For good or ill, whether I wished it or not, it seems I am indeed . . ." He grinned. "The last man standing."

*In the following pages
you are cordially invited to a tea party
in which the author has invited some of her
favorite characters to discuss all sorts of things.
Join the discussion already in progress . . .*

Guests for *afternoon tea*

∞

Name *Pandora, Countess of Trent*

Address *c/o The Wedding Bargain*

Name *Marianne, Marchioness of Helmsley*

Address *c/o The Marriage Lesson*

Name *Gillian, Countess of Shelbrooke*

Address *c/o The Husband List*

Name *Rebecca*

Address *undetermined*

Name *Jocelyn, Viscountess Beaumont*

Address *c/o The Prince's Bride*

Name *Elizabeth, Lady Collingsworth*

Address *c/o A Visit from Sir Nicholas*

*Princess Valentina Pruzinsky
of the Kingdom of Greater Avalonia*

Continued from What Λ Lady Wants . . .

" $\mathcal{N}$ ow then." Princess Valentina Pruzinsky, of the Kingdom of Greater Avalonia, sipped her tea. Her gaze slid around the circle of women gathered in my living room and she smiled in a pleasant manner. "What else did you want to know about men?"

I cringed to myself but tried to keep my smile as natural as possible. It wasn't easy. I'm pretty sure instead of the pleasant expression I was going for, it probably came off more like I had just eaten something yucky and was trying not to let anybody know. You know, that look you get when somebody, usually at a very upscale party, has just made you taste an hors d'oeuvre they swear is to die for, and the moment it hits your mouth you realize it's something you cannot stand.

You struggle to keep from showing that whatever you've just tasted is disgusting, make a *yummy* kind of noise, and try to figure out if you can actually swallow without choking, or even better, spit it out unnoticed into a napkin or potted plant.

What did my nice, properly brought up heroines want to know about men that a reformed, although previously extremely wicked, princess who had been married twice and certainly had a far different attitude about sex than they did, could tell them?

This wasn't at all what I'd had in mind when I'd invited some of my favorite heroines to have tea at my house. It had seemed like such a good idea but nothing had gone exactly as I'd expected from the beginning. They were shocked by my lack of servants (I should have made some up), my inability to actually pour tea (who knew there was a trick to it?) and the fact that my style of living was nowhere near their grand nineteenth-century standards (at which point I should really should have pointed out to them that they are fictional while I am real, but that would have been rude). None of which should surprise me. I had written them to be independent and outspoken and know their own minds. I had just never been on the receiving end of it before.

"First of all." Jocelyn Shelton Beaumont (Viscountess Beaumont) studied the princess with a mix of curiosity and suspicion. "I'm curious as to the appeal of older men rather than younger men."

Valentina raised a brow. "Surely you're not serious?"

Jocelyn's sister-in-law, Gillian Effington Marley Shelton (Countess of Shelbrooke), traded glances with her cousin, Pandora Effington Wells (Countess of Trent).

Jocelyn's sister, Marianne Shelton Effington (Marchioness of Helmsley), set her teacup on my coffee table with a sigh. "I'm afraid she is."

"I thought the answer to that was obvious," Pandora said in an aside to Gillian.

"As did I," Valentina said wryly.

I thought it was obvious too since Valentina's two marriages, both to men significantly older who had had the nerve, or the decency, to die within the first few years of wedded bliss, leaving Valentina substantially better off financially than she had been before.

"Money, of course," Marianne said thoughtfully.

Not that as a princess of the fictional Kingdom of Greater Avalonia, Valentina hadn't once had her own fortune, but one could never have too much money when one was trying to fund the overthrow of a government and foment revolution. Of course, that was before her reformation. When she last appeared in a book, she was homeless, penniless, and dependent upon the kindness of the very relatives she had once tried to bring down.

"And power too I would think," Marianne added.

"Very good." Valentina narrowed her eyes. "And?"

"Experience," Gillian said eagerly, and I had the weirdest feeling that I was on some sort of bizarre game show. "Wisdom if you will."

"Especially about women." Pandora grinned with triumph as if she had just picked door number two and won a car. "What women like, what women want, what makes women happy, that sort of thing."

Valentina smiled a slow, decidedly wicked smile. Oh, I had written her well. "There is little better than a man who knows what a woman wants."

I take it back. Valentina looked like the one who had just won the car. And the all-expenses-paid trip to Hawaii.

"Still," Jocelyn said in that stubborn way only Jocelyn could manage. "They are so very old."

"Not old, my dear. *Aged.* Like fine wine." Valentina stirred a spoonful of sugar into her tea. "If a man is handsome in his youth and refrains from excessive indulgence in food or drink, the chances are excellent he'll be handsome as well as distinguished and most desirable as the years pass." She glanced at me. "No doubt, Victoria can think of an example."

"No one you'd know," I said under my breath, although Sean Connery immediately came to mind, who has been my own personal favorite older man pretty much since I was old enough to recognize the appeal of men in general.

"Aside from everything else," Valentina continued, "they don't have all that . . ." She glanced at me. "What is the word I'm thinking of?"

I stared back. "I have no idea."

"Arrogance, I think, yes that's it. Oh, they can certainly be arrogant enough, but it's a different sort of arrogance from that of younger men. They don't have that annoying attitude that somehow you should be grateful simply to be in their presence. Older men"— Valentina smiled pleasantly—"are grateful to be in yours."

"There's something to be said for that," Pandora murmured.

"And they don't last very long either," Jocelyn snapped.

"Conveniently enough, no." Valentina studied the

younger woman. I had invited each heroine here at the point in their lives when their book had ended. Even though they might have appeared in a subsequent book, the end of their own stories was when I knew them best. "You don't like me very much do you."

"You tried to kill me!" Jocelyn glared.

"I did not." Indignation sounded in Valentina's voice and she glanced at me. "Did I?"

"Not technically." I thought for a moment. "It was your, I don't know, co-conspirator, lover, henchman, whatever you want to call him who tried to kill her."

"Ah, the good old days," Valentina said with a sigh. "I do miss having henchmen. Couldn't I have one now?"

I shook my head. "Sorry, you've reformed.

"What about a minion or two?"

"No minions, no henchmen."

"Lovers?"

"I believe when I last wrote you, I left you in the arms of the hunky Capt. Dimitri," I said firmly. "You should thank me for that."

"I remember him," Marianne murmured. "Very nice."

"Indeed he is and I'm not ungrateful . . ."

Jocelyn narrowed her eyes. "I think you're all missing the point. She's done some truly bad things. Revolution—"

"Unsuccessful," Valentina murmured.

"Murder—"

"Again, for the most part, unsuccessful?" Valentina glanced at me and raised a brow. I nodded.

Jocelyn ignored her. "And you're treating her like she is one of the family."

"I believe she is." Marianne thought for a moment.

"After all you married her cousin and her other cousin married Pamela."

"And she has reformed," Pandora murmured.

"Besides her . . ." Gillian searched for the right word. "Misdeeds—"

"Misdeeds?" Jocelyn gasped.

"For want of a better word," Gillian said firmly. "—were a long time ago. . . What?" She looked at me. "Six books ago?"

I shrugged. "Eight I think."

"*I think*," Marianne began, "it's past time you moved on, Jocelyn, and forgot all about what the princess did. Perhaps even forgive her."

Jocelyn gasped. "Forgive her? Never."

"Oh, come now, Jocelyn." Pandora huffed. "After all, you survived quite nicely and are now living happily ever after."

"No thanks to her." Jocelyn glared.

"No," I said firmly. "Thanks to me." It was time that I took charge of the conversation. After all, these were my characters. I had made them up and I should be able to control them. "As Pandora said, you—all of you—are living happily ever after."

"I'm not," Valentina said. "Not in any official sense, that is."

Marianne leaned toward me and lowered her voice. "You do realize these last few pages have been all about her?"

"I'm not sure how that happened," I murmured.

"As well it should be all about me." Valentina turned an icy, evil-princess glare on me. Very scary. Maybe I had written her too well. "I've been meaning to speak to you about that."

"Have you?" I said in as innocent a manner as I could manage even though I knew what was coming.

"I think I should have my own story. My own book." Valentina taped her fingernail against the teacup. "My own happy ending."

"She seemed rather happy to me," Gillian said under her breath. "That captain of hers . . ."

I shook my head. "I'm not sure—"

"I deserve it." Valentina raised her chin. "You've taken everything away from me. My country, my fortune, my family—"

"That wasn't my fault," I said quickly. "That was entirely your doing."

"Nonsense." Valentina scoffed. "You wrote me that way."

"She does have a point," Pandora said to Gillian.

"Oh?" Jocelyn stared at the other women. "Now you're siding with the wicked princess?"

"Victoria reformed her," Marianne pointed out. "She's not wicked anymore."

"Well, she's still a little wicked," I murmured. "You're all a touch wicked." I like a heroine whose behavior isn't perfect. Who sees the benefits of a well-thought-out lie or a finely tuned scam.

"She's in a different category altogether." Indignation sounded in Jocelyn's voice. "She's been bad, not merely wicked but bad. Evil if you will—"

"That's rather strong." Valentina huffed.

"And . . ." Jocelyn crossed her arms over her chest. "She's a secondary character. She's not the stuff heroines are made of."

"I could be." Valentina nodded in my direction. "It's entirely up to her. She's already reformed me, it wouldn't take that much to completely redeem me."

"You'd have to do something really, really good," Pandora said thoughtfully. "To be redeemed, that is."

"Perhaps you could adopt an orphan or two?" Marianne suggested in a helpful manner.

"She'd need to adopt an entire herd of orphans to be redeemed," Jocelyn snapped.

"Helping the poor is good, especially at great personal sacrifice," Gillian said under her breath. "Very heroic."

"I can't believe you are encouraging making this . . . this witch—"

"You're too kind." Valentina smiled in a modest manner.

"A heroine with her own book while poor, dear Becky—"

Becky—Rebecca Shelton—was Marianne and Jocelyn's youngest sister. She had originally been sitting on my sofa with the others but had lacked, well, substance, because I'd never written her story and had just sort of faded away. It was a little creepy.

"—who certainly deserves her own story far more than any wicked princess does, remains two dimensional. Vague and unformed." Jocelyn rose to her feet. "Well, I for one, will not put up with it any longer."

"I rather like that idea." Valentina ignored Jocelyn and leaned toward me. "Could you do that? Could you make me a witch?"

Jocelyn snorted. "More of a witch, you mean."

Valentina ignored her. "You could give me, I don't know, magical powers. Oh, that would be great fun. I would like that."

"I'm leaving," Jocelyn warned, but no one except me seemed to notice.

Marianne patted Valentina's hand. "You would have to use your powers then for good rather than evil."

"Oh, I would," Valentina said in a sincere manner I wasn't sure I believed. "I definitely would."

Gillian shook her head. "It would be a huge temptation, you know. You haven't been reformed all that long."

"Nonsense." Valentina scoffed. "I'm certain I wouldn't have any trouble—"

"This is entirely too much." Jocelyn huffed and vanished.

I felt kind of bad for her. Jocelyn was somewhat spoiled and used to getting her own way, precisely as I had written her. I should have known she would never forgive the role the princess had played in Jocelyn once being terrorized by Valentina's henchman and more or less shot.

She wasn't the first guest we had lost either. Aside from that uncomfortable moment when Becky had faded away, Elizabeth—Marianne's daughter—had left our group when she realized she really didn't want to know exactly what her mother and aunt thought about men, especially her father and uncles.

"I wouldn't even mind remaining a secondary character if I had magical powers." Valentina drew her brows together. "And a wand. Magical powers and a wand."

"Oh, and a book of spells," Gillian said brightly. "That would be fun."

"Yes, yes, I like that." Valentina nodded. "Magical powers, a wand, and a book of spells." She paused.

"And you have my word, my sacred vow as a princess of Avalonia, that I would use it all for good rather than evil. Although ultimately, Victoria, it is entirely up to you."

"I don't know what to say," I said weakly.

"I know I've already had my story," Pandora said slowly. "But I'd rather like a wand as well. And a magical power or two."

"As would I." Gillian grinned. "And a book of spells."

"I think we all would." Marianne glanced around the circle of women and they all nodded. "We're in agreement then. We'd like a new book, if you please, in which we all have magical powers, wands, and a book of spells."

"I don't think so." I stared at them. "There's no way I'm giving you magic. Besides, your stories have all been written."

"Mine hasn't," Valentina muttered.

"Yeah and I'd give you magic?" I snorted. "Right." I shook my head. "That's it. This was a huge mistake. I thought it would be interesting to have you all visit my world for a while, but it's just not working out."

Marianne's eyes widened. "But we're having a lovely time."

"I appreciate the sentiment but I'm not sure I believe it. And let's face it, one of you has faded away, one left because she was embarrassed by the frank nature of the conversation, and one vanished in a cloud of indignation."

Pandora winced. "It doesn't sound at all good when you put it that way."

"I am sorry. I don't know what I expected. Each and

every one of you is exactly as I wrote you. I shouldn't be the least bit surprised that this whole afternoon has gotten completely out of my control. So, ladies." I drew a deep breath. "As much as this has been fun, in an awkward and uncomfortable sort of way, I think I've had enough. More than enough."

"As have I." A distinctly male chuckle sounded behind me and just like in my books, an actual shiver of excitement raced up my spine. Even though I had never heard his voice in anything other than my head before, I knew exactly who it was.

To be continued. . .